EDWARD MARSTON was born and brought up in South Wales. A full-time writer for over forty years, he has worked in radio, film, television and theatre and is a former chairman of the Crime Writers' Association. Prolific and highly successful, he is equally at home writing children's books or literary criticism, plays or biographies.

edwardmarston.com

TIMETABLE OF DEATH

EDWARD MARSTON

Allison & Busby Limited
12 Fitzroy Mews
London W1T 6DW
allisonandbusby.com

First published in Great Britain by Allison & Busby in 2015.
This paperback edition published by Allison & Busby in 2016.

A CIP catalogue record for this book is available from
the British Library.

10 9 8 7 6 5 4 3

ISBN 978-0-7490-1817-7

Typeset in 10.5/15 pt Adobe Garamond Pro by
Allison & Busby Ltd.

The paper used for this Allison & Busby publication
has been produced from trees that have been legally sourced
from well-managed and credibly certified forests.

Printed and bound by
CPI Group (UK) Ltd, Croydon, CR0 4YY

With love and thanks
to Judith
who helped me with my research in Derbyshire
and who enjoyed watching the County Cricket team so much that she
encouraged me to weave the game of cricket into the narrative

PREFACE

This is a work of fiction and I have had to bend certain facts to make them fit into the narrative. I had to create a vacancy for the post of chairman of the Midland Railway and take a few liberties with the publication of the *Derby Mercury* and with the policing arrangements in Spondon in 1859. At the time, St Werburgh's church was known as St Mary's. It was rededicated to St Werburgh in the early 1890s. When I visited the church, a wedding was taking place. By contrast, the novel begins with a funeral. The murder of Enoch Stone in 1856 was an actual event. The case remains unsolved.

CHAPTER ONE

Spondon, 1859

Perched on the top of a hill, the parish church of St Mary looked down on the people of Spondon with the fond and caring eye of a doting parent. When it was built at the end of the fourteenth century it had been an imposing Gothic structure that seemed too large and grandiose for a small Derbyshire village and, even though it now served a parish of over fifteen hundred souls, its pre-eminence, architecturally and spiritually, remained. Among its multiple functions, it was the social centre of the village, the place where the faithful gathered every Sunday in their best attire to mingle with their friends and neighbours, to exchange news, to share confidences and to develop stronger bonds.

The main topic of conversation that Sunday morning had been the untimely death of Cicely Peet, a lady of some standing in the community, cut down cruelly by disease when still short of her fiftieth birthday. As the congregation listened to the handsome tribute paid to her by the vicar during his sermon, her grave had already been dug in the churchyard and the funeral was already assured of a sizeable number of mourners. There was a pervasive mood of sadness and regret and many a handkerchief was pressed into service. When it was finally over, people came slowly out of St Mary's to shake the hand of the Reverend Michael Sadler and mumble a few departing words before glancing involuntarily in the direction of the fine house where Mrs Peet had lived for so many years. It was a long time before everyone had dispersed.

A blanket of sorrow lay over the whole village. Respect for the dead was not, however, a universal feeling. On the very next day, it was certainly not in evidence in the behaviour of two of the younger inhabitants.

'Aouw!'

Lizzie Grindle had pushed her younger brother and made him yelp.

'Chase me!'

'Don't mank abaht,' he complained.

'I'm farster than ter.'

'Gerraht!'

'Carn't ketch me for a penny cup o' tea!'

To provide more encouragement, she shoved him so hard this time that he stumbled and fell to the ground. He scrambled to his feet with the intention of striking back at her but she'd already taken to her heels. Sam Grindle gave chase even though he could never outrun his sister. While she was a tall, rangy, long-legged girl of twelve, he was a short, chubby ten-year-old with a freckled face and piggy eyes. Ordinarily, he couldn't even begin to keep up with her, but the urge for revenge gave him both additional speed and a sense of purpose. Surprisingly, he began to gain on her. Lizzie was delighted that she'd provoked a response. Tormenting her younger brother was her chief pastime and she was particularly adept at causing trouble then blaming it on him. She was far more guileful and inventively dishonest than

Sam. As a result, it was the boy who, more often than not, felt the anger of his father's hand.

The children of Walter Grindle, the blacksmith, were familiar figures in the village, always arguing, always making a noise, always darting about, always up to some kind of mischief, or so it appeared to onlookers. What they saw early on that Monday morning was a girl shrieking madly as she was pursued by a podgy lad issuing all kinds of dire threats against her. On the day before a funeral, it was unseemly. Tongues were clicked and dark looks exchanged. But they had no effect on Lizzie Grindle. She was in her element, goading her brother and pretending to be frightened of him before turning to give him a contemptuous giggle. While she ran on with the ease of a natural athlete, his legs began to tire and his lungs to burn. Sam was soon reduced to a painful plod.

Lizzie immediately changed the rules of the game. Instead of being a race that only she could win, it became an exhilarating exercise in hide-and-seek. She concealed herself in doorways, ducked under carts and disappeared behind a horse for several minutes at one point. Each time, her brother eventually found her but, before he could grab her, she was off in a flash to her next fleeting refuge. When she reached Church Hill she still had enough strength to run up it and enough devilry to stand there and mock him with rude gestures. Panting audibly and hurting badly, Sam lumbered bravely on, determined to get even with her somehow.

The churchyard offered a whole range of hiding places and Lizzie went skipping between the headstones in search of the best one. She quickly found it. The open grave of Cicely Peet beckoned. It was perfect. Her brother would never dream of looking in there. Untroubled by any thoughts of the impropriety of using someone's last resting place as a source of childish fun, she hared across the grass and jumped happily into the grave.

It was only then that she discovered it was already occupied.

Lizzie's Grindle's scream of terror could be heard half a mile away.

CHAPTER TWO

The invention of the electric telegraph had been a boon to Scotland Yard. Messages that might have taken several hours to deliver by other means could now be sent in a matter of minutes. A national network was slowly being set up along the routes taken by railways and canals. Communication had therefore quickened by leaps and bounds. There was, however, an element of frustration for the recipient because the information transmitted by telegraph was often terse.

Edward Tallis voiced his usual complaint.

'Why can't they give us more detail?' he asked.

'We must accept the limitations of the service, sir,' said Robert Colbeck, tolerantly. 'By its very nature, a telegraph encourages abbreviation. We should be grateful for what it *can* do and not criticise it for being unable to send an exhaustive report of a particular crime.' He glanced at the missive in Tallis's hand. 'From where did this one come?'

'Derby.'

'What's the name of the victim?'

'Mr Vivian Quayle. He was a director of the Midland Railway, hence their call for immediate assistance.'

They were in the superintendent's office. Wreathed in cigar smoke, Tallis was seated behind his desk with the telegraph in his hand. It would have been easier to give it to Colbeck so that he could read it for himself but a deep-seated envy made Tallis draw back from that. What the inspector was not told was that there was a specific request for him to be sent. Because his record of solving crimes on the railway network was unmatched, the press had dubbed him the Railway Detective and it was a badge of honour that Tallis resented bitterly. It grieved him that Colbeck invariably collected praise that the superintendent felt should instead go to him.

Tallis was a solid man in his fifties with short grey hair and a neat moustache. His spine had a military straightness, his eyes glinted dangerously and, when roused, his rasping delivery could penetrate the walls of his office with ease. Colbeck, by contrast, was tall, slim, handsome, lithe, soft-spoken and twenty years younger. He was also something of a dandy with an elegance that Tallis thought inappropriate in one of his detectives. Since the two men could never like each other, they settled for a mutual respect of each other's considerable virtues.

'May I see the telegraph, please?' asked Colbeck.

Tallis put it in a drawer. 'There's no point.'

'Who sent it?'

'Mr Haygarth – he's the chairman of the company.'

'The headquarters are in Derby. Sergeant Leeming and I will go there at once.' Colbeck gave a non-committal smile. 'Do you have any instructions, sir?'

'Yes, I do,' said Tallis, ominously. 'First, I expect you and the sergeant to maintain the high standards that I set for all officers in the Detective Department. Second, I'm counting on you for a speedy solution to this crime. When there's so much work for them here in London, I can't have my men tied up in the provinces for any length of time. The capital takes priority. Third,' he went on, rising to his feet and brushing cigar ash from his sleeve, 'I insist that you send me a full report at the earliest opportunity and keep me informed at every stage of the investigation. Fourth and finally—'

'I think I can guess what that is, sir,' said Colbeck, interrupting him. 'Fourth and finally, if we don't make rapid progress, you'll come to Derby in person to take charge of the case.'

'I will, indeed.'

'Yet a moment ago you said that the capital must take priority.'

'And so it must.'

'Then it will surely be foolish of you to desert London in order to devote your energies to a murder investigation in Derbyshire. You're needed here, Superintendent. When you are at the helm, the underworld quivers.'

Tallis glared. 'Do I detect a whiff of sarcasm?'

'Your senses are far too well tuned to make such a mistake.'

'Don't you dare mock a superior, Colbeck.'

'I'm simply acknowledging your superiority,' said the other, seriously. 'The commissioner, after all, is largely a figurehead. In reality, it's you who bears most of the responsibility for policing the capital and – since you do it with such exemplary style and effectiveness – that's why you should remain here.'

Edward Tallis was unsure whether to be flattered by the praise or irritated by the smoothness with which it was delivered. By the time the superintendent made up his mind, it was too late. Colbeck had left the room.

Panic had seized the village of Spondon. The shocking discovery of a murder victim in their churchyard had unsettled everyone and set off fevered speculation. Though he did his best to reassure his parishioners, the vicar was unable to quell the mounting alarm. Michael Sadler was a short, slight man in his fifties with the remains of his white hair scattered in tufts over his pate. What made him so popular with his congregation was his kindness, his lack of condescension and the merciful brevity of his sermons. More discerning worshippers also admired the soundness of his theology and the sheer breadth of his learning. Qualities seen at their best inside the church, however, did not fit him for heated confrontations. When he found himself caught up in one that morning, he was clearly out of his depth.

'I insist!' yelled Roderick Peet.

'So what?' retorted Bert Knowles.

'Do as you're told, man.'

'I done it already.'

'Don't be so exasperating.'

'Now, now, gentlemen,' said the vicar, trying to intervene. 'There's no need for discord. I'm sure that this matter can be settled amicably.'

'We're talking about my wife's funeral,' said Peet, shaking with rage.

Knowles pointed a finger. 'Then theer's 'er grave.'

'Damn your impudence!'

'Please,' chided the vicar, a hand on his arm. 'Let's moderate our language, shall we, Mr Peet? Never forget that we're on consecrated ground.'

Peet bit his lip. 'I do apologise, Vicar.'

'*You'd* do well to remember that this is a churchyard, Bert.'

Knowles shrugged. 'Aye, 'appen I should.'

But he was clearly unrepentant. Knowles was a sturdy man in his sixties with a gnarled face, a farm labourer who supplemented his low wages by digging graves and doing odd jobs in the village. He was not a churchgoer. Peet, on the other hand, was a pillar of St Mary's and one of its most generous benefactors. He was a tall, lean man in his seventies with great poise and dignity. He was wearing funereal garb. As a member of the local gentry, he expected the common people to defer to him at all times and most of them did. Knowles was the exception. The gravedigger hated any sign of aloofness and called no man his master.

Sadler understood the positions of the two combatants all too well. Horrified that an interloper had appeared out of the blue in his wife's grave, Peet wanted a new one to be dug instantly. The original, he felt, was contaminated beyond redemption. For his part, Knowles argued that he'd done exactly what he was told to do and that was the end of it. He saw no reason why his grave could not receive the body of Ciccly Peet as planned.

'There was a murdered man in there,' howled Peet.

'Well, 'e's not theer now,' countered Knowles.

'It's a bad omen.'

'I don't see as 'ow it is, Mr Peet. A grave's a bleedin' grave.'

'Bert!' shouted the vicar in dismay.

Knowles raised a grubby palm. 'Sorry.'

'So you should be.' His voice softened. 'Mr Peet's request is very reasonable. He wants a fresh grave for his dear, departed wife.'

'Dunna axe me to dig it.'

'You'll get paid. I'll happily provide the money myself.'

'There's no need for you to do that, Vicar,' said Peet. 'I'll meet the cost.'

Knowles folded his arms. 'No.'

'Then we'll find someone else.'

'No,' repeated the other, gruffly. 'Nobody steals my job.'

'Bert *is* our official gravedigger,' admitted the vicar. 'We never had the slightest cause to complain about his work in the past. As you see,' he added, indicating the open grave, 'he does an excellent job.'

'Then let him do it again,' said Peet, struggling to hold in his temper. 'Doesn't this idiot understand an order when he's given one? I'm not making a polite request. What I'm issuing is a demand. And it must be obeyed.'

'Matter o' principul,' said Knowles, stubbornly. 'If my grave en't good enough for ter, bury the missus somewheer else.' He pulled out a pipe and thrust it in his mouth. 'Gorra bit of bacca abaht thee, Vicar?'

It was too much to expect Victor Leeming to enjoy a journey that took him away from his wife and family, but at least he didn't launch into his standard litany of objections to steam locomotion. Settling back in a seat opposite Colbeck, he suffered in silence. The train to Derby had set out from King's Cross station, the London terminus of the Great Northern Railway. Because it had no terminus in the capital, the Midland Railway had been forced to come to an agreement with one of its chief rivals, making use of the latter's tracks between London and Hitchin. Beyond there, trains ran on lines owned by the Midland. As a company it had endured some very difficult times but, although he was well aware of them, Colbeck saw no point in trying to interest the sergeant in the vagaries of running a railway company. Instead, he pointed out the benefit of their present assignment.

'Detective work is not merely fascinating in itself,' he said. 'It gives us a geography lesson each time.'

'I'd prefer to stay in London, sir.'

'I don't believe it, Victor. Even you must have been uplifted by the wonders of Scotland, the scenic delight of Devon and the novelty of all the other places we've been taken to in the course of our work. And what you've seen and experienced you doubtless pass on to your children, so they are getting an education as well.'

'I never thought of that,' confessed Leeming. 'And you're right about the boys. Whenever I've been away, they always pester me for details of where I've been. So does Estelle, for that matter.'

'Madeleine is the same. In her case, of course, she has been able to join us from time to time. My dear wife is still talking about our adventure in Ireland.'

'Let's hope that the superintendent never finds out about that. If he realised that we had the help of a woman during a murder investigation, he'd have a fit.'

Since they occupied an empty compartment they were able to talk freely. Leeming was a stocky individual of medium height with the kind of unsightly features more suited to a ruffian than to a detective sergeant. Indeed, though he wore a frock coat and well-cut trousers, he still contrived to look like a villain on the run from the law. Years of being teased about his ugliness as a boy had served to toughen him and he'd become so proficient at punching his detractors that they'd learnt to hold their tongues. Colbeck admired him for his strength, tenacity and unwavering loyalty.

'Why can't the police in Derby handle this case?' asked Leeming.

'Someone clearly thinks it's beyond their competence.'

'That means we'll get a frosty welcome. Nobody likes to be told that detectives are being brought in over their head.'

'We've coped with that situation before,' said Colbeck with a sigh. 'Some constabularies have been extremely helpful but we do tend to meet with jealousy and suspicion as a rule. It's understandable.'

'The railway police are the worse, sir.'

'I agree, Victor. They never accept that they have no power to investigate major crimes on the network. Some of them always try to do our work for us. There's no knowing what we'll face when we get there but we'd better brace ourselves for resistance of some sort. One thing is certain,' he said, philosophically. 'There won't be a brass band waiting to greet us at Derby station.'

Donald Haygarth walked so quickly up and down the platform that his companion had difficulty in keeping up with him. Haygarth was a big, barrel-chested man in his fifties with an expensive tailor, paid to conceal his customer's spreading contours. For all his bulk, he moved at speed and exuded self-importance. Trotting beside him was Elijah Wigg, the cadaverous Superintendent of Derby Police, the brass buttons of his uniform gleaming like stars and his boots brushed to a high sheen. Wigg's side whiskers were so long and luxuriant that they threatened to join forces under his chin and blossom into a full beard. Weary of trying to have a conversation on the hoof, he put a skeletal hand on Haygarth's shoulder and pulled him to a halt.

'There's no need to wear out the soles of your shoes,' he said, spikily. 'It won't make your famous Railway Detective come any sooner.'

'He'll be here any minute,' said Haygarth, fussily. 'I know the train that he caught because he had the forethought to inform me by telegraph. If it's running on time, as it should be, I expect him to be only a mile or so away from us.'

'I'm glad to hear it. The next train to London arrives here in twenty minutes. Inspector Colbeck can go straight back where he came from.'

'And why on earth should he do that?'

'*We* will be handling the investigation, Mr Haygarth.'

'I've called in an acknowledged expert.'

'An acknowledged expert on *what?*' demanded Wigg. 'He doesn't know this part of the country, he doesn't understand the people and he won't be able to make head or tail of the Derbyshire dialect. Why have a complete stranger blundering around when we have a police force equipped with local insight?'

'Be honest, Superintendent,' said Haygarth. 'This case is too big for you.'

'I deny it.'

'It's a complex murder inquiry.'

'We can handle it better than anyone.'

'That's patently untrue.'

Wigg bristled. 'What do you mean?'

'I mean that you already have one unsolved murder on your hands. Need I remind you that it's three years since a man named Enoch Stone was killed in Spondon and that nobody has yet been brought to book for the crime?'

'That investigation continues. We'll find the culprit eventually.'

'I want a quicker result in this case,' said Haygarth, acidly. 'That's why I've turned to Scotland Yard. I don't have three years to wait for the arrest and conviction of the man who murdered Mr Quayle. You keep chasing your tail over the Enoch Stone case, Superintendent. I need Inspector Colbeck to take charge of this one.'

Elijah Wigg spluttered. Before he could reply, however, he was diverted by the sound of a train's approach and saw it powering towards them in the distance. When he took his watch from his waistcoat pocket, Haygarth was delighted to see that the train was punctual. He walked briskly back up the single platform with Wigg scampering at his heels.

When the train finally squealed to a halt, there was a tumult of hissing steam, acrid smoke and the systematic clamour of compartment doors being opened. While passengers were waiting to climb aboard, others were welcoming those who'd just alighted. Haygarth didn't need to find the detectives. As soon as he stepped onto the platform, Colbeck had spotted the police uniform and made straight for it. Introductions were performed. Wigg glowered, Haygarth beamed, Colbeck tossed an approving glance at the station itself and Leeming stretched.

'I'm so glad that you've come,' said Haygarth, pumping the hands of the newcomers in turn. 'I've reserved rooms for each of you at the Royal Hotel. You will, of course, be staying at the expense of the Midland Railway.'

'Thank you, sir,' said Colbeck. 'But the sergeant and I are still very much in the dark. What we'd like to do in the first instance is to visit the scene of the crime and learn what steps have been taken by the police.'

'We've done all that's appropriate,' said Wigg, officiously. 'We are not bumpkins in some rural backwater, Inspector. You're standing in one of the nation's finest manufacturing towns and it has a police force worthy of its eminence. We follow the correct procedures here. My suggestion is that we have your luggage sent to the hotel so that you can accompany me to Spondon.'

'We just stopped there,' said Leeming. 'Is that where the murder occurred?'

'It is, Sergeant.'

'Do you have a police station there?'

'No, but we have six constables, all local men.'

'They're well-meaning fellows,' observed Haygarth, 'but they are not trained detectives. In fact, they're still struggling to solve a murder that took place in the village three years ago.'

'That's irrelevant,' snapped Wigg.

'I beg leave to doubt that, Superintendent,' said Colbeck. 'The overwhelming majority of villages in this country, I'm pleased to say, have never had a single homicide yet Spondon, it appears, has had two in the space of three years. The place has already aroused my interest. Did Mr Quayle, the more recent victim, have any connection with the village?'

'None whatsoever,' replied Haygarth. 'He lived in Nottingham.'

'Then what was he doing there?'

'I'll be grateful if you could find out, Inspector.'

'How was he killed?'

'We're not entirely sure. We await the results of a post-mortem.'

'This case gets more intriguing by the second,' said Colbeck, smiling. 'It is positively swathed in mystery. Thank you for inviting us here, Mr Haygarth. I have a feeling that Derbyshire is going to yield a whole battery of surprises.'

Leeming turned to Wigg. 'Do you have any suspects?' he asked. 'Are there any people who would profit directly from Mr Quayle's death?'

'Yes,' said Wigg, seizing a chance to embarrass Haygarth. 'One of them is standing right next to you, Sergeant.'

'How dare you!' exclaimed Haygarth.

'Facts are facts, sir. There's a vacancy for the chairmanship of the Midland Railway. Vivian Quayle was the obvious candidate but you also threw your hat into the ring. His death leaves the field clear for you,' said Wigg, enjoying the other man's obvious discomfort. 'What's more, you know Spondon intimately because you were born there.' He stroked a side whisker as if it were a favourite cat. 'I'm bound to find that a cause for suspicion.'

CHAPTER THREE

Peace had finally been restored at St Mary's church and, although both disputants still nursed hurt feelings, a compromise had been reached. The Reverend Michael Sadler might know little about exerting control over a furious argument but he knew a great deal about grief and its corrosive effects. Having persuaded Roderick Peet to return home, the vicar had worked subtly on Bert Knowles, urging him to show compassion towards a bereaved husband and reminding the gravedigger of how he had felt in the wake of his own wife's death some years earlier. Seeds of doubt were planted in the man's mind. They were irrigated in the vicarage where Knowles was offered the rare treat of a glass of sherry and, when he'd downed that in an unmannerly gulp, a second glass. The memory of his loss was still a raw wound for Knowles. Tears welled up in his eyes as he recalled it and, while he still smarted at Peet's display of arrogance, he came to see that they did have a kinship of sorts. Both had felt the pain of losing a beloved wife. When the vicar asked him how *he* would have reacted if a murder victim had suddenly appeared in the grave destined for Margery Knowles, the question was like a stab in the heart for Knowles and he at last capitulated, agreeing to dig a second grave for Cicely Peet.

When he left the vicarage, Knowles did so with a meditative trudge in place of his usual brisk stride. The vicar, meanwhile, offered up a prayer of thanks to God then poured himself another glass of sherry. He had managed a first, delicious sip before his wife came bustling into the room.

'There are three strangers in the churchyard,' she said, querulously.

'Surely not, my dear – there's a constable at the gate to keep everyone out.'

'I could have sworn that I saw them.'

Enid Sadler was a pale, thin wraith of a woman with poor eyesight and a habit of nodding her head whenever she spoke. The discovery of the dead body in a grave dug for someone else had shredded her nerves and her hands still shook.

'Leave it to me,' said the vicar, solicitously, helping his wife to a chair then handing her the glass of sherry. 'Drink this – I won't be long.'

On the short train journey to Spondon the detectives had been given all the salient details. When the corpse had been found in the churchyard, it had been identified from the business card in the man's wallet. There were no marks of violence on Vivian Quayle and, since he had a pocket watch and money on him, robbery could be ruled out as a motive for his murder. It was the local doctor who'd established that the man had been poisoned but he was unable to say which particular poison was used or how it had been administered. The body had been removed to the home of Dr Hadlow where it was awaiting a post-mortem.

Colbeck, Leeming and Wigg stared into the open grave. In the course of removing its uninvited guest, two of the local constables had inadvertently kicked some of the earth piled up beside it into the cavity and left their footprints along its edge. The neat handiwork of Bert Knowles had been badly disturbed.

'I feel sorry for the girl,' said Colbeck. 'When she jumped in there, she must have been frightened to death.'

'Who wouldn't have been?' asked Leeming, sympathetically.

'In my view,' said Wigg, bluntly, 'she got what she deserved. Lizzie Grindle and her brother shouldn't have been playing in the churchyard. If they were my children, I'd have given them a good hiding.'

'Do you *have* children, Superintendent?'

'No, Sergeant – as it happens, I don't.'

'I thought not,' said Leeming. 'Being a father makes you look at things very differently. I have two sons. If one of them had been through this experience, I'd have wanted to help them cope with it. The poor girl in this case is young and vulnerable. She may have nightmares for years to come.'

Wigg was brusque. 'Serves her right.'

'How was he found?' asked Colbeck, staring at the grave. 'I mean, in what exact position was he lying?'

'He was stretched out on his back, Inspector.'

'So he wasn't just tossed in there?'

'Apparently not.'

'Was his clothing torn in any way?'

'No,' replied Wigg. 'It was sullied, of course, but that was inevitable. You'll be able to judge for yourself when I take you to meet Dr Hadlow. The coroner has been informed and is sending someone out to conduct the post-mortem.'

'How did Enoch Stone die?'

'That's immaterial.'

'We're always interested in unsolved murders.'

'We'll solve it one day,' said Wigg, stoutly. 'Have no fear.'

'You haven't answered the inspector's question,' said Leeming. 'Who was Enoch Stone and how was he killed?'

'I can tell you that,' said the vicar as he walked towards them. 'I'm relieved to see that *you're* here, Superintendent. Unable to see you properly, my wife was afraid that you were grave robbers.' He gave a dry laugh. 'Technically, I suppose, it was Mr Quayle who deserves that appellation. It was he who robbed Cicely Peet of her grave. A new one is going to be dug.' He looked at Colbeck and Leeming. 'Welcome to St Mary's, gentlemen. I'm Michael Sadler, the vicar.'

There was an exchange of handshakes as Colbeck introduced himself and the sergeant. When he told the vicar that they'd taken charge of the investigation, he saw the superintendent wince. Evidently, Wigg was going to be a problem for them. In his eyes, it was the Scotland Yard detectives who were the grave robbers. They'd stolen the case from right under his nose.

'In answer to your questions,' the vicar began, 'Enoch Stone was a man of middle years who worked as a framework knitter.' He saw the bewilderment on Leeming's face. 'Anyone in Spondon will tell you what that is, Sergeant. One night in June, 1856, Stone was found on the Nottingham road with severe head injuries. He'd been battered to the ground, then robbed.'

'There's no need to preach a sermon about it, Vicar,' said Wigg, impatiently. 'We're here to investigate the murder of Mr Quayle.'

'Let the vicar finish,' said Colbeck. 'We're learning something about this village and the information is invaluable.'

'Thank you,' resumed the vicar. 'In brief, Stone was still alive after the assault and was carried to the home of Dr Hadlow. Though nursed throughout the night, he succumbed to his injuries and died. Everyone was shocked. Stone was a quiet and well-respected man who was universally popular, all the more so because he was also a musician. When a reward of a hundred pounds was offered, the people of Spondon were quick to add another twenty pounds to the amount. Sadly, it failed to bring forth information leading to the arrest of the malefactors.'

'That's enough of Enoch Stone,' said Wigg, testily.

Colbeck raised an eyebrow. 'Were you in charge of the investigation?'

'I was, Inspector, and I still am. The search for the killer continues.'

'I admire your dedication.'

'We never give up.'

'But this is a relatively small village,' observed Leeming. 'That should have made your task much simpler. We've had to solve murders in major cities where killers have to be winkled out of a large population.'

Wigg was nettled. 'If you think it's easy to solve a murder in Spondon,' he said, rounding on the sergeant, 'I'll be interested to see how you fare with the present case, especially as you're doing so with no knowledge whatsoever of this village and its inhabitants.' He jabbed a finger at Leeming. 'Show me how it's done.'

'We gladly accept your challenge, Superintendent,' said Colbeck, suavely, 'but don't underestimate our capacity for learning and for doing so quickly. It seems that we've come too late to catch the person or persons responsible for the death of Enoch Stone but we can assure you that whoever murdered Mr Quayle will not remain at liberty for long.'

'Derby?'

'Yes, Father,' she said. 'There's been a murder at a village nearby.'

'Then I pity Robert.'

'Why is that?'

'He'll have to travel on the Midland Railway,' said Caleb Andrews. 'It's a dreadful company – even worse than the GWR.'

'The victim was a director of the Midland Railway.'

'That proves my point. The killer was probably a discontented customer and there are plenty of those, believe me.'

Madeleine Colbeck was so struck by the absurdity of her father's claim that she burst out laughing. It only encouraged Andrews to repeat his claim. Having retired after a lifetime's service on the railway, the former engine driver had contempt for all the companies except the one for whom he'd worked. In the past, he'd reserved his bitterest criticism for the Great Western Railway but, Madeleine now discovered, he was ready to pour even more scorn on the Midland.

'It's a complete hotchpotch, Maddy,' he said. 'It's made up of three companies who should have been strangled at birth – North Midland, Midland Counties, Birmingham and Derby Junction. Not one of them could provide a decent service. When they joined together to form the Midland Railway, they fell into the hands of a money-grubbing monster named George Hudson.'

'Yes, I know. Robert has told me all about the so-called Railway King. He was forced to resign in the end, wasn't he?'

'He should have been lashed to the buffers of one of his own engines.'

'But he was hailed as a hero at one time.'

'Not by me, he wasn't. From the very start I thought he was a crook.'

Madeleine let him rant on. When her father was in such a mood, he was like a locomotive with a full head of steam and had to be allowed to let some of it off. They were in the house in John Islip Street that she shared with her husband and was always pleased when her father came to visit, especially as he'd finally become accustomed to the notion of her having servants at her beck and call. Andrews was a short, wiry man with a fringe beard now salted with white hairs. Rocked by the death of his wife years earlier, he'd been helped through the period of mourning by his daughter who'd had to accommodate her own anguish at the same time. It had drawn them closer, though there were moments when Madeleine reminded him so much of his beautiful wife that Andrews could only marvel at her.

She had undergone a remarkable transformation, moving from a small house in Camden Town to a much larger one in Westminster and leaving a crotchety father to live with an indulgent husband. What united all three of them was a mutual passion for railways. There was only one disadvantage to that. With a son-in-law dedicated to solving crimes connected with railways, Andrews kept trying to appoint himself as an unpaid assistant.

'Robert should have come to me before he left,' he asserted. 'I'd have told him all that he needed to know about the Midland Railway.'

'Valuable as it would have been,' she said, tactfully, 'he didn't have time to listen to your advice. When the summons came, he dashed off to Derby without even coming home first. Robert sent word of where he'd gone.'

'When you hear more about this murder, let me know.'

'I will.'

'I may be able to help in some way.'

'You're not a detective, Father.'

'I've got a sixth sense where railways are concerned, Maddy. Look at that threat to the royal family. I was the first person to realise the danger.'

'That's true,' she conceded.

'I made a big difference in that case,' he boasted, 'and I may be

31

able to do exactly the same again with this one. Be sure you tell me all the details. I could be useful.'

Madeleine wondered why it sounded more like a threat than a kind offer.

Augustus Hadlow was a sharp-featured, stooping man in his forties with a low voice and a pleasant manner. The son of a country doctor, he'd followed his father into the medical profession and had worked in Spondon for well over a decade. When they called at his house, a fine Georgian edifice with classical proportions, the detectives were given a cordial welcome before being conducted to the room in which the cadaver of Vivian Quayle was being kept. Herbs had been used to combat the smell of death. Quayle lay naked beneath a shroud and Colbeck noted how carefully his clothing had been folded before being draped over a chair. After checking the label, he examined the frock coat briefly. Though soiled by its contact with bare earth, it was not torn and the buttons were intact. Quayle's shoes stood beside the garments but something was missing.

'Where is his hat?' asked Colbeck.

'He didn't have one, Inspector,' replied the doctor.

'A gentleman like Mr Quayle would never travel without a hat.'

'Then it must have been stolen by the killer,' surmised Leeming. 'Why take a hat yet leave a wallet and a watch behind?'

'That's one more mystery for us to unravel, Sergeant. Tell me, Doctor,' he went on, turning to Hadlow, 'what made you decide that he'd been poisoned?'

'I couldn't think of any other possible explanation for his death,' said Hadlow. 'When I got him back here and was able to examine him properly, I saw puncture marks on his arm.' He pulled back the shroud to reveal the corpse. Hadlow indicated a mark on one arm. 'Something lethal was injected into the vein.'

'Have you any idea what it could be?'

'No, Inspector, I'm not an expert on poisons, I'm afraid.'

'What struck you when you first saw the body?'

'Well, I couldn't believe that I was looking at a murder victim. It's a strange thing to say about him but . . . it was almost as if he looked at peace.'

Wigg fell prey to light sarcasm. 'Are you suggesting that he climbed into the grave of his own volition then met his Maker by injecting himself with poison?'

'Of course not, Superintendent – there was no syringe.'

'And there was no reason to take his own life,' said Colbeck. 'Didn't you say that Mr Quayle was in line to be the next chairman of the Midland Railway?'

'It was a foregone conclusion,' said Wigg. 'Mr Quayle was an ambitious man with a lot to live for. He'd never commit suicide. His death allows Mr Haygarth to collect the spoils. In the emergency, during the interregnum caused by the resignation of the previous chairman, he'd appointed himself as the acting chairman.'

Colbeck remembered that, in the telegraph sent to Scotland Yard, Haygarth was described as the chairman. Before the board approved of his appointment, he had already promoted himself. Both detectives had been studying the corpse and trying to work out what Quayle must have looked like when alive. Though he was reportedly in his late fifties, he seemed much younger and was passably handsome with dark, curly hair and a well-trimmed moustache. Even in that undignified position, he somehow looked a more imposing figure than Donald Haygarth.

Responding to a nod from Colbeck, the doctor covered the body up again.

'Can I ask you a question, Dr Hadlow?' said Leeming. 'You

were involved when Enoch Stone was killed, weren't you?'

'Do we have to drag that case up again?' protested Wigg.

'You told us that the investigation was ongoing, Superintendent.'

'Yes, but you're not here to meddle in it. One murder is enough to keep you occupied, I fancy. Please confine yourself to that.'

'We're bound to wonder if there's any link between the two killings.'

'None at all,' said Wigg. 'Don't you agree, Doctor Hadlow?'

'On the face of it,' replied the other, 'I'd have to endorse your opinion. Stone was the victim of a brutal assault while Mr Quayle seems to have escaped violence. Then, of course, their stations in life were far apart. One came from humble stock while the other was extremely wealthy, if his attire is anything to judge by. I see no connection between the two crimes, Sergeant.'

'Except the obvious one,' added Colbeck. 'Both men were killed in Spondon. Was that a bizarre coincidence?'

'I don't know, Inspector.'

'I do,' said Wigg, firmly. 'Yes, it *was* a coincidence, so can we please forget Enoch Stone and concentrate our efforts on finding out who killed Mr Quayle?'

After plying the doctor with some more questions, Colbeck signalled to Leeming that it was time to leave and the two of them stepped out into the street. Since the superintendent stayed in the house for a few minutes, they were able to have a private conversation at long last.

'What's your feeling, Inspector?'

'Wigg is an encumbrance.'

'It's a pity that *he* wasn't found in that grave.'

'Now, now, Victor, let's not be vindictive.'

'That's what *he* is, sir. He reminds me of Superintendent Tallis.'

'Oh, no,' said Colbeck with a laugh. 'You're comparing a

molehill to a mountain. Wigg doesn't have the intelligence or the ruthlessness to replace our beloved superintendent.'

'What's our next step, sir?'

'I think that we should take a walk around Spondon and get to know the geography of the village. I noticed some public houses on our way here. Keep a sharp eye out for any others.'

'Why is that?'

'It's because you will have to choose between them.'

'I don't follow, sir.'

'This crime was committed in Spondon but I'll wager anything that its roots are a long way from here. Finding those roots is my job. That's why I'll use the hotel in Derby as my base. You, meanwhile, will be staying here in a local hostelry while you search for any clues and talk to potential witnesses.'

Leeming's face fell. 'Are you leaving me alone in this godforsaken wilderness?'

'It strikes me as a rather nice place to live.'

'Then why don't *you* stay here?'

'I'll be dealing with the family of the deceased and looking more closely into Mr Quayle's relationship with the Midland Railway. Don't worry, Victor. I'm not cutting you adrift. We'll spend the first night at the Royal Hotel then you can come here tomorrow morning. Spondon is only a few miles away from Derby.'

'What exactly must I do here?'

'Your first task will be to attend the funeral of Mrs Peet. The vicar did tell us that a lot of people were expected. Study them carefully,' advised Colbeck. 'The killer might well be among them.'

CHAPTER FOUR

'This is the reward notice, Mr Haygarth,' Cope said, handing it over. 'I've arranged for copies to be put up in Spondon itself and all over Derby.'

'We must go further afield than that.'

'We will do.'

'A supply must be sent to Nottingham.'

'That's already in hand.'

'This is good,' said Donald Haygarth, examining the notice. 'It's clear and precise. A reward of two hundred pounds should be enough to encourage anyone with relevant information to come forward.'

'I hope so, sir.'

Maurice Cope was a short, stringy, thin-faced man in his late thirties with a self-effacing manner and an eagerness to please. He'd worked at the head office of the Midland Railway since its formation and watched the internal battles on its board of directors attentively so that he could align himself with the more influential members. Impressed by Haygarth's character and determination, he'd campaigned in secret on his behalf and was gratified that he was now working for the future chairman. There were, however, clouds on the horizon.

'I should warn you that there have been rumblings,' he said.

'About what, may I ask?'

'They're about the size of the reward for a start, sir. Some people have complained that it's far too high and that there should have been a board meeting in order to authorise it.'

'Nonsense!' exclaimed Haygarth with a dismissive gesture. 'In a crisis such as we face, immediate action was called for. That's why I took it upon myself to summon Inspector Colbeck and have these reward notices printed. If we'd had to wait days until members of the board could be brought together for discussion, we'd have lost all momentum.'

'I agree, Mr Haygarth.'

'*Someone* had to step into the breach.'

'You were the ideal person,' said Cope, ingratiatingly, 'and we are fortunate to have you. Inevitably, however, there has been criticism of the way that you took control of the situation.'

'Mr Quayle and I were the only candidates for the chairmanship. When he was murdered it was only natural that I should assume the office.'

'Thank goodness you did, sir.'

'I wish that all my colleagues saw it that way.'

'I'm sure that they'll come to do so in time.'

They were in the headquarters of the Midland Railway, the place from which its complex network of services was controlled. Years earlier, Haygarth, the owner of some lucrative silk mills, had been persuaded to invest some of his substantial wealth in the company. In return, he was given a seat on the board of directors and immediately began to gather like-minded people around him. Intelligent, ambitious and politically adroit, he'd waited until a vacancy had occurred for the chairmanship then put himself forward. He'd been needled when the general preference seemed to be for Vivian Quayle.

'Mr Quayle had many virtues,' he said, 'and I'll be the first to admit that. He was industrious, far-sighted and wholly committed to the expansion of the Midland Railway. As a man, I admired him. As a future chairman, on the other hand, I had the gravest of reservations about him. In the present circumstances, those reservations are now quite irrelevant. We must bring his killer to justice and we must console his family in every way possible. In posting a large reward and in bringing the Railway Detective here, we are sending out a message that any enemies of this company will be swiftly hunted down.'

'Your prompt action is to be commended, Mr Haygarth.'

'I've given statements to the press and much of what I said will be included in the obituaries of Mr Quayle. He will be deservedly mourned. As for my critics,' he went on, waving the poster in the air, 'you may tell them that the costs of printing and distribution will not fall on the company. Along with the reward money, I will gladly pay them out of my own pocket.'

'That's extraordinarily generous of you, sir.'

'I want my colleagues to know the sort of man that I am.'

'They'll be impressed. But there's just one question I'd like to ask.'

'What's that?'

'If the crime is solved by Inspector Colbeck, will *he* get the full reward of two hundred pounds?'

Haygarth's face darkened. 'We'll have to see about that.'

Big, solid and with a commanding presence in the town, the Royal Hotel offered good accommodation and an excellent menu in its dining room. As they enjoyed their meal there that evening, Robert Colbeck had no cause for complaint. Victor Leeming, however, kept glancing wistfully around. From the next day onwards, he knew he'd be eating plainer fare and sleeping in a far less comfortable bed above a noisy bar in a Spondon public house. Sensing the sergeant's dismay, Colbeck tried to cheer him up.

'You'll like it there, Victor. It's what you've yearned for, after all.'

Leeming was baffled. 'Is it?'

'Yes, I've lost count of the times you've moaned about bringing up your family in a big city with all the dangers that that implies. Whenever our work has taken us to smaller communities – Dawlish was a case in point – you said how nice it would be to live in such a place.'

'That's true,' admitted the other. 'The air would be a lot cleaner than it is in London and it would certainly be a lot safer and quieter.'

'There you are, then. Spondon answers all your needs. It's a pleasant village, just the kind of place for you, Estelle and the boys.'

'No, it isn't. I'd soon tire of it.'

'Why?'

'There's so little to do in a small village. Nothing ever happens there.'

Colbeck grinned. 'I wouldn't describe two murders in three years as a case of nothing ever happening. There are six constables there, remember, so there must be a lot of petty crime to police.'

'Throwing drunks out of a bar and keeping naughty children out of the churchyard is not my idea of work, Inspector. I thrive on action.'

'Don't treat naughty children with such contempt. It was two of them who first discovered that a murder had occurred. They set this investigation in motion. Bear that in mind. You should make a point of meeting the pair of them.'

'I will, sir,' said Leeming, 'and I'm sorry to complain. It's only right that one of us explores Spondon properly. If truth be told, I'll feel more at home in a village pub. Luxury like this always makes me uneasy.'

'It's a strange paradox. Comfort makes you uncomfortable.'

'I'm like a fish out of water here. It's Spondon for me. That's where the crime took place and where, in all probability, the killer lives.'

'Why do you say that?'

'He knew that there was an empty grave handy at St Mary's.'

'That could have been a case of serendipity.'

Leeming frowned. 'You've used that word before but I forget what it means.'

'It means that, if you stumble upon something that serves your purpose, you take full advantage of it. When the killer chose St Mary's, he may have been unaware that there was an appropriate place for a dead body. He's obviously somebody who knows the village,' Colbeck agreed, 'but that doesn't mean he still lives there. What we do know about him is that he has a macabre sense of humour. Most killers try to conceal their victims in order to slow down the process of detection. This man did the opposite. He *wanted* that corpse to be found.'

'I keep thinking about that missing top hat.'

'If we find that, it will have the name of Mr Quayle inside it.'

'How do you know?'

'I checked the label on his coat. His name was sewn into it. Among the many places I need to visit is the Nottingham tailor patronised by Mr Quayle. He was a man of exquisite taste.'

'Where else will you go, sir?'

'I'll visit the home of the deceased and make discreet enquiries there and I'll certainly need to look into the workings of the Midland Railway. Mr Quayle was intimately involved in them. He had power and that always creates enemies.'

'Mr Haygarth was one of them,' said Leeming, recalling their meeting with the acting chairman. 'He made a song and dance about the importance of catching Mr Quayle's killer but I didn't get the impression that he was really sorry that the man had died. Secretly, he must be delighted. He's just too cunning to show it.'

'My feeling exactly, Victor.'

'Do you think that someone from the Midland Railway is behind it all?'

'It's not impossible,' said Colbeck, thanking the waiter with a smile as the man cleared away their plates. 'It's equally possible that someone employed by a rival company is implicated. One sure way to disable the Midland is to get rid of the man who is about to become its chairman. Think of the impact on the morale of all the employees of the company. This will have shaken them badly.'

'It didn't shake Mr Haygarth.'

'I noticed that.'

'I know that Superintendent Wigg only said it by way of a jest but should we put Haygarth on the list of suspects? I can't see him killing another man but he looks capable of hiring someone to do his dirty work.'

'We must keep an open mind, Victor.'

'I like to have something to bite on in an investigation.'

'The cheese will be served very soon. Bite into that.' They both laughed. 'I'll warrant that you won't find the same quality in the Malt Shovel or the Union Inn or wherever you choose to stay.'

'I'll be where I fit in better,' said Leeming.

'Exactly,' said Colbeck. 'You can blend into that village in a way that I can't. There are times, I readily accept, when my educated vowels are a positive drawback. You're more down to earth and you're a good listener. It's one of your strengths.'

Leeming pulled a face. 'I didn't know that I had any.'

Colbeck laughed and patted his companion's shoulder. 'You're awash with them, Victor.' He saw the waiter approaching. 'It looks as if our cheese is on its way.'

But the waiter was bringing something more than just a selection of cheeses. After setting down the platter on the table, he put a hand inside his coat to extract a letter.

'This is for you, Inspector,' he said, giving it to him. 'It was handed in by someone at reception and passed on to the head waiter.'

'Thank you,' said Colbeck, scrutinising it and noting the neatness with which his name had been written. The man nodded and walked away. 'Let's see what we have here, shall we?' He opened the letter and took something out. 'Well, well, well . . .'

'What is it, sir?'

'It's a reward notice, Victor. A very tempting amount of money is being offered for information that leads to the arrest of the killer of Mr Quayle.' He turned the paper over. 'However, that's not all we've been given.' He passed it over to Leeming. 'Do you see what someone has written on the back?'

After reading details of the reward, Leeming looked at the reverse side.

'Gerard Burns – is he the person who sent this to you?'

'I don't think so.'

'Then who is he?'

'As of now,' said Colbeck, 'I fancy that he's our prime suspect.'

The day began early at the vicarage. Funerals were always unsettling occasions for Michael Sadler but he was looking forward to the latest one with real trepidation. In view of what had happened to the grave originally dug, he was afraid that he'd lost the hitherto unquestioning support of Roderick Peet, the bereaved husband. Other members of the family might also look askance at him. The fact that he'd finally persuaded Bert Knowles to dig a fresh grave might not be enough to win back the Peet family. It was something he should have done instantly, before Peet was drawn into the blistering row with Knowles. Deeply troubled, the vicar hardly touched his breakfast and heard very little of his wife's customary wittering.

The fact that it was a dull day with a promise of rain only added to his feeling of dread. He'd known and been very fond of Cicely Peet but it was not her tragic death that filled his mind. What preoccupied him was the image of a murder victim in the grave prepared for her. Fearful that something untoward might have occurred in her new resting place, he bestowed a token kiss on his wife's forehead then let himself out of the vicarage. When he walked around the church to the site of the fresh plot, he saw movement behind a neighbouring headstone and his heart constricted. The figure of a man rose up as if part of some weird ritual of resurrection. The vicar was now trembling all over. It was only when the initial shock wore off that he realised he was looking at Bert Knowles.

'I slept the night 'ere,' explained the gravedigger, stretching himself. 'Nobody was goin' to jump into *this* 'ole I dug. I made sure o' that, Vicar.' He bared his teeth in a hopeful grin. 'Is there any charnce o' some o' that theer sherry o' yours to wake me up proper?'

Victor Leeming was no stranger to funerals. There'd been a worrying sequence of them in his own family and he'd watched his grandparents, parents, two brothers and a sister laid to rest over the years, increasing his sense of being a lone survivor. In the course of his work, too, he'd been obliged to attend a number of funerals. Some were of police colleagues, killed in the execution of their duties, and others – as in the latest case – were of murder victims.

When he walked towards St Mary's church, a steady drizzle was falling. He'd heard enough about Cicely Peet during his earlier visit to Spondon to be aware of her exalted position in the community. Even so, he was taken aback by the number and quality of vehicles stretching down Church Hill and beyond. No women attended but a sizeable male congregation had come to pay its respects to the deceased. Leeming was glad. It was easier to remain anonymous in a crowd. When he joined the queue of solemn men filing into the church, he picked up several comments about Cicely Peet. She was not only held in high regard by everyone. Her beauty was also recalled and praised. What saddened the mourners was that such a lovely woman should have died so suddenly instead of gracing the village for many years to come. The general feeling was that her husband, devastated by his loss, would not be long in following her to the grave.

The mourners were not confined to members of the gentry who could afford expensive carriages and retain coachmen to drive them. Villagers were also there in force. Leeming heard local traders talking about the pleasure they always had from serving such a delightful lady. A hefty man with a full beard and a gravelly voice talked about her generosity whenever he'd shoed her horse. Leeming suspected that he might be the blacksmith whose daughter had actually found the interloper in the earlier grave and that the man had felt impelled to attend the funeral as a result. The sergeant's supposition was confirmed when he overheard someone asking the blacksmith if his children had recovered yet from their grim discovery.

'Lizzie hasn't slept a wink since,' replied Walter Grindle.

'What abaht thy lad?'

'Sam's all of a shek.'

'Who could've done sich a thing?'

It was a question that Leeming was there to answer if enough evidence presented itself but there was no sign of it so far. He made a point of sitting in the back row in the nave with his ears pricked to gather the muttered remarks of those nearby. When the coffin was brought in by the bearers with due solemnity, there was an audible sigh of grief. Leeming made no contribution to it. Nor did he hear much of the burial service. He was there to look and listen rather than to be caught up in the emotion of the occasion. What he did notice was that the vicar seemed extremely nervous for someone who must have presided over a large number of funerals in the course of his ministry. The Reverend Michael Sadler was slow and hesitant. In his eulogy of Cicely Peet, he spoke with great care as if fearing that he might offend her family by a misplaced word or a jarring sentiment. Leeming felt sorry for him. The vicar was clearly going through an ordeal.

In a gathering of lowered heads and sorrowful expressions, it was difficult to pick out anyone who might be a potential suspect. As time went on, however, one person did arouse Leeming's curiosity. He was a young man with pleasant features and a flitting gaze. Since he sat on the end seat in the back row, he was only a matter of yards away from Leeming who could see him across the aisle. Like the detective, he was taking less interest in the service than in those attending it. No grief registered in his face or behaviour. He kept glancing around at those near him. When the service came to an end, the long procession to the churchyard began and Leeming had the opportunity of taking a closer look at the young man. There was something odd about him that made him stand out but the sergeant couldn't decide what it was.

Eventually, it was time for the back rows on both sides of the nave to disgorge their occupants. Leeming tried to get close to the young man but there were too many people in the way. Over the heads of mourners, he could see him talking to a number of people in turn but he didn't get the feeling that he was a local man. He seemed to be as much a stranger as Leeming himself. As the congregation gathered around the grave, Bert Knowles lurked nearby with his spade, seemingly unaffected by the gravity of the event and simply waiting for his moment. Leeming never got near enough to see anything of the committal or to watch the drizzle adding a slippery coating to the coffin. His eyes remained on the young man, who now seemed more and more detached from what was going on. All of a sudden, he turned on his heel and headed towards the gate as if he'd got what he wanted and was anxious to sneak away. Leeming went after him.

The young man was walking briskly in the direction of the railway station. It required a sustained effort for Leeming to catch him up. Placing a firm hand on the man's shoulder, he brought him to a halt and spun him around.

'Excuse me, sir,' said Leeming, politely. 'I'd like a word with you.'

CHAPTER FIVE

After having breakfast with Leeming at the Royal Hotel, Colbeck had set off to make his own enquiries. He'd already found out from the hotel management that nobody could remember who had delivered the letter for him. Apparently, it had just been slapped down on the reception desk by someone who left immediately. How much notice he should take of the name he'd been given, Colbeck didn't know but he was certain that Gerard Burns had not been plucked at random out of the air. The man definitely existed and needed to be found.

Colbeck was waiting on the platform at Derby railway station when a possible source of information materialised beside him. It was almost as if Superintendent Wigg had followed him there.

'Might I ask where you're going, Inspector?' he said.

'I'm going where I need to go,' replied Colbeck, levelly.

'My men are, of course, ready to offer help whenever you need it.'

'Thank you, Superintendent. I may well need to call on them at some stage.'

'We await your summons.'

'Is there any news about the post-mortem?'

'It's not yet been completed. My understanding is that . . . well, it is proving more difficult than at first assumed. When they're available, I'll make sure that you have full details.'

'I'd value that information.'

'We understand the significance of a post-mortem, Inspector,' said Wigg, pointedly, 'so please don't treat us like country cousins. We're a young force but no less effective for that. When the Derbyshire Constabulary was established two years ago, we had eight divisions with Belper Police Station as its Divisional Headquarters. That arrangement proved unsatisfactory so it was moved this year to Derby instead and I was put in charge of it.'

'I'm sure that you deserved your promotion,' said Colbeck without irony. 'But since you come from these parts, does the name Gerard Burns mean anything to you?'

'I've never heard of him.'

'Are you quite sure?'

'I'm absolutely certain,' insisted Wigg. 'I have an excellent memory for names. How did this Gerard Burns come to your attention?'

'His name was written on the back of a reward notice and sent to me.'

Wigg laughed harshly. 'Then you can forget all about it. The fellow probably doesn't exist or, if he does, he'll have no connection whatsoever with the murder investigation. Someone is trying to stir up trouble for him, I daresay. As for that reward notice,' he went on, 'we've had several names sent to the police station. One person is certain that Prince Albert is the killer while another cites Her Majesty, the Queen. Two people have come up with the name of the late Duke of Wellington and it's only a matter of time before we get equally ridiculous suggestions designed to cause us annoyance.'

'Gerard Burns does not belong among the hoaxes, Superintendent.'

'How do you know that?'

'It's a question of instinct.'

'I may lack your detection skills, Inspector, but I do know how to pick up a scent and follow a trail.' He fixed Colbeck with a stare. 'What will happen if I and my men solve this crime before you and Sergeant Leeming?'

'I thought that you were offering to help us?'

'We're at your command,' said Wigg, spreading his arms, 'but it's not wholly impossible that, through our own individual efforts, *we* bring this investigation to the desired end.'

'What – as you did so in the case of Enoch Stone?'

Wigg gritted his teeth. 'Please answer my question.'

'If that happens,' said Colbeck, pleasantly, 'I'll be the first to shake your hand and to congratulate you. I'll also point out to Mr Haygarth that, instead of bringing us all the way from London, he should have relied on the local police force instead.'

'Haygarth will never admit that he made a mistake.'

Colbeck studied him. 'Why do you dislike the man?'

'It's not so much a question of dislike as of distrust.'

'He struck me as being very decisive.'

'Haygarth is *too* decisive, Inspector. He exceeds his authority. Mr Quayle would never have done that. I had my reservations about the man but they can be disregarded. As a future chairman, he had all the right qualities.' Wigg sniffed loudly. 'That's not the case with Donald Haygarth.'

'When we first met you,' remembered Colbeck, 'you jokingly put his name forward as a possible suspect.'

'There was no joke involved, I promise you.'

Colbeck was taken aback. 'Are you being serious, Superintendent?'

'I was never more so,' said Wigg. 'I may have made the

suggestion in a light-hearted way but that was deliberate. If you want to compile a list of suspects, you can cross out the name of Gerard Burns and insert Haygarth in its place. He's involved in this crime somehow and I hope to be the person to place him under arrest.'

'How long have you been there?' asked Leeming.

'Three years.'

'Do you like the work?'

'I love it, Sergeant. It's opened my eyes in every way.'

'What did you think of the service?'

'It was very dignified.'

'Is that what you'll say in your report?'

'Yes,' said Philip Conway, 'but I can't guarantee that my words will be printed. The editor always trims my articles to the bone. The main thing he wanted me to get were the names of all the bigwigs who attended. People like to be mentioned in a newspaper – in the right way, that is.'

Victor Leeming had warmed to the young reporter. Conway had looked shifty at first but, on further acquaintance, he'd turned out to be an enthusiastic young man with a questing intelligence. As soon as the sergeant had introduced himself, Conway had fired half-a-dozen questions about Scotland Yard at him, and he was still wide-eyed about meeting a man who worked alongside Inspector Colbeck.

'I've followed his career,' he explained, 'so I must have seen your name as well. We have all the London newspapers here, you know. They're delivered by train at a surprisingly early hour.' He gave a sheepish grin. 'My ambition is to work on one of those papers one day.'

They were in the Malt Shovel, the public house where Leeming had booked the room and where he'd invited Conway to share a pint of beer with him. From the table where they sat, they could see a malt shovel perched on two hooks above the bar. The beer was exceptional and the atmosphere flavoursome. Leeming had taken to the place immediately.

'I've got some cuttings about the Railway Detective's cases,' said Conway with a boyish grin. 'You saved the royal train from being blown up, didn't you?'

'We were lucky enough to do so,' replied Leeming, modestly.

'Then there was a case somewhere in Yorkshire.'

'The village was called South Otterington. Actually, Spondon reminds me of it in some ways. I can't say that I enjoyed my stay in Yorkshire very much but there was an unexpected bonus.'

'What was that, Sergeant?'

'We found a village named Leeming.'

They shared a laugh then sipped their drinks. Ordinarily, Leeming would have been very circumspect when talking to a reporter. Colbeck had warned him to say too little to the press rather than too much. Some editors had an agenda that included biting criticism of the Metropolitan Police Force. The *Derby Mercury* had no such axe to grind. In its edition that day it had given an account of the murder and welcomed the arrival of the detectives from Scotland Yard. Besides, Leeming decided, the young reporter was not there to denigrate them in any way. Conway was in awe of them. He was also a native of Derbyshire and therefore able to relate more easily to local people. Leeming had not just made a new friend, he'd acquired an assistant.

'Then there was that case in Wales,' recalled Conway.

'Let's forget our past successes,' said Leeming, firmly. 'If we spend all our time talking about them, we won't be able to add to the list. I need to know this village inside out. You may be able to help me.'

'I'll do what I can, Sergeant, but I have to answer to an editor. He tells me where and when I can go. I was sent here to attend the funeral and to gauge the reaction of Spondon to the murder. The second bit is easy. This village has been knocked senseless by the crime.'

'Who have you spoken to so far?'

'Lots of people,' said Conway, fishing a notebook out of his pocket and leafing through it. 'The first person I interviewed was Walter Grindle. It was his daughter who leapt into the grave where Mr Quayle was lying.'

'I saw the blacksmith as well. On the way into church, he stood close to me. I heard him say what an effect the discovery had had on his children.'

'They're terrified.'

'In the same circumstances, mine would be as well.' Leeming sat back and his chair creaked. 'What exactly did Mr Grindle say to you?'

Nottingham was a thriving manufacturing town with a population that had increased markedly in the past decade. It owed much of its reputation to a textile industry in which the quality of its lace, in particular, stood out. Yet it had by no means lost all of its charm and its picturesque aspects. When he glanced through the window of his compartment, Colbeck saw a community sited conveniently on the navigable River Trent and still possessing striking relics of its past such as its Norman castle, now in ruins but with undeniable grandeur. News of the murder in the neighbouring county had caused great upset in Nottingham because the victim had hailed from there and was a well-known figure. As soon as he left the train, Colbeck overheard people speculating on the identity of the killer and his motivation. The name of Vivian Quayle seemed to be on everyone's lips.

When he left the station, Colbeck made for the cab rank. He had not needed to ask anyone where Quayle had lived because the man's address had been printed in that morning's edition of the *Derby Mercury*. The cab drove to the edge of the town before turning into the gateway of an estate. Filtered by the trees, bright sunshine was casting intricate shadows over the winding track. When he emerged from a hundred yards or more of woodland, Colbeck saw ahead a well-tended lawn edged with flower beds and, beyond it, a large Jacobean mansion in an impressive state of repair. Having met many railway magnates in the course of his work, Colbeck was used to seeing the high standard of living that they enjoyed, but Vivian Quayle's abode was more sumptuous than most.

The cab stopped well short of the house because a uniformed policeman stood in its path with his hand raised. He came over to eye the passenger.

'This is a house of mourning,' he said, crisply. 'No visitors are allowed.'

'I'm not a visitor, Constable. My name is Inspector Colbeck and I've been summoned from Scotland Yard to lead the murder investigation. It's imperative that I talk with a member of the family.'

The man was suspicious. 'How do I know you are who you say you are?'

'You simply have to look into my eyes.'

Colbeck gazed at him with an intensity and a sense of authority that made the policeman back away. Producing a weak smile of apology, he stood aside and waved the cab on. The man had been officious but Colbeck approved of his being there to keep unwanted visitors at bay. Quayle's murder would have set the local press buzzing and the last thing that the family wanted at such a time was a demand from reporters to make a statement. They would still be reeling from the thunderbolt that had hit them. Colbeck needed to behave with the utmost tact.

When the cab drew up outside the house, he asked the driver to wait then went to the front door. It opened before he could even reach for the bell and he was confronted by a beetle-browed butler who seemed as intent on sending him on his way as the policeman. Having heard who Colbeck was, however, the man grudgingly admitted him and took the visitor along to the study. Colbeck was left alone to gauge something of the character of Vivian Quayle from the room in which he'd worked. Patently, he was not a reading man. Though two walls were lined with bookshelves, there were very few books on them. Pride of place had instead been given to delicate porcelain. It occupied the majority of the shelves and the most attractive objects stood in a glass-fronted cabinet.

Above the gleaming marble fireplace was the item that told Colbeck most about the dead man. It was a full-length portrait of Vivian Quayle, standing in front of a locomotive with an engine shed in the background. Well dressed and well groomed, Quayle had a smile on his face that spoke of unquestioning confidence in his abilities. He cut an incongruous figure against the industrial grime behind him but the fact that he'd asked the artist to paint the portrait in such a place showed a genuine love for the railway. Colbeck had more than a passing interest in the locomotive itself because his wife had developed her artistic skills to a point where she could sell her paintings of locomotives and he was pleased to see how superior her work was to the one before him. While the portrait painter had captured the essence of Vivian Quayle, he'd struggled to make the locomotive and the engine shed look at all realistic.

'He loved that painting dearly,' said a voice.

Colbeck turned to see a tall, sleek man in his thirties who had just opened the door noiselessly and entered the study. At a glance, Colbeck could see that the newcomer bore a close resemblance to the figure in the portrait.

'I'm Stanley Quayle,' the son went on without offering a handshake. 'You've come at an awkward time, Inspector Colbeck.'

'I appreciate that, sir, and I'm deeply sorry to intrude.' He glanced up at the painting. 'The locomotive is from the Jenny Lind class, isn't it?'

'You're very observant.'

'It's a later model so it was probably built in Derby. The original Jenny Lind, of course, was built in Leeds by E. B. Wilson and Company. Mr Kirtley, the esteemed locomotive superintendent of the Midland Railway, improved on the design. But,' he said with a smile of apology, 'you don't wish to hear me rambling on about locomotives.'

Quayle motioned him to the sofa then made a point of sitting in the chair at the desk as if signalling that he had just claimed part of his inheritance. While he was looking Colbeck up and down, the latter was appraising him.

'What can you tell me, Inspector?' asked Quayle.

'First, let me offer you my sincere condolences, sir. I can imagine how great a shock this has all been to you.'

'When will the body be released to us?'

'That will happen as soon as the post-mortem is concluded.'

'Do you need such a thing?' demanded Quayle. 'My father was murdered. Must you add to our grief by cutting him open like an animal on a butcher's slab?'

'It's important for us to know the precise way in which he was killed, sir. We know that he was poisoned by lethal injection. If we can identify the nature of that poison, we may have a valuable clue.'

'Why is it taking so long?'

'I've no answer to that, sir.' He glanced towards the door. 'Is the whole family here at the moment?'

'Most of us are,' replied the other. 'My younger sister lives here and my brother has a house nearby. Both are far too distressed to speak to you. As for my mother, I fear that this whole business may be the death of her. Mother is frail at the best of times. She's taken to her bed. Only the capture of the villain who committed this foul crime could hope to revive her.'

'You may leave that in my hands, sir. You said that most of the family were here. Are you expecting anyone else to join you?'

'No, we're not. My other sister went away years ago and is . . . estranged from events here. She may not even be aware of what's happened.'

'What will she do if she *does* become aware of them?'

'That's a private matter.'

'On receipt of such terrible news about her father, any daughter would wish to return home, surely?'

Quayle's eyes flashed. 'As I told you, Inspector, it's a private matter.'

'As you wish, sir.'

'So I should hope. Now, what action have you taken?'

'We're looking closely at the place where the murder occurred. Can you suggest any reason why your father should have gone to Spondon in the first place?'

'No, I can't.'

'Did he ever mention the village to you?'

Quayle shook his head. 'Why should he?'

'When did you last see him?'

'It must have been three or four days ago.'

'So you're unable to give me details of his movements on the day leading up to the murder. What about your brother or your sister?'

'Neither of them can help you, Inspector. Father was a tireless workhorse. He was always on the move. Lucas saw very little of him and, even though she was under the same roof, Agnes spent almost no time with Father. She's been too busy nursing our mother, a task that has suddenly become more pressing.'

While he felt sympathy for the man, Colbeck resented the note of arrogance in his voice and the way that he was staring impatiently at his visitor as if anxious to get rid of him as soon as possible. The inspector did not sense a willingness to cooperate or an acknowledgement of his status as the person charged with solving the crime.

'There's a question that I'm bound to ask you, Mr Quayle.'

'I'm not one to flinch,' boasted the other, jutting out his jaw.

'Did your father have any enemies?'

'He was a successful man, Inspector, and, as such, excited a lot of envy.'

'Envy rarely leads to murder, sir.'

'That depends how high the stakes are.'

'Are you referring to the chairmanship of the Midland Railway?'

'If that's the construction you wish to place on my remark, so be it. As for long-standing feuds with anyone, one or two may have existed. But in general, my father was a sociable man with a wide circle of friends. Messages of condolence have already started to pour in.'

'But you're not prepared to name any likely suspects, is that it?'

Quayle was blunt. 'You're the detective – flush them out.'

'Any help you could give us would be appreciated, sir.'

'I've expressed my feelings,' said the other, rising to his feet, 'and I'm unable to give you any more time. The one place where you won't find the killer is inside this house.' He opened the door meaningfully. 'Start looking elsewhere, Inspector.'

'One last question,' said Colbeck, getting up. 'Do you, by any chance, happen to know a man by the name of Gerard Burns?'

Quayle's cheeks reddened and his body tensed. For a moment, it looked as if he was about to resort to physical violence and Colbeck prepared for an assault. In the event, it never came. Instead, Quayle walked to the door and opened it wide.

'That's all the time I can give you, Inspector.'

Colbeck had his answer.

CHAPTER SIX

Since their husbands had worked so closely together for a number of years, a friendship had grown up between Madeleine Colbeck and Estelle Leeming, and they tended to get together whenever their husbands were involved in a case that took them away from London. As it happened, the visit that Estelle made that afternoon to John Islip Street had been arranged a fortnight in advance. It coincided with the departure of both men to Derbyshire. Knowing that her guest would bring her two boisterous young sons, Madeleine had taken the precaution of inviting her father and it was not long before Caleb Andrews led the boys out into the garden to play. Their whoops of pleasure could be heard clearly inside the house.

'It's so kind of Mr Andrews to take charge of them,' said Estelle. 'It means that we can have a proper conversation for once.'

'My father enjoys their company.'

'They can be difficult to control sometimes.'

'He manages somehow.'

'When they're not at school, finding something to do with them is always a problem. Separately, David and Albert would be no trouble but, as soon as they get together, the sparks begin to fly.' More yells were heard from the garden. 'I hope they don't tire your father out.'

'Don't worry about him, Estelle. He's much tougher than he looks.'

'The boys can wear you down, Maddy.'

Estelle Leeming was a pretty woman in her thirties with a slim body and auburn hair that she'd passed on to both of her sons. Living in a small house, she was always rather intimidated by the Colbeck residence. After all the years as the wife of a policeman, she still worried about her husband whenever he went to work.

'It was worse in the old days,' she confided, 'when Victor was still in uniform. I knew that he'd always come home with bruises or scratches on his face yet it always took me by surprise somehow. When he turned up with a terrible black eye one night, I had a job recognising him. He got it when he arrested a burglar he caught climbing out of a house.'

'Robert always says that he's bound to be injured from time to time. He never complains about pain. If he gets his coat torn in a fight, however, or if someone damages his hat, then he's livid.' They both laughed. 'He cares far more about his appearance than he does about his safety.'

'That's certainly not true of Victor.'

'What did he tell you, Estelle?'

'All he sent me from Scotland Yard was a short letter saying that he was off to Derby for some reason. He gave no details.'

'Then I can at least provide you with some information because Robert's letter was more explicit. A director of the Midland Railway has been murdered. They were summoned by telegraph.'

'I suppose that we ought to feel proud that they're always in demand,' said Estelle with a sigh, 'but I do miss Victor. Apart from anything else, the boys are much more of a handful when he's away. Still, you'll find out the problems of being a mother when you have children of your own.'

'I already have a child.'

Estelle sat up. 'Do you?'

'Yes,' said Madeleine, pointing to the window. 'He's out there in the garden with the boys. Since he retired, my father's entered his second childhood.'

'I daresay that he'd like grandchildren of his own.'

'That's in the lap of the gods, Estelle.'

'It's certainly not something you can control,' admitted the other. 'We had to wait. When it happened, we were so grateful to have two healthy boys. It completed the family somehow.'

'I'm sure that it did,' said Madeleine, keen to get off the subject. 'It's time for tea, I think.' She rang the bell for a servant. 'They'll have worked up an appetite by charging around the lawn.'

Victor Leeming was quietly elated. When he mistook Philip Conway for a potential suspect, he made a new friend and learnt a great deal about Spondon. The reporter had not only talked to several people in the village, he recalled details of recent crimes there, recorded in editions of his newspaper. Leeming was surprised to hear how much of it there had been. Apart from thefts from various premises, there had been a spate of vandalism, a drunken brawl that led to three arrests and a case of sexual assault. Beneath the even tenor of the village, there was clearly a worrying undercurrent. As he talked to the young reporter, Leeming came to understand the full meaning of serendipity. Chancing upon Conway had been a stroke of good fortune.

'What about the murder of Enoch Stone?' he asked.

'That will never be solved.'

63

'Why is that?'

'Too much time has gone by and any clues have long since disappeared. I don't think the killer was a local man. Stone was well liked here. My guess is that he was set on by a traveller of some sorts who battered him to the ground, stole his money then fled. They'll never find him, Sergeant.'

'Yet they're still looking.'

'They might as well chase moonbeams.'

'I've arrested quite a few moonbeams in my time,' said Leeming with a chuckle. 'Just when you're ready to abandon a particular case, something always turns up out of the blue to help you solve it.'

'I'm glad you mentioned turning up,' said Conway, glancing at the clock on the wall, 'because that's what my editor is expecting me to do. We've been here almost two hours. I'll have to go, I'm afraid.'

'That's a pity.'

Conway got up. 'I'll probably be in Spondon again tomorrow.'

Leeming shook his hand warmly. 'You know where to find me.'

'Goodbye, Sergeant.'

When the reporter went out, Leeming followed to wave him off. He then turned in the opposite direction and went in search of Walter Grindle. The moment he got within earshot of the forge, he could hear a hammer striking the anvil with rhythmical power. He arrived in time to see the blacksmith fitting a shoe to a shire horse. Bert Knowles was holding the animal's bridle and smoking his pipe. Unable to understand more than a few words of what they were saying to each other, Leeming had to wait until the work was finished. As soon as he introduced himself, both men took an interest. Grindle demanded that the crime be solved quickly so that his children would stop fearing that a killer was stalking the streets of the village. He explained how distressed they both still were. For his part, Knowles had seen someone putting up a reward notice and, since he was barely literate, had got the man to read it out to him.

'Two 'undred!' he said, moving the pipe from one side of his mouth to the other. 'I could sup a lot o' beer wi' a windfall like thar.'

'Do you have any information that could lead to the killer?' asked Leeming.

'I might 've.'

'What is it?'

'Look arter Samson, will ter?' said Knowles to the blacksmith, handing over the horse. 'The sergeant's gonna buy me a pint.'

Leeming was dubious. 'Have you really got something useful to tell me?'

'Yes,' replied Knowles, indignantly. 'I dug the bleedin' grave where thar dead body turned up.'

As soon as he saw the window display at Brough and Hubbleday, Tailors Ltd, Colbeck's heart lifted. Everything on show was of the highest quality. He entered the premises to be greeted by Simon Hubbleday, a round-shouldered little man in his sixties who had worked there since the day the shop had opened. Peering over the top of his spectacles, he took one look at Colbeck and clapped his hands in appreciation.

'Nothing we could make for you would be an improvement on what you already wear, sir,' he said, honestly. 'The cut and cost of your attire tells me that you hail from London and keep a tailor in Bond Street or somewhere nearby.'

'You have good eyesight.'

'I only wish that Mr Brough was still alive to admire that cravat and that waistcoat. But my erstwhile partner – I am Simon Hubbleday, by the way – died a few years ago and left me alone with the task of making the gentry of Nottingham look both smart and respectable.'

'Your window display does you credit, Mr Hubbleday.'

'Praise from a man with your meticulous attention to detail is praise indeed.' He beamed at Colbeck. 'How can we be of service to you, sir?'

'I'd like to say that you could make something for me Mr Hubbleday, but the truth is I come only in search of information. One of your customers, I believe, was Mr Vivian Quayle.' The old man's face clouded. 'I see that you've heard the sad news about him.'

'Mr Quayle has been a customer for many years and so, I may add, have both of his sons. What happened to him is quite appalling. A nicer gentleman does not exist in the whole of Nottingham. It was a privilege to serve him.'

Colbeck introduced himself and asked if they might have a word in private. After summoning an assistant from the inner reaches of the shop, Hubbleday took his visitor off to an office that was barely big enough to accommodate both of them.

'Fortunately,' said the old man, 'Mr Brough was even smaller than me. The two of us could fit in here without any difficulty. Now, Inspector, what do you wish to know?'

'Tell me about Mr Quayle's top hat.'

'It was something about which he was very particular.'

'Really?'

'Don't ask me why. We sell top hats by the dozen. Our highest price is five shillings and sixpence but most customers settle for something slightly cheaper. Mr Quayle, by contrast, paid even more for his because he wanted the very finest silk. It was, if I may say so, a top hat of top hats.'

'In other words, it would be very distinctive.'

'Any man of discernment would covet it, Inspector.'

'That may explain why it disappeared.'

'I don't understand.'

Colbeck told him that the hat was missing from the open grave in which the dead man was found. Opening a drawer in his desk, Hubbleday took out a pile of drawings and began to leaf through them.

'I'm inclined to agree with you that it was stolen rather than simply discarded,' he said.

'Did you sew Mr Quayle's name inside it?'

'Oh, yes, he insisted. Ah, here we are,' he continued, plucking a drawing from the pile and passing it over. 'That's the hat we made for him.'

'It's highly individual,' observed Colbeck, 'and almost nine inches in height. That curly brim is a work of art.'

'Mr Quayle wanted it to stand out in a crowd. Everyone wears top hats these days. You'll see bargees on the river with them, and conductors on omnibuses. They used to be the sign of a gentleman,' said Hubbleday, nostalgically, 'but people of the lower sort get hold of them these days.'

'This is very useful,' said Colbeck. 'I'd recognise that hat anywhere.'

'Keep the drawing if it's of any use, Inspector. I hate to say it but Mr Quayle will never be in need of a new hat.'

'And you've never designed a similar one for anybody else?'

'No, I haven't.'

'What about Mr Quayle's sons?'

'Oh, they have very different tastes,' said Hubbleday with a smile. 'Lucas, the younger of the two, is something of a peacock and always leans towards ostentation. Stanley, his elder brother, is more conservative.'

'I met Stanley Quayle earlier,' said Colbeck. 'He seems to have taken charge at the house. I gather that his mother is not in the best of health.'

'Mrs Quayle has been ailing for several years, Inspector. Her husband was devoted to her. When you came down the street, you'll have passed the florist. He told me that, because his wife was so fond of flowers, Mr Quayle placed an order for a fresh supply of roses or lilies to be delivered every Monday morning.'

'I should have thought there'd be plenty of flowers on the estate.'

'Those were only for show,' said Hubbleday, 'or so I was told. Mrs Quayle liked to sit in the window of her room and look out on them. Mr Brough and I were invited to a function at the house once. You'll have seen the flower beds at the front but perhaps you missed the formal garden at the rear of the property. It is truly a thing of beauty.'

'Unfortunately,' said Colbeck, 'I wasn't there to admire the garden. I simply wanted to make contact with the family.'

'Did you meet Lucas Quayle? He's a delightful fellow.'

'No, I only spoke to his elder brother.'

There was a significant pause. 'Stanley Quayle is very single-minded,' said Hubbleday, measuring his words. 'He always seems much older than he really is. By repute, he's an astute businessman.' His frown melted into a smile. 'Nobody would ever say that about Lucas Quayle. He's always striking out in new directions even if some of them are ill-advised. Their father used to tell me that he had one reliable son and one irresponsible one. Curiously, he seemed fonder of the madcap.'

'There are two daughters as well, aren't there?'

'Don't ask me about those, Inspector. I sell nothing that they might want.'

'I understand that one of the daughters was estranged from the family.'

'I'm in no position to comment on that.'

'When I called at the house, Stanley Quayle informed me that the elder sister might not even attend the funeral.'

Hubbleday was scandalised. 'That's disgraceful!'

'The rift with the family must indeed be serious.'

'Death has a habit of uniting a family, Inspector. I pray that it might do so in this case.'

'So do I,' said Colbeck. 'I'd be very interested to meet the lady.'

Lydia Quayle sat alone at a table in a London tea room and read the item in the newspaper for the third time. She was a smart, shapely woman in her late twenties with brown curly hair framing a face whose unforced beauty was marred by an expression that veered between sorrow and anger. Putting the newspaper aside, she sipped her tea then took a first nibble out of one of the cakes on the plate beside her. It was afternoon in London and, through the window, she could see heavy traffic in the road outside. Lydia was distracted by the sight of a tiny bird perched on a stationary cart and hopping from one place to another. When the bird landed on the rump of the horse between the shafts, the animal took no notice. It was only when the creature hopped along its back and onto its mane that the horse shook its head violently and sent the bird flying into the sky.

Lydia picked up the newspaper and read the article about her father's murder once more. Getting up abruptly from the table, she abandoned the tea and cakes, tossed the newspaper aside with disdain and left the restaurant.

* * *

The short time that Victor Leeming spent with the gravedigger gave him more amusement than information. Over a pint of beer guzzled down at enormous speed, Bert Knowles told him that on the night in question he'd been drinking with friends at the Union Inn and, when he rolled out of there, a sense of duty made him walk to the churchyard to make sure that the grave he'd dug for Cicely Peet was still sound and that none of the sides had caved in. When he got there, he claimed, he felt that somebody was watching him though he saw nobody even though he stayed in the churchyard for a long time. Knowles insisted that the invisible watcher must have been the killer, biding his time until it was safe to put the dead body into the ground.

Leeming felt sorry for the man. He earned a pittance as a labourer and work at the church was intermittent. But the sergeant was firm, telling him that the tale about a phantom in the dark was not worth one penny of the reward money. Knowles promptly burst out laughing, slapped him on the arm and said that his story, freely acknowledged as being fictitious, had been 'worth a try'. Yet the purchase of a pint of beer for him had been a profitable investment. Thanks to Knowles, word of Leeming's presence there would be quickly disseminated throughout the village. Those who felt they had something of importance to tell him would certainly do so when they read the reward notice. The sergeant was pleased with himself. In the space of a few hours, he'd befriended a reporter who'd given him a brief criminal history of Spondon, and a local character who was also a mine of information about the village.

Having walked back to the forge with Knowles, he waited until the labourer had taken the horse back to the farm then asked if he could speak to the blacksmith's children. Walter Grindle agreed with the proviso that he had to be present. When he met Lizzie and Sam, Leeming realised that he'd get very little of value out of them. The girl kept collapsing in a flood of tears when she recalled her moment of discovery and her brother was paralysed with fear in the presence of a detective from Scotland Yard. The interview with the children was mercifully short for all concerned.

As he strolled along the street Leeming heard the sound of running feet behind him. He stopped and turned so that a lanky, dishevelled man with unusually large and staring eyes could catch up with him. Leeming put his age close to forty.

'Are you the sergeant?' asked the man.

'Yes, sir – who are you?'

'My name is Barnaby Truss,' said the other, breathlessly, 'and I just had a word with Bert Knowles when he went past my shop. He's an old friend and always stops if he sees me. I'm a glove-maker, sir, like many people in this village.'

'What kind of gloves?'

'*Silk* ones – the best you can buy.'

Leeming saw a chance to educate himself about local industry.

'Someone mentioned a stocking frame. What exactly is that?'

'Oh,' said Truss, 'you won't find many of them in Spondon because this is a place for gloves. Happen you've heard the sound of our frames as you've walked along the street. They're worked by hands and feet and make a lot of noise.'

Leeming was gratified to talk to someone who didn't lapse into the dialect that he found incomprehensible. In every sense, Truss was a cut above Bert Knowles. The glove-maker read his mind.

'Oh, I can talk the language as well as any of them, if I've a mind to,' he explained, 'but I've got ambitions, Sergeant. I want to go into local politics in Derby one day. That means a lot of public speaking so I've took lessons. You can probably tell.'

'Oh, yes,' said Leeming without conviction.

The only thing he could tell was that Truss's ambitions were doomed. Of the man's sincerity he had no doubt, but Truss was altogether too tentative and subdued for the cut-and-thrust of political debate. Besides, the staring eyes would frighten away any potential voters. However, the man's commitment had to be applauded so the sergeant passed a few encouraging comments.

'What can I do for you, Mr Truss?' he asked.

'I've got something to report.'

'I can see that Mr Knowles has told you about the reward.'

'Oh, I'm not looking for any money,' said Truss as if hurt by the suggestion. 'I'd just feel guilty if I didn't report something I saw. Of course, it may be nothing to do with the murder but, then again, it just might.'

'Go on, sir.'

'Well, Sergeant, what I witnessed was this . . .'

As he launched into his story, Truss began to wave his hands about in the air as if showing off a pair of his silk gloves. The gestures were so inappropriate as to be another deadly strike against his hopes of ever making his mark in local government and Leeming felt that whoever had been giving the man instruction in public speaking had no right to take a fee for his service. The glove-maker's evidence was markedly more interesting than the cock-and-bull story invented by Knowles. On the night when the murder occurred, Truss had been returning home when he saw something that he first dismissed from his mind as being unimportant. In view of what had happened, he wondered if he'd instead accidentally bumped into the killer.

'What time was this?' asked Leeming.

'Oh, it was well after midnight, Sergeant.'

'That was rather late to be out, wasn't it?'

The hands fluttered wildly like a pair of doves suddenly released from a cage.

'I was . . . on my way home f-from a f-friend,' said the other, introducing a stutter that had never been there before. 'I was coming down Church Hill when I saw him.'

'How far away was he, Mr Truss?'

'It must have been twenty or thirty yards.'

'Could you see him at all clearly in the dark?'

'No, I couldn't,' replied the other, 'but I saw enough to know that a man was pushing a wheelbarrow and that there was something in it covered with a cloth. I took no notice, to be honest, because it's not an unusual sight in Spondon. We've had to wheel Bert Knowles home in a barrow more than once when he's been drunk. But this barrow was heading for the church and the person pushing it was struggling as if he wasn't used to doing anything like that. A dead body can be heavy. Suppose *that's* what was under the cloth? I've been asking myself that ever since.' His arms fell to his sides and he grinned inanely. 'Was I right to tell you, Sergeant Leeming?'

'You were indeed, Mr Truss, and I'm very grateful.'

'Please don't mention to anyone else that I told you. It could be . . . awkward for me, you see.'

Leeming suspected that the real awkwardness would be felt by the friend whom Truss had called on that evening. From the man's behaviour, he guessed that the glove-maker had had a rendezvous with a woman and that he was anxious to protect her from any gossip and embarrassment. After reassuring him, Leeming sent him on his way and reviewed what he'd just learnt. As he did so, he recalled the old adage that bad news always came in threes. Could it be equally true that good news also came in triplicate? That's what had happened to the sergeant. Since he'd arrived in Spondon, he'd met Philip Conway, recruited Bert Knowles to his cause and heard about the nocturnal adventures of a glove-maker. He'd had three pieces of good news to pass on to Colbeck.

Something told him that the last of them was by far the best.

CHAPTER SEVEN

Robert Colbeck had enjoyed his visit to the tailor's shop in Nottingham. He felt wholly at ease in such an environment and was so struck by the quality of items on display he had purchased a new cravat there. But it was the missing top hat that had taken him to the establishment and he left with a drawing of it in his pocket. Much as he'd liked Simon Hubbleday and revelled in their conversation, he'd been unable to prise from him all the information about the Quayle family that the tailor clearly knew. Hubbleday had been both discreet and professional, yielding a few details about his customers while holding many others back. Colbeck was certain that the man could have said far more about Stanley Quayle, for instance, and about the reason that drove one of his sisters away from the house.

His next port of call was the police station where a pleasant surprise awaited him. Having met with muted hostility from the Derbyshire Constabulary, in the person of Superintendent Wigg, he was given an affable welcome by the duty sergeant, Thomas Lambert, who was quick to offer any help that he could. Lambert was a stolid man in his forties with a flat face enlivened by rosy cheeks and a pair of mischievous eyes. He seemed to radiate goodwill. Colbeck's reputation ensured him a firm handshake.

'Ask me anything you wish, Inspector,' said Lambert, obviously thrilled to take part, albeit tangentially, in a murder investigation. 'We knew Mr Quayle well. We want his killer brought to book.'

'That's a common objective for all of us, Sergeant.'

'He was a kind and charitable man. At least, that was how we saw him. I don't think there was much kindness and charity in his business life, mind. At meetings of the board of directors and such like, I daresay he'd have had to fight tooth and claw. Where big decisions need to be made, blood usually flows.'

'What do you know of Donald Haygarth?'

Lambert sniffed. 'I know little to his credit, Inspector.'

'He was Mr Quayle's rival.'

'There were whispers he was hatching a plot to seize control of the company.'

'Where did you hear that?'

'You pick up things in this job,' said Lambert, tapping the side of his nose.

'How well do you know Mr Quayle's family?'

Lambert grinned. 'I'm not exactly on visiting terms at their house, but I've come across them all over the years. Mrs Quayle – God bless her – is a poor old dear who's been dogged by all kinds of maladies. She's a wealthy woman in her own right. Old money,' he said, knowingly. 'It's the best kind, in some ways. Her husband made his fortune out of coal and, since he sold so much of it to various railway companies, it was only natural that he should join the board of the Midland Railway. He was very rich. The Quayle family lives in style.'

'I know,' said Colbeck. 'I've been to the house. It wasn't the best time to call but I'd have appreciated slightly more cooperation than I was offered.'

'That means you met Stanley Quayle.'

'It was not a meeting of true minds. He was quite rude to me.'

'He's like that with most people, Inspector. He's taken over the running of the coal mines from his father and it's gone to his head. Fair's fair, he very efficient and conscientious but – well, if you want it in plain language – he can be a bastard.'

'What about his brother?'

The duty sergeant chuckled. 'Lucas Quayle is an altogether different person,' he said with a twinkle in his eye. 'He's open, friendly and full of life. In his younger days, he had a few brushes with the law but they were minor incidents and settled out of court. Marriage quietened him down a bit – that and his big brother.'

'Does he work alongside Stanley?'

'He works *beneath* him, sir.'

Lambert talked at length about the relationship between the two brothers before being forced to break off when two constables brought in a prisoner they were having great difficulty in controlling. The duty sergeant came out from behind his desk, pinioned the man's arm behind his back and marched him off to one of the cells at the rear of the building. Colbeck heard the iron door clang shut.

'I'm sorry about that, sir,' he said when he returned. 'That was Jake Daggett, a regular customer of ours. He hit the landlord of The Red Lion over the head with a chair this time.' When a yell of rage came from the cell, Lambert closed the door to muffle the sound. 'Now, then, where was I?'

'You were telling me about the two brothers,' Colbeck reminded him, 'but what I really want to hear is something about the two sisters.'

'If the two men are like chalk and cheese, Inspector, the two ladies are as different as coal and chocolate. I don't mean this unkindly because she's a good woman, by all accounts, but Agnes Quayle is as plain as a pikestaff. They say that she gave up her chances of marriage to look after her mother. If you ever meet her, you'll see that any chances were very thin on the ground.' He lowered his voice. 'I speak as the father of two daughters. You're always worried that they may be unable to find husbands and hang around your neck forever.'

'Tell me about the elder sister.'

'Lydia is a real beauty, sir – a lot of young men took an interest.'

'Did she marry one of them?'

'No, Inspector – and I'm only passing on a rumour here – she believed that she was already spoken for. However . . .'

'Her parents opposed her choice,' guessed Colbeck.

'They did more than that. They packed her off to Europe on a tour and they sacked the fellow straight away. He was their head gardener.'

One mystery was solved. 'It was Gerard Burns, I'll wager.'

'It was, indeed.'

'That explains why Stanley Quayle was so angry when I mentioned him.'

'I'm not surprised.'

'Why?' asked Colbeck. 'Was Burns such an ogre or did the family think that his low status made him a highly unsuitable attachment?'

'I reckon they turned their noses up at him. Money does that to people. Nice as pie as he could be on the surface, Mr Quayle stamped out his daughter's romance.'

'What happened to her?'

'I don't rightly know, Inspector. Talk was that she's in London.'

'Apparently, there's a doubt over her return for the funeral.'

'She must come back for that,' said Lambert with passion. 'Her father was *murdered*, for heaven's sake!'

'Quite so.'

'It's unnatural.'

'Let's go back to Gerard Burns.'

Lambert pursed his lips. 'Shame to see him go, Inspector.'

'Why – did you know him?'

'Not personally, but I watched him many a time. Do you have any interest in cricket, Inspector?'

'Yes, I do,' replied Colbeck. 'I loved playing it in my younger days.'

'Burns was not only a canny gardener,' said Lambert, 'he was the best bowler in the county. Nottinghamshire's loss is Derbyshire's gain.'

'Is that where he went – over the border?'

'He couldn't stay here. Mr Quayle made that very clear.'

'So where exactly is he?'

'Oh, he's fallen on his feet in one way,' said Lambert. 'It's a promotion of a kind. He looks after the gardens at Melbourne Hall.'

Gerard Burns was a tall, lean, sinewy man in his thirties with a mop of fair hair imprisoned under his battered hat. The gardens under his aegis were among the finest in the county, comprising broad tracts of lawn, avenues of trees, explosions of colour in the flower beds and tasteful statuary. As he walked around the edge of the Great Basin, he watched the insects buzzing merrily above the water. Burns took great pride in his work and made every effort to maintain the high quality of grounds constructed a hundred and fifty years earlier after consultation with no less than the royal gardeners. He turned along a path that led to the ponds and saw two men busy with their hoes. One of them suddenly bent down to retrieve an object from behind a shrub. He held it up for Burns to see.

'Iss thar ball the children lost,' he called out. 'You'd best 'ave this, Mr Burns. Catch it.'

He threw it high in the air but the head gardener caught it easily with one hand. Burns rolled the ball over in his palm. Aware of his skill on the cricket field, the undergardeners were both watching him expectantly. He obliged them with a demonstration. After walking away from it, he turned to face the Birdcage, the outstanding feature of the gardens, a large and elaborate wrought iron arbour created by a celebrated ironsmith at the start of the previous century and still retaining its full majesty. Burns, however, was not there to admire it. Having measured out his run-up, he set off, accelerated, then flung the ball with all his strength. Flashing through the air, it struck the arbour and bounced harmlessly off. The undergardeners gave him a round of applause.

'I told ter,' said one of them to the other. 'He's like a strick o' lightnin'.'

Victor Leeming was gazing reflectively into the empty grave in the churchyard. He tried to envisage what Vivian Quayle had looked like when he lay there on his back. Fortunately, the dead man had fitted into the cavity without difficulty. A much taller or broader corpse would have been crumpled up.

'What are you doing here, Sergeant?' asked the vicar, coming up beside him.

'I'm just thinking.'

'This is a day for contemplation. I made that point in my address.'

'Yes, yes, I remember,' said Leeming. 'It was . . . very moving.'

'Thank you. I've just come from the family. They're still bemused by the suddenness of it all. A month ago, Mrs Peet was a healthy, active lady with decades ahead of her – or so it seemed. Then the headaches began and she went downhill with indecent haste. The brain tumour was a silent enemy growing in stealth. It's ironic.'

'What is, Vicar?'

'Well, my dear wife is plagued by all sorts of minor ailments and has never been very robust, yet she will probably go on forever. A fit and lively person dies without warning while a near invalid soldiers on from year to year.'

'Death can be very cruel.'

'Yet it's always the working out of God's purpose. There must have been a reason why he called Mrs Peet into his presence. What that reason was, I've yet to decide.' He looked across at the other grave, now hidden under a mound of fresh earth. 'You, too, are still looking for reasons, of course.'

'Yes,' said Leeming, 'I'm wondering how and why Mr Quayle ended up in Spondon. It's the first thing I'll ask the killer when we catch him.'

'I spotted a reward notice on my way back here. It should bring results.'

'It's already brought your gravedigger to me.'

'What did Bert Knowles have to say?'

'Oh, he made up a story about being in here on the night of the murder and feeling that he was being watched. When I told him his evidence was worthless, he admitted he'd made the whole thing up and had a good laugh.'

The vicar sighed. 'That's typical of Knowles. He's incorrigible.'

'Actually, he was very helpful. He told someone why I was here and the man, a Mr Truss, came running to see me. He really did have something useful to say.'

'Yes, I know Truss. He's a sound, God-fearing fellow.'

'Is he a married man?'

'No,' said the vicar, 'he can be a little alarming until you get used to those eyes. I think he's accepted that he holds no attraction for the gentler sex.'

Leeming didn't disillusion him by telling him about Truss's night-time activity. After taking the funeral then trying to comfort the family, Sadler was already in a delicate state. The loss of faith in one of his parishioners would be painful to him and, in any case, Leeming would not break his promise to the glove-maker.

'I really came to look for the marks of a wheelbarrow,' he explained.

'You won't find many of those, I'm afraid. A lot of feet have trampled across the churchyard today.'

'Some marks are still visible.'

'Then they were put there by Bert's wheelbarrow. It's monstrously heavy but he shoves it around as if it's as light as a feather.' He turned to point. 'He keeps it out of the way behind the tool shed.'

'I know, Vicar. I made a point of finding it.'

'Why do you have such a fascination with a rusting old wheelbarrow?'

'I wanted to eliminate it,' explained Leeming. 'There are traces of it all over the place. But there's also the marks of another wheelbarrow and they end right here beside the grave. Do you see, Vicar?' He bent down to pat the earth. 'This wasn't made by the wheel on Knowles's barrow. So I'm bound to ask where it did come from. Mrs Peet arrived for the funeral in a glass-panelled hearse,' he said. 'I'm wondering if Mr Quayle got here in a meaner form of transport.'

* * *

When Lucas Quayle went in search of his brother, he found him seated at the desk in the study and flicking through the pile of papers he'd taken from a drawer.

'What are you doing in here, Stanley?' he asked.

'I'm searching for Father's will.'

'Mother would tell you where that's kept.'

'She's far too unwell to be bothered,' said Stanley. 'Besides, according to Agnes, the doctor has given her something to make her sleep. Mother needs rest.'

'Are you certain that the will is actually here?'

'I'm convinced of it.'

'Father must have lodged it with his solicitor, surely.'

'He'll have kept his own copy. He did everything in duplicate.'

'That's true.'

Annoyed at the intrusion, Stanley put the papers aside and rose to his feet.

'Why do you need to bother me, Luke?'

'There's something we must discuss.'

'If it's what I think, you're wasting your breath. That matter is long over and done with. Forget all about it.'

'Lydia is our *sister*. We can't just ignore that fact.'

'She left this family of her own accord and she is not coming back to it.'

'I disagree.'

Lucas Quayle usually lost any arguments with his brother because the latter had established his dominance over a long period. This time, however, the younger man would not give way. Tall and well built, he had something of his father's good looks and had cultivated a similar moustache. The resemblance ended there. While Vivian Quayle had been wholly committed to his responsibilities as the owner of some profitable coal mines, his second son had been more wayward, embarking on two or three different careers before abandoning each in turn, and feeling the lash of his father's tongue and that of his elder brother's. It was only when he'd married after a succession of dalliances that he'd introduced any stability into his life. It irked him that his brother still treated him like the aimless drifter he'd once been.

'I think that we should get in touch with Lydia,' he declared.

'I won't hear of it.'

'She has a right to be here, Stanley.'

'Lydia spurned this family and lost all claim on it as a result. When I finally find the will, I'll guarantee that her name is never mentioned in it.'

'Our sister is not expecting it to be. She and Father . . . broke apart decisively. I accept that. But the nature of his death will surely wipe away the old bitterness. Lydia needs to be told that she's welcome in this house again.'

Stanley stamped a foot. 'It will never happen while I'm here.'

'Think of Mother. She'd want to see her daughter.'

'Don't drag Mother into this. I'm the head of the household now and my writ runs here. No more argument, Luke,' he affirmed. 'Lydia is *persona non grata* here.'

His brother was appalled. 'Do you hate her so much?'

'I don't even acknowledge her existence.'

'What's happened to you, Stanley? You've changed since you took over the mines. Father could be callous when forced to be but you make a virtue of it. I don't have to ask Mother or Agnes how they feel. I know that, in their hearts, they're ready to forgive and forget. They'd love to see Lydia again.'

'Well, it won't happen.'

'You can't keep her away from the funeral if she chooses to come.'

'Yes, I can. I'll see that she's turned away.'

'Would you really *do* such a thing?' asked his brother.

'I'm confident that it won't come to that,' said the other, softening slightly, 'but I'll do what Father would have wanted and that's to shun her completely. As for getting in touch with Lydia, we don't even know where she is.'

'I do,' said the other.

For a few seconds, his brother was stunned. His eyes smouldered and, when he spoke again, his voice was dripping with accusation.

'You *dared* to maintain a correspondence with her?' Stanley grabbed his brother's lapels.

'I'm entitled to make my own decisions about Lydia.'

'How long has this been going on?'

Lucas waved a hand. 'It doesn't matter.'

'How *long*, I asked?' demanded his brother.

'I tracked her down a few months ago.'

'Whatever for?' he shouted, veins standing out on his temples.

'I was curious.'

Stanley Quayle released him and stood back, eyeing him with complete disgust. Before he could say anything, there was a tap on the door and the butler entered with a telegraph. Aware of the taut atmosphere, he simply handed it to the elder brother and left at once.

'If it's a telegraph, it must be important,' said Lucas Quayle.

After glaring at him, his brother tore open the missive and glanced at it.

'The post-mortem has been completed,' he said, curtly. 'Father's body will be released to us tomorrow.'

* * *

85

Staying at the Malt Shovel was a mixed blessing. While he enjoyed its food and relished its beer, Victor Leeming found himself under siege. At the end of the working day, a stream of people came in turn to see him, each with what they felt was information worthy of attention and, possibly, of reward. Some of it was clearly fabricated and therefore easily dismissed, some was so confused as to be of no help at all and the rest was well meant but irrelevant. In the interests of maintaining goodwill, however, he took down all the statements and thanked each witness. When there was a lull in activity, he was tempted to slip off to his room but another person came through the door, a basket-maker from Potter Street. He was an old man with watery eyes and a croaking voice but his memory seemed unimpaired. Having taken his dog out for a walk on the night in question, the basket-maker recalled seeing a man pushing a wheelbarrow towards the church. He was too far away to see what was in the barrow but said that it was moving slowly.

Leeming was so glad for the corroboration of Barnaby Truss's evidence that he bought the man a drink. He then retired to his room to sift through the statements he'd taken in the course of the day and to have a quiet moment alone. His escape was short-lived. The landlord pounded on the door before flinging it open.

'There's someone to see you, sir,' he grunted.

'Tell him to wait.'

'He said he'd come up here, if you prefer.'

'This room is not big enough for two of us,' complained Leeming. 'Oh, all right, I'll come down at once,' he said, getting up from his chair. 'But I can't spend the whole evening down there. The world and his wife want to see me.'

When he clattered down the stairs, he was in a resigned mood but his face brightened when he saw who his visitor was. Colbeck was seated at a table in the corner with two tankards of beer on it.

'This is good,' he said, taking another sip. 'What about the food?'

'It's wholesome, sir.'

'How does it compare with the menu at the Royal Hotel?'

'The pork pie is grand but the choice is a bit limited.'

After taking the seat opposite Colbeck, the sergeant downed the first couple of inches of his beer before using the back of his hand to wipe the froth from his mouth. He gave an abbreviated account of his day and was pleased with the way that Colbeck complimented him on his visit to the churchyard to search for marks of a barrow.

'This could be an important sighting,' said the inspector.

'It was verified by a second man.'

'Then you have to find out if someone else was abroad at that time of night. What's the latest train to get into Spondon? Who was on it and which way did they walk home? I suppose it's not unusual for someone to be pushing a wheelbarrow about in a village like this.'

'It is if there's a dead body in it, sir.'

'We don't know that for certain.'

'What else could he have been taking up that hill?'

'Did anyone actually see him enter the churchyard?'

'No,' conceded Leeming, 'but I found those wheel marks there. They were quite deep and obviously caused by a heavy load. Anyway,' he went on, taking another long drink, 'what have you been up to, sir?'

'Oh, it's been a full day.'

Colbeck's version of events was concise and lucid. He talked about his visit to Nottingham and what he'd learnt there about the Quayle family. He'd returned to Derby, called in at the hotel and found an important letter awaiting him.

'What was it, sir?'

'It was a copy of the post-mortem report, Victor. It appears that the victim was sedated before he was injected with a poison. Since he's not an expert toxicologist, the man who conducted the post-mortem was not entirely sure of all the elements in that poison but his conclusion is that death would have been fairly swift. Whoever killed Mr Quayle knew exactly what he was doing.'

CHAPTER EIGHT

Lost in thought, Lydia Quayle walked along the Thames embankment in the fading light of a warm evening. She was torn between family loyalty and an abiding hatred, nudged by an impulse to return home for the funeral yet repelled by the memory of the man who would be lowered into his grave. Years of deep anger could not be so easily laid to rest. When she'd made the decision to leave Nottingham and all its associations behind her, she'd vowed never to return, trying to create a new life for herself elsewhere. Lydia had even persuaded herself that she was happy being independent and free from the dictates of others. But the move to London had not been without its disappointments and limitations. It had taken her time to adapt to them.

When she first saw the newspaper report about the murder of her father, she'd felt an instant elation and wanted to meet the killer in order to thank him for doing something that she had considered doing in her darkest moments. Shame had quickly set in, to be replaced by a distant pity but that, too, had soon evaporated. Recalling what her father had done and – above all – said to her, the bitterness had returned afresh. Devoid of love for him, she could not even find an ounce of regret, still less of forgiveness. If she went back home, it would be to rejoice in his death.

Lydia made an effort to put her father aside and to consider the other members of her family. Her mother might be glad to see her, though she'd offered her elder daughter little support when the turmoil had occurred. On the other hand, she was a sick woman and that had been taken into account. She'd had no strength to oppose the wishes of her husband or to protect Lydia in some way and had therefore appeared to condone what was going on. Stanley would certainly not welcome her and might even forbid her to enter the house. He was simply a younger version of their father with the same implacable resentment towards her. Nor would Stanley's wife speak up for her. She was far too dutiful and submissive.

Agnes lacked the spirit or the desire to stand up against her elder brother. She and Lydia had never been close. They had played together as young children but any bond between them had soon been stretched to breaking point. Lydia had been the clear favourite of their parents and of the wider family. She was more attractive, appealing, intelligent and venturesome. Living in her sister's shadow, Agnes had been almost invisible. Since Lydia had shown little care or sympathy for her, she could expect none in return. In the years since she'd been cut off from her family, Lucas was the only member of it that she really missed. Significantly, he was the one who had got in touch with her.

While she had never really enjoyed the company of her sister or her elder brother, Lydia still had fond memories of Lucas Quayle. He was bright, engaging and had a streak of wildness that had got him into trouble in earlier days. Agnes had been horrified by some of his escapades and Stanley had been as outraged as their father but Lydia had always admired his youthful bravado and was sorry that it had slowly been suppressed. She and her younger brother had too much in common to grow completely apart. Lydia decided that she would like to see him again, but he was only one member of the family and she had good reason to avoid the others. On balance, therefore, she felt that it would be wiser to stay away from Nottingham.

Preoccupied as she was, Lydia hardly felt a shoulder brush hers.

'Oh,' said the man, raising his top hat, 'I do apologise.'

'That's quite all right,' she murmured.

'It was my mistake.'

His voice was soft and educated and her first impression was that he was a polite, well-dressed man of middle years who'd been strolling harmlessly along the embankment when he'd made unintended contact with her. Lydia then saw the look in his eyes. It was no accident. Mistaking her for a prostitute, he had deliberately sought her out. His gaze was a compound of interest, invitation and sheer lust. A burning disgust coursed through her whole body but a stronger emotion followed. What she saw in front of her was not a complete stranger but the figure of her father, compact, stern, arrogant and entitled to everything he wanted in the way that he wanted it. As the man smiled at her and offered his arm, she pushed him angrily away and emitted a long, loud, high-pitched scream of pure hatred.

'How much do you know about the Midland Railway?' asked Haygarth.

'I'm more well-informed than most people, I fancy.'

'Big changes have taken place in the last decade.'

'They were forced upon you, Mr Haygarth.'

'I'd rather draw a veil over our former manager, if you don't mind. George Hudson did wonderful things for us in the early days, one must acknowledge that, but he . . . left us with problems. That chapter in our history is closed.'

'The succeeding one had much to recommend it.'

'We like to think so.'

'Mr Ellis was the ideal choice as your chairman.'

To Haygarth's chagrin, Colbeck gave a brief and accurate outline of the recovery of the Midland Railway under its recently retired chairman, thereby robbing the other man of the chance to lay claim to some of the improvements. With Maurice Cope in attendance, they were at the company headquarters, Haygarth occupying the chair behind the desk like a usurper seated on a throne. He and Cope had been impressed and sobered by the inspector's detailed knowledge of the history of the Midland. It warned them that they could not make unjustified assertions without being challenged by him.

After explaining what he'd done the previous day, Colbeck told them that Sergeant Leeming had made what appeared to be progress in Spondon itself. While Haygarth was pleased to hear it, Cope made no comment and remained watchful.

'What it all boils down to,' said Colbeck in conclusion, 'is this. Should we be looking for someone inside the company or outside it?'

'Oh, outside it, surely,' bleated Cope, breaking his silence.

'Do you agree, Mr Haygarth?'

'You must leave no stone unturned,' replied the other, sonorously.

'Does that include *Enoch* Stone?' asked Colbeck, unable to resist the comment and swiftly apologising for it. 'So I have complete access to the company?'

'Of course – Cope will make sure of that, Inspector.'

'Yes,' said Cope with a marked absence of enthusiasm. 'You may call on me.'

'During my brief conversation with him,' said Colbeck, 'Stanley Quayle was of the opinion that his father might have had enemies among his fellow directors. I'm not suggesting in any way that you incited them to commit murder, Mr Haygarth, but passions can run high in a contest and you wouldn't be the first person embarrassed by the zeal of one of your supporters.'

'I accept that,' said Haygarth, urbanely, 'but you'll find no killers in my camp, Inspector. They are all law-abiding individuals.'

'I can vouch for that,' added Cope.

'Then you'll be happy to give me a list of all board members,' said Colbeck.

'Well . . .' Cope looked for a prompt from Haygarth.

'We'll be quite happy,' said the acting chairman. 'We have nothing to hide.' He shot Cope a glance before turning back to Colbeck. 'What help have you had from Superintendent Wigg?'

'Not a great deal,' replied Colbeck. 'Apart from the fact that he sent a copy of the post-mortem report, he's done very little beyond mocking me for claiming that I had the name of a suspect.'

'Oh?'

'It was written on the back of a reward notice and delivered to my hotel. When I mentioned the name to the superintendent, he said the man probably never existed.'

'And does he?'

'Oh, yes. Stanley Quayle confirmed that.'

'Who is the fellow?'

'Gerard Burns.'

Haygarth frowned. 'I've heard that name before somewhere.'

'I gather that he's a talented cricketer.'

'Ah, that's it, of course!' said the other, snapping his fingers. 'I have no interest in cricket myself but Vivian Quayle had something of an obsession about it. Burns was his head gardener,

I think. Every summer Mr Quayle used to host a couple of cricket matches. His elder son, Stanley, used to captain a team made up largely from household servants and the estate staff. Because of this man, Gerard Burns,' said Haygarth, 'they won every match.'

'He was good enough to represent the county, I hear.'

'That may well be so, Inspector.'

'Why was he named as a suspect?' asked Cope.

'He was dismissed by Mr Quayle,' said Colbeck. 'To get rid of his finest cricketer, he must have had good reason. I'm told that Burns left in disgrace.'

'I knew nothing of that,' claimed Haygarth. 'Vivian Quayle and I saw very little of each other socially so I was not aware of events at his home any more than he knew about my private life. What about you, Cope?'

'The name is entirely new to me, sir.'

'Are you taking him seriously as a suspect, Inspector?'

'I must do,' replied Colbeck. 'He appears to have had a motive and, being young and strong, would have the means to overpower his victim. Whether or not he had the opportunity to do so, of course, is another matter.'

'Where is he now?'

'He works in the garden at Melbourne Hall. I'll visit him today.'

'Good gracious!' exclaimed Haygarth. 'You'll be in exalted company. Do you know who happens to live at Melbourne Hall?'

'I'm afraid that I don't.'

'It's the prime minister – Lord Palmerston.'

Having taken the wheelbarrow from the churchyard, Victor Leeming had borrowed two sacks of potatoes from a greengrocer so that he was pushing a substantial weight. He even covered them with a cloth. He took his cargo to the bottom of the hill and began the slow ascent. In reconstructing what he believed might have been the route taken by the killer, he hoped that he might jog the memory of a passer-by who'd happened to have been in the vicinity on the night of the murder. Disappointingly, the only villagers he encountered were two old ladies and a postman. They all asked him what he was doing but none was of any help to him.

The load was heavy and even someone of Leeming's considerable strength was feeling the strain. Before he reached the gate to the churchyard, he was confronted by a big, broad, rugged man in his thirties with a swagger. The newcomer was carrying a pair of riding boots.

'You must be Sergeant Leeming,' he said with a lazy grin.

'That's right. Who might you be?'

'Oh, I'm Jed Hockaday, sir. I'm a cobbler by trade but I was also sworn in as a special constable, so you might say we're in the same business. What are you doing?'

'Were you anywhere near here on the night of the murder?'

'No, sir, I was visiting friends in Duffield.'

'Then you're of no use to me.'

Hockaday was wounded. 'Don't say that, Sergeant. I was hoping you'd call on me. I've been involved in a murder case before, you see.'

'Was that the one involving Enoch Stone?'

'Yes – he was a good friend of mine.'

'I was told he was killed by a traveller.'

'No, no,' argued the other man. 'The murderer lives here in Spondon. I'd swear to that. Most folk in this village are good, kind, honest people. They'd do anything to help someone in a spot of bother. Then there are the others,' he went on, glancing around, 'those who keep themselves to themselves. You never know who's hiding behind a closed door, do you, or what they might be planning? I hate to say it because I've probably mended his shoes at some point, but Enoch's killer is one of us.'

Leeming had seen enough of Hockaday to realise that he was a man of limited intelligence. His sheer bulk and his willingness had recommended him for police work and he would be very effective at dealing with anyone in a brawl. As an assistant in a murder investigation, however, he would be a handicap.

'I'll be standing by all the time, Sergeant,' said the cobbler. 'You're staying at the Malt Shovel, aren't you? My shop is farther along Potter Street.'

'Thank you. I'll remember that.'

'A man dressed like you shouldn't be pushing a wheelbarrow. Would you like me to take over from you?'

Leeming was affronted. 'No, I wouldn't. I can manage on my own.'

'Then I'll leave you to it and deliver these boots. Remember my name.'

'I will, Mr Hockaday.'

'Everyone here calls me Jed.'

He treated Leeming to another lazy grin then swaggered off. Though there was a link between them, Hockaday was no Philip Conway. Both men were excited to make the acquaintance of a Scotland Yard detective. While the young reporter was a reliable source of information, however, the cobbler was better left to his trade. In the hands of such amateur constables, Leeming believed, the murder of Enoch Stone would remain unsolved until Doomsday. Grasping the handles of the barrow again, he gave it a shove and it creaked into action but he did not get as far as the church. A horse and cart came into view with a pungent load of manure piled high on it. The driver was enraged by what he saw.

'Leave my barrer alone!' yelled Bert Knowles. 'Thass stealin', thar is.'

* * *

Since the railway had yet to reach Melbourne, Colbeck was obliged to take the train to the nearest station then hire a cab. It took him through rolling countryside with pleasing vistas wherever he looked. Derby might be a railway town, with its works contributing liberally to the regular din, smoke and grime, but whole areas of the county were still untouched by industry. Colbeck found the leisurely journey both restorative and inspiring. Melbourne was a small village in the Trent valley that still retained its rustic charm. Standing at the south-east end, the Hall was by far the largest and most striking house in the area, a fitting place of residence for a prime minister. The cab went down the hill towards it, giving Colbeck the opportunity to see the smaller houses and cottages of ordinary mortals.

When he reached the house, his attention instead went straight to the church of St Michael with St Mary, standing close to the stables and the servants' quarters of the Hall. One of the finest Norman churches in the kingdom, it was a truly magnificent structure with a size and quality worthy of a cathedral. Colbeck promised himself that he would take a closer look at the place before he left Melbourne. The Hall itself was an arresting edifice in an idyllic setting. Its origins were medieval but it had fallen into such a state of disrepair during the later years of Elizabeth's reign that its new owner had pulled down and rebuilt large parts of it. Substantial alterations were also made in the next century and, over the years, each new owner felt the urge to stamp his mark upon the house.

Colbeck was unable to take in all the architectural felicities. He was there simply to speak to the head gardener. The garrulous housekeeper insisted on telling Colbeck that Melbourne Hall actually belonged to the former Emily Lamb who'd inherited it from her brother, Frederic, who had himself acquired the place at the death of his elder brother, William Lamb, erstwhile Lord Melbourne, another prime minister. Colbeck didn't wish to alarm her by saying that he was treating the head gardener as a murder suspect so he merely said that he hoped Gerard Burns would be able to help him with enquiries relating to an estate in Nottinghamshire on which he once worked.

When he met the gardener himself, he was able to be more forthright. After introducing himself, he explained exactly why he had come to Melbourne. Gerard Burns stared at him with what seemed like genuine surprise.

'Mr Quayle is *dead*?' he asked in disbelief.

'Have you not heard the news?'

'How could I? We are very cut off here.'

'Reports of the murder have been in all the newspapers, Mr Burns.'

'I've no time to read newspapers, Inspector. Looking after these gardens takes up all of my time.' With a sweep of his arm, he indicated the grounds. 'It's hard work to keep them in this condition all the time.'

'You're obviously very proficient at your trade, sir.'

'Thank you.'

'Though I suspect it's rather like the one in which I'm engaged. It's never possible to master it because one always has to learn new things.'

'That's very true of horticulture,' said Burns, 'because new plants and shrubs arrive from abroad all the time. You have to learn how to nurture them. Then there are the new ways they keep inventing to kill weeds.'

Burns spoke openly but there was an underlying surliness in his voice and manner. He clearly wanted to be left alone to get on with his job. What he least wanted to do was to talk about his time with the Quayle family but Colbeck needed answers and pressed on.

'Where were you three nights ago, sir?' he asked.

'Why do you want to know?'

'Were you here in Melbourne?'

'No, I wasn't,' admitted the other. 'I went over to Ilkeston to play cricket.'

'Yes, I've heard about your prowess as a bowler. I believe that you played for the county when you lived in Nottinghamshire.'

Burns smiled. 'We beat the All-England team once. I took seven wickets.'

'And you also played for a team organised by Mr Quayle, I'm told.' The glowing pride vanished instantly from the gardener's face. 'Thanks to you, victory was assured every time. What sort of a captain was Stanley Quayle?'

'That world is long behind me, Inspector.'

'I should imagine that he liked to throw his weight around.'

'If you don't mind,' said Burns, sharply, 'I'd rather not talk about all that.'

'I'm afraid that you'll have to, sir. Otherwise, I may have to invite you to accompany me to the nearest police station where we can have a more formal interview. A pleasant chat out here in these wonderful gardens is surely preferable to that, is it not?' Burns gave a reluctant nod. 'Why did you leave Mr Quayle's employ?'

'I think you already know that.'

'All I have is one side of the story. I'd like to hear yours.'

'It was a mistake,' said Burns, vehemently. 'I broke their rules and I was dismissed. When you work for people like that, there are lines you're never allowed to cross. I strayed over them and paid the penalty. Mr Quayle not only had me thrown off the estate, he made sure that I'd never get another job in the county again.'

'So how did you end up here?'

'One of the gentlemen who ran the county cricket team had some influence here. He gave me a letter of introduction and I was taken on. When the head gardener retired, I'd done enough to show that I could replace him.'

'You've done well for yourself,' observed Colbeck, looking around. 'But you must have had regrets when you left your former post.'

Burns shifted his feet. 'I had no regrets on my own account.'

'Yet I daresay you felt sorry for the lady herself.'

'That's as maybe, Inspector.'

'Have you seen Miss Lydia Quayle since?'

There was a studied pause. 'No, I haven't.'

'Did you *want* to see her?'

'As I told you,' snapped Burns, 'that world is behind me. I've put down roots here. I'm married now. I've got all I want.'

Colbeck took a long, hard look at him. Burns met his gaze with a mingled bitterness and defiance. Someone had identified him as a killer and there were aspects of his character that easily qualified him for the role. Yet he'd taken pains to distance himself from the Quayle family and had started afresh in a quiet, rural refuge. Colbeck wondered just how deep his acrimony still was.

'That's a beautiful church you have on your doorstep, Mr Burns.'

'Yes, it is.'

'Do you worship there?'

'My wife and I go most Sundays.'

'Then you're obviously acquainted with Christian virtues,' said Colbeck. 'I'm going to take a look inside the church. It will give you time to think over what you've told me. Some of it is very plausible yet I have a nagging sensation of being deceived. When I come back, I hope that you'll realise the importance of being completely honest with me. See it as an opportunity of getting something off your chest.'

'I've nothing new to add, Inspector,' insisted Burns.

'In that case, you might wish to subtract from your statements.'

'You'll be wasting your time if you come bothering me again.'

'We can talk about cricket,' said Colbeck, airily. 'That's never a waste of time, is it? If you played against the All-England XI, you'll no doubt have encountered the redoubtable Mr Stephenson.'

Burns straightened his shoulders. 'I bowled him out.'

'Why did H. H. Stephenson play for that team when Gerard Burns did not?'

'Gardening's what I love. Cricket's just for fun.'

Colbeck appraised him again. Lydia Quayle's romance with him was understandable. Apart from his physical attractions, Burns was well spoken, self-possessed and highly skilled. The inspector was bound to wonder which of them had made the first move. Had he set his cap at one of the daughters of the house or had she been the one to initiate things? Colbeck would be interested to find out.

'When I told you about Mr Quayle's death,' he recalled, 'you were surprised but there was no other reaction from you.'

'Why should there be?'

'Don't you feel even the slightest regret at his murder?'

'No,' said Burns, stoutly. 'To be honest, I am delighted.'

CHAPTER NINE

When the family gathered in the drawing room, there was a surprise in store for them. Harriet Quayle, widow of the murdered man, insisted on being present. Though she had to be helped to her seat by her daughter, Agnes, a spindly young woman with an anxious face, she was determined to be involved in what would be an important discussion. Stanley Quayle was irritated by her arrival, not least because it would inhibit him slightly. He tried to get rid of her.

'Are you sure that you feel well enough to be here, Mother?' he asked.

'I do feel poorly,' she confessed, 'but I'm staying.'

'It may be a long debate.'

'I'll manage to remain awake somehow.'

'We can tell you afterwards what's been decided.'

'You won't have to, Stanley. I can help to make any decisions.'

'Very well,' he said, resignedly.

'Mother is entitled to be here,' said Lucas Quayle. 'I agree that both my dear wife and Stanley's wife are best excluded. They're only members of the family by marriage and, in any case, neither of them felt that it would be right to join us.'

'All needed are now here,' said Stanley.

'All except Lydia, that is,' said his brother, waspishly.

'Let's keep her name out of this, please. This doesn't concern her.'

They all looked towards Harriet for a word or sign of confirmation but she said nothing. Sitting deep in an armchair, she seemed frailer than ever. Stanley was the only person still on his feet. He struck a pose.

'Father's body has been returned to us,' he began, 'so we can make all the necessary funeral arrangements. Lucas and I have already had a preliminary talk on that subject but now is the time for anyone else to offer their opinion as to how the event should be planned. Under other circumstances, we would invite mourners back here after the event but – given Mother's weakened condition – that would put far too big a strain on her.'

'I'll be the judge of that, Stanley,' she said.

'Stanley is right,' argued his brother. 'Your health comes first, Mother.'

'That's nonsense, Lucas. The person you should first consider is your poor father. This is his funeral not mine. We must ask ourselves what he would have wanted and I think that we all know the answer. He would like a dignified ceremony followed by a gathering of family and friends under this roof.'

'I agree,' Agnes piped up.

'So do I,' said her younger brother.

'Well, I'm not so sure,' said Stanley Quayle, irked that they were all of one mind. 'There are other factors to consider. Father, alas, did not die a natural death. He was the victim of a cruel murder.'

Harriet clutched at her throat. Agnes quickly put a comforting hand on her shoulder and shot a look of reproof at Stanley for being so carelessly explicit. Her elder brother surged on regardless.

'In the first instance,' he declared, 'it might be better to have a small, private service for the immediate family. After a decent interval to allow for the investigation to continue, and for an arrest to be made, we can hold a memorial service for all and sundry. By that time, Mother may be fully recovered and more able to cope.'

'By that time,' said Harriet, wryly, 'I may well be dead myself.'

'Mother!' exclaimed her daughter.

'I don't have unlimited time, Agnes.'

'You shouldn't even think such things.'

'I agree,' said Stanley Quayle. 'It's morbid.'

'My view is this,' said his brother, sitting up. 'Please listen carefully.'

The argument had started and it went on for a long time, rising in volume and growing in intensity. Agnes was the surprise. Normally so subdued, she spoke up for once and did so to some effect. Lucas Quayle seemed more intent on opposing his brother's views than on putting forward an alternative plan and it caused a deal of friction between them. It was the elder brother who first started shouting. Harriet took a full part in the quarrel and it was only when she lost her voice that it came to an abrupt end. They sat there in silence, looking around at each other and feeling embarrassed that they'd descended into an unseemly squabble at a time when they should have been mourning the death of Vivian Quayle.

Several minutes went by before Stanley Quayle finally spoke. His voice was low and almost sepulchral. He looked from one to the other.

'I've not had an opportunity to tell you all that a detective from

London called here yesterday,' he said. 'An Inspector Colbeck has been put in charge of the case.'

'What kind of man was he?' asked his brother.

'He seemed competent but I was too distracted to spend much time with him.'

'You should have let me talk to him, Stanley.'

'That's precisely what I didn't want to do. We must be discreet and restrained, Lucas. I didn't want you blurting out family secrets to him.'

'If he's any kind of detective, he's bound to find out the full facts about Lydia's departure from here.'

'Don't bring *her* name up again,' pleaded Agnes.

'We can't just pretend that she never existed.'

'That's exactly what we must do.'

'Be reasonable, Agnes.'

'Remember what Father told us. She must be banned from coming here.'

'Wait a moment,' said Harriet, regaining her voice. 'What's this about a detective from London?'

'He's from Scotland Yard,' explained her elder son. 'He's far more likely to solve the crime than the police in Derbyshire.'

'Who sent for him? Was it you, Stanley?'

'No, Mother, I should imagine that it was Mr Haygarth.'

'Keep that dreadful man away from me,' wailed Harriet in distress. 'I won't have him in this house. He's been plotting against your father for years. If that inspector is hunting the killer, he should look no further than Donald Haygarth.'

'Mr Haygarth tried to poach me away from the estate,' said Burns.

'But he told me that he only knew you as a cricketer.'

'Then he was lying.'

'He said that he'd simply heard about your feats as a demon bowler.'

'It was my gardening expertise that he prized, Inspector. He didn't approach me in person, mark you, but he sent a man to sound me out. Somehow, he knew exactly how much I was paid and was told to offer me more.'

'But you declined the offer.'

'Yes, I did, and for two good reasons.'

'I think we both know the first one,' said Colbeck, tactfully. 'You had emotional commitments to a member of the family. What was the other reason?'

'Mr Haygarth didn't really want me for what I could do to his garden. He just wanted to spite Mr Quayle. When I realised that I sent the go-between away.'

'Who was the man? Did he give you a name?'

'Yes – it was Maurice Cope.'

Colbeck was not surprised. When he'd seen them together that morning, he'd worked out the relationship between the two of them without difficulty. Cope was Haygarth's henchman, a company employee who was in a good position to know everything that went on at the headquarters of the Midland Railway and who reported it immediately to his master. Haygarth's crude attempt to lure away the head gardener was yet one more instance of the bad blood between him and Vivian Quayle. Colbeck was ready to wager that it would have been only one of many such attempts to annoy or wound his rival.

The second visit to Melbourne Hall was more productive. After a long and fascinating exploration of the church, Colbeck had returned to find that Gerard Burns was less defensive. He talked a little more about his romance with Lydia Quayle and admitted that it had reached the point where they'd considered marriage, even if it involved an elopement. Evidently, it was no passing attachment. The pair had been betrayed by one of the servants who'd seen them together in the woods. Dismissal was instant. Lydia was locked in her room and Burns was hustled off the property and forbidden to return.

'I misled you earlier,' said Burns, contritely. 'I did make an effort to see Lydia afterwards. She'd never have forgiven me if I hadn't at least tried.'

'What happened?'

'I was seen and chased away again.'

'Did you make a second attempt?'

Burns hung his head. 'I intended to,' he said, 'but he changed my mind.'

'Who did?'

'Lydia's father.'

'What did he do?'

'Mr Quayle sent two men to the house where I was staying. They were paid ruffians, Inspector. There's no other word for them. I put up a good fight and bloodied their noses but they were too strong for me. When they made their threat, I knew that they were deadly serious.'

'What threat was that?'

'I still shudder when I remember it.'

'Tell me what they said,' urged Colbeck.

Burns needed a full minute to compose himself before he did so. Long-suppressed memories streamed through his brain and the agony showed in his face. Eventually, he licked his lips before speaking.

'They said that, if I tried to get anywhere near Lydia again, they'd cut off my right hand. They meant it, Inspector. They'd take away my livelihood without a second thought. One of them sneered at me and said I wouldn't be able to bowl a cricket ball again.'

'Are you certain that Mr Quayle put them up to it?'

'They never mentioned his name but who else could it have been?'

'Why didn't you go to the police?' asked Colbeck.

Burns gave a hollow laugh. 'What use would that have been?' he said, sourly. 'They've no power over a man like Mr Quayle. It would have been my word against his. Besides, I'd already been frightened off by those two men. They said that, if I dared to go to the police, they'd cut off *both* my hands and that they wouldn't stop there. From that day on, I've always had this with me,' he went on, pushing back his coat so that he could take a long knife from its sheath. 'It's my protection.'

'Mr Quayle can't hurt you now.'

'I'd like to spit on the bastard's coffin!'

Colbeck understood the sentiment. What he wanted to know was whether or not Burns would do anything to put the man *into* the coffin. In view of the treatment meted out to the gardener, he felt sorry for him but he also realised that what he was hearing was a powerful motive for murder. With a knife in his hand, Burns looked more than capable of using it. Had he waited for a few years before wreaking his revenge? The bond between him and Lydia Quayle had been broken asunder and his subsequent marriage to someone else had proved that. But the urge for revenge could lie dormant for a long time before bubbling back to the surface again. Had that happened in the case of Gerard Burns? He'd freely confessed that he'd been playing cricket in Ilkeston on the day of the murder. Colbeck knew enough of Derbyshire geography to realise how easy it would have been to get to Spondon the same night. The revelation about the wheelbarrow could also be pertinent. As they were talking, a barrow was standing no more than a few yards away. It was part of a gardener's stock-in-trade.

Burns sheathed his knife. 'Will that be all, Inspector?'

'Yes, Mr Burns – for the time being, anyway.'

'There's no need for you to come back, is there?'

'One never knows.'

'I did *not* kill Mr Quayle.'

Colbeck looked him in the eye. 'I'd like to believe that.'

He took his leave and strolled away, taking a few moments to admire the landscaping. Melbourne Hall clearly had its own Garden of Eden. Colbeck walked on past an avenue of cedars. Tucked away behind them was a garden shed and he took the trouble to stroll across to it. Since the door was unlocked, he eased it open and glanced inside. A copy of the *Derby Mercury* lay among the implements on the table. It appeared that Gerard Burns did find time to read newspapers, after all.

Victor Leeming was pleased to see Philip Conway back in the village again. The reporter had picked up various snippets of information in Derby and he passed them on. The one that interested Leeming most was the fact that Superintendent Wigg had been overheard pouring scorn on the efforts of the Scotland Yard detectives and boasting that he would solve the crime before them.

'Then where is he? The murder was committed *here*.'

'But it may have been planned somewhere else, Sergeant.'

'We've already accepted that. What does the superintendent know that we don't? If he's holding back anything from us, Inspector Colbeck will tear him to pieces. The man is supposed to help.'

'Derbyshire police can be very territorial.'

'It's a common weakness among certain constabularies.

Thinking they can handle complex investigations themselves, they get into a terrible mess then call on us to bail them out. Superintendent Wigg is only one of a kind.'

They were sampling the beer at the White Swan in Moor Street. Arriving with high expectations, Conway was disappointed that there'd been no apparent progress.

'I was hoping you'd have . . . something to tell me,' he said.

'I do have something,' said Leeming. 'This beer is nowhere near as good as the stuff at the Malt Shovel. You should have warned me.'

'You wanted to get around the village. Men who drink here wouldn't go anywhere near the Malt Shovel or the Union Inn or the Prince of Wales, for that matter. Like any other village, Spondon is a collection of little groups.'

'I found that out.' He put a hand on the reporter's arm. 'I need a favour from you, Mr Conway.'

'It's granted before you even ask it.'

'There's something you could put in your newspaper for me.'

Leeming told him about the double sighting of a man with a wheelbarrow at a crucial time on the night of the murder. The post-mortem had been unable to give a precise time of death but it did specify the likely hours between which it must have occurred. The barrow had been seen well inside that wide spectrum of time. Leeming wanted an appeal for anyone else who might have spotted it to come forward and he suggested that the reward on offer be mentioned once again. Conway agreed to do his bidding and began to speculate on the murder.

'Why push him up the hill in a wheelbarrow when the killer could have driven a horse and carriage right up to the church gate and unloaded the body there?'

'People were about that night. Two of them, at least, saw the barrow. I fancy that a few more would have seen something as conspicuous as a horse and carriage outside the church. That would have attracted too much attention. Someone would have been bound to be curious.'

'I never thought of that.'

'If that's what the killer used,' said Leeming, 'it was safer for him to leave the horse and carriage out of sight. That's my theory, anyway. Earlier on, I borrowed the wheelbarrow from the churchyard and went back down the hill. I found a likely place to tuck away a horse and carriage. When I pushed the barrow uphill, I discovered what a struggle it was and I was only carrying some sacks of potatoes.'

'You were being very thorough.'

'I was hoping someone would see me who'd been out and about on the night of the murder. I wanted to jog their memory.'

'And did you?'

'I'm afraid not. The only person who stopped to talk to me was one of the village constables.'

'Which one was it?'

'He was a burly fellow named Jed Hockaday.'

'Yes,' said Conway, 'I've met him. He's a cobbler.'

'He didn't strike me as being all that intelligent. But he was very keen to help. He boasted that he'd been involved in the Enoch Stone case. Hockaday told me that he and Stone had been good friends.'

'Then he was telling a barefaced lie, Sergeant.'

'What do you mean?'

'I've read all the reports of that investigation and Hockaday's name pops up more than once. Far from being a friend of the victim, he was one of Stone's enemies. The two of them came to blows over something. Hockaday deliberately misled you.'

'Why should he do that?'

'He was trying to impress you.'

'What do you think of him?'

'I wouldn't trust him an inch,' said Conway.

'He insisted that the killer still lived in the village.'

'Did you believe him?'

In the light of what he'd just heard, Leeming's view of the cobbler had altered considerably. He'd been inclined to dismiss the man as someone of no practical use to him. Looking back, he remembered Hockaday's size and obvious strength. Behind the lazy grin and the confident manner, there could be a more calculating person than he'd realised. Though unaware of the full details of the earlier murder case, Leeming had a strange presentiment.

'I wasn't sure if I believed him, but I do now. He spoke with such certainty that he seemed to have definite proof. There's one sure way that he could have got that, Mr Conway.'

'Is there?'

'Yes,' said Leeming, voicing a possibility. 'Hockaday *knows* that the killer is still here because the man looks back at him in the shaving mirror every morning.'

Lydia Quayle read the newspaper report with a mixture of interest and repulsion. Though she wanted to throw it aside, something made her read on. There were some outline details about the nature of her father's murder but no new information about the likely identity of his killer. When she saw that Scotland Yard detectives had been called in, she wondered how deeply they would rummage into the family life of the man she'd grown to despise so much. In the end, she tore herself away from the article, folding the newspaper up and dropping it into the wastepaper basket.

There was a light tap on the door, then it opened to admit a short, plump woman of middle years with an enquiring smile.

'May I come in, please?'

'Of course you may,' said Lydia. 'This is your house.'

'The house may be mine but this room is exclusively your territory. I made that clear from the start. Everyone is entitled to have a place that is solely theirs.'

'I agree with that, Beatrice, and I'm deeply grateful.'

Lydia indicated a chair and her friend sat down opposite her. Beatrice Myler had been her salvation. She was a kind, gentle, sympathetic woman who made no demands on her. They had met in Rome when both of them were on sightseeing tours. In the wake of the discovery of Lydia's secret romance, she had been sent off to Europe with her former governess in the hope that the trip would expunge all her feelings for Gerard Burns. In fact, it did quite the opposite. She thought about him constantly and blamed herself for getting him summarily dismissed from a job that he enjoyed so much. Lydia kept wondering how he would cope and if he was still thinking fondly of her. It was only when she'd bumped into Beatrice Myler in the crypt of a little Italian church that she found herself able to forget about her past life for a while.

They were two intelligent women with shared interests in music and literature. Beatrice also had a passion for Italian culture and she fired the younger woman with her enthusiasm. Neither was travelling with ideal companions. Lydia was partnered by the elderly governess who was, in essence, her gaoler, paid to watch her carefully and keep her well away from England. Beatrice was there with her uncle, a retired archdeacon in his seventies with an arthritic hip. He and the governess were quite happy to sink down on any available seating and leave the others to their own devices.

'I don't know what I'd have done without you,' said Lydia.

'You'd have won through somehow. You have an instinct for survival.'

'It was more like desperation to get away from my home. I was suffocated there, Beatrice. They wouldn't allow me to breathe properly.'

'You did the right thing in striking out on your own.'

'I was in a complete daze at first,' admitted Lydia, 'and very frightened. I thought that Nottingham was a big town, but it's so small compared to London. I'd just never *seen* so many people.'

'You were very brave to come here, Lydia. This is no place for a young woman by herself.'

'I soon learnt that.'

Within her first week there, she'd found herself a target for unwanted male interest and had had to move from one hotel to another in order to shake off admirers. Lydia had money enough to look after herself but no anchor to her life. After months of loneliness in the capital, she'd plucked up the courage to take up the invitation given to her by Beatrice Myler to call on her if she was ever in London. When she entered the cosy house in the suburbs, Lydia had found her new home.

'I had a letter from my uncle this morning,' said Beatrice.

'How is he?'

'Oh, you know what he's like. Uncle Herbert had to have his customary moan about arthritis. I think he feels rather cheated. Because he spent all of his working life in holy orders, he believes that God should have given him a special dispensation.'

'He's a dear old soul. I enjoy his company.'

'As it happened, his letter was all about you.'

Lydia gaped. 'Was it, really?'

'Uncle Herbert is very fond of you. He wants you to know that you're in his prayers.' Beatrice smiled. 'You're in mine, too, of course. I haven't said anything before because I knew that if you wished to talk about it, you'd already have done so. But I've seen the immense strain you've been under since . . . you heard the news. And this morning's letter has made me want to speak out. Do you mind?'

'No,' said Lydia, squeezing her hand. 'You're entitled to speak out.'

'You may not like what I'm going to say.'

'It will be worth hearing, Beatrice. You're always so sensible.'

'Then my advice is this,' said the older woman. 'Go back home, Lydia. This is a time of trial for the whole family. Go back home and build bridges.'

Having had a meal at a public house in Spondon on the previous evening, Colbeck decided that he didn't want to repeat the experience. Besides, it was only fair that Leeming should have some consolations for being shunted off to the village. The sergeant had therefore been invited to join him at the Royal Hotel for dinner. As well as guaranteeing the high quality of the cuisine, it gave them a chance to discuss the case in comparative luxury. Colbeck had, as usual, been assiduous. After the meeting with Donald Haygarth and Maurice Cope, and the visit to Melbourne Hall, he'd returned to Derby with the intention of calling on some of the other board members of the Midland Railway. But he did not need to go looking for them because three of them came in search of him. When he interviewed them separately, each had told him more or less the same thing. Vivian Quayle had the vision to be chairman of the company. Haygarth did not. Obliquely, they all hinted that the latter was more than capable of engineering the death of a rival. They also named Maurice Cope as his fellow conspirator.

'Has anyone got a good word to say about Mr Haygarth?' asked Leeming.

'Yes, Victor, I do. He chose this hotel for me.'

'I wish he'd chosen it for me as well. The Malt Shovel has its charms but the floorboards creak and my bed is padded with anthracite. Anyway, do go on, sir.'

'Well,' said Colbeck, 'After talking to Mr Quayle's colleagues on the board, I made a point of finding the man who'd performed the post-mortem, then – just in case he was missing me – I called in at the police station to see Superintendent Wigg.'

'He's been sniping at us behind our backs, sir. Philip Conway told me.'

'Don't take it too seriously, Victor. I rather like that kind of thing. It spurs me on. I asked him what he knew about the Quayle family and, to my amazement, he'd been collecting what information he could about them. He was actually helpful.' He picked up the menu and ran an eye over it. 'What about your day?'

Leeming gave him an edited version of events in Spondon. He told Colbeck about the effort of pushing a heavy wheelbarrow up a hill and about his meetings with Jed Hockaday and Philip Conway. He'd also spoken to the stationmaster in Spondon and learnt how many people had got off the last train on the night of the murder. Curiously, the cobbler had been one of them. The rest of Leeming's day had been spent fending off people with lurid imaginations and an eye on the reward money.

'To be honest, sir,' he said, 'I was glad to escape for the evening. I think I must have spoken to everyone in the village by now.'

'Then there's no point in your staying there.'

Leeming's face glowed. 'I can move back in here?'

'No, Victor,' replied Colbeck. 'You can go home. To be more exact, you can return to London tomorrow to deliver a report on the situation here. I've already sent letters to Superintendent Tallis but you'll be able to give him the latest news. Before that, of course, I'd like you to drop off a letter at my house and assure Madeleine that I'm in good heart and thinking of her.'

'I'll gladly do that. Will I have time to see Estelle and the boys?'

'You can spend the night with them.'

'That's wonderful!'

'I haven't arranged a family reunion for your sake,' warned Colbeck. 'Frankly, it's another family reunion that I have in mind. If she's in London, I want you to find Lydia Quayle. Because of what Burns said about her, she interests me.'

'How on earth am I supposed to find her, sir?'

'You'll think of a way, Victor. Besides, you won't be on your own.'

'Who's going to help me?'

'My wife, of course,' said Colbeck, putting the menu back on the table. 'The superintendent would be aghast, naturally, but I think we need a woman on this case. It may involve delicate negotiations and – with respect – that is not your strong suit. Madeleine will be at your side.' He clapped Leeming on the shoulder. 'You and she will make an excellent team.'

CHAPTER TEN

It was an unwritten rule that when they had breakfast they never discussed anything of real moment. Neither Lydia Quayle nor Beatrice Myler wanted to start their day with a subject that might lead to argument and impede their digestion. Over their meal that morning, therefore, they confined themselves to domestic trivia. It was only when they'd finished and when the maidservant had cleared away the plates that they felt able to move on to a more serious matter.

'The decision, of course, is entirely yours,' said Beatrice.

'I know,' said Lydia, her throat tight.

'It's a real dilemma.'

'It's more than that, Beatrice. There's no right way to proceed. I'll be damned if I do go back and damned if I don't.'

'You'll hear no criticism from me.'

'I won't need to. I'll provide more than enough censure myself.'

'Oh, this must be preying on your mind dreadfully. What if . . .'

Thinking better of it, Beatrice lapsed back into silence and reached for her tea. Lydia was eager to know what her friend was about to say and eventually cajoled her into telling her what it was.

'I was only going to pose a question,' said Beatrice. 'What

if your father had died of natural causes? Would you have been tempted to go back then?'

'No,' said Lydia, 'definitely not.'

'You sound very convinced of that.'

'I am, Beatrice.'

'And what if your mother had passed away? You've often told me how fragile she is. Would that draw you back to Nottingham?'

'To be honest, I don't know. But it's a decision I may have to face soon.'

'It should be easier now that your father is . . . out of the way.'

'Where my family is concerned, there are no easy decisions.'

Beatrice felt sorry for her but there was little she could do beyond offering her unqualified sympathy. Her own family life had been so different. It had been happy and blissfully uneventful. Never having the desire or the opportunity to get married, she'd found fulfilment elsewhere. Having come into a substantial amount of money on the death of her parents, she could afford to live in a delightful house and visit Italy whenever she chose. But the truth of it was, she now realised, that she'd never been forced to make a decision of the magnitude that now confronted Lydia. It was therefore impossible for her to put herself in her friend's position. She had never met any of the other members of the family or experienced the deep divisions that they appeared to have.

'Whatever you do, Lydia, you'll have my full support.'

'That means everything to me.'

'I won't presume to offer you any more advice.'

'What about your Uncle Herbert?'

'Oh,' said Beatrice, chortling, 'he was an archdeacon. He'll give you advice whether you ask for it or not. Uncle Herbert would see it as his duty.'

'How much have you told him about me?'

'It wasn't necessary to tell him anything, Lydia. People like him just know.'

Lydia spooned sugar into her tea and stirred it, contrasting the life she now led with the one that she'd escaped. When she'd been at home, she had a family, a position in the community and an ability to follow her interests whatever the costs involved. It was the friendship with Gerard Burns that had been the catalyst for change. Slow to develop, it had started at a cricket match when she saw him in supreme form. As a bowler, he'd terrorised the batting side. Suddenly, he was much more than simply a gardener. Though he was increasingly fond of her, he was held back from making even the smallest move in her direction because she seemed quite unattainable. For anything to happen between them, therefore, it had been up to Lydia to take the initiative and that was what she'd finally done. She'd been shocked at her boldness but thrilled with his response. They began to meet in secret and the attraction eventually burgeoned into love.

As she looked across the table, she realised that Beatrice had never had that sense of madness, that fire in the blood, that conviction that nothing else mattered than to be with the man she adored. It had somehow been beyond her friend's reach. What Beatrice had in its place was something that Lydia had come to cherish because it brought a peace of mind she'd never felt before.

'I'd rather stay here with you, Beatrice,' she said.

And the discussion was over.

Madeleine Colbeck took advantage of the bright sunlight flooding in through the window of her studio and started work early that morning. While she knew that there were other female artists in London, she flattered herself that she was the only one who'd forged a reputation for painting steam locomotives and railway scenes. Her father was her greatest source of technical advice but he was also her sternest critic. When she heard the doorbell ring, she feared that he'd called unexpectedly and would come to view her latest work before it was ready to be seen. Opening the door, she listened for the sound of his voice. In fact, it was Victor Leeming who was being invited into the house. After putting her brush aside and wiping her hands on a cloth, Madeleine went downstairs to greet him.

'What are you doing here, Victor?' she asked.

'I'm to act as a postman,' he replied, handing over a letter. 'The inspector said I was to deliver this before reporting to Scotland Yard.'

'Come in the drawing room and tell me *everything*.'

She led the way into the room and sat beside him on the sofa. Anxious to open her letter, she felt that it would be rude to do so until she'd talked to her visitor.

'Is Robert still in Derby?'

'Yes, he is, and likely to be there for some time.'

'Have you made any headway in the investigation?'

'I like to think so but I daresay you'll read about it in the letter.'

'Why did Robert send you back to London?'

'He has work for me to do here, Mrs Colbeck. I'm to stay the night.'

'That will please Estelle,' she said. 'By the way, she came here for tea with the boys a couple of days ago. We had a lovely time.'

'Did my lads behave themselves?' he asked, worriedly.

'They were as good as gold. My father saw to that. Between you and me, I'm very glad that he's not here at the moment. If he were, he'd insist on telling you how to solve the murder.'

'I wish somebody would. I'm completely confused.'

'Why is that?'

'It's too complicated to explain and I don't want to repeat what the inspector has told you in his letter. Besides, I need to see Superintendent Tallis. I don't know why,' he said, despondently, 'but whenever I go into his office, I feel as if I'm about to face a firing squad.'

Madeleine laughed. 'He's not that bad, is he? Robert enjoys teasing him.'

'I'd never dare to do that. He'd have me back in uniform in a flash.' He got to his feet. 'It's a pleasure to see you again, Mrs Colbeck, and to know that I'll be in a more comfortable bed tonight than the one I spent the last two nights in.'

She rose to her feet. 'I'll show you out.'

'There's no need. You enjoy reading your letter.'

'I'm dying to open it.'

'Then prepare yourself for a surprise. I'll see you again this afternoon.'

'Do you need to come back?'

'Those are my orders,' he said with a smile. 'You and I are going to be working side by side. Open your letter and find out why.'

To work up an appetite for breakfast, Colbeck had taken a walk around Derby before its streets were bustling with people and noisy with traffic. He liked the town. Its rich medieval legacy was still visible and there was a sense of civic pride that he admired. When he'd had his breakfast, he went off to find Maurice Cope.

'Derby is a good blend of the old and the new,' he remarked. 'It's full of lovely, narrow, winding streets as well as big, solid, purposeful buildings. You must enjoy living here, Mr Cope.'

'Actually,' said the other, 'I live in Kedleston. Not in Kedleston Hall, I hasten to add – that's far too grand for me. I live in the village.'

'Does it have a railway station?'

'Not yet, but I hope that it will one day.'

'I could say the same of Melbourne. A branch line there would have saved me a lot of time. How do you get into Derby every day?'

'I ride,' said Cope. 'I find a steady canter very invigorating of a morning. It's only three miles away from Derby.'

Colbeck was surprised. In his view, Cope was an unlikely horseman. Indeed, he looked as if he got very little physical exercise. Yet, although he worked for a railway company, he chose to live somewhere yet to be served by it. That seemed perverse. They were in an office that seemed to reflect Cope's character. It was clean, well organised and dull. There was nothing to excite the eye or stimulate the brain.

'How did you get on in Melbourne?' asked Cope.

'I thoroughly enjoyed my visit. The Hall itself and the church nearby are exceptional.'

'I was referring to your meeting with Mr Burns.'

'He was quite exceptional as well, in his own way,' said Colbeck. 'He's a first-rate gardener and an outstanding cricketer. Few of us have two such strings to our bow.'

'What did you make of him, Inspector?'

'I have something to find out before I make a final judgement.'

'Is he a credible suspect?'

'Why do you ask that?'

'I'd like to pass on the observation to Mr Haygarth. He wants to know about every stage of your investigation.'

'Then you may tell him that we are still gathering evidence across a wide front. Given the fact that he worked for Mr Quayle and fell out with him, Mr Burns must be considered as – how shall I put it – a person of interest to us. What was your estimate of him, Mr Cope?'

'I've never met the fellow and nor has Mr Haygarth.'

'So you've never seen Gerard Burns playing cricket?'

'It's a game I have no time to watch, Inspector.'

Colbeck glanced at a framed photograph on the wall of the Derby Works.

'There's another reason why I like this place,' he said. 'It's a railway town but quite unlike most of the others. Places like Crewe, Swindon and Wolverton have their works near the heart of the town, and so does Ashford in Kent. Yours is on the outer edge of Derby.'

'Other industrial developments got here first, Inspector.'

'I'd value the opportunity to take a look around the works.'

'You won't find any murder suspects there.'

'I just want to satisfy my curiosity, Mr Cope.'

'Then I'll ensure that you're made welcome there. Will Sergeant Leeming want to accompany you on a tour of inspection?'

'No,' said Colbeck with a laugh. 'He doesn't share my enthusiasm for rail transport. In any case, he'll be back in London by now.'

Cope was astonished. 'What's he doing there?'

'He's widening the search.'

'You seem to have strange methods of investigation, Inspector.'

'They usually bring gratifying results, I assure you.'

'There's something I wish to say,' said Cope, clearing his throat for what was plainly a rehearsed speech. 'Donald Haygarth is part of the backbone of this company. He's essential to its future success. Since he is the person to profit most from the unfortunate demise of Mr Quayle, it's only natural that some people would name him as a suspect. I know that Superintendent Wigg has done so. I can see it in his eyes.'

'The superintendent has made no secret of the fact.'

'He needs to understand that nobody is more committed to unmasking the killer than Mr Haygarth. It was he who sent for *you*, Inspector.' He hunched his shoulders interrogatively. 'Do you think he'd be rash enough to do that if he had any blood on his hands?'

He paused for an answer that never came. Early in his career, Colbeck had been summoned to solve a murder by the very man who'd committed it and who was certain that he would be absolved from suspicion by making contact with Scotland Yard. Ultimately, his hopes had been dashed. There was no proof so far that Haygarth was attempting the same sort of bluff but he had certainly not been eliminated as a possible suspect working in conjunction with others.

'What is your next step, Inspector?' asked Cope.

'I'm going to pay a visit to Ilkeston.'

'Why do you need to go there?'

'There's an alibi that needs to be checked. It's one of those tedious jobs that a murder investigation always throws up but it can't be ignored.' He looked Cope up and down. 'Tell me, sir, would you say that you had a good memory?'

'I have an excellent memory, as it happens.'

'And would you describe yourself as honest?'

Cope bridled. 'I find that question rather offensive,' he said. 'Speak to anyone in this building and you'll find that I'm known for my honesty.'

'Gerard Burns would think differently.'

'What has he got to do with it?'

'If your memory was as sound as you claim, you'd remember. You once approached him on Mr Haygarth's behalf to entice him away from his job by offering him more money. Has that slipped your mind?'

'I deny it flatly,' said Cope, standing his ground.

'Are you claiming that Burns has made a mistake?'

'No, Inspector, I'm claiming that he's told you a downright lie. But, then, what can you expect from an unprincipled rogue who wormed his way into the affections of one of Mr Quayle's daughters?'

'When we spoke about him in Mr Haygarth's presence, you insisted that his name was new to you. How is it that you've suddenly become aware of his reason for leaving Mr Quayle?'

Cope held firm under Colbeck's accusatory gaze. 'I, too, have been making enquiries,' he said. 'You're not the only one who can do that, Inspector.'

The anomaly had been pointed out to him many times. Victor Leeming was one of the bravest detectives at Scotland Yard, justly famed for his readiness to tackle violent criminals and for his disregard of personal injury. His courage had earned him many commendations and won him promotion to the rank of sergeant. Yet when he had to spend time alone with Edward Tallis, he had an attack of cowardice. Taking a deep breath and pulling himself to his full height, he knocked on the superintendent's door and received a barked command to enter. Leeming went into the room and closed the door gently behind him Head bent over a document he was perusing, Tallis kept him waiting. When he finally looked up, his eyes widened.

'Is that you, Leeming?' he demanded.

'Yes, sir.'

'What the devil are you doing here?'

'Inspector Colbeck sent me to deliver this report,' said Leeming, stepping forward to put the envelope on the desk then jumping back as if he'd just put food through the bars of a lion's cage. 'He sends his regards.'

'Does he, indeed?'

Tallis opened the letter and read the report with a blend of interest and exasperation. His grunts of disapproval were warning signals. Leeming was about to become the whipping boy yet again.

'So,' said Tallis, glaring at him, 'the Inspector is scouring the Midlands for an unusual top hat and you have been amusing yourself by pushing a wheelbarrow uphill. Is that the sum total of your achievements?'

'There's more to it than that, sir.'

'Then why is there little else in the report?'

'The missing top hat and the wheel marks of a barrow in the churchyard might turn out to be useful clues.'

'Then again, they might not.'

'We shall see, Superintendent. Does the inspector make no mention in his report of Gerard Burns, one of our suspects?'

'Yes, he does,' said Tallis, 'but Colbeck seems more interested in telling me about his ability as a fast bowler than about his potential as a killer. And what's this nonsense about a search for Miss Lydia Quayle?'

'The inspector believes that she will give us information that can't be obtained elsewhere. In the shadow of a murder, you expect a family to retreat into itself but, in this case, they've shut us out completely. Inspector Colbeck called at the house and had short shrift from Stanley Quayle. He's the elder son. You'd have thought he'd have wanted to help those of us who are trying to catch the man who murdered his father but he's shown no interest. His sister may be able to tell us why.'

'Lydia Quayle had a disastrous relationship with this fellow, Burns.'

'That's why it's important to find her, sir.'

'You and Colbeck were sent to Derby to solve a heinous crime. I don't want the pair of you poking into a misalliance between a gardener and a lady who should have known better. This is work for detectives of another kind,' said Tallis with utter contempt. 'I refer to that odious breed of private investigators that enjoy peeping through keyholes and eavesdropping on conversations. We are dealing with murder, Sergeant, not with sexual peccadilloes.'

'The inspector called it a true romance.'

'Well, he'd better not do so in my hearing.'

'They must have loved each other to take such a risk.'

'Don't you dare invite me to speculate on the stratagems to which they resorted,' said Tallis, leaning forward aggressively. 'This attachment was never going to be sanctified by marriage. All that it did was to estrange a young woman from her family and give a dissolute fast bowler a reason to hate her father.'

'Oh, he wasn't dissolute, sir.'

'Don't argue with me, you idiot!'

'Inspector Colbeck described him as a responsible person.'

'And look at what he was responsible for!'

'It happened years ago, sir.'

'He ruined this young lady's life and drove her apart from her family. And now,' he continued, glancing at the report, 'he's had the gall to get married.'

'It's not a crime,' retorted Leeming, emboldened by the scorn in Tallis's voice. 'If it is, you must arrest the inspector and me because we've both found someone with whom to share our lives. What happened between Gerard Burns and Lydia Quayle has a direct bearing on this case. One of them has been found,' he stressed. 'It's important that we track down the other.'

Tallis was so stunned by the unaccustomed forthrightness of his visitor that he could find nothing to say. Instead, he scanned the report again so that he could take in the fine detail. When he'd finished, he looked up at Leeming.

'As you wish, Sergeant,' he said, chastened. 'Find the lady.'

Though Ilkeston was in Derbyshire, it was much closer to Nottingham than it was to the county town that Colbeck had just left. It was an archetypal industrial community, owing its wealth to coal, ironworks and textile manufacture. When he got his first look at the place, Colbeck despaired of ever finding a cricket pitch there. It was so defiantly urban that the few trees he could see were like nervous guests afraid to step fully into a room. The ironworks stood at New Stanton to the south of the town and it soon made its presence felt. One of the three blast furnaces on the banks of the Nutbrook Canal suddenly boomed out and made the ground quake. Colbeck mused that even an experienced bowler like Gerard Burns would find it hard to maintain the rhythm of his run-up if disturbed by the deafening noise from the Stanton Ironworks.

The cab driver had a pleasant surprise for him. There was indeed a cricket pitch half a mile out of the town and he spoke fondly of it. Colbeck asked to be taken there. Having watched matches at Lord's Cricket Ground in London, he was bound to compare the Ilkeston equivalent unfavourably with it. Small, oval and encircled by trees, it also served as a park and a few tethered goats were grazing on it. Yet it was relatively flat and had a pavilion of sorts, a long wooden shed with a verandah in front of it. An old man was coming out of the pavilion. When Colbeck approached him, he discovered that he was talking to the groundsman.

'How often are matches played here?'

'Not often, sir.'

'Is there a regular team here?'

'Not really, sir.'

'How much money is spent on the upkeep of the ground?'

'Not much, sir.'

'I see that you've got goats here.'

'Better'n sheep, sir – far less dung.'

There was an element of pride in the man's voice. What was a rather sorry pitch in Colbeck's eyes was a source of pleasure to him. It was he who kept the grass cut and marked everything out. Ramshackle as it was, the pavilion had a fairly recent coat of white paint.

'You had a match here a few days ago.'

The man chuckled. 'We beat a team from Matlock, sir.'

'Why was that?'

'We 'ad best bowler in't county.'

'Gerard Burns?'

'Aye, thass 'im.'

He went into rhapsodies about the game and described how none of the Matlock team could handle the speed, aggression and accuracy of Burns's bowling. The Ilkeston team was gathered from the surrounding area. Miners, ironworkers and those employed in textile factories showed little interest in cricket. They saw it as a game for gentlemen and preferred rougher sports. Yet a cluster of spectators had turned out to watch Ilkeston destroy Matlock.

'It were a treat, sir.'

'I wish I'd seen Burns in action,' said Colbeck. 'I've heard a lot about him.'

'The lad were champion.'

'What happened after the game?'

'We drank till we dropp'd.'

The old man's reminiscences were so filled with excitement and spiced with the local dialect that Colbeck didn't understand much of what he said but he heard the salient details. Burns had been invited to join the team by someone who'd seen him play for Nottinghamshire and knew of his move to Melbourne. It had taken time to persuade the gardener to represent Ilkeston as a guest player but, once he'd committed himself, he gave of his best. The celebrations went on into the evening and Burns had drunk more than his share of beer.

'Then he went back to Melbourne, I suppose,' said Colbeck.

'No, sir. I were on't cart wi' 'm when it took us ter station.'

'So where did he go?'

'Derby.'

Colbeck felt a minor thrill of discovery. Flushed with alcohol, Gerard Burns sounded as if he had been in the right place and at the right time to kill the man he hated. How he had contrived to get Vivian Quayle to Spondon was not so easily explained. Nobody had been able to tell Colbeck where exactly Quayle had been in the twenty-four hours leading up to his murder. He was as ubiquitous as he'd been industrious. Was it possible that Burns had somehow become aware of the man's movements that night? He had, after all, returned to what was part of the Quayle fiefdom. The coal mines in Ilkeston and beyond were owned by the family. They employed large numbers of people from the town. Burns would have been well aware of that. Was that the reason he'd come to Ilkeston in the first place?

Colbeck's speculations took him all the way back to the railway station. When he descended from the cab, he paid the driver and thanked him for his help. He was just about to walk away when a carriage rolled past nearby. The passenger could be seen clearly. He appeared to be wearing funeral garb but it was his top hat that made Colbeck stare. Tall and with a delicately curved brim, it looked remarkably like the one missing from the murder victim. At that moment, the passenger turned his head idly in the direction of the detective and there was a searing moment of recognition between them.

Colbeck was looking at the face of Stanley Quayle.

CHAPTER ELEVEN

When Caleb Andrews called in unexpectedly at the house, his daughter was on tenterhooks, fearing that Victor Leeming would soon turn up as well and that the two men would meet. There would be no way to get rid of her father then. He'd insist on knowing the latest developments in the case and – after a volley of derisive comments about the Midland Railway – he'd offer his help in the investigation. Madeleine was therefore greatly relieved when he announced that he was off to visit a former colleague from the LNWR.

'He should have retired years ago,' said Andrews, disparagingly. 'Silas always had poor eyesight and he was slow to react to things. You can't be in charge of a locomotive when you're like that. It's how accidents happen and he's had a few of those. I was different,' he went on, thrusting out his chest. 'My eyesight was always perfect and I had a quick brain. I'm still as fit as I always was, Maddy. I could go back to work tomorrow.'

'You've put all that behind you, Father. Enjoy your retirement.'

'I need something to keep me active.'

'You talked about getting an allotment.'

'That wouldn't suit me.'

'What would attract you?'

'You know the answer to that. Whenever he starts a new case, I'd like Robert to call on me for advice. I've lived and breathed railways, Maddy. I *know* things.'

'Then you can discuss them with Silas Pegler. You'll have shared memories.'

'You can't have a serious talk with Silas,' he complained. 'He's a likeable old fellow but he's got no conversation.'

What that meant, she knew, was that her father dominated any discussion with his friend and allowed him few opportunities to speak. It was a situation she'd seen with virtually all of his railway colleagues. Andrews was a fluent talker but a bad listener. Eager to send him on his way, she made no comment and he eventually took his leave. They exchanged a farewell kiss then she waved him off from the doorstep. His departure was timely. Five minutes later, Victor Leeming arrived. He and Madeleine adjourned to the drawing room. The sergeant was in an almost ebullient mood.

'How did you get on with the superintendent?' she asked.

'I put him in his place for once.'

'You told me that it was like facing a firing squad.'

'I was the one with a rifle in my hands this time,' he bragged. 'When he said that there was no need to find Lydia Quayle, I made him see that it was vital.' His buoyancy faded. 'We're now left with the small problem of exactly *how* to find her, of course. London is a huge city with a population of over three million. She could be anywhere.'

'Didn't Robert give you any instructions?'

'He simply told me where to start.'

'And where is that?'

'We have to visit some libraries,' he explained. 'How much has the inspector told you about the case?'

'His letter was very detailed,' replied Madeleine. 'I know about the friendship between Miss Quayle and the gardener, and I know that she was sent abroad by her father to keep the two of them apart.'

'Inspector Colbeck learnt something about her travels from Burns. He said how fondly she'd always talked of Italy. That's the most likely place she'd have gone. Burns had no way of confirming it, of course, because they'd lost touch completely, but it's logical. He told the inspector something else about her as well.'

'What was that, Victor?'

'Lydia Quayle loved reading. She was always talking about the latest thing she'd read. When it was the gardener's birthday, she gave him a book of poems.'

Madeleine smiled inwardly. Early in their relationship, Colbeck had given her a poetry anthology. She had read something from it every night. In her case, it had been a treasured gift but she doubted if the gardener got quite as much pleasure out of the volume he'd been given.

'I can see how my husband's mind is working,' she said. 'A young woman with a passion for books is likely to borrow some on a regular basis. If she lives alone, she'll have plenty of time for reading and she's now free from the social commitments that she must have had when she lived at home with her parents.'

'I'm not a reading man myself,' said Leeming, apologetically. 'I don't have a leaning that way. As for libraries, I wouldn't even know where to find one.'

'Then we must start with the London Library. That's in St James's Square.'

'I've never had call to go there.'

'There's the British Museum, of course, but that's for more scholarly books and I don't think you're allowed to borrow them. It seems to me as if Miss Quayle would be more interested in reading novels, books of poetry or something about Italy, perhaps. She may also buy books, I daresay, but an avid reader would also belong to a library.'

'You're starting to sound like the inspector.'

'I'm trying to think like him, that's all.'

'I never tell Estelle anything about my work. It would only upset her to know how much danger we come up against. Besides, there's no point. She wouldn't be able to do what you can do.' He grimaced. 'I hope we're lucky, Mrs Colbeck. I've just thought what would happen if we *don't* find the woman.'

'You'd have to go back to the superintendent and admit that you failed.'

Leeming gulped at the prospect. 'It'd be worse than a firing squad in that case. He'd let loose the artillery on me.'

An atmosphere of gloom and apprehension pervaded the whole house. Servants moved about in silence as if frightened to speak. The murder of Vivian Quayle had had a profound effect on them and on those who worked outside on the estate. If someone as important and as well protected as their master could be killed, they worried about their own safety. Family members and servants all wore funeral attire. When Agnes helped her mother slowly downstairs, there was a rustle of black taffeta. Though her daughter advised against it, Harriet Quayle insisted on being taken out for a drive. Having been penned up indoors for days, she said that she felt that the house was oppressive and that she needed fresh air.

'At least, let me come with you,' volunteered Agnes.

'I prefer to be alone.'

'But what if you're taken ill?'

'Stop fussing over me, Agnes.'

'I worry about you.'

'If anything untoward happens,' said Harriet, 'I'm sure that Cleary will bring me back at once. I just want to experience *freedom*.'

It was a strange word to use but Agnes knew that her mother was more than capable of coming out with odd remarks or making peculiar demands. There was a capricious streak in her that had not been entirely quelled by almost forty years of marriage to one of the leading industrialists in the county. The butler was there to open the door wide for them and the driver was standing beside the landau with its door opened and its step folded down. When he saw the old lady emerge, he hurried across to her and offered his arm. Harriet took it gratefully.

'Thank you, Cleary,' she said. 'You can let go of me now, Agnes.'

'You're not to stay out for long, Mother.'

'I just want to be able to breathe again.'

'Take good care of her, Cleary,' said Agnes.

'Yes, Miss Quayle,' he replied.

Cleary was a tall, thin, lithe man in his thirties with a gaunt face and a dark complexion. Though he'd been born in the area, he had a slightly foreign look to him. After helping his mistress into the carriage, he put a blanket over her legs even though it was a warm day. Agnes watched as he climbed up on the box seat and used a whip to set the horses in motion. As the vehicle swept off, its wheels made a loud scrunching noise on the gravel that sounded almost sacrilegious near a house of mourning.

Agnes went back into the building in search of her younger brother. She found him in what had once been their father's study, poring over some documents. When he looked up at her, she gave a sigh of despair.

'I couldn't stop her, Lucas.'

'We must give Mother her head.'

'She can be so determined.'

'It's a family trait,' said Lucas Quayle. 'You don't build empires with a faint heart. Everything that Father achieved would have been impossible without Mother. Until her health collapsed, she helped him a great deal in the early days. That's why it was such a strong marriage.'

Agnes made no reply. Talk of marriage always embarrassed her. Shorn of her own chances by her lack of appeal to the male sex, she'd been compelled to look after her mother and put up with the old lady's idiosyncrasies. Nobody else in the family, she felt, understood how unfair it was on her. She got scant reward and was taken for granted by everyone. She recalled how quickly her mother had abandoned her to take Cleary's arm instead. That kind of petty rebuff had happened a hundred times. It might, however, be about to end soon.

'The doctor is very worried about her,' she said.

'We're all worried, Agnes.'

'He doesn't think she's taking the tablets he's given her.'

'You should know if that's the case.'

'I can't stand over her every minute of the day, Lucas.'

'No, no, I accept that.'

'It's almost as if she's . . . inviting death.'

'Don't be melodramatic.'

'Her behaviour has been so weird since we learnt about Father.'

'I suspect that all our behaviour has been like that, Agnes. I know that mine has. I've been swinging between grief and anger like a pendulum. And you've seen how tense Stanley has become. It's an abnormal situation,' said Lucas. 'We're bound to react in abnormal ways.'

Agnes nodded. She could talk to Lucas in a way that was impossible with her other siblings. While Lydia had taunted her, Stanley had largely ignored her. Lucas at least seemed to notice that she existed.

'What are the police doing?' she asked.

'That's something I want to know as well,' he said, decisively. 'When the detective came from Scotland Yard, I wasn't even allowed to meet him. Stanley had him out of the house in minutes. We should have helped the inspector. We know things about father that nobody else could tell him.' He stood up. 'In fact, in half an hour, I'm catching a train to Derby to meet this Inspector Colbeck.'

'Have you told Stanley?'

'I don't need his permission, Agnes.'

'He'll think that you do.'

'Well, he's not here to stop me, is he? I'll do as I please.'

'Where is he?'

'Stanley went into Nottingham to sort out the funeral arrangements. After that, he was going to call in at a pit near Ilkeston.'

'Why is he doing that?' she cried with sudden annoyance. 'It's so typical of him. Our dear Father was murdered and all that Stanley wants to do is to visit a mine. Doesn't he *care*, Lucas? He's supposed to be in mourning.'

Because he was wedded to his work, Stanley Quayle saw little of his wife and even less of his children. They formed a decorous background in his life. Even the death of his father could not keep him away from one of the family pits. His visit to the funeral director had been short to the point of rudeness. He'd simply given the man a list of requirements he'd written out, answered a few questions from him then gone off to Ilkeston. Keeping on the move, he discovered, was a useful distraction from the sorrow enveloping the rest of the family. Someone else could deal with the cards and the messages of condolence that kept coming in. He had more important things to do.

The glimpse of Inspector Colbeck was worrying. He could think of no reason why the detective should be in Ilkeston. What he'd seen in the man's face was a fleeting suspicion and it was as disturbing as it was irritating. It was almost as if Colbeck had just had something confirmed in his mind. Quayle had been at pains to keep his distance from the investigation and he made sure that nobody else in the family was involved. Lucas, in particular, was likely to be thoughtless and indiscreet. Family secrets best kept hidden could unwittingly be revealed and it could lead to embarrassment.

As the carriage turned in through the main gates of the estate, he made a mental note to speak to his brother again and impress upon him the need to close ranks. The outside world should know nothing of the rift with Lydia, for instance, or of the other ugly skeletons in the closet. Stanley Quayle was an expert in repression, hiding things from the past so cunningly that nobody even knew that they were there. Reclining in the carriage, he rehearsed what he was going to say to his brother. It never occurred to him that at that very moment Lucas Quayle was on his way to Derby and that it was too late to rein him in.

The visit to the London Library was an overwhelming experience for Victor Leeming when he called there that afternoon with Madeleine Colbeck. He'd never seen so many books before. Endless shelves were packed with a variety of reading matter for those who used the place regularly. Leeming had very few books in his own home. Colbeck had an extensive and wide-ranging stock but his collection could not compare with what was on display in the library. In reply to a polite enquiry, the man on duty behind the desk refused point-blank to reveal the names of their subscribers. It was only when Leeming explained that he was involved in a murder investigation that he got some cooperation. The man searched through the long list of readers but he was unable to find the name of Lydia Quayle among them. Reluctantly, Madeleine and the sergeant withdrew.

'We'll have to try elsewhere,' she suggested.

'What if she *does* use this library?'

'Her name was not on their list.'

'I know that, but perhaps she's using a different name now. If she's cut herself off completely from the Quayle family, she might have taken on another identity. It's something that criminals often do.'

'She's not a criminal, Victor.'

'The family seem to treat her like one.'

As they came out into St James's Square, he glanced nervously up and down in case any policemen were about. If he was recognised by one of them, it might be reported to Scotland Yard and he would have to answer awkward questions about why he was seen in the company of a woman when he was supposed to be conducting a search on his own. When an empty cab came in sight, he flagged it down. Madeleine gave the driver an address in New Oxford Street and they climbed in.

'How did you know the number, Mrs Colbeck?' he asked.

'I borrow books from this library,' she said. 'It was one of the presents I had on my last birthday. Robert paid for my membership.'

'Even I have heard of Mudie's Lending Library.'

'It's been opened for less than twenty years but it's been a huge success. In fact, there are so many books there now that they don't have room to display them all. They had to move to larger premises but there still aren't enough shelves.'

'Libraries are a closed book to me,' he said, artlessly.

When Madeleine laughed, he realised what he'd said and apologised for the unintended pun, sinking back into his seat and listening to the steady clip-clop of the horse's hooves. Leeming was not sanguine about their hopes of success. Sensing his pessimism, Madeleine sought to raise his spirits.

'We'll find Miss Quayle somehow,' she said, brightly. 'We *have* to.'

When Colbeck returned to the Royal Hotel that afternoon, he found someone waiting for him. Lucas Quayle leapt up from his seat and accosted the detective. Having first gone to the police station in Derby, he'd been sent on to the hotel. Pleased to meet him, Colbeck felt rather conspicuous standing beside a man in mourning wear.

'How did you pick me out so easily?' he asked.

'Superintendent Wigg gave me a description of you.'

Colbeck smiled. 'I can imagine that it was not altogether flattering. But you didn't need to ask him, surely. Your brother could have told you what I looked like.'

'Stanley gave us no information whatsoever about you,' said Lucas Quayle. 'We were merely told that you'd come and gone.'

'That sums up my visit perfectly. It was a very short interview. Your brother was too . . . preoccupied.'

'He often is, Inspector.'

'Does he know that you've come to see me?'

'No, he doesn't. If I'd told him in advance, he'd have tried to stop me.'

'But we need all the help we can get, Mr Quayle. Anything we can learn about your family is valuable to us.'

They adjourned to a quiet corner of the lounge and lowered themselves into armchairs. Colbeck had the feeling that his visitor would be much more forthcoming than his brother. He anticipated the first question.

'You'll no doubt wish to know what progress we've made so far.'

'Yes, I would,' said Lucas Quayle.

'I'd be happy to furnish you with a list of suspects but, unfortunately, we don't have one as yet. There are one or two people who've . . . come to our attention, let us say, but an arrest is still a long way off.'

'I appreciate that it may take time, Inspector.'

'We've gathered a lot of evidence, however, and it's pointing us in certain directions. That's all I can tell you at present, sir.'

'We put our trust in you, Inspector.'

'What we still have are gaps to fill regarding your family.'

'Ask me what you need to now.'

'Then let me start where your brother ended my conversation with him,' said Colbeck, testing him out. 'What can you tell me about Gerard Burns?'

Lucas Quayle did not flinch. He gave an honest reply, explaining that Burns had been a personable young man who did his job well and improved the gardens immeasurably. Nobody in the family had been aware of the fact that Lydia had fallen in love with the gardener. When the relationship came to light, Stanley Quayle had been as vengeful as their father. They both subjected Lydia to a verbal onslaught that left her distraught. While he didn't entirely approve of the romance with Burns, Lucas Quayle had been more sympathetic towards his sister. He admitted that he'd had one or two foolish dalliances in his past and argued that it gave him a degree of understanding of Lydia's position. Colbeck stepped in.

'With respect Mr Quayle,' he said, 'I don't think that there's any similarity between you and your sister here. You confess quite openly that you were briefly led astray but the relationship between Burns and your sister was far more committed. They even considered elopement.'

Lucas Quayle was thunderstruck. 'Who told you that?'

'It was Mr Burns himself.'

'You've spoken to him?'

'After the way that your brother reacted to the mere mention of his name, I simply had to. Burns was certainly no philanderer. His love for your sister was deep and genuine, and it was requited.' The other man nodded sadly. 'Burns told me that he was thrown off the estate and that your sister was sent abroad.'

'That was Stanley's idea. If it had been left to him, Lydia would have ended up at the North Pole but they compromised on Italy. She'd always wanted to go there. Father believed that three months of Mediterranean sunshine would remind her of her duty to the family and wipe the memory of Gerard Burns from her mind.'

'The plan didn't work, sir.'

'I know that. Lydia was still infatuated with him.'

'Are you aware that your father took steps to keep Burns away from her?'

'He used his influence to ensure that the fellow would never work in the area again. Father could be brutal on occasion and so can my brother. They watched Lydia like hawks. It was demeaning for her.'

Colbeck realised that he was clearly unaware of the threats of violence made against Burns but decided against telling him. Lucas Quayle might disbelieve him. If he did, there was no point in blackening the image of his father in a younger son's mind days away from the funeral. The tense situation at the house, he learnt, did not last indefinitely. When she reached her twenty-first birthday, Lydia had come into enough money to support herself in relative comfort. It also gave her the confidence to challenge her father and then to defy him. Though he didn't know the full details, her younger brother said that there'd been a fierce argument before his elder sister had left the house for good.

'Did none of you keep in touch with her?' asked Colbeck.

'We were ordered not to, Inspector.'

'How did you feel about that?'

'I was very upset. I'd always liked Lydia. She had so much more life in her than Agnes, my younger sister. As long as she stayed at home, however, Lydia was having that life squeezed out of her. It was painful to watch.'

'Tell me about your father, sir.'

'If you've met Stanley, you already know the essence of his character.'

'Are they so alike?'

'Yes, Inspector, they love to be in charge.'

While he spoke with some affection for his father, Lucas Quayle did not disguise the man's driving ambition and his determination to get the better of his rivals in whatever walk of life. Vivian Quayle had had two passions – one was for collecting the fine china that Colbeck had seen on display in the study, and the other was for the game of cricket.

'If you've spoken to Burns, you'll have heard about our matches.'

'Yes,' said Colbeck, 'I understand that he was your prize asset.'

'Frankly, we'd never have won without him.'

'I believe that your brother was captain of the team.'

'Stanley insisted.'

'Did he have any special talent for the game?'

The other man laughed. 'No, Inspector, I think his highest score was eleven. He couldn't bowl to save his life and he wasn't mobile enough to be any use in the field. Yet he strutted around as if he'd just scored a century. We had three good players in our team – Burns was one, Cleary, the coachman, was another and I was the third. I was a far better batsman than Stanley,' he went on, 'but there was never any chance of my being captain. Do you have an elder brother?'

'Unfortunately, I don't. I was an only child.'

'Then you can count yourself, lucky, Inspector. The worst thing to be in my family is a younger brother.'

'Forgive me for saying so, Mr Quayle,' argued Colbeck, 'but it seems to me that that unwelcome distinction should go to your elder sister. You stayed and remained on amicable terms with your parents. Your sister was effectively banished.'

Lucas Quayle was contrite. 'You are quite right to remind me of that,' he said. 'Taking everything into account, I've had a remarkably happy life. Lydia has never enjoyed that same contentment and that upsets me.'

'It must also upset your mother and your other sister.'

'Mother has been unwell for years, Inspector. She was rocked when Lydia left home but could do nothing to stop her. Poor Agnes must have been sorry to lose her sister but she's never spoken about it. She was too scared of Father and of Stanley. There you are, Inspector,' he added. 'Agnes is another member of the family worse off than me. She's trapped there in perpetuity. I had the chance to escape.'

'Mr Quayle,' said Colbeck, 'there's something that I put to your brother and he was unable to help me. I'm hoping that you can. What possible reason could your father have had for going to Spondon?'

The other man's brow wrinkled in concentration. 'I can't think of one, Inspector,' he said at length.

'Nor could your brother, I fear. That leaves me with alternative explanations.'

'What are they?'

'Your father either went there under compulsion or he was killed elsewhere and taken to the village. He may, of course, have had a connection with Spondon in the past that nobody seems to know about.'

'I can't for a moment imagine what it could be, Inspector. My father was a Nottinghamshire man through and through. He rather despised Derbyshire.'

'Thank you, Mr Quayle,' said Colbeck. 'I'm very grateful that you came here. You've filled in many of those empty gaps I mentioned. Will you tell your brother about this meeting?'

'Yes,' replied the other, 'I'll tell him the truth. I'm already braced for an almighty row with him. It won't be the first one, alas. Stanley and I locked antlers over Lydia. I was all for inviting her to the funeral. Stanley was apoplectic.'

'How can you invite her when you don't know where she is?'

'I hired someone to find her, Inspector. I love my sister. I wanted her to know that there was at least one member of the family who cared about her.' He saw the smile on Colbeck's face. 'Have I said something amusing?'

'Not at all, Mr Quayle – I'm smiling at this unexpected good fortune. As we speak, someone is scouring London for her at my behest. His job would have been made far easier if you'd just given him the address.'

Mudie's Lending Library occupied several rooms at the address in New Oxford Street. Victor Leeming was once again dazzled by the sheer number of books under one roof. They were helped this time by a tall, bespectacled woman of middle years. She took them into

147

an office and produced a list of members in alphabetical order. It ran to several thousand. After going through it with meticulous care, she looked up with a sweet smile of apology.

'I'm sorry,' she said, 'but we have nobody of that name.'

Madeleine was disappointed. 'I could have sworn we'd find her here.'

'You can see the list yourself, if you wish.'

'No, thank you.'

'We might as well go,' said Leeming. 'She's obviously not here.'

'Wait a moment – I've had a thought.' Madeleine turned to the woman. 'Do you keep a record of borrowings, by any chance?'

'Oh, yes,' replied the woman. 'We have to, Mrs Colbeck. We need to know exactly where our books are at any given time. Reading habits are fairly constant. Almost half of the books borrowed are novels but that's hardly surprising, I suppose. History and biography account for over half of what remains.'

'What about travel?'

'Yes, that is very popular with some members. Over ten per cent of our borrowings relate to travel and you can subdivide that in different groups. People tend to have a particular interest in one country or in one part of the world.'

'The person we're after is fond of Italy.'

'We have a large collection of books on Italy and its culture.'

'This lady, it appears, is a fervent admirer of the country.'

'She's not here, Mrs Colbeck,' said Leeming. 'We must accept that.'

'She may not be here as Lydia Quayle,' said Madeleine, 'but she might have become a member under another name. You suggested that possibility.'

'It's true – I did.'

'Then let's see if we can find her by her reading habits rather than by name.'

The librarian was already ahead of Madeleine, flicking her way through a ledger that contained borrowings over recent months. Every so often, she would stop to jab at something with a finger before moving on.

'We do have someone who is clearly devoted to Italian culture,' she told them. 'As soon as a new book on the subject comes out, she is the first to borrow it. But her name is not Lydia Quayle, I'm afraid.'

'What is it?' asked Madeleine.

'It's Miss Beatrice Myler.'

CHAPTER TWELVE

Philip Conway was disappointed to learn that Leeming had gone back to London without any explanation. The reporter had been hoping to hear about the progress of the investigation. Instead, he was forced to gather what evidence he could on his own, talking to local people of all kinds and seeing if the newspaper appeal regarding the wheelbarrow had borne fruit. Distressingly, most people had not even been aware of the appeal because they didn't read the newspaper. None of those who did actually buy the *Derby Mercury* could recall having seen a wheelbarrow on the night of the murder. Conway baulked at the prospect of returning to his editor with nothing new to say about the case so he made continuous sweeps of the village, asking questions of everyone he met. His rewards were scant. It was when he walked past the church that he had his most interesting encounter. Spotting a familiar figure in the churchyard, he went over to him.

Jed Hockaday was staring intently at the grave of Cicely Peet.

'What are you doing here, Mr Hockaday?' asked Conway, joining him.

'Oh.' The cobbler looked up. 'I'm just paying my respects.'

'Did you know Mrs Peet well?'

'She was a customer of mine and kind enough to praise my work. When she needed something repaired, of course, a servant always brought it to me but, if ever I did bump into Mrs Peet at the annual fair or such like, she always had a good word for me.'

'Most people do – you're proficient at your trade.'

'Kind of you to say so, Mr Conway,' said the other with a lazy grin. 'Though, between you and me, I'd rather be thought of as a constable than as a cobbler at the moment.' He nudged the reporter. 'What's the latest news?'

'Why ask me?'

'I've seen you nestling up to the sergeant.'

'I'm paid to get the facts, Mr Hockaday.'

'Then what are they?'

'Read the *Mercury* and you'll know all that I do.'

'Don't be like that, Mr Conway,' said the cobbler. 'I got your measure. I spoke to the landlord at the Malt Shovel. Sergeant Leeming stayed there and I'm told the pair of you was chirping away together like two birds in a nest.'

'The sergeant wanted to know about the Enoch Stone case.'

Hockaday squinted at him. 'What did you tell him?'

'I told him the truth. It'll never be solved.'

'It will one day. We owe it to Enoch.'

'I thought that you and he fell out over something.'

'Oh, that was forgot as soon as it happened,' said Hockaday, dismissively. 'Me and Enoch were friends, really. We went to school together. I always liked him.' His voice hardened. 'That's why I want to catch the villain who battered him to death.'

'The killer is long gone.'

'No, Mr Conway – he's right here. I'll dig him out eventually.'

'You've had three years to do that.'

'That means he thinks he safe – but he's not. If I catch up with the rogue, I'll strangle him to death with my bare hands.' His anger subsided and he grinned again. 'That's a silly thing for a constable to say, isn't it? I've been sworn in to follow the due processes of law. I'll have to hand him over to the court.'

'Did you ever mend Enoch Stone's boots?'

'That's a strange question to ask!'

'What's the answer, Mr Hockaday?'

The cobbler shook his head. 'No, I didn't. Enoch mended his own boots.'

'I thought you were friends.'

'We were – but we didn't live in each other's pockets.' He slapped the reporter on the arm. 'Good to see you, Mr Conway. Be sure to let me know what's afoot if the sergeant turns up again.'

'You can ask him yourself.'

'He's taken to you. You're the only one he'll give the real titbits.'

After a final glance at the grave, Hockaday ambled off, leaving the younger man to wonder why the cobbler had been there in the first place. The chances of his having ever spoken more than a few words to Cicely Peet were remote. If he was likely to visit any grave to pay his respects, it would have been that of Enoch Stone, his alleged friend. Conway was baffled. As he was turning away, he saw the vicar trotting towards him. There was an exchange of greetings.

'What did Jed Hockaday have to say to you?' asked Sadler.

'It was rather odd, Vicar. Is he a religious man?'

'He doesn't come to church very often, if that's what you mean. You can always tell when he does. Walk past him and you catch a strong whiff of leather.'

'He was standing beside Mrs Peet's grave.'

'That's the second time today, Mr Conway.'

'Oh?'

'He was here first thing this morning, holding a vigil here then walking over to look into the open grave.'

'Does he have an obsession with death?'

'I didn't ask him. I was just grateful when he was chased away.'

'Who chased him?'

'I was speaking figuratively. Bert Knowles drove past on his cart. When he saw Hockaday beside the first grave he'd dug for Mrs Peet, he yelled out a warning to leave it alone. I won't give you his exact words,' said Sadler, meekly, 'because they were rather ripe. What they amounted to is this. If Hockaday so much as touched the earth piled up beside the grave, Bert threatened to bury him alive.'

When the cab dropped them off outside the house, Leeming paid the fare then turned to look up at it. It was an attractive terraced property with a small garden in front of it. He and Madeleine opened the gate and went through it to the front door. A ring on the doorbell brought a maidservant who opened the door and looked from one to the other with a pleasant smile.

'May I help you?' she said.

'Does a Miss Beatrice Myler live here?' asked Madeleine.

'Yes, she does.'

'May we speak with her, please?'

'I'll handle this, Dora,' said a voice from behind her and the servant immediately moved away. The newcomer appraised the callers. 'I'm Beatrice Myler. Can I help you in any way?'

'I'm afraid not,' said Madeleine, hopes vanquished by the sight of a middle-aged woman.

'I told you it was the wrong house,' said Leeming.

'We do apologise for disturbing you, Miss Myler. We thought you might be someone else, you see.'

'But obviously you're not Miss Lydia Quayle.'

'No,' said Beatrice, defensively. 'You'll have to look elsewhere.'

'You share the same interest in Italy with her,' explained Madeleine. 'That's how the mistake arose. You and Miss Quayle are obviously kindred spirits.'

Beatrice was keen to send them on their way but Lydia suddenly appeared.

'Did I hear my name?' She looked at the visitors. 'I'm Lydia Quayle.'

'Oh,' said Leeming. 'We were led to believe that—'

'We've found you at last,' said Madeleine, interrupting him and ignoring the fact that Beatrice had lied to them. 'May we have a word with you, please?'

'If you wish,' said Lydia, guardedly. 'Please come in.'

She stood aside to let them enter the house. Beatrice was less welcoming. As they went through the door, Madeleine could feel that the older woman resented their arrival. It had aroused her protective instinct.

Colbeck had found the conversation with Lucas Quayle illuminating. He now had far more insight into the mechanics of the family. Having secured the address where Lydia was living, he went to Derby railway station and sent a telegraph that would eventually reach Leeming at Scotland Yard. When he stepped out of the office, he saw Donald Haygarth standing on the platform. In a remarkably short space of time, Haygarth was behaving as if already appointed to the post of chairman of the Midland Railway. A distinct air of ownership surrounded him.

'Good day to you, sir,' said Colbeck.

'Hello, Inspector,' replied the other. 'What brings you here?'

'I've been making use of your telegraph station. Thank you

for putting Mr Cope at my disposal, by the way. He's been very helpful.'

'Cope is both knowledgeable and loyal, two qualities I happen to admire.'

'He told me that he rides here from Kedleston every day.'

'Yes, he's much more robust than he looks.'

'How did he get on with Mr Quayle?'

'He treats every member of the board in the same way,' said Haygarth, smoothly, 'and was on excellent terms with Vivian Quayle. Men like Cope are true servants of this company.'

'That confirms my impression.'

'Do you have anything to report, Inspector?'

'We continue to make progress, sir.'

'But you're nowhere near making an arrest yet, I fancy.'

'There's a lot more evidence to collect before we can do that,' said Colbeck. 'What happens when a train comes into the station?'

'Apart from the ear-splitting noise, there's a lot of smoke and steam.'

'It's the same with a murder investigation, sir. At the start, everything is covered with smoke and steam. It takes time for it to clear. We're starting to make out the shape of the carriages and even the outline of the locomotive. What we can't yet see is the killer on the footplate.'

'Will he have had a fireman to help him?'

'It's possible, Mr Haygarth, or he may be on his own.'

'What have you been doing since I last saw you?'

'The most significant development was a breach in the wall of silence around the Quayle family. Stanley Quayle was virtually unapproachable.'

'How did you get through to them?'

'I didn't,' replied Colbeck. 'In fact, *they* got through to me. To be more precise, I had a visit from Lucas Quayle. He was vastly more informative than his elder brother.'

'Did he tell you anything that advanced the investigation?'

'I think so. He put flesh and bone on a number of nebulous characters. I have a much clearer image of the family now. He also had something interesting to say about Gerard Burns.'

'He still sounds the most likely killer to me.'

'If you have any evidence to support that view, sir, I'd be happy to see it.'

Haygarth was peevish. 'You said yourself that he had to be considered as a suspect.'

'He's only one of a number, sir.'

'Who are the others?'

'I'm not at liberty to tell you at the moment.'

'But you do have people in mind?'

'Oh, yes,' said Colbeck. 'We have a list of possible names.'

'What about Sergeant Leeming? Has he turned up anything of interest in Spondon?'

'The sergeant always uncovers useful information. But he's not in the village at the moment. I sent him back to London.'

'What on earth is he doing there?'

'He's following a line of inquiry, sir. I suppose that I should have asked him to speak to you,' Colbeck went on before the other man could question him further. 'If he wanted information about Spondon, you could have given it to him. After all, you were born there.'

'That's beside the point.'

Hiding his irritation, he glanced down the line at the approaching train.

'Superintendent Wigg didn't seem to think so.'

'The superintendent can be a troublemaker at times. It's one of

157

the reasons I didn't want him to handle this case. He has too many axes to grind.'

'How long did you live in Spondon?'

'We moved when I was only a boy.'

'But you were baptised in the local church, I take it.'

'Yes, I was.'

'And you know the geography of the village.'

'I've probably forgotten most of it, Inspector. I haven't been near Spondon for decades. My time is divided between making sure that my silk mills are operating at maximum efficiency and keeping the Midland Railway under surveillance.'

'That's a taxing demand on any man.'

'I've learnt to bear responsibility lightly.'

'Then you deserve congratulation, sir.'

'It's something that Vivian Quayle was unable to do,' said Haygarth as the train got ever closer. 'When he got involved with this company, he handed over the control of his coal mines to his elder son. I like to keep my hand on the tiller. I've given my sons managerial positions but retained overall control of the mills. Unlike Quayle, I'm able to wear more than one hat at a time.'

Colbeck was about to ask him another question but the train surged past and made conversation impossible. Haygarth was lost in a fug of smoke and steam. When it began to clear, he had disappeared into a compartment.

It took time to win Lydia Quayle's confidence. When she realised why they'd called, Lydia was tempted to ask them to leave and Beatrice was patently anxious to get rid of them. But Madeleine was very persuasive and Leeming had the sense to let her do most of the talking. Alone, he knew, he would have been unable to draw anything out of Lydia. He could now understand why Colbeck had suggested that his wife should be involved in tracing the exiled member of the Quayle family. She had a lightness of touch that Leeming signally lacked.

'Let me assure you,' said Madeleine, 'that we are not here to advise you to return to Nottingham. We'd have no right to do so. That's a personal decision for you, Miss Quayle.'

'It certainly is,' said Beatrice. 'And that decision has already been made.'

'How did you find me?' asked Lydia.

'We went to Mudie's Lending Library.'

'But I'm not even a member.'

'Miss Myler is.'

When Madeleine explained that Lydia's predilection for Italy had helped them to run her to earth, Lydia was impressed.

'That was very enterprising of you, Mrs Colbeck.'

'It was my husband's suggestion. He's had a lot of experience at finding missing persons.'

'I don't wish to be pedantic,' said Beatrice, 'but Miss Quayle does not qualify as a missing person. When she parted company with her family, she came to London because she preferred to live here. Nobody came in search of her because she was not really missing.'

'What do you wish to know?' asked Lydia.

Madeleine was apologetic. 'We'd have to intrude on your private life.'

'That's not permissible,' Beatrice interjected. 'Miss Quayle has put that whole world behind her. She has no wish to revive unpleasant memories.'

'Everybody must want to have a murder solved,' said Leeming, 'especially if the victim happens to be their father.'

'The sergeant is right,' conceded Lydia.

'You don't have to do this,' Beatrice argued.

'I feel that I do.'

'You've turned your back on Nottingham.'

'The situation there has changed. If I can help the investigation in any way, then I ought to do it. There's no danger. I've learnt to confront my past.'

Madeleine was unable to read the glance that was exchanged between the two women but she could see that Beatrice Myler was very unhappy. Lydia, however, was offering to answer questions so Madeleine pressed on.

'It's only fair to tell you that my husband has already spoken to Mr Burns.'

'I see,' said Lydia.

'He talked very candidly about the reason he left your father's employ.'

'Need we dredge all that up again?' asked Beatrice, tetchily.

'If it's relevant,' said Lydia, firmly, 'then we must.'

'It would be like opening a wound that's starting to heal.'

'My father was murdered, Beatrice. *He* was the person who inflicted the wound. It no longer smarts so much now that I know he's dead.'

It was Madeleine's turn to communicate with a glance and Leeming read it correctly. It was the sort of look that his wife gave him when she wanted to have a private discussion with a female neighbour who'd just called in. He rose to his feet.

'I feel I'm rather in the way,' he said. 'I'll wait outside.'

'Beatrice will take you into the other room,' said Lydia, indicating that she'd rather be left alone with Madeleine. She smiled at her friend. 'Would you mind?'

'Of course not,' replied Beatrice, her face impassive as she got up from the chair. 'Follow me, Sergeant Leeming.'

She led him out then closed the door harder than she needed to have done.

'I may have to tell you something rather distasteful,' warned Madeleine.

'Don't hold back on my behalf, Mrs Colbeck. I've received some terrible blows in my life and I managed to survive them all.'

'It concerns your friendship with Mr Burns.'

'Let's call it by its proper name, shall we?' said Lydia. 'It was a romance, an ill-advised one, perhaps, but it meant everything to me at the time.'

'I can understand that.'

'I knew from the start that it was an impossible dream but that's what drove me on, somehow. I wanted to shock and defy convention. Have you ever harboured impossible dreams, Mrs Colbeck?'

'Yes,' answered Madeleine, thinking of her marriage to Colbeck and her career as an artist. 'In my case, the dreams came true.'

'Did you have no opposition from your father?'

'None at all – he's approved of what I've done.'

'Then he must have been a lot more tolerant than mine.'

'What about your mother? Did she take your side?'

'She was never consulted properly. All that Mother was told was that I was in disgrace and had to be punished. As you doubtless know, I was taken abroad.' Lydia pulled a face. 'Going to Italy had always been my ambition but not under those circumstances. It was an ordeal – until I met Beatrice, that is.'

'When you lived at home, did you see much of your father?'

'I saw very little. He was not really interested in me any more than in Agnes, my younger sister. We were simply part of the furniture. Father only took proper notice of my brothers, Stanley and Lucas. They were raised in his image, though Lucas was something of a rebel.' She smiled fondly. 'That's why I got on with him so well. At heart, we were two of a kind.'

'You must have been to social gatherings of one kind or another.'

'Oh, yes, we were all dragged off to those – Mother, Agnes and me. Father hardly noticed us. He was too busy shaking hands with people who might be useful to him one day.'

'You strike me as an observant woman, Miss Quayle. Did you ever see any sign of . . . enmity towards your father? I don't mean outright hostility. People are far too careful to show that. But I fancy that you'd have been able to sense if some of the so-called friends were not quite as friendly as they appeared.'

'Yes,' said Lydia, 'I was. When you've nothing to do but sit on the sidelines, you notice all manner of things that give people away.'

'Did you pick out any false friends of your father's?'

'Two of them picked themselves out, Mrs Colbeck.'

'One of them, I suspect, was Mr Haygarth,' said Madeleine, recalling what she'd read in Colbeck's letter. 'He was your father's rival, wasn't he? Who was the other person you spotted?'

'His name is Elijah Wigg. He's a police superintendent.'

Madeleine was caught off balance. There'd been no mention of Wigg in her husband's long and detailed missive. She wondered what Vivian Quayle had done to make an enemy in the police force.

'Why he and father were at odds with each other,' said Lydia, 'I don't know, but they were bound to meet at certain functions. There was a dinner when we found ourselves sitting at the same table as the Wigg family. Father didn't exchange a single word with him.'

'How strange! Let's move on to Mr Burns,' suggested Madeleine. 'I do apologise if this is embarrassing for you.'

'Years have passed since then. I'm a different person now.'

'Your friend gave my husband a very clear account of . . . what had happened between you and him. There was even talk of an elopement, I believe.'

'You snatch at anything to be with the person you love, Mrs Colbeck. We were talking about it the night we were seen together.' Her face showed anger for the first time. 'That put a stop to all our plans.'

'Yet you tried to get in touch on your return from Italy.'

'I tried and failed – so did Gerard.'

'Do you know why, Miss Quayle?'

'They kept him away from me.'

'There was rather more to it than that,' explained Madeleine. 'This is what I meant when I said I might have to pass on something distasteful. Your father paid two ruffians to assault Mr Burns and they warned him that, if he dared to get anywhere near you again, he'd suffer even more injury.'

'I can guess the nature of that injury,' said Lydia, quietly, 'because my father made the same threat to me. I was not as familiar with the ways of the world then so you can imagine the profound shock that it gave me. I was horrified.'

'What did your father threaten to do?'

'He said that if I made any attempt to get in touch with Gerard again . . .' She broke off and wiped away a tear that had just trickled out of her eye. 'It was the way that Father said it that turned my stomach. Keep well away from him, I was told, or the man I'd loved would be castrated.'

Philip Conway had returned to the offices of the *Derby Mercury* to discover that the editor was not there. Expecting a reprimand for not bringing back from Spondon the latest news about the murder investigation, Conway was heartily relieved. He was able to write an article on an unrelated subject. Instead of vanishing altogether, however, the chastisement had only been postponed. When the editor finally turned up, he summoned the reporter to his office and asked for details of the latest developments. Unable to provide them, Conway was given a verbal roasting and sent off to the Royal Hotel to speak to the man in charge of the case.

The Railway Detective was in the lounge, talking to Superintendent Wigg. From the gestures made by the latter, Conway deduced that an argument was taking place. He lurked nearby until Wigg's temper had cooled then drifted across to them. The superintendent's manner changed at once. He always made an effort to cultivate the press even if only dealing with a young reporter.

'Ah, come on over,' he invited, beckoning with a finger. 'This is Philip Conway from the *Mercury*, Inspector, but I daresay that you've met.'

'As a matter of fact, we haven't,' said Colbeck, 'but Sergeant Leeming has mentioned him favourably to me. How do you do, Mr Conway?'

'I'm pleased to meet you, Inspector. The sergeant worships you.'

'*I* certainly don't,' said Wigg under his breath. 'Well, I'll be on my way, Inspector, but do bear in mind what I said.'

Colbeck rose from his chair in tandem with Wigg and they exchanged a farewell handshake. The superintendent beamed at the reporter.

'Do give my regards to the editor,' he said.

Conway gave a dutiful nod and stood aside so that Wigg could leave. After sizing the newcomer up, Colbeck waved him to a chair, asked if he would like a drink then summoned a waiter to place an order for two glasses of whisky. The reporter was clearly delighted to be in his presence.

'I didn't realise that the sergeant had returned to London,' he said.

'It's only a temporary return.'

'Is he there in relation to the investigation?'

'Yes,' said Colbeck in a tone that announced he would give no details. 'I've read your articles in the *Derby Mercury*. They've been reassuringly accurate.'

'Thank you, sir.'

'The sergeant will have told you how often we get traduced or misrepresented in the London press. They always expect us to solve a crime instantly, whereas it may take weeks, if not months. Look at the other murder in Spondon.'

'I meant to tell you about that, Inspector.'

'They present a curious contrast, don't they?' observed Colbeck. 'On the one side, we have Mr Quayle, a native of Nottingham without any discernible link to the village, being found dead in its church. On the other, we have a local man robbed and killed on a road leading out of it. Compare the nature of their deaths. The wealthy industrialist is dispatched with poison while the framework knitter was battered to the ground. Which of the crimes is easier to solve?'

'Neither has been solved yet.'

'The latest one will be.'

'What about the earlier one?'

'That should have been solved three years ago. The sheer brutality of the attack tells us something about the character of the attacker. The facts would suggest to me that he's a local man, aware of the route home that Enoch Stone would take after a night drinking in a public house.'

'Most people believe it may have been a traveller, seizing his opportunity.'

'Were any strangers seen in the village that day?'

'Not as far as I know, Inspector.'

'Then I'd plump for someone in Spondon. I took the trouble to find out the wage earned by a framework knitter and it's not a large one. The killer didn't get away with a lot of money so perhaps robbery was not the motive, after all. It was made to look as if it was. What prompted the murder might have been something else entirely.'

'I agree,' said the reporter.

'Now in the case of Mr Quayle,' said Colbeck, 'there was a sizeable amount of money in his wallet and he had an expensive pocket watch. Neither was stolen. How do you explain that?'

'I don't but, then, I'm not a detective.'

'Don't be modest. You ferret out stories so you're in an allied trade.'

The waiter arrived with the whisky on a tray. He set a glass down in front of each of them then withdrew. Colbeck sampled his drink before speaking.

'You said earlier that you meant to talk to me about Enoch Stone.'

'Sergeant Leeming may already have mentioned this.'

'No, he hasn't said anything to me about it.'

Conway took a hasty sip of his whisky and had a minor coughing fit. When he'd recovered, he described his visit to Spondon that day and his encounter in the churchyard with Jed Hockaday. He quoted the vicar then recalled Leeming's assessment of the cobbler. After listening carefully, Colbeck said that he would make a point of speaking to the man himself. Hockaday's behaviour was too peculiar to be ignored and it called his status as a constable into doubt.

'I'll pass on your comments to Sergeant Leeming.'

'Is he on his way back here this evening?'

'No,' replied Colbeck, 'he'll spend the night at home then catch an early train. Before then, he may find a surprise awaiting him at Scotland Yard.'

After what he saw as his earlier triumph over the superintendent, Victor Leeming entered the office without the usual tremors. Indeed, there was a spring in his step and a radiant smile igniting his features. He and Madeleine had succeeded in their task. Lydia Quayle had been located and a fund of information about her family had been elicited from her. The person who'd drawn it out, of course, was Madeleine but there would be no mention of her part in the visit. Congratulations were in order and Leeming was ready to enjoy them.

'Good evening, Superintendent,' he said, airily.

'What kept you?' snarled the other.

'I had to follow a twisting trail, sir.'

'You've been away for hours.'

'But I did what the inspector asked me to do,' Leeming contended. 'By dint of careful research, I found out the address where Miss Quayle is living.'

'It's number thirty-eight, Bloomfield Terrace, Pimlico.'

'That's right, sir. Thirty-eight, Bloomfield Terrace . . .' His smile froze and his confidence died instantly. 'How on earth do you *know*?'

'Colbeck sent me a telegraph with the details.'

'But I had to spend ages finding the place.'

'All you found was something we already know. Now, then,' said Tallis, reaching for a cigar. 'Since you were so certain that you'd collect vital evidence from the young lady, tell me what you actually discovered.' He lit the cigar, had a few puffs to make sure that it was fully alight then issued a grim challenge. 'Come on, man. *Impress* me.'

Leeming could hear the firing squad shuffling into position.

CHAPTER THIRTEEN

Stanley Quayle was in a vile mood. The first person to feel the lash of his tongue was John Cleary, the coachman. They were outside the stables and Quayle's voice echoed around the yard.

'Whatever did you think you were doing?' he demanded.

'Mrs Quayle asked to be taken for a drive, sir.'

'My mother is ill. She needs complete rest. The doctor advised that she remain in bed until further notice. The last thing she should be doing is leaving the house.'

'I only did what I was told, sir,' said the other, politely.

'You should have talked to me first.'

'You were not here, Mr Quayle.'

'Then you should have sought my brother.'

'Your mother was very insistent, sir. She's always enjoyed being taken for a drive in the country, and the weather was warm.'

'This is nothing to do with the weather,' shouted Quayle. 'It's to do with my mother's health. She's very poorly and coping badly with her bereavement. If you'd had any sense, you'd have realised that. You should have refused to take her.'

'That would only have upset Mrs Quayle.'

'It's what you should have done, Cleary.'

He continued to berate the coachman. Everyone within earshot felt sorry for Cleary but the man himself withstood the onslaught with relative equanimity. The fact that the coachman remained so calm under fire only enraged Stanley Quayle even more and he threatened to dismiss the man.

'I was employed by your father, sir,' Cleary reminded him. 'Now that he's no longer here to give orders, I'm answerable to Mrs Quayle instead.'

'Damn your insolence!'

After ridding himself of another torrent of bile, Quayle turned away and stormed back into the house. Roused by the first confrontation that evening, he was pulsing with fury as he went off to the second one. When he found his brother in the drawing room, he went straight on the attack.

'Why, in God's name, did you let it happen?'

Lucas Quayle shrugged. 'What are you talking about?'

'Mother is dying in front of us and you let her go gallivanting around the countryside in the landau.'

'She said that she needed fresh air, Stanley. That seemed to me a very reasonable proposition.'

'It will have taxed her already waning health.'

'Only the doctor can decide that,' said his brother. 'But I'm told that she looked well enough when she came back. Even Agnes admitted that and she did everything to prevent Mother going out in the first place.'

'Well, it won't happen again. I've just given Cleary orders to that effect.'

'You can't *stop* Mother going out, Stanley.'

'It's in her best interests.'

'She loves the countryside around here.'

'For heaven's sake, Lucas, she's in *mourning*!'

'So are you, for that matter,' responded his brother, tartly, 'yet it didn't stop you traipsing off to one of our coal mines.'

'Someone had to make the funeral arrangements.'

'I agree, but you didn't have to go on to Ilkeston afterwards.'

'I had things to check up on,' said the other, angrily, 'so I won't be called to account by you. I'm in charge now and that means I make all the decisions. In fact, that's what I really want to talk about. I had a legitimate reason to go out, Lucas. You didn't. Agnes tells me that you went to Derby to see Inspector Colbeck.'

'That's right,' said the other, defiantly. 'I wanted information.'

'I gave the inspector all the information he required.'

'That's nonsense, Stanley. You told him almost nothing and had him out of the house in a matter of minutes. It was absurd. Don't you *want* to catch the man who killed our father?'

'Of course, I do.'

'Then why didn't you offer proper assistance to Inspector Colbeck?'

'I had too many other things to do.'

'The investigation takes precedence over all of them.'

'Nothing that's happened within these four walls has any bearing on the case. That's why I was not prepared to waste time talking to the police. Above all else,' he said, sternly, 'I'm not having our dirty linen washed in public.'

'Inspector Colbeck is very discreet.'

'But you aren't, Lucas. You blurt things out before you realise what you're doing. You had no cause to leave this house.'

'I wanted to know what was going on, Stanley. That's what normal people do. If a loved one is murdered, they want every scrap of information they can get about the police investigation. It's only natural.'

'I don't want strangers prying into things that don't concern them.'

'The police need our *help*,' Lucas emphasised.

'Keep away from them.'

'The inspector said how useful I'd been.'

'You shouldn't have been allowed within a mile of him.'

'Stop giving me orders, Stanley. I'm old enough to make up my own mind about things. Power goes to your head sometimes. It was the same when we played cricket. I told the inspector about it.'

His brother was puce with indignation. 'What are you talking about?'

'Your insistence on being in control,' said Lucas. 'You *had* to captain the team even though people like Burns, Cleary and me were much better players. You went round bawling commands at us as if you really knew what you were doing.'

'I *did* know, Lucas. That's why we always won the matches.'

'Gerard Burns was the real match-winner not Stanley Quayle.'

'Captaincy was the deciding factor. I set the field and I chose the bowlers.'

'You also selected yourself as our opening batsman even though you hardly ever got into double figures. That was appalling captaincy.'

The row escalated at once and the brothers stood toe to toe, exchanging insults. Though they talked about cricket, they were really arguing about the lifelong tension and inequality between them. Stanley Quayle became more and more like his father, cold, authoritative and uncompromising, while his brother regressed into the rebel he'd been in his younger days. All of the old dissension between them came to the surface. They were still trading accusations when their sister came into the room.

'Whatever's going on?' she asked in alarm. 'I could hear you upstairs.'

Sobered by her intervention, Lucas apologised to her but

Stanley Quayle was determined to shift any blame from himself. He claimed that his brother had let the whole family down by talking to Colbeck. At a time as fraught as the present one, the one thing they had to guard was their privacy. It was deplorable, he said, that the police were allowed to peer into their lives and learn about their past upheavals. Agnes agreed that it had been a mistake for her younger brother to go to Derby but he defended himself vigorously.

'I learnt things of importance to us,' he asserted.

'You should have stayed here to mourn Father,' said Agnes.

'I prefer to help in the search for his killer.'

'What could you say that would have been of any help?'

'I talked about Lydia, for a start.'

'That's exactly what I mean,' railed his brother. 'There was absolutely no need to open that Pandora's box. It should have been left firmly closed.'

'The inspector already knew the truth. He'd spoken to Burns.'

'Don't mention that hateful name again!'

'We have to face facts, Stanley. He may be involved here. Burns would have more reason than anybody to want Father killed. He has to be a suspect.'

'He wouldn't *dare*,' snapped the other. 'We scared him away.'

'You never understood what happened between him and Lydia, did you?'

'I understood enough to know that it was a grotesque misalliance.'

'That was what I felt as well,' said Agnes. 'Lydia was so reckless.'

'Did you really want your sister married to a *gardener*?' asked Stanley, curling his lip. 'That cunning wretch led her astray, Lucas. I daren't think what he did to Lydia. It's too unsettling. Burns should have been horsewhipped.'

'The inspector told me something that I didn't know,' said Lucas. 'We don't want to hear it.'

'That's your trouble, Stanley. You never want to learn the truth. You just close your ears and block everything out. How can you make a fair judgement on anything until you're aware of all the facts?'

'The main fact was all I needed to know – Burns tried to seduce our sister.'

'Oh, I don't think it went that far,' protested Agnes.

'That's all he was after.'

'You're quite wrong about him,' said Lucas, 'and so was I. The inspector told me something that's made me revise my opinion of Burns and showed me just how much he meant to Lydia.' He paused for a few moments. 'It was no passing fancy. They were planning to elope and get married.'

Lydia knew that her friend was deeply upset. The moment that the visitors had left, Beatrice retired to her room and stayed there for well over an hour. Nonetheless, Lydia felt that she'd been right to speak to Madeleine Colbeck. It was foolish to pretend that she had no interest in the murder inquiry. Part of her wanted to know what had happened and when the person responsible would be caught. Madeleine had probed gently away without causing the slightest offence or discomfort. When she was leaving with the sergeant, Madeleine had given her an address where she could be reached in case she thought of anything that might be useful to the inquiry. Lydia had felt soothed. In the wake of Beatrice's departure upstairs, the sensation quickly evaporated. There would be repercussions and Lydia was not looking forward to them.

Beatrice finally emerged from her room and came downstairs but she made no immediate contact with Lydia. Instead, she wandered about the house from room to room as if deliberately avoiding her. It was left to Lydia to make the first move. She intercepted Beatrice outside the kitchen.

'We must talk,' she said.

Beatrice feigned indifference. 'Must we?'

'To begin with, I owe you an apology. When all is said and done, this is still your house. I had no right to invite someone in when you clearly objected to them.'

'That's certainly true.'

'I'm very sorry, Beatrice.'

'What I'm sorry about is that you made me look foolish and deceitful. If you heard them mention your name, you must also have heard me telling them that they'd made a mistake in coming here. Then out you pop and contradict me.'

'It wasn't like that at all.'

'They knew I'd been lying. I felt betrayed.'

'Why didn't you simply tell them that I live here?'

'I didn't want them interfering,' said Beatrice, petulantly. 'I didn't want strangers to walk in off the street and . . . take you away.'

'They made no suggestion about taking me anywhere.'

'I'm talking about your *mind*, Lydia. They filled it with all the things that you ran away from. When they did that, they took you away from me.'

Lydia touched her arm. 'But I'm still here, Beatrice.'

'Only in body – your mind is back in the Midlands.'

'I can't just ignore what happened to my father.'

'You've managed to do that very effectively, so far. After a month of living here, you stopped mentioning his name. It was as if he didn't exist.'

'In that sense, he still doesn't.'

'Then why did you spend such a long time talking about him?'

'I was answering questions about the family.'

'You were being drawn back into a past you swore to escape. And while you were doing that,' said Beatrice, unhappily, 'I was trapped in the other room with that ugly detective. He frightened me, Lydia.'

'Then that's something else I have to apologise for,' said the other, 'but he did the right thing in leaving me alone with Mrs Colbeck. I could talk to her in a way that would have been impossible with a man.'

'What did you say to her?'

Lydia chose her words with care. Though she'd taken her friend into her confidence about the reasons for coming to London, she had spared Beatrice the more disturbing details. She had said nothing about the threat made to her about Gerard Burns by her father or about the violence she'd suffered. When she'd dared to defend her actions, Vivian Quayle had lost his temper and struck her across the face. He'd then grabbed her by the shoulders and shaken her before hurling her to the floor. On the following day, when he'd calmed down, he'd mumbled an apology but the damage was irreparable by then. All that Lydia could think about from that point onwards was her eventual escape. When the break came, she'd resolved never to see her father again and she'd kept her vow.

'It wasn't my fault that they came here,' she pointed out. 'It was yours.'

Beatrice tensed. 'What do you mean?'

'You're the one who belongs to the Lending Library. How clever of them to find this address by asking about readers with a passion for Italy! I'd never have thought of doing that.'

'There are other ways to discover where you are, Lydia.'

'Nobody else has any reason to find me.'

'That's not true.'

Lydia felt as if she'd just walked into something very solid and she was dazed for a moment. Beatrice's revelation was stunning. Evidently, she knew. Lydia had concealed from her the fact that her younger brother had learnt her address by employing a private detective and had then written to her. The only way that her friend could possibly know about the correspondence was by going into Lydia's room and finding the letter in the bedside drawer. There was profound awkwardness on both sides. Lydia was shocked that her privacy had been violated and Beatrice was horrified that her friend had kept something so important from her. The taut silence lasted for minutes.

'I should have been told, Lydia,' said the older woman at length.

'It would have been hurtful to you.'

'It was far more hurtful to learn that you hid the truth from me.'

'You had no call to search my bedroom.'

'I had to find out the truth.'

'How did you even know that I'd received a letter? You were out at the time.'

'Dora told me.'

'Then why not ask me directly?'

Beatrice's tone sharpened. 'Why not save me the trouble of asking?'

The awkwardness between them suddenly intensified and the whole balance of their relationship seemed to shift. Beatrice knew that her friend had not been entirely honest with her and, by the same token, Lydia knew that the older woman had gone behind her back to search for something. Neither of them knew what to say. Beatrice felt both let down and guilty while Lydia was at once hurt and chastened. She wanted to tell Beatrice that she had replied to her brother and told him not to contact her again but the words simply would not come. For her part, Beatrice had an urge to enfold her in a tearful embrace yet she was quite unable to move.

Two close friends had just reached an impasse, unable to decide if they'd somehow been drawn closer by their respective mistakes or if their relationship had been shattered beyond recall.

Since he knew the train that Leeming would catch in London that morning, Colbeck walked to Derby station to meet it. When an earlier train steamed in, one of the passengers who alighted was Elijah Wigg, adjusting his hat and jacket. He was obviously so proud of his uniform that Colbeck wondered if the man could ever be persuaded to take it off. Wigg strode across to him.

'Where are you going, Inspector?' he asked.

'I'm waiting for someone to arrive, actually.'

'My day clearly starts much earlier than yours. I was in Spondon at eight o'clock to see what, if anything, the local constables had managed to discover. I'm known for my sudden inspections. It keeps men on their toes.'

'Has any new evidence come to light?'

'If it has, they didn't get a sniff of it. I told them where and how to look.'

'Ah,' said Colbeck, 'I'm glad that you mentioned the Spondon constables. One of them accosted Sergeant Leeming. He's a local cobbler by the name of Jed Hockaday.'

'Yes, he's very committed and you can't say that of all of them. Hockaday's a man of low intelligence but I like that in a policeman. It's more important to have someone who obeys orders at once than someone who thinks too much.'

'Then we must agree to differ, Superintendent,' said Colbeck. 'Given the choice, I prefer a thinking policeman every time. He usually knows that discretion is the better part of valour and never rushes in regardless.'

'I can't see you rushing in anywhere,' joked Wigg. 'It might crease that impeccable attire of yours.'

'Oh, you'd be surprised how often I've had torn garments and scuffed shoes. During a case I handled in Kent,' recalled Colbeck, 'my frock coat acquired a nasty tear when someone shot at me. As a *thinking* policeman, I had the presence of mind to fall to the ground and feign injury.'

'Hockaday would never dream of doing that.'

'How long has he been a constable?'

'He volunteered when Enoch Stone was killed.'

'According to that reporter, Philip Conway, the fellow is still carrying out a one-man investigation into the murder.'

'It's not confined to one man,' corrected Wigg. 'That case remains open.' He stroked a whisker and grinned. 'I see that the love affair with Mr Haygarth is over.'

'I can't imagine what you mean.'

'When he sent for you, he told me that you were the cleverest detective in England. His enthusiasm has waned a bit since then. After I left you at the Royal last night, I bumped into him outside the Midland headquarters. Haygarth was less than complimentary about you.'

'He's entitled to his opinion,' said Colbeck, easily. 'I daresay that even you have your detractors, Superintendent, impossible as it may seem.'

Wigg leant in close. 'Haygarth is not your detractor,' he said, quietly. 'His fear is that you'll do your job too well and discover that *he's* implicated in this murder somehow. I told you that he had to be a suspect. His change of attitude to you is clear proof of it.' He tugged his jacket into shape. 'And where Haygarth goes, that slimy creature of his called Maurice Cope goes as well. Watch your back, Inspector. They're dangerous men.'

Of all the members of the family, Agnes Quayle had been the one most unnerved by the news of the murder. Her life might be dull and repetitious but at least, she had always consoled herself, it was both comfortable and supremely safe. Those guarantees had suddenly disappeared. She was profoundly discomfited and no longer felt safe at the house. If her father could be killed in mysterious circumstances, then the rest of the family might also be in jeopardy. The thought made her afraid to leave the house alone for her daily walk. Her main concern, however, was for her mother. In defying her children and going for a drive in the landau the previous day, Harriet Quayle had been taking an unnecessary risk, yet she'd returned with a touch of colour in her cheeks. Even so, Agnes agreed with her elder brother's argument that their mother should be kept inside the house and more or less confined to her room. While Stanley and Lucas would pop their heads in to exchange a few words with her, the burden of looking after the old woman would fall as usual on Agnes. It was a burden that was feeling increasingly heavy.

With the disappearance of the man who had dominated the house for so long, there would be considerable changes. None of them, Agnes feared, would be of any advantage to her. The open antagonism between her brothers was worrying but she lacked the ability to reconcile them. She would now be at the mercy of her elder brother's dictates and Stanley Quayle tended to treat her more like one of the servants than a member of the family, assigning her tasks rather than involving her in any discussions about the future. Lydia would not have allowed herself to be treated in that way. While never daring to strike out on her own like her sister,

Agnes wished that she'd had something of Lydia's bravado. And secretly, in her darkest moments, she'd even wished that there'd been a Gerard Burns in her life to add the excitement that was so cruelly missing. When she remembered what the outcome of the liaison between Lydia and the gardener had been, however, she was relieved that her life had been so uneventful.

As she went up the stairs that morning, she envisaged another day of sitting at a bedside and she gritted her teeth. Agnes tapped on the door of her mother's bedroom and expected an invitation to go in. When it never came, she opened the door gently and peeped in to see if her mother was still asleep. But Harriet Quayle was not even there. The bed had clearly been slept in but the sheets had now been thrown back. There was no sign of the old woman. Agnes conducted a frantic search but it was in vain. Wondering what had happened and fearing that she would be blamed, Agnes was so distressed that she slumped to the floor in a dead faint.

'I felt like a complete fool, Inspector.'

'You did nothing wrong, Victor.'

'I spent all that time and effort finding that address, only to discover that the superintendent had it already.'

'It fell into my lap when you'd already set off on your search,' said Colbeck. 'I sent the address by means of a telegraph in case you failed to locate the house.'

'Where did you get the information?'

'Lucas Quayle came to see me. It was quite fortuitous.'

Having met Leeming at the station, Colbeck was walking down the street with him. The sergeant had caught the designated train from London and brought a letter from Madeleine and a stream of complaints. Not only had he had to leave his wife and family again, he was still haunted by his last confrontation with Edward Tallis. It was time to apply balm to his wounds.

'You'll be staying with me at the Royal Hotel from now on, Victor.'

'Oh,' said the other, partially mollified, 'that's a relief.'

'I think you've seen all you need to of the Malt Shovel in Spondon.'

'It was such a pleasure to spend the night in a soft bed.'

'How were Estelle and the boys?'

'It was wonderful to see them again.'

'You deserved a treat. A happy family is the perfect antidote to any harsh treatment at the hands of the superintendent.'

'I just hope that he never finds out that Mrs Colbeck was involved in the search for that address. If he does, both of our necks will be on the block.'

'It was a risk worth taking.'

'I'd never have succeeded on my own,' admitted Leeming. 'When we met Miss Quayle, she was very hesitant and I could see that the woman with whom she lives didn't like me at all. It was only because Mrs Colbeck spoke to her alone that we got what we came for. Lydia Quayle trusted her.'

'What did you learn?'

'The full details are in the letter but what interested me was what she said when asked if her father had any enemies. Two names were put forward.'

'The one is self-evident, Victor.'

'Yes, sir, it's Mr Haygarth. The other was more of a surprise.'

'Why was that?'

'It was Superintendent Wigg.'

'That *is* a surprise,' said Colbeck, recalling his earlier meeting with the man. 'How did the two of them even meet? Wigg is a Derbyshire man through and through while Quayle's world revolved around Nottingham. In the normal course of events, you wouldn't have thought their paths crossed very much.'

'I'm only going on what Lydia Quayle said.'

'It's the last name I'd have expected.'

'What have you been doing while I was away, sir?'

'Well, my main achievement was to gather some new information about the inner workings of the Quayle family. They came by courtesy of Lucas Quayle who is a much more amenable person than his brother. In addition to that,' Colbeck went on, 'I had a brief meeting with Mr Haygarth and a chat at the hotel with Superintendent Wigg. He was even more peppery than usual until your young friend turned up.'

'Philip Conway – is that who you mean?'

'It is, Victor, and he was good company. In fact, he's helped me determine what we should do this morning.'

'And what's that, sir?'

'Well, when we've left your luggage at the hotel, we're going to catch the next train to Spondon. Apparently, that cobbler you told me about has been acting very strangely. I think it's time that I made the acquaintance of Jed Hockaday.'

The news that Harriet Quayle had disappeared threw the whole house into turmoil. A servant had found Agnes stretched out on the floor and raised the alarm. When she'd been rallied with smelling salts, she explained what had happened. Stanley Quayle took control and ordered a thorough search of the house, even including the attic rooms and the cellar. He also sent for the doctor. If his mother could wander off without telling anybody, there was obviously something wrong with her.

'It wasn't *my* fault, Stanley,' said his sister, close to tears.

'You must take your share of the blame.'

'Mother is entitled to her privacy. I can't sit with her indefinitely.'

'No,' he agreed, 'but you might have had the sense to lock her bedroom door.'

Agnes was appalled. 'I'm not her gaoler,' she cried, 'I'm her daughter.'

'It was your job to look after Mother.'

'How was I to know that she'd go missing?'

'This is the second time you've failed, Agnes,' he chided. 'Yesterday, you let her go off in the landau and today she's escaped again.'

Before she could reply to the charge, her young brother came to her rescue.

'It's unfair to blame Agnes,' he said. 'She's looked after Mother with great care. You should remember that, Stanley. Now let's concentrate on the search.'

'Where the devil is she?' yelled his brother.

'Well, she's certainly not in the house. I've widened the search to the grounds. I wanted to alert you before I go and join in the hunt.'

'I'll come with you, Lucas,' said his sister.

Stanley was vengeful. 'If Cleary has dared to take her for another ride in the landau,' he warned, 'I'll flay him alive.'

But the coachman was not the culprit. When they went outside, they found the gardeners and the estate workers awaiting orders. The coachman was among them and swore that he'd never seen Mrs Quayle that morning. Everyone was told to fan out and search every inch of the property. While her elder brother was barking orders, Agnes made sure that she slipped off with the younger one.

'I feel dreadful, Lucas,' she confided.

'You deserve a medal for what you've been doing,' he told her. 'If anyone is to blame, it's Stanley and me. We put too much responsibility on you. Mother is our problem just as much as yours.'

'It's so unlike her to disappear, especially when she's so unwell.'

'That may be the explanation, Agnes.'

'What do you mean?'

'Mother has had a profound shock. It's bound to have affected her mind in some way. She probably doesn't know what she's doing half the time.' He inhaled deeply. 'I just hope that we find her still alive.'

Agnes blanched. 'You don't think . . . ?'

'We must be prepared for anything.'

It was not long before Harriet Quayle was found. One of the gardeners called out and they all converged on the summer house. Wrapped in a shawl, she'd been sitting in a basket chair and had fallen asleep. The commotion had roused her and she looked in dismay at the anxious faces all round her. Agnes pushed forward to put an arm around her.

Harriet was dismayed. 'Who are all these people?'

Lucas got rid of them all with a wave of his arm. When the others went quickly off, only his mother, sister and he remained. He knelt down beside the chair.

'What are you doing out here, Mother?' he asked, gently.

'I was remembering something, dear,' she replied with a wan smile.

'But why did you come here?'

'Your father proposed to me in this summer house.'

CHAPTER FOURTEEN

Even his worst enemies conceded that Donald Haygarth had his virtues. He was tireless, single-minded and had the knack of getting things done quickly. He also had a gift for remembering names that endeared him to those who liked to be recognised. It was part of his strategy for befriending influential people, though his critics pointed out that he only lured them into his social circle for the purpose of exploiting them in some way. Haygarth was a bundle of contradictions, steely, supple, ruthless, caring, assertive, detached, manipulative and easy-going by turns. When he entered the office that morning, Maurice Cope wondered what mood he would find the acting chairman in. Haygarth looked up with a welcoming smile. Cope relaxed.

'Good morning, Cope.'

'Good morning, sir,' said the other, deferentially. 'I thought I'd get here before you for once.'

'To do that, you'll have to start taking a train instead of riding a horse. I set out at the crack of dawn every day.'

'You can only see so much out of the window of a train. When I'm on horseback, I feel as if I'm part of the landscape instead of just being an observer of it.' He saw the pile of papers on the desk. 'You've been as busy as usual, I see.'

'Yes,' replied Haygarth, sitting back in his chair. 'I've been going through this projected scheme to link Nottingham directly with London. It was Vivian Quayle's dream but it will have to wait. We don't have a direct line from Derby yet. That's something I've pledged to get for us. We need a new London terminus so that we can be free from our financial obligations to the GNR.'

'They've given us running powers on their tracks, sir, so we ought to be grateful. It's not an ideal situation, I agree, and it's something Mr Quayle vowed that he would change.'

'Forget his vows. They have no relevance now. His plans for Nottingham will have to be put aside. It will never be at the heart of the Midland.'

'But it doesn't have to remain quite so isolated,' said Cope, reasonably. 'It really ought to be on the main line.'

'Mr Quayle is dead,' said Haygarth. 'His scheme died with him.'

Cope accepted the rebuke with a penitential nod. 'Yes, sir, it did.'

'Let's hear no more of it.'

'No, sir.' He brightened. 'I did what you asked, Mr Haygarth.'

'What did you find out?'

'Inspector Colbeck has talked to a number of people on the board,' said Cope, handing him a sheet of paper. 'Their names are listed there. The ones with a cross against them went voluntarily to see him.'

'I'll remember that,' said Haygarth, scanning the list. 'Knowing one's enemies is always an asset. What else has he been doing?'

'The inspector has continued to gather evidence patiently.'

'Has he been bothering you in any way?'

'No, sir, he hasn't been looking too closely at the operation of the Midland.'

'That's reassuring to hear.'

'He's diverted by other things.'

'Let's hope it stays that way. Keep an eye on him, Cope.'

'I have my spies.'

'Did they tell you what Sergeant Leeming was doing in London?'

'No, Mr Haygarth,' replied the other, 'but I'm told he's just come back. The inspector met him at the station.'

'What else do you have to report?'

'Superintendent Wigg had an argument with him at the hotel yesterday. I can't tell you what it was about but the inspector clearly won the dispute. He remained calm while the superintendent ranted and raved.'

'I've seen Elijah Wigg when he's roused. His wrath gets the better of him.'

'After he left,' explained Cope, 'the inspector had a drink with someone else. He's a young man named Philip Conway.'

'That name rings a bell. He's a reporter, isn't he?'

'Yes, sir, he's been digging around in Spondon on his own account.'

'Has he now?' said Haygarth, rubbing his chin. 'I'd be very interested to know what the young man found out.'

When the detectives reached Spondon, the first thing they did was to visit the churchyard. A mound of earth stood over the grave of Cicely Peet. In time it would settle down of its own accord into a level patch covered in well-tended turf. A marble headstone, engraved with a moving tribute, would eventually stand there. Wreaths of all sizes and colours adorned the plot. The detectives each said a silent prayer for the soul of the deceased. They then went across to the open grave.

'I wonder why they haven't filled it in,' said Leeming.

'The gravedigger must have a reason.'

'Bert Knowles would leave it like that just to be awkward, sir. You should have heard his language when he saw me with his wheelbarrow. I had to put him in his place good and proper.'

'Perhaps he's expecting another funeral in the near future.'

'That might be the explanation. He's a lazy devil. Why dig a new grave when there's already one there? That's what he'll say.'

'He has a point, Victor.' Colbeck glanced round. 'Philip Conway said that he might be in the village today. You've obviously impressed him.'

'That was because I bought him a drink or two.'

'Don't be modest. He said you were a good detective – and you are. He also told me something about Mr Haygarth. It turns out that he has a nasty habit of descending on the editor if there's the slightest criticism of the Midland Railway in the local newspaper.'

'I had a feeling that he was a bully.'

'Picking a fight with the press is never a sensible thing to do. But he's a combative individual. When I last spoke to him, I was met with a flash of defiance.'

'Why should he defy *you*?'

'You may well ask, Victor.'

Leeming shrugged. 'I thought he was keen to help us.'

'When we take an interest in *other* people, he'll give us all the help that he can. What he doesn't like is any scrutiny of *him*.'

'Is there something he doesn't want us to know?'

'That's the logical supposition.'

'Superintendent Wigg is convinced that he was behind the murder.'

'If what you gathered from Lydia Quayle is true,' said Colbeck, pensively, 'the superintendent himself ought to merit our attention. He had good cause to loathe her father, it seems, and we've both seen enough of him to know that he's a man who bears grudges.'

Leeming rolled his eyes. '*We* have a superintendent like that.'

'Fair's fair, Victor. Edward Tallis is good at his job. I discovered that when he was absent from work for a while and I became acting superintendent in his place. I struggled badly,' confessed Colbeck, 'and was very grateful when he came back. He's far better in the role than I could be. Wigg is nowhere near as efficient as him.'

'I couldn't take my eyes off those side whiskers of his. I keep thinking they're going to grow into each other one day and spread down his chest like so much ivy.' He chuckled. 'But I agree, sir. He can't hold a candle to Mr Tallis.'

'What separates the two men is this. Our superintendent usually gets results while Wigg walks about with an unsolved murder hanging around his neck like the albatross in *The Ancient Mariner*.'

Leeming goggled. 'Can you say that again, sir?'

'It's a poem by Coleridge.'

They left the churchyard and made their way to Potter Street. As they passed the Malt Shovel, Leeming glanced in through the window and gave the landlord a friendly wave. They carried on until they came to Jed Hockaday's shop. Bent over a last, he was hammering nails into the sole of a shoe. When he looked up and saw who they were, he abandoned his work at once. Hockaday wiped his hands on a rag before extending a palm to Colbeck.

'You must be the Railway Detective,' he said, almost agog.

Colbeck shook his hand. 'There's no need to guess who you might be,' he said. 'As soon as we got within yards of here, we could smell the tang of leather. You're Mr Hockaday, the cobbler.'

'I'm cobbler and constable, actually. When I finish here at the end of the working day, I go on patrol.'

'That's very public-spirited of you, Mr Hockaday.'

Leeming was uneasy. 'How can you work with this smell of leather?'

'You get used to it, Sergeant,' said the cobbler, smiling. 'Is there anything I can do for you? I'm only too glad to help.'

'That's a kind offer,' said Colbeck. 'We'll bear it in mind. I really wanted to ask you why you were staring at the graves in the churchyard yesterday.'

Hockaday's smile faded. 'Who's been telling tales?'

'You spoke with Mr Conway, I believe.'

'I may have done.'

'You told him that Mrs Peet was a customer of yours.'

'That's right.'

'A lady like her would never have deigned to come in the shop, surely,' said Leeming. 'Mrs Peet would have sent a servant.'

'She was a gracious lady. I'll miss her. As for what Mr Conway may have told you,' said Hockaday with annoyance, 'there's no law that stops you from paying respects to the dead.'

'You're right – there isn't.'

'But it wasn't only Mrs Peet who interested you,' said Colbeck, 'was it? I believe that you also looked into the grave where the body of Mr Quayle, the murder victim, was found. Then you discussed the Stone case at length.'

'That makes three deaths,' commented Leeming.

'One was natural and the other two were not.'

Hockaday backed away and hunched up defensively. His eyes darted from one to the other and back again. He chewed his lip before speaking.

'It was Mr Conway who brought up Enoch Stone. He knew

I'd been looking for my friend's killer for years. As for the empty grave,' he added, 'I was just wondering if anybody would want to use it after what happened. If it was left to me, I'd fill it in. Bad memories like that should be buried.'

'That won't make them go away.'

'No, Inspector, but it will stop children sneaking into the churchyard to peer into that grave. I chased a couple of them away this morning. Bert Knowles needs to get busy with his spade.'

'Then why doesn't he?'

The smile was back. 'Bert is a law unto himself.'

'On the night of the murder,' said Leeming, 'you were in Duffield, or so you told me. Is that right?'

'Yes, Sergeant, I stayed with friends.'

'Can they vouch for you?'

'Why should they need to?'

'I just want to establish the facts, sir.'

'I was *there*,' insisted Hockaday.

'Then why did the stationmaster here remember you getting off the last train that night? I asked him if he recognised anyone who got off at Spondon. Your name was the first one he mentioned.'

'You can't have been in two places at once,' said Colbeck.

'Which one was it, Mr Hockaday,' asked Leeming. 'Duffield or Spondon?'

The cobbler glowered at them.

As they sat around the bed, it was difficult to know if their mother was asleep or not. Her eyes were closed and her breathing shallow but she seemed to react to comments they made. Stanley and Lucas Quayle had been impressed by the way that their sister had handled the situation. Once their mother had been found, Agnes had brought her back to the house and taken her up to her room. The doctor eventually arrived to examine the old woman and decided that, though her early morning venture out of the house had caused no visible harm, she needed rest. Her sons joined her daughter at Harriet Quayle's bedside. Without warning, she opened her eyes.

'What are you all doing here?' she asked.

'We're looking after you, Mother,' replied Agnes.

'I pay a doctor to do that.'

'You need company,' said Stanley.

'Then where have you been for the last few days? I needed company then but you didn't come anywhere near me.'

'I did,' said Lucas, softly. 'I looked in whenever I could.'

'But I was the one who actually stayed with Mother,' said Agnes, virtuously.

Stanley was critical. 'Then how did she manage to get out of the house?'

'That's unjust,' said Lucas. 'We owe Agnes a great deal. This little incident has shown that.'

'Well, it mustn't happen again.'

'I went for a walk, Stanley,' said his mother. 'Surely I can do that.'

'It might have harmed you, Mother.'

'But it didn't – the doctor agreed.'

'You've got limited strength and you must conserve it.'

Harriet said nothing. She lay back and looked at each of her children in turn. Agnes was a picture of sympathy, Lucas was concerned and Stanley was anxious to leave. As she studied her elder son, Harriet felt that he looked more like his father than ever, impatient, animated and eager to get back to work. She gave an incongruous giggle.

'You don't need to sit around my deathbed yet,' she said.

Stanley was shocked. 'That's a terrible thing to say, Mother.'

'I don't think it is,' said Lucas, getting up to kiss her on the forehead. 'I think it's a good sign. Get some rest, Mother.'

'I was resting quite happily in the summer house until I was disturbed,' she pointed out. 'Why didn't you leave me there?'

'You're safer here.'

'Agnes will look after you,' said Stanley, rising to his feet.

'Yes,' murmured his sister, 'Agnes will look after you.'

As all three of her children hovered over her, Harriet raised a skinny hand.

'Away with you,' she said, weakly. 'I want to sleep.'

The meeting with Philip Conway was a happy accident. The detectives were approaching the Union Inn when he came into view. After an exchange of greetings, they stepped into the inn and found a table. Colbeck ordered drinks and they were able to talk at leisure. The reporter was interested to hear about their confrontation with Jed Hockaday.

'What did he say when you caught him lying?' he asked.

'Oh, he came up with all sorts of excuses,' replied Leeming. 'The one he finally settled on was that he got so drunk in Duffield that he didn't realise his friends had probably put him on the train that night to Spondon.'

'Did you believe him?'

'No,' said Colbeck. 'And when we asked for the names of the friends with whom he spent that evening, he prevaricated for minutes. We had to chisel their names out of him. He was understandably resentful. As a constable, Hockaday is used to asking awkward questions instead of being forced to answer them.'

Leeming issued a warning. 'You'd best keep out of his way, Mr Conway.'

'Why is that?' asked the reporter.

'He'll blame you for setting us on to him.'

'All I did was to describe his behaviour in the churchyard.'

'He lied about that as well,' said Leeming. 'I wouldn't have a man like that under me. I think we should report him to Superintendent Wigg.'

'No,' decided Colbeck. 'Let's make sure that we have proper grounds for dismissal before we do that. We've frightened him and people don't always act sensibly when they're in that state. Keep an eye on him, Sergeant.'

'What do you think he'll do?'

'Well, I wouldn't be at all surprised if he didn't rush off to Duffield at some stage to tell these friends of his what to say when questioned. We know they exist because Hockaday wouldn't dare to give us false names.'

'You can see why he's not that popular in the village,' said Conway.

'Policemen never are,' moaned Leeming. 'When you put on a uniform, you lose a lot of friends. I discovered that. In Hockaday's case, there's another problem. He tries hard to be liked but he's just not very likeable.' He tasted his drink. 'This is the best beer I've tasted in Spondon.' He put the tankard down. 'The inspector was telling me what you said about Mr Haygarth.'

'What *did* I say?'

'That your editor finds him a nuisance.'

'Mr Haygarth is always complaining about something or other.'

'What about the late Mr Quayle?' asked Colbeck. 'Did you have the same trouble from him?'

'No, not at all – he was on amicable terms with the *Mercury*. He certainly didn't charge into the office breathing fire the way that Haygarth does. My editor says that Haygarth is the opposite of the superintendent. Elijah Wigg does everything he can to butter us up but all that Haygarth does is to find fault. However,' he went on, 'they have one thing in common. They possess foul tempers.'

'I know. I've had both of them shouting at me.'

'They should be grateful that we came here,' said Leeming.

'We'll never get gratitude out of the superintendent,' warned Colbeck. 'He sees us as trespassers. Mr Haygarth couldn't have been happier to see us at first. But the moment I started to ask about his link with Spondon, he became angry.'

'I thought he was born here.'

'He was, Victor, but he doesn't like to be reminded of the fact. He left the village as a boy and hasn't been back here for decades.'

Conway was astonished. 'Is that what he told you, Inspector?'

'Yes, and he did so in no uncertain terms.'

'Then he has a very poor memory. He attended Mrs Peet's funeral.'

'I didn't see him there,' said Leeming.

'Then he must have made sure that you didn't for some reason.'

'It was easy to miss him in that sea of hats.'

'Not really – his hat was somewhat taller than the others.'

Colbeck's ears pricked up. 'Are you certain that it was him?'

'I daren't make mistakes about things like that, Inspector. It's an article of faith with me. If you look at the list of names we printed with the obituary, you'll see that Donald Haygarth is among them.'

Anyone involved with the Midland Railway knew the difference between the two men. Vivian Quayle had had a genuine love of the railway system. He was fascinated by each new technical development in the production of steam locomotives and rolling stock and was a frequent visitor to the Derby Works. He would spend hours talking to the chief engineer about the manufacturing process. Those who toiled in the pattern shop, the foundry, the carriage shop, the machine shop and the boiler shop knew Quayle as a regular and respected visitor. They'd never set eyes on Donald Haygarth. His realm was the boardroom and the public platform. He was known to have a desire to stand for Parliament. His ambition for the company was clear. He wanted to maximise its profits and turn the Midland Railway into the best in the country. But he refused to get his shoes dirty as he did so.

He was studying the accounts when Maurice Cope knocked before entering the office. Haygarth was too involved in what he was doing to pay him any attention. Cope had to wait until the other man finally glanced up.

'What do you want?' asked Haygarth.

'This just arrived for you, sir,' said Cope, handing over a letter. 'I think that it's the information you've been waiting for.'

'It's about time, too.'

As the acting chairman opened and read the letter, Cope watched him like a cat hoping to be tossed a morsel. Haygarth smiled with satisfaction. He could have waited until the announcement was made in the *Derby Mercury* but he was too impatient for that. He always wanted advance notice.

'Was I right, sir?'

'Yes – it's the details of the funeral.'

'Is that an invitation?'

Haygarth smirked. 'Oh, they won't invite me.'

'Then why were you so keen to learn when it's taking place?'

'I intend to go uninvited,' said Haygarth. 'It may cause something of a stir but I need to be seen there. Stanley and Lucas Quayle will probably ignore me. That's to be expected. But everyone else will think it only proper that I pay my respects to the man I've replaced. And there's something else.'

'What's that, sir?'

'The press will be there in force. I'll have publicity.'

They had settled into an uneasy and watchful truce. Though Lydia Quayle and Beatrice Myler were excessively polite to each other, there was no contact at a deep level. It remained to be seen if their former rapport had been lost or simply misplaced. The fact was that each had seen the other in an unflattering light. Lydia had been revolted by the discovery that her room had been searched and Beatrice had been wounded by the knowledge that someone from the family had got in touch with her yet she'd said nothing about it. While they took their meals together, they tiptoed around each other for most of the day. The servants too were all aware of the charged atmosphere.

In the end, it was Lydia who offered an olive branch.

'We mustn't let this come between us, Beatrice.'

'Unfortunately, it already has.'

'If we both make an effort, we can put it behind us in time.'

'You shouldn't have invited them into my house.'

Lydia was stung. 'You used to call it *our* house.'

'Yes, I did, didn't I?' said the other, wistfully.

'I've been so contented here.'

'So why did you wish to spoil it all?'

'It wasn't deliberate. You must see that.'

But her friend was in no mood to make concessions. Lydia was made to feel that she was there on sufferance. Something had snapped. Beatrice showed no interest in wanting to repair it. They were sitting opposite each other in the drawing room. Both held books but neither had actually been reading. They'd been simmering away quietly. Not wishing to risk rejection again, Lydia held her tongue and thought about her visitors instead. Their arrival had given her hope yet left her despondent. Madeleine Colbeck had convinced her that Lydia might know something that would help a terrible crime to be solved but, in coming through the front door with Victor Leeming, she'd brought the real world and all its hideous associations into the haven of peace and harmony that the two women had created. A cosy and uncomplicated life had suddenly been snatched away from Lydia and, by extension, from Beatrice. An estranged daughter had a new reason to hate her father. Vivian Quayle had destroyed her happiness from beyond the grave.

'What are you reading, Beatrice?' she asked, softly.

'It's that new book about Venice.'

'Is it from the Lending Library?'

'Yes, it is.'

'What are the illustrations like?'

'They're very good. They bring back pleasant memories.'

Lydia smiled. 'I'm glad that something does.'

'It's made me want to go there again. Venice is so magical.'

'When are you thinking of going?'

'I'll need to look in my diary.'

'Are you intending to travel alone?'

It was a nervous question and it received no answer. Beatrice simply buried her head in the book and pretended to read. The old companionship had withered. Lydia prayed that it might not be beyond recall. But the other woman was ignoring her as if she was not even there. She was not only punishing her friend. Beatrice seemed to be taking pleasure from doing so.

Hockaday was worried. Determined to impress the detectives, he'd instead ended up being exposed as a liar. He feared that it could cost him his post as a constable and that would deprive him of a status he relished. After brooding at length on his ill-fated conversation with Colbeck and Leeming, he came to a decision. He abandoned his work, took off his apron and put on a coat in its place. Thrusting a hat on his head, he locked up the premises and walked to the station as quickly as he could. People he passed on the way got only a curt response to their greeting. The cobbler's mind was elsewhere. When he arrived at the station, he bought a ticket and asked about the next available train that would take him to his destination. He then went out onto the platform and marched up and down.

Victor Leeming, meanwhile, entered the railway station cautiously. Sitting in the window of the Union Inn, he'd seen the cobbler go past in a hurry and followed him at a discreet distance. He already knew that a train to Duffield was imminent because Colbeck had consulted the copy of *Bradshaw* he usually had with him. Leeming bought a ticket then remained out of sight until the train arrived and the cobbler got into a compartment. Making sure he was not seen by the other man, the sergeant chose the last of the carriages.

During their brief acquaintance, Colbeck had grown to like Philip Conway. He had a mind like a sponge that soaked up information whenever and wherever he found it. Crucially, he was treating the pursuit of the killer as a mission in which he could both learn and be of practical assistance. At his first meeting with Superintendent Wigg, Colbeck had been unaware that the man would later be named by Lydia Quayle as one of her father's enemies. The detective could not understand why until the reporter enlightened him. Armed with the information, he returned to Derby and made straight for the police station. He was shown into Wigg's office immediately.

'I'm glad you've come, Inspector,' said the superintendent.

'That's a welcome change. When we first arrived here, you felt that we were intruders. Have we somehow won your approval?'

'I wouldn't go that far.'

Colbeck smiled disarmingly. 'I had a feeling you'd say that, Superintendent. Tell me,' he went on. 'I recall your saying at one point that you had reservations about Mr Quayle. May I know what they were?'

'One should never speak ill of the dead.'

'That's a pious platitude, in my view, and should be disregarded by anyone in our profession. The dead person in this instance is a murder victim and we need to be able to probe his vices as well as his virtues. Mr Haygarth has no problem in listing his rival's shortcomings. Your perception of Mr Quayle, I suspect, may be different.'

Wigg was suspicious. 'What's behind this question?'

'The simple desire to get as much information about the deceased as possible,' replied Colbeck. 'You didn't like the man, did you?'

'We had our differences.'

'I fancy that it went deeper than that,' said Colbeck.

'Don't listen to tittle-tattle, Inspector.'

'My informant was that young reporter from the *Derby Mercury* and he's no purveyor of tittle-tattle. Indeed you went out of your way to congratulate him on his work when he joined us at the hotel last night.'

'What has Conway been telling you?'

'I'd rather hear it from you, Superintendent.'

Wigg folded his arms. 'If you have an accusation, make it.'

'Very well,' said Colbeck, meeting his gaze. 'Before you joined the Derby Constabulary, you were a superintendent in the railway police here. Somewhere along the line, you fell foul of Mr Quayle and he had you dismissed. Is it true or false?'

'It's partially true,' admitted the other.

'What Mr Conway didn't know was the nature of your crime, if that's what it was. But he did point out that you joined the constabulary instead and rose quickly within the ranks to your present position. I admire you for doing that.'

'The past is the past, Inspector. We've all made mistakes in our time. Mine was in falling out with a man in a position of authority. It wasn't a "crime". It was a misjudgement on my part. Even you must have made those.' He gave a thin smile. 'In fact, you might be making one at this very moment.'

'That's conceivable.'

'Let's leave the matter there, shall we?'

Colbeck agreed. He'd made Wigg aware that he knew about the animosity between the superintendent and Vivian Quayle and that it might have a bearing on the investigation. But he didn't press the man too far. He needed to have firm evidence of Wigg's involvement in the murder before he could do that.

'You said that you were glad that I'd come.'

'I am,' said Wigg. 'I have some news for you.'

'What is it?'

'The pathologist has consulted someone with more thorough knowledge of poisons and, as a result, he's able to give us slightly more detail about what was injected into Mr Quayle.'

'Excellent.'

'He was killed by a compound of different poisons, some of which were detected at the post-mortem. One of them was not.'

'What was it?'

'See for yourself,' said Wigg, picking up a sheet of paper from his desk and handing it over. 'I don't know much about chemicals.'

Colbeck read the name. 'This one is likely to be very corrosive.'

'I asked the pathologist how someone could get hold of it.'

'What was his answer?'

'He said that it's sometimes found in powerful weedkillers.'

Colbeck thought about a garden shed in Melbourne Hall.

CHAPTER FIFTEEN

Weapon at the ready, Gerard Burns knelt motionless behind the bushes and waited for his moment. The bird circled, hovered for an instant then descended to the fence and scanned the ground below. Burns pulled the trigger and the crow was instantly blown off its perch by the shotgun blast. The gardener's dog scampered out from its hiding place to retrieve the bird and bring it back to its master. Burns took it from the animal's jaws and walked across to the shallow pit he'd already dug, tossing the lifeless body into it then using a boot to cover it with earth. He hated crows more than anything else and killed them whenever possible. The noise of the shotgun had made the other birds scatter in a crescendo of squawks and screeches so he was able to put the weapon aside and reach for his spade to fill in the grave properly.

One of the undergardeners came around the angle of the house.

'What have you shot this time, Mr Burns?'

'It was another crow.'

'Wood pigeons are better. You can eat those.'

'I'll kill any pests I can.'

'Slugs are the worst.'

'There's poison in the shed. Use it.'

'Yes, Mr Burns.'

Recognising that the head gardener was in no mood for conversation, the other man went off to hoe some flower beds. Burns, meanwhile, went back to the shed with the spade and the shotgun. Ejecting the empty cartridge, he dropped it into the bin he kept for rubbish. Everything was in full bloom during the summer so there was a lot to do in the garden and he worked long hours to keep everything under control. However, his time was not entirely taken up with horticulture. Reaching behind some tarpaulin in the corner, he brought out a heavy object and tested it for balance. It was not ready yet, he decided. There was still plenty of work to do on it but Burns loved the feel of it in his hands. Stepping outside the shed, he tried a few practice strokes with his new cricket bat. He heaved a sigh, conscious that his days of real prominence on a cricket field were over. What he missed most was the applause for a ball well struck or for the latest wicket he'd taken. Burns was no longer the leading light of a county team. He was now condemned to take part in lesser contests where spectators were few and ovations non-existent.

The new bat was part of a dream. He played one final cover drive, saw an imaginary ball hurtling through the air like a bullet, then went back into the shed. It was time to return to reality.

The train journey to Duffield did not take very long. In earlier days, the village had stood in an area of scenic beauty at the lower end of the Pennines. Situated near the junction of two rivers, the Derwent and the Ecclesbourne, it was like many other Derbyshire villages, agricultural communities that had been transformed by the growth of industry and the development of the railways. When first opened in 1841, the railway station there was little more than a halt but it was now a solid permanent structure. Farm labourers existed in dwindling numbers in tied cottages and the new houses in the village had, in many cases, been built by the Midland Railway for its employees who travelled to the Derby Works each day by train.

Victor Leeming was not interested in the history of Duffield. His only concern was to follow Jed Hockaday in order to confirm the alibi that had been given to the detectives. When the train steamed into Duffield station, therefore, he stayed in his compartment until the other passengers had alighted. Only when the train was about to depart again did he leap out onto the platform and slam the door shut behind him. Leeming looked around to see in which direction his quarry had gone. Over a dozen people were in view but Hockaday was not among them. Leeming had the lurching sensation that he'd been tricked. It looked as if the cobbler had been aware that he was being followed and, instead of getting off at Duffield, had simply stayed on the train. There was a consolation. The sergeant had the names and addresses of two people with whom Hockaday claimed to have spent time on the night of the murder. More to the point, he would not have been able to reach them first in order to tell them what to say to the detective. The journey to Duffield was not in vain, after all.

The cottage in King Street was little more than a hovel. Clearly, Hockaday's friends were in straitened circumstances. A rusty bell hung outside the front door. When he rang it, Leeming had to wait some time before the door was opened by a wizened old man bent almost double. Having established that he was talking to Seth Verney, the sergeant explained why he was there.

The mention of Hockaday's name put some animation into the old man.

'Yes, sir, Jed was here that night.'

'What time did he leave?'

'He caught the last train back home.'

'Had he been drinking?'

Verney cackled. 'Oh, yes – he likes his beer.'

'But he should have been on patrol in Spondon and constables are not allowed to drink on duty.'

'It were his day off, sir.'

'How long was he here?'

'Jed's never here for long but we loved seeing him.'

'He told us he was in the village for some hours.'

'That's as maybe. We only saw him at the very end of the evening.'

'So where did he go before he came here?'

'I don't know, sir, but he'd been drinking.'

'How often do you see him?'

The old man cocked his head to one side. 'What's this got to do with that murder you talked about?'

'I'm not sure,' admitted Leeming.

'Jed is a constable. He's one of *you*, Sergeant.'

'I appreciate that, Mr Verney.'

'He's not in any trouble, is he?'

'No, no, I'm just . . . checking up on something he told us.'

'Why're you doing that? Don't you trust his word?'

'It never does any harm to confirm certain facts.'

But the other man was increasingly defensive. Leeming found it hard to get the information he was after. What surprised him was Verney's age and obvious penury. He seemed an unlikely friend for Hockaday, especially as the old man claimed that he'd signed the pledge and was thus no drinking companion of the cobbler. Leeming couldn't imagine what they'd have to talk about. He was wondering with whom Hockaday had spent time before he came to see Verney and his wife.

'Let me go back to a question I asked earlier,' said Leeming.

'Which one?'

'How often do you see Mr Hockaday?'

'He only comes every now and then.'

'Why is that, sir?'

'Shouldn't you be back in Spondon, trying to catch that killer?' asked the old man with a burst of anger. 'It wasn't Jed, I tell you. I'd swear to it.'

'Why do you say that, sir?'

'It's because he only comes here when he has money to give us.'

'Is he a relative of yours, Mr Verney?'

The old man looked over his shoulder to make sure that nobody inside the cottage could hear him, then he leant forward to confide in Leeming's ear.

'I'm Jed's father.'

Harriet Quayle's health had swiftly declined. Though there'd been no apparent ill effects from her sojourn in the grounds, she later became visibly unwell. Even though she was in a warm bed, she began to shiver. Her face whitened and her breathing was irregular. She complained of pain in her limbs. But the biggest change was in her attitude. Hitherto, she'd made an effort to cope with the devastating news of her husband's murder and had even been able to go for a ride in the landau. It was almost as if the ugly truth had finally sunk in. She had lost the man who'd been beside her for so many years and who'd fathered her four children. Her grief was exacerbated by the fact that one of those children was no longer there to comfort her.

'Mother is getting worse,' said Agnes.

'Give her something to help her sleep,' advised her elder brother. 'The doctor left those tablets.'

'She's rambling, Stanley. Her mind is crumbling.'

'Stay with her. If Mother doesn't improve, send for the doctor. I'll look in on her when I get back.'

'Where are you going?'

'I've business in Nottingham.'

'I feel so much better when you're *here* – everybody does.'

'Goodbye, Agnes.'

After brushing her cheek with a token kiss, he ignored her plea and left the house. The landau was waiting for him on the drive. Standing beside it and holding the door open was John Cleary. He acknowledged Stanley Quayle with a nod. After clambering into his seat, the passenger turned on the coachman.

'Do you see what you did, Cleary?'

'I don't know what you mean, sir,' said the other, folding the step into position and closing the door.

'Thanks to you, my mother is very ill.'

'I'm sorry to hear that, sir.'

'You should have considered her health before you agreed to take her for a drive. Her constitution was too weak for an outing.'

'Mrs Quayle seemed well enough to me, sir.'

'It wasn't your place to make such a judgement.'

'No, sir,' said Cleary. 'I know that.'

'My mother left the house against the express wishes of my sister. You must have been aware of that when they came out together.'

'I was too busy helping Mrs Quayle into her seat, sir.'

'You've displeased me, Cleary,' warned the other.

'I didn't mean to,' said the coachman, earnestly, 'and I didn't think that it would do Mrs Quayle any harm. I was as worried as anybody when she disappeared. Well, you saw me, sir. I helped in the search for your mother and I was very relieved when she was found.'

Stanley Quayle looked at him with undisguised contempt. Unable to decide if the coachman was being honest or merely obsequious, he repeated his warning that Cleary's job hung in the balance. If he was given the slightest cause for annoyance, Quayle would have him dismissed.

'Do you understand, Cleary?'

'Yes, sir.'

'When I make a threat, I always mean it.'

The coachman's manner was courteous. 'Yes, Mr Quayle.'

The passenger sat back in his seat and waved a lordly hand.

'Take me to the railway station.'

Whether on the cricket field or off it, Gerard Burns always committed himself to the task in hand. In the time that he'd worked in the gardens at Melbourne Hall, he'd suggested a number of initiatives. Though some had inevitably been turned down, those that had been implemented proved to be universally successful. He was always looking for ways to improve vistas and add floral refinements. His latest project concerned the fountains and he was studying them yet again when he realised that he had a visitor. Robert Colbeck seemed to have materialised out of thin air.

'I never expected to see you again, Inspector,' said Burns.

'I'd hoped it might not be necessary, sir.'

'It's not really convenient for me to talk now.'

'Then I'll wait for you in the police station, Mr Burns, and we can have the interview there. It might not be quite so private, I'm afraid.'

Colbeck's threat had the desired effect. If Burns was seen giving a statement in the police station, it would soon become common knowledge. Several people were employed at the Hall. One of them was certain to catch wind of the development and taunting was sure to follow. If it was known that Burns was a suspect in a murder inquiry, his job might be at risk. Changing his mind, he led Colbeck to a quieter part of the garden and they sat on a bench in the sunshine.

'What would you like to know, Inspector?' asked the gardener.

'I'm sure that you recall that cricket match in Ilkeston.'

'Very clearly.'

'I went there,' said Colbeck, noting the look of surprise from the other man. 'I have to say that I've seen better pitches.'

Burns recovered quickly. 'If you took the trouble to check up on me, you'll know that what I told you was the truth. I did play cricket there on that day.'

'It's not what you told me that's at issue here, Mr Burns. It's what you deliberately held back from me.'

'And what was that?'

'After the match, you took a train to Derby.'

Burns shrugged. 'Is that a cause for suspicion?'

'Why did you go there?'

'That's a personal matter.'

'Did you go to see a friend or were you drawn there by an enemy?'

'Speak more plainly, Inspector.'

'If you were in Derby late that night, you were not far from Spondon.'

'That doesn't mean I went there.'

'No, but it raises the possibility that you *could* have.'

'I could have done all sorts of things.'

There was an underlying smugness in the reply that alerted Colbeck. He sensed that Burns had reverted to the posture he'd adopted at their first meeting when he'd been evasive and unhelpful. It was at their second encounter that he'd been far more honest. The gardener was behaving as if he'd expended his reserves of honesty and was falling back on prevarication. Waiting for the next question, he offered a challenging smile. Colbeck jolted him out of his complacency.

'We've spoken to Miss Lydia Quayle.'

Burns was startled. 'Where is she?'

'The lady lives in London now, sir. I didn't have the pleasure of meeting her myself but I've had a full report of what transpired.' He could see the gardener's extreme discomfort. 'You may be relieved to know that Miss Quayle did not talk about you at any length.'

'Oh, I see.'

'You belong to an episode in her life that she has left behind her.'

'It's the same in my case, Inspector.'

'When we last spoke, you told me of a threat made against you. The same vile threat was repeated to Miss Quayle by her father. It was the final straw that broke the bond between them. And, of course,' added Colbeck, 'it severed the bond between you and the young lady.'

There was a lengthy pause. Burns gritted his teeth and looked him in the eye.

'If you're waiting for a comment,' he said, eventually, 'I don't have one to make except to say that I wish Lydia . . . Miss Quayle well.'

'I've no doubt that those are her sentiments with regard to you, sir.'

A note of aggression crept in. 'So why are you really here, Inspector?'

'An odd coincidence has occurred, Mr Burns.'

'What is it?'

'Before I tell you that,' said Colbeck, gazing around, 'can you tell me how you keep these gardens in such pristine condition. The lawns are like brushed velvet and the flower beds have nothing but flowers in them. How do you control weeds?'

'We dig them out by the root.'

'Some will already have propagated.'

'I treat those with a herbicide,' explained Burns. 'Horticulture is a science that is constantly changing and you have to keep up with the changes. The Americans have done a lot of research on herbicides but I get my inspiration from the Germans.'

'What do they recommend?'

'It used to be sodium chloride but some scientists experimented with sulphuric acid and iron sulphate. As it happens, I prefer a herbicide that uses both.'

'May I see it, please?' asked Colbeck.

Harriet Quayle had rallied enough to be able to sit up in bed and to talk with more coherence than she'd earlier managed. Watching her with concern, her younger daughter and her younger son sat either side of the bed.

'Where's Stanley?' asked Harriet.

'He's gone to Nottingham,' replied Lucas.

'Why?'

'He didn't say, Mother.'

'He should be here, mourning with the rest of the family.'

'I agree,' said Agnes. 'Nothing is more important than that.'

'Stanley is attending to business somewhere,' said her brother. 'That's the one certain thing I can tell you. It proves what I've believed all along. He doesn't *feel* things the way that the rest of us do. Stanley has no heart.'

'Let's have no backbiting, Lucas,' warned his mother.

'It's just an observation.'

'Where could your brother have gone?'

'We honestly don't know, Mother.'

'He was driven off in the landau,' said Agnes. 'That's all I can tell you.'

'It's so inconsiderate of him,' scolded their mother. 'Stanley was my firstborn. He was such a delight as a baby. He had such a pleasant disposition.'

'There's no sign of that now,' said Lucas under his breath.

'In fairness to Stanley,' said Agnes, 'he's taken responsibility for things that neither Lucas nor I really wanted to do. We should acknowledge that.'

'I agree, Agnes. He's borne the brunt.'

Harriet went off into a trance for a few minutes and the others waited in silence, communicating by looks and gestures. Their mother finally spoke.

'If he went to Nottingham,' she said, 'he might have been going to the undertaker because the premises are in the town. Stanley may have gone somewhere else, of course, and I'd like to know where.'

'There's no need to do that, surely,' he said.

'I'm curious.'

'Then wait until Stanley comes back and ask him.'

'I want to know *now*,' Harriet told him. 'If Cleary took him to the station, he might know what Stanley's destination was.'

She clenched her fists and the veins stood out on the backs of her hands. 'My elder son should be here. I want to know where he is and what he's doing there.'

Victor Leeming had arranged to meet Colbeck back at the hotel so that they could compare notes but, when he got there, the sergeant saw no sign of him. He was not long without company. As soon as Leeming went into the lounge, Stanley Quayle rose from an armchair and came across to him. He was still in black garb.

'Superintendent Wigg told me I might find the inspector or a Sergeant Leeming here.'

'That's me, sir.'

'I'm Stanley Quayle.'

'I guessed that you might be,' said Leeming.

'Where's Inspector Colbeck?'

'I'm not entirely certain, sir, but he'll be collecting evidence somewhere.'

'Then I'll have to talk to you, I suppose.'

There was a note of resignation in his voice that Leeming did his best to ignore. Working all the time in Colbeck's shadow, he was used to being undervalued and disregarded. Quayle resumed his seat and Leeming took the chair next to him.

'First of all,' said the other, 'I must apologise for being so uncooperative when the inspector called at the house.'

'I understand, sir. You were distracted.'

'That doesn't excuse my rudeness.'

Though the words were trotted out smoothly, Leeming couldn't hear a vestige of sincerity in them and the expression of disdain on the other man was unmistakable.

'Your brother came to see the inspector, sir. He was very helpful.'

'It was my brother's visit that prompted this one. I wanted to correct any misleading statements he made.'

'That's a matter between you and your brother, surely.'

'It has a bearing on this investigation,' said the other. 'Lucas may have given you the impression that we were a disjointed and unhappy family. It's a travesty of the truth, Sergeant. Most of the time, I can assure you, we live in perfect harmony with each other. If my brother and I were not on such amicable terms, we could not run the coal mines so efficiently together.'

'I thought that *you* ran the business and that your brother merely assisted.'

'Lucas has clearly misled you on that score.'

'I never actually spoke to him, Mr Quayle. I'm only going on what the inspector told me.'

'Then I must correct some misapprehensions.'

Stanley Quayle was still unwilling to divulge any new information about the family that might assist the investigation. He simply wanted to portray it in a more favourable light than his brother. He spoke of a loving father who'd imbued his sons with the aspirations that drove them on. While conceding that his brother had been wayward at times, he insisted that Lucas was now following in the Quayle tradition of enterprise. The other reason for coming to Derby was to find out if there had been any developments in the case. Leeming was succinct, explaining that they'd made some encouraging progress but were in no position to make an arrest as yet.

'What we really need to know is where your father was on the day when he was murdered. Didn't he keep a diary?'

'Yes,' said Quayle, 'and he filled it in scrupulously. If we could find it, a lot of things would become clearer, but it's disappeared. You'll have to manage without it, I fear.' He sighed. 'But you do have suspects in mind, I take it?'

'There are people at whom we're looking more closely, sir,' said Leeming, guardedly. 'That's all I can tell you.'

'Mr Haygarth is one of them, I hope. And then, of course, there's . . .'

Quayle drew back from mentioning the name of Gerard Burns.

'That gentleman has been interviewed, sir,' said Leeming.

'He was no gentleman, Sergeant.'

'But he was a good cricketer, I'm told.'

'I don't want to talk about that,' said the other, curtly. 'We indulged the fellow in all manner of ways and he repaid us with . . .' He gestured with both hands. 'My brother will have told you about the betrayal we suffered.'

'We've heard about it from all sides, Mr Quayle.'

'Don't believe a word that Burns told you.'

'Yet his version of events was supported by your sister.'

'What?' cried the other, aghast. 'You've *seen* Lydia?'

'Yes, sir, we did. We tracked her down in London.' There was fury in the other man's eyes. 'Your sister had a right to know what was going on, sir,' argued Leeming. 'After all, it's *her* father as well as yours.'

Stanley turned away. 'I don't want to hear any more.'

'Your sister has no intention of coming home.'

'No more!' snapped Quayle. 'We have enough problems without getting embroiled in that one again. As far as I'm concerned, my elder sister does not exist.'

'Your brother takes a different view.'

'Lucas will do what he's told.'

'Don't you wish to know where Miss Quayle has been since you parted?'

'The subject is closed, Sergeant, and so is this conversation. I'm sorry that I was unable to see the inspector instead of having to put up with your impertinent questions.' He got up. 'I'll bid you farewell.'

'One moment,' said Leeming, also on his feet. 'There's another name that's come to our ears and it's a most unlikely one. We gather that this person might bear ill will against your father.'

'Who is it?'

'Superintendent Wigg.'

'I'd forgotten him.'

'Should we treat him as suspect?'

Stanley Quayle pondered. 'Yes,' he said at length. 'Yes, you should.'

Now that the shock of the murder was wearing off in Spondon, people were starting to remember things that had seemed irrelevant at the time. The reporter was therefore able to pick up scraps of information here and there that might be of use to the detectives. Having become a familiar figure in the village, he'd won the trust of most of the inhabitants so they were more ready to confide in him. When his work was done, he strolled towards the railway station with the feeling that his day had been well spent. Before Conway reached the building, however, he saw Jed Hockaday emerging from it. Spotting the reporter, the cobbler bore down on him with a vengeance.

'I want a word with you,' he said, angrily.

'You can have as many as you like,' replied the other, coolly.

'Stop telling lies about me to those two detectives.'

'You're the one who's been telling lies, Mr Hockaday. According to you, on the night of the murder, you weren't even in Spondon. Yet when the sergeant had a word with the stationmaster, he discovered that you got back here on the last train.'

'I'd been drinking,' said Hockaday. 'I was confused.'

'You were sober in the morning. When you woke up in your own bed, you must have realised that you got back home somehow.'

'That's none of your business.'

'If it's relevant to the murder investigation, it *is* my business.'

'I had nothing to do with the murder,' said the cobbler, brandishing a fist, 'so you can stop saying that I did. I never even knew the dead man.'

'Are you sure?' challenged Conway.

'I'm *very* sure.'

'What about Mr Haygarth?'

Hockaday glared. 'Who?'

'Donald Haygarth – did you know him?'

There was a momentary delay in replying that gave the cobbler away and his manner was shifty. Though he insisted that he was neither friend nor acquaintance of Haygarth, his claim was unconvincing. The question had put him on the defensive and it irked him. He went back on the attack again.

'Keep away from Spondon,' he warned.

'It's a free country. I can come here, if I want to.'

'You're not welcome.'

'You don't speak for the whole village,' said Conway. 'Most people have been very friendly. They've been glad to help, especially as it may get their names in the *Mercury*.'

Hockaday stepped in close. 'Don't spread lies about me – or else.'

'Are you threatening me, Mr Hockaday?'

'There's such a thing as slander.'

Conway laughed. 'Do you think I don't know that?' he said. 'I work for a newspaper so I've had the laws of libel and slander drummed into me. It's the reason I always tell the truth. Malicious lies can be expensive.'

'You'd do well to remember that.'

Hockaday stood over him as if about to strike a blow. In the end, he took a step to the side so that the reporter could go past. Conway paused.

'Let me ask you again,' he said. 'Do you know Donald Haygarth?'

Unable to contain his anger, Hockaday stalked off.

Colbeck was intrigued. Of all the people involved in the case, he found Gerard Burns the most interesting and not only because of his prowess as a cricketer. On the journey back to Derby, he reflected on the character of the gardener. Until his romance with Lydia Quayle, he'd been viewed as an ideal employee, honest, dependable, hard-working, keen to improve the gardens he tended and ready to lend his skills to the family on the field of play. Yet he was also capable of dishonesty, entering into a relationship that called for systematic deception on his part. Having heard from Leeming what an attractive young woman she was, Colbeck could understand how Burns had been drawn to her but he sensed that there was another element at work. Gerard Burns was a man who liked danger and who would be drawn into a romance by the very thing that should have kept him at bay. He might have been beaten by hired ruffians, but he'd taken care to point out that he'd given both men a good fight before he was overpowered.

Where had he been after the match in Ilkeston? The groundsman there had placed him in Derby on the night of the murder and Burns had admitted it freely. What he refused to say was what he was doing there and who might vouch for his whereabouts at a time when Vivian Quayle was being lowered into a grave in Spondon. Colbeck had left Melbourne Hall with many questions unanswered. Burns had been unmoved when it was pointed out that poison similar to that in the herbicide he used had been found in the murder victim. Of the main suspects – Burns, Wigg and Haygarth – the gardener was the one most likely to have committed the crime on his own. The others would probably have used a trusted confederate. As a policeman, Wigg seemed the least likely candidate but Colbeck had arrested a murderous sergeant in his time so he knew that a police uniform was no proof of innocence. Wigg might have had a ready assistant in someone like Jed Hockaday and Haygarth merely had to call on Maurice Hope.

His meditations took him all the way back to the headquarters of the Midland Railway. Colbeck felt that the warm welcome he received from the acting chairman was a trifle forced. Haygarth pressed for details. When he heard that Colbeck had made a return visit to Melbourne Hall, he wondered why the inspector had not arrested Gerard Burns on the spot.

'I had insufficient evidence, sir,' explained Colbeck.

'You had him lying about where he was on the night of the murder and you discovered that he uses a weedkiller which contains a poison found in the victim's body. What else do you need?'

'Mr Burns didn't lie to me. He merely withheld the truth and that's a slightly different thing. As for the herbicide, he's not the only gardener who uses it.'

'But you just told me that it came from Germany. How many people would even know that such a product existed?'

'Good horticulturalists are observant people,' said Colbeck. 'They read articles about developments abroad. Mr Burns is luckier than most in that he's encouraged to keep abreast of the latest news.'

'I think you've got enough to put him behind bars.'

'Then you have an inadequate grasp of the law.'

'I don't think so. On the evidence we have – including his hatred of Vivian Quayle – a clever barrister could send him off for a rendezvous with the hangman.'

'I dispute that,' said Colbeck, firmly, 'and I speak as a former barrister. When you prosecute an innocent man, it can be embarrassing and not without consequences. To begin with, the police can be sued for wrongful arrest. Before you go to court, you must ensure that you have watertight evidence of guilt.'

'But you have it, Inspector. Burns is the obvious killer.'

'The burden of proof still lies with us.'

'Arrest him now before he makes a run for it.'

'Where would he go, sir?' asked Colbeck. 'Burns has a wife and a child on the way. It's one of the factors that I deem important. He loves his job. Would he risk losing everything by committing a murder?'

'Yes,' asserted Haygarth, 'if he could get away with it.'

'Most killers suffer from that delusion.'

The remark produced a long, heavy silence. Haygarth pretended to look for something on his desk then opened a drawer to continue the search. He slammed it shut in annoyance.

'There was something I wanted to show you,' he said, 'but I can't find it.'

'Give it to me another time, sir.'

'It was the list of the new locomotives being built for the Midland. I thought you might be interested in it.' He looked up. 'And you still haven't visited the Works, have you? Cope is ready to show you round.'

'Thank you.'

Colbeck knew that he was just trying to change the subject. In an office as tidy as his, Haygarth would know exactly where everything was. He'd instituted the false search because he'd been knocked off balance. Colbeck exploited the weakness.

'Is it true that you haven't been to Spondon for decades, sir?'

'Yes, it is. I told you so.'

'Then you must have a twin, Mr Haygarth. I have reliable reports that someone looking remarkably like you attended the funeral of Mrs Peet.' He gave a quizzical smile. 'Have you any idea who that might have been?'

CHAPTER SIXTEEN

The situation was intolerable. They both felt that. Lydia Quayle and Beatrice Myler still had their meals together but they were ordeals rather than occasions for pleasure. They were conducted largely in silence and what conversation they did manage was brief and brittle. Blaming herself for what had happened, Lydia kept more and more to her room, the one place in the house where she didn't feel that she was intruding. Beatrice, too, often sought privacy. Yet even though they were physically apart, they felt each other's presence keenly. When they did move about the house, it was as if they were walking on eggshells, each afraid that she might accidentally bump into the other. Mutual love and understanding had perished.

Unable to stand it any longer, Lydia came to a decision. When she found her friend in the drawing room, she tried to sound as pleasant as possible.

'I think that we need some time apart, Beatrice,' she said.

'Yes, I've been thinking the same thing. Where will you go?'

'I don't know.'

'Oh, I fancy that you do, Lydia.'

'Truly, I don't.'

'You want to go *there*, don't you?' said Beatrice, accusation hanging on the air. 'In spite of everything you promised, you intend to go home.'

'That's not the case at all. I simply . . . don't want to be in the way.'

Beatrice made no reply. Lowering her eyes, she sat in silence. The tension between them was almost tangible. For several minutes, they wrestled with words that refused to come out of their mouths. It was only when Lydia was about to move off that her friend recovered her voice.

'How long will you be away?'

'How long do you *want* me to be away?'

'I'm not sure.'

'But you'd value a break from me, is that it?'

'We'd both profit, Lydia.'

It was gone. The ability that each of them had had to read the other's mind had vanished. They were like strangers, meeting for the first time, unable to get beyond a surface politeness, bereft of any affection. Lydia suddenly noticed what a plain and unbecoming woman she was and, by the same token, Beatrice was struck by the fact that there was so little about her companion to interest her. Neither would believe that they had lived together so agreeably.

'Are you still reading that book about Venice?' asked Lydia.

'Yes, I am.'

'And you still want to go there again?'

'I need a holiday.'

'Would you need one if I wasn't here?'

Mildly put, the question had explosive power. Beatrice recoiled.

'I didn't say that, Lydia.'

'Would you?'

'I haven't thought about it.'

'I'll wager that you've thought about nothing else.'

'All right,' conceded the other, 'it has crossed my mind.'

'In other words,' said Lydia, grasping the nettle and speaking more forcefully, 'you'd be better off without me.'

'I might be.'

'Why can't you be honest about it?'

'Why can't you be honest about your plan to go home?'

'I don't *have* a plan.'

'Yes, you do, I can see it in your face. It's been fomenting in your mind ever since Sergeant Leeming and that woman came here. Their visit changed your attitude towards your family somehow.'

It was true and Lydia was unable to deny it. Her conversation with Madeleine Colbeck had altered her perception of the world she'd left behind in Nottingham. While she didn't feel a strong urge to return, she did view her family with less bitterness than hitherto. Attuned to her moods, Beatrice had been aware of it at once.

'They ruined everything,' she said, abruptly. 'Until they came here – until that vile man and that interfering woman arrived – we'd always enjoyed peace and contentment, but not any more.'

'You can't blame the sergeant and Mrs Colbeck. They're trying to solve a murder and must take whatever steps are necessary.'

Beatrice spoke with coldness. 'That's the other thing.'

'What is?'

'Most people in my position would find it intolerable,' she said, giving full vent to her anger. 'When you came to London, you drifted from one hotel to another. I offered you a place of sanctuary and you brought murder into my house. Yes, I know,' she went on, quelling Lydia's protest, 'it wasn't *your* fault that your

227

father was killed. That's not the point. The simple fact is that you are inescapably linked to a heinous crime. Some people would find that highly embarrassing in a lodger yet I was ready to accept it and to support you through a difficult period. In the name of friendship, I did everything humanly possible to offer you succour. When I did that, of course, I was unaware that you'd started a correspondence with your brother.'

Full of pain and recrimination, the words poured out of her but Lydia heard only one of them. It was enough to wound her deeply. Beatrice had described her as a 'lodger'. The older woman had invited her to move in as a dear friend yet Lydia's status was now that of someone who merely rented a room.

'I'll leave immediately,' said Lydia.

When they met at the hotel, they had a lot of information to exchange. Colbeck told him about the second visit to Melbourne and about his clash with Donald Haygarth. The acting chairman had shrugged off his question about the funeral.

'He claimed that it did not constitute a proper visit to Spondon because he was so preoccupied with the service that he saw nothing of the village.'

'Why was he there in the first place?' asked Leeming.

'It turns out that he's a friend of Mr Peet and went out of courtesy.'

'Mr Haygarth could have told us that before.'

'I think that there are lots of things he could have told us, Victor. One by one, I suspect, we'll go on finding them. But what do you have to report? Did you follow Hockaday to Duffield?'

'He didn't go there, Inspector.'

Leeming explained what had happened and how he had met an old man who confided that he was Jed Hockaday's father. Where the cobbler had gone, he didn't know because Hockaday had given the sergeant the slip.

'Not necessarily,' said Colbeck. 'He may not even have known that you were following him. You've always been adept at shadowing people.'

'I felt cheated, sir. He shook me off.'

'Then he's cleverer than we gave him credit. On the night of the murder, he was in Duffield, as he told us, but he only called on Mr and Mrs Verney at the end of the evening. Where had Hockaday been beforehand?'

'I'll tackle him about that.'

'What else have you discovered, Victor?'

'Oh, I had a surprise, sir,' said Leeming. 'Stanley Quayle came here to see you. He wasn't very pleased to deal with me instead but we had an interesting talk. That was the surprise. He may have looked down his nose at me but he's not the ogre you took him for when you first met him.'

After listening to an account of the conversation between the two men, Colbeck was sorry to have missed Stanley Quayle. Some valuable information had been gleaned and the most telling fact concerned the murder victim's whereabouts in the hours leading up to his death.

'His appointments diary was stolen by the killer,' decided Colbeck, 'because it would have told us where he would have been.'

'His elder son didn't know, sir. His father was always away somewhere on business, he said. Stanley Quayle and his brother were working at one of their pits. They assumed that their father would have been involved with the Midland Railway.'

'Yet neither Haygarth nor Cope saw him that day.'

'That's what they claim.'

'The appointments diary was probably kept in the office where the self-appointed acting chairman now sits so he could have been in the best position to take possession of it.'

'The finger points at Haygarth once again.'

'That doesn't mean we forget the other suspects,' warned Colbeck. 'Did Stanley Quayle admit that his father had particular enemies this time?'

'Yes,' said Leeming, 'but he added no new names to the list and he missed out Superintendent Wigg. When I mentioned him, Mr Quayle had a long think then said that we should keep the superintendent in mind. Talking of which . . .'

'Don't worry, Victor. I sent another report to Superintendent Tallis. He would have got it today, after you'd left London. I gave the impression that I'd made slightly more progress than I actually had while you were away but it should be enough to pacify him. Our superintendent is like a caged tiger,' said Colbeck with a nostalgic smile. 'The only way to stifle his roar is to feed the beast on a regular basis.'

Edward Tallis returned to his office after a testing interview with the commissioner. While he exercised power over his officers, he was answerable to Sir Richard Mayne, the man who'd run the Metropolitan Police Force since the death of the other joint founding commissioner four years earlier. Though Tallis and Mayne had a mutual respect for each other, the meeting that day had been highly uncomfortable for the superintendent. He was roundly criticised for his lack of success in the fight against crime. It was only when he reached the safety of his office, and was smoking a consolatory cigar, that he realised why the commissioner had been in such a bad mood. The satirical magazine, *Punch*, had somehow got hold of Mayne's standing orders to uniformed policemen and made much of the fact that the commissioner had decreed that, however inclement the weather, his men were not to carry umbrellas. Mayne was lampooned mercilessly. Having himself been ridiculed in cartoons, Tallis had some sympathy for the commissioner but it didn't lessen the sting of the barbs directed at him. The superintendent wanted to pass on the pain.

As he looked at the pile of documents on his desk, he saw that the latest letter from Colbeck was at the very top. Tallis read through it again. It was a model of how a report should be delivered. Written in a neat hand, it was literate, well organised and informative. No other detective at Scotland Yard could have sent such a crisp yet apparently comprehensive account of an investigation. At a first reading, it had been very satisfying. But the superintendent knew Robert Colbeck of old. The inspector could use words to beguile and distract. When he looked at the report again, Tallis read between the lines before slapping it down on the desk and drawing on his cigar. After he'd exhaled a veritable cloud of smoke, he spoke aloud.

'What are you up to this time, Colbeck?'

Much as he liked to see his daughter, Caleb Andrews rationed his visits carefully, mindful of the fact that Madeleine needed time to work on her paintings. For the most part, therefore, he called on her by prior arrangement so as not to interrupt her time at the easel. When he came to the house that day, he knew that she'd finished her daily stint and would give him a welcome. Over a cup of tea, he told her about the visits he'd made to other retired railwaymen and how they'd all agreed that the standard of driving a locomotive had fallen since they'd ceased to occupy a footplate. Madeleine listened to it all with an amused tolerance.

'Is there any word from Robert?' he asked.

'Yes, I had a letter from him yesterday.'

'What's the latest news about the case?'

'He said very little about that,' replied Madeleine, trying to guide him off the subject. 'He's still collecting evidence.'

'Did you pass on my offer of help, Maddy?'

'Robert knows that you're always standing by.'

'Why hasn't he sent more details? I need something to work on.'

'Let him do his job, Father,' she advised.

In fact, the letter she'd received from Colbeck that morning had been full of details about the case but Madeleine didn't wish to divulge any of it to her father. She would certainly never admit that Victor Leeming had recruited her help and that she'd been directly involved in the inquiry. Powered by envy, her father would pester her for every morsel of information. Instead, therefore, she talked about the locomotive that she was currently putting onto canvas. Since it belonged to his beloved LNWR, he waxed lyrical about its features and asked to see it. Madeleine told him to wait, preferring to show him a finished painting.

'Why do you never put *me* on the footplate?' he asked, tetchily.

'I never put any figures in my paintings.'

'Are you ashamed of your old father?'

'No,' she replied, squeezing his arm, 'I'm proud of what you did as an engine driver. But when you're an artist, you have to do what you do best and keep away from things you're not good at. I'm not a figurative artist.'

'You're the best artist I've ever seen, Maddy.'

'You wouldn't say that if you'd seen some of the figures I've tried to paint. I'm much safer with locomotives and rolling stock. Somehow I just can't make people look *real* on canvas.'

'You could make me look real.'

'I've tried to put you in a painting many times, Father, but it never works.'

'Is that my fault or yours?'

'It's mine,' she confessed. 'That's why I stick to what I *can* do.'

'But you can do anything if you really try,' he argued. 'You're like me, Maddy. I worked on the railway but I also found that I had a gift for solving crimes so I developed that gift.'

Madeleine had to suppress a smile. She heard the doorbell ring and, since she was not expecting a visitor, wondered whom it could be. Moments later, a servant came into the room to say that a lady had asked to see her but would not give her name. Madeleine excused herself and went into the hall. When she saw who her visitor was, she was grateful that her name had not been divulged in her father's hearing.

Lydia Quayle was standing there.

Victor Leeming was delighted to see him again. Apart from the landlord at the Malt Shovel, the reporter was the only person he'd befriended in Spondon. The vicar had been helpful to him but it was Philip Conway with whom the sergeant had formed any sort of bond. Since he was staying at the hotel at the Midland Railway's expense, Leeming had no compunction about putting the cost of two more drinks on the bill. He and Conway found seats in the lounge. After giving the sergeant an attenuated account of his day, the reporter told him about the friction he'd experienced with Jed Hockaday.

'Yes,' said Leeming, 'it was the cobbler who caused *me* a headache as well.'

'I thought he was going to assault me.'

'Did he actually hit you?'

'No, but he certainly wanted to. Hockaday was angry because I told you things about him. He warned me to keep my mouth shut. But what happened to you?' asked Conway. 'When we saw him walk past the Malt Shovel, you went after him.'

'I tried to, anyway.'

Leeming repeated the story he'd told Colbeck but it had a deliberate omission. There was no reference to the fact that Seth Verney claimed to be the cobbler's father. While he was a friend, Conway was not a detective who could be trusted with every item of interest that was unearthed. In the light of Hockaday's threat to the reporter, Leeming didn't want him to confront the cobbler about his parentage. It was a treat that the sergeant was reserving for himself.

'If he didn't go to Duffield,' said Conway, 'where did he go?'

'It must have been somewhere farther up the line. On the other hand,' said Leeming, 'he might simply have got off at the next station and caught the first train back to Spondon. I still think he must've spotted me. Hockaday is cunning.'

'He's cunning and dangerous, Sergeant.'

'I just wish I knew where he went earlier on. Anyway, I came back here and was amazed to find Stanley Quayle keen to help us.'

'And so he should. His father was the murder victim, after all.'

'He was dressed from head to foot in black but he didn't really seem to be in mourning. Most people who are bereaved are quiet and withdrawn. He talked down to me as if I was one of his miners.'

'I've heard that he likes to crack the whip.'

'This is only my opinion, mind you,' said Leeming, thoughtfully, 'but he was less interested in his father's actual death than he was in the fact that it's made him head of the family. Stanley Quayle loves power.'

'Like father, like son.'

'He thinks the killer is a choice between Mr Haygarth and

Gerard Burns. At least, that was until I put another name into his head.'

'And who was that?'

'Superintendent Wigg.'

'Oh, yes,' recalled Conway, 'the inspector asked me about him. I explained why he was no friend of Vivian Quayle. You must know the story.'

'I do. What else can you tell me about the superintendent?'

'He keeps the streets of Derby fairly safe. I have to admit that.'

'What about his private life?'

Conway became defensive. 'I don't know much about that,' he said. 'He's a married man but I've no idea what his interests are or, indeed, if he has any. Running the police force is a full-time job. He doesn't have time for anything else.'

'I can sympathise with him there,' said Leeming, soulfully. 'You're never really off duty in the police.'

There was a long pause. He couldn't understand why the reporter was being so reticent. On any other subject, Conway was a mine of information. Reading the question in Leeming's eyes, the other man explained.

'The superintendent is very close to my editor,' he said. 'They dine together sometimes. It means that the *Mercury* gets the first whiff of any crime but it also means that none of us is allowed to look too closely at Elijah Wigg. In a town like this, he's untouchable.'

'If he's involved in the murder,' said Leeming, 'we'll certainly touch him.'

'But you'll have a job finding any evidence.'

'We like a challenge.'

'Wigg is a freak,' said Conway. 'He loves to be seen abroad in Derby but he remains invisible somehow. Nobody has really got the measure of him, not even my editor. Isn't that strange?'

'There must be *something* you can tell me.'

Conway needed a meditative sip of his drink before he recalled something.

'Superintendent Wigg has a brother in Belper.'

'So?'

'He's a pharmacist.'

Madeleine Colbeck hated having to lie to her father but there was no alternative. Having ushered her visitor to another room, she returned to Andrews and told him that the caller had come to the wrong address. She then made a supreme effort to look relaxed and to signal that he could stay as long as he wished. In the event, her father soon began to yawn and decided that it was time to wend his way home. Madeleine saw him off at the door with a kiss then went straight to Colbeck's study. Standing in front of the fireplace, Lydia Quayle was admiring the painting of *Puffing Billy*.

'This has your name on it,' she said in wonderment.

'I always sign my work.'

'So you really *did* paint this?'

'Yes,' said Madeleine. 'My husband was kind enough to take me all the way up to Wylam Colliery in Northumberland so that I could make sketches of it.' She indicated the painting. 'This is the result.'

'It's magnificent,' said Lydia. 'I had no idea you were so talented. But why paint a funny old steam engine. It's so . . .'

'It's so unwomanly?' suggested Madeleine.

'Well, yes, I suppose that's what I mean.'

'Let me take you somewhere more comfortable and I'll explain why I'd rather paint a locomotive than anything else in the world.'

Madeleine conducted her into the drawing room and told her

how her passion for the railways made her want to paint and how Colbeck had encouraged her to develop her talent. Lydia was duly impressed. Madeleine's long recitation had the advantage of taking some of the stress out of her visitor.

It was Lydia's turn to speak now and she did so haltingly.

'You told me that I could come here, if I felt the need to,' she began.

'I was pleased to see you, Miss Quayle. I'm just sorry that you called when my father happened to be here. I hope you didn't mind being locked in my husband's study for so long.'

'No, I loved it. There were even more books than we have. It's a wonderful place to sit and read.'

'Unfortunately, he has very little time to do that.'

'Beatrice and I read all the time.'

Her face clouded as she realised that she should have spoken in the past tense. The long hours of reading were behind her and the library she'd shared so pleasurably was now out of her reach. Lydia manufactured a smile of apology.

'I'm so sorry for troubling you like this, Mrs Colbeck.'

'You're most welcome, I do assure you.'

'I wish I could say that I've remembered something that might be of help to your husband, but it's not so. I came here for another reason.'

'Whatever it was,' said Madeleine, 'you are still welcome.'

She could see the change in Lydia Quayle. When they'd met before, it had been in a house where Lydia had seemed to belong and to enjoy a cosy, cultured, leisurely way of life with a close friend. That sense of a settled existence had now faded. Lydia had somehow been cut adrift. It was not Madeleine's place to ask why. She simply wished to offer what help she could to her visitor.

'You've awakened something in me, Mrs Colbeck,' said Lydia.

'It's a feeling of guilt, I suppose. You reminded me that I had a family.'

'Did you need reminding? News of your father's murder was in all the newspapers. You were well aware of it when we called on you.'

'I was aware of it but determined not to respond to it. You'll probably find that rather heartless of me.'

'I make no judgement, Miss Quayle. I fully understand why there was a rift between you and your father. My situation is different,' said Madeleine. 'If I learnt that my father had cut himself shaving, I'd rush off to be with him.'

'What if he'd stopped you marrying the man you loved?' asked Lydia. 'My guess is that you'd never forgive him.'

'You're probably right.'

'It's my mother who worries me, you see. You stirred up my guilt about her. This will probably kill Mother. Before that happens, I'd like to make my peace with her.' There was a pleading note. 'Do you think I should?'

'I can't make that decision for you, Miss Quayle.'

'What would you do?'

'If it was at all possible,' said Madeleine, 'I'd try to heal any wounds.'

'That's what I needed you to say.'

'Why come to me? Miss Myler would have given the same advice, surely.' Lydia's head drooped. 'Oh, I see. We obviously caused problems, coming to your house as we did.'

'It's not *my* house, Mrs Colbeck.'

'But you were so at home there.'

'Yes,' said Lydia with a pale smile. 'I was, wasn't I?' She looked around the room. 'Do you have children, Mrs Colbeck?'

'No, we don't – not as yet.'

'This would be a nice house in which to raise a family and that's what will probably happen one day. I made the decision *not* to have children and, in many ways, it was a momentous one.'

'I agree.'

'If they couldn't be fathered by Gerard . . . by the man I told you about, then I had no interest in motherhood. That may sound odd to you. Being a spinster must seem a dull, arid, unfilled sort of life but it's not. There are rewards that I never dreamt of and I've never regretted my decision to remain single.'

'Each of us finds happiness in a different way, Miss Quayle.'

'*You* still have it – I don't.' Lydia reached out to grasp her by the wrist. 'I can't face going back there alone, Mrs Colbeck,' she admitted. 'I need to ask a big favour of you. Will you come with me?'

Concern over Harriet Quayle's health had steadily increased. The doctor was honest. He was unable to guarantee that she would survive for long. Agnes sat beside the bed and, during her mother's more alert moments, read to her from a poetry anthology. Her brothers paid regular visits to the bedroom, as did their respective wives, but the constant coming and going put even more strain on the patient. The whole family came to accept that one funeral might soon be followed by another.

To give his sister some respite, Lucas Quayle offered to take over the vigil on his own. His mother seemed to be asleep so all that he had to do was to sit there and leaf through the poems, pausing at one that he'd been taught to memorise as a child.

'Is that you, Lucas?' murmured Harriet, eyelids fluttering weakly.

'Yes, Mother,' he said, closing the book.

'Where is everybody?'

'Do you want me to call them?'

'No, no, it's peaceful in here. Too many people fluster me.'

'How are you feeling?'

'I'm still here,' she said with a quiet defiance. 'What's happening?'

'We're carrying on as best we can.'

'I'm not talking about you. What's happening with . . . the investigation?'

'Inspector Colbeck is still making enquiries, Mother.'

'Has he asked to see me?'

'No, no,' said her son, 'he understands that you are . . . not in the best of health. I've spoken at length to him and Stanley went to Derby to see him. The inspector was not there so Stanley talked to Sergeant Leeming instead.'

'What have these detectives found out?'

'All that they've managed to do so far is to identify some suspects. But I have faith in the inspector. He's a very experienced man.'

'Does he think he'll ever find out the truth?'

'Yes, he does, Mother. But you shouldn't be worrying about that. Remember the doctor's advice. Try to get as much sleep as possible and keep your mind off any unpleasantness. That's difficult in a house of mourning, I grant you, but it's best if you don't concern yourself with the murder inquiry.' He saw his mother gasp as if she'd felt a stab of pain. 'Are you all right?'

'It was that word, Lucas – murder. It's so sudden and final. If someone is ailing, you have time to prepare for the worst. The blow is not so painful. When someone is killed abruptly, however . . . well, you know what I'm trying to say.'

'I do, Mother.'

She put a hand into his palm. 'Will you do something for me, please?'

'You only have to ask.'

'I know that you've been in touch with Lydia. Write to her again,' said Harriet softly. 'I'd like to see her before I die.'

It was a balmy evening as they walked along St Peter's Street in Derby and glanced in the windows of the shops. They passed an ironmonger, a glove-maker, a family draper, a baker, a grocer and many other tradesmen. Victor Leeming was reminded of a street near his own house in London.

'The only difference is that it's much noisier there,' he said, 'and there's far more traffic. Then, of course, there's the stink.'

'Every major city has its individual flavour,' said Colbeck, drily. 'London's happens to be the worst.'

'I'd still rather be there than here, sir.'

'Our return is easily achieved, Victor. We simply have to solve a murder.'

'This one may take ages. I don't know where to look next.'

'Well, my suggestion is that you might start in Belper. Your chat with Philip Conway may have given us a useful clue. If Superintendent Wigg's brother is a pharmacist there, he might be the source of some of the poison that killed Mr Quayle.'

'But he'd never admit it, surely,' said Leeming.

'Why not?'

'He'd want to protect his brother.'

'That would make him an accessory before the fact,' said Colbeck, 'and I don't believe for a moment that Wigg would ask for something able to kill a human being. Poisons can be bought for other reasons. If he *did* purchase some – and we have no proof that he did – the superintendent would have palmed his brother off with a plausible excuse.'

'I'll go to Belper first thing in the morning,' decided Leeming.

'After that, I'd like to see what a certain cobbler has to say about his train journey today.' He looked at Colbeck. 'What about you, sir?'

'I'm going to pay a second visit to the victim's house.'

'Is that wise? We were more or less kicked out last time.'

'Lucas Quayle came to see me of his own volition and his brother has obviously mellowed if he went out of his way to make contact with us. Neither, alas,' said Colbeck, 'was able to give us any indication as to where their father was on the day of the murder but I'm hoping to find someone who can. After that,' he went on, 'I am giving myself a treat.'

'Are you going back to London to see Mrs Colbeck?'

'That's not a treat, Victor, it's a positive luxury and hopelessly beyond my reach at the moment. No, I'm going to have a tour of the Derby Works.'

Leeming was shocked. 'You're going to look at *engines*?'

'I want to see the whole production process.'

'What's that got to do with a murder case?'

'It may have more relevance than you think,' said Colbeck. 'While you were talking to that young reporter, I had a word with Mr Cope about visiting the Works. He was only too glad to arrange it and to accompany me. In other words . . .'

'He wants to keep an eye on you and report back to Mr Haygarth.'

'Maurice Cope is his spymaster. He seemed to know exactly what we've been doing since we got here. It's one of the reasons I suggested a walk before dinner. At least we can talk freely out here in the street without fear of being overheard.'

'Do you think they've had someone following us?'

'Cope is getting his information somehow, Victor.'

'I'd better start looking over my shoulder.'

They strolled on companionably in silence until the Royal

Hotel eventually came into view. When they saw a sturdy figure standing outside the main entrance and paying a cab driver, Leeming gave a short laugh.

'What's the trouble, Victor?'

'For one horrible moment, I thought that man was Superintendent Tallis.'

'Your eyes did not deceive you,' said Colbeck, easily. 'It *is* him. I had a feeling that he'd turn up sooner or later because my reports weren't able to disguise the fact that we've made no significant advances in this investigation. He'll be able to join us for dinner.'

'I won't be able to eat a thing with the superintendent there.'

'His presence won't hamper my digestion in the least. Strangely enough – and don't ask me to explain this – I'm rather pleased to see him.'

CHAPTER SEVENTEEN

Female company was something that Madeleine Colbeck had learnt to do without. There were maidservants and a cook in the house but that was not the same as having a woman with whom she could talk on equal terms. Though her aunt paid occasional visits, the age gap between them inevitably steered the conversation in set directions. Being an artist meant that Madeleine had of necessity to spend a great deal of time on her own and she relished that solitude. It was only when she was not at work that she felt lonely. Now that she had a guest of her own age, she realised how much she had been missing.

'It was so kind of you to offer me accommodation,' said Lydia Quayle. 'I'd expected to stay at a hotel.'

'You're very welcome here.'

'Thank you, Mrs Colbeck.'

'It's a pleasure, Miss Quayle.' Madeleine laughed. 'This is ridiculous,' she said. 'If we're going to have dinner together, I think we can dispense with the formalities, don't you? Please use my Christian name.'

'And you must do the same, Madeleine.'

'I will, Lydia.'

It was a step forward and each of them appreciated it. Madeleine had not merely invited her to stay out of kindness. She wanted her visitor to have time to consider her decision to return home in the certain knowledge that there would be some domestic upheaval as a result. Lydia had been ready to set off there and then but she was persuaded to postpone the journey to Nottingham until the following day. It gave them the opportunity to get to know each other better.

'Why didn't you give your name when you called here?' asked Madeleine.

'I wasn't sure that you'd wish to see me.'

'But I volunteered my address.'

'You did that out of kindness,' said Lydia. 'I wasn't certain that you'd really want me to come here with my tale of woe. Because I didn't give my name, I knew I'd at least get to see you. Curiosity would have brought you out.'

'It did. I was puzzled.'

They were in the drawing room, awaiting the summons to dine. Lydia was relieved and reassured. In coming to the house, she'd not only found someone who'd accompany her to Nottingham, she'd made a real friend. Something else struck her. Alone with Madeleine, she was able to act and feel her own age. Looking back, she saw that life with Beatrice Myler had put unlived years on her. Lydia had dressed, thought and behaved as an older woman. Maturity had been a comforting shell into which she'd willingly climbed. Now, however, the comfort came from being with someone who made her feel younger and more alive.

'I didn't realise that the police employed women,' she said.

'They don't,' said Madeleine, 'and you must never tell anyone that I came to see you. Scotland Yard would never dream of letting women become detectives. I've only been involved because my husband believes that I have something to offer that neither he nor Sergeant Leeming possesses.'

'It's true. I could never have talked as openly to the sergeant as I have to you.'

'I take that as a compliment.'

'I trusted you, Madeleine.'

'Then I hope I can repay that trust,' said Madeleine. 'On one issue, I'm afraid, I have to disappoint you. I won't be able to go to your home. I'm happy to accompany you to Nottingham to lend some moral support but, if I'm introduced to your family as Inspector Colbeck's wife, it could well compromise the whole investigation.'

'I don't wish to get you or the inspector into any trouble.'

'Thank you, Lydia.'

'Would your husband lose his job as a result?'

'Oh, I don't think they'd be foolish enough to dismiss him altogether. He's far too valuable a detective to cast aside. But there would be a lot of embarrassment and he might even be demoted.'

'I don't want that to happen,' said Lydia, worriedly.

'Neither do I. As it happens, I have been in a position to help with certain investigations in the past but that fact has had to be suppressed. Superintendent Tallis takes a dim view of women altogether,' said Madeleine. 'If he knew that my husband had actually dared to call on my services, the superintendent would roast him alive.'

Edward Tallis surprised them both. Instead of descending on them in a fit of wrath, he'd come, in the spirit of enquiry, to find out exactly what was going on. His manner was calm and his tongue lacking its usual asperity. Colbeck and Leeming could not remember the last time he'd been in such a quiescent mood. Neither of them realised that, in coming to Derby, he'd been escaping from London and from the scorn of the commissioner. At the bookstall in King's Cross railway station, Tallis had taken the trouble to buy a copy of the offending edition of *Punch* and he'd chuckled at the way his superior had been pilloried, his amusement edged with relief that he hadn't been the target this time.

Instead of being unable to touch his food, Leeming ate heartily and left the senior officers to do most of the talking. All three of them found the lamb and mint sauce to their taste. Tallis dabbed at his mouth with a napkin to remove the specks of gravy from his moustache.

'How would you summarise this case, Colbeck?'

'I'd do so in two words, sir.'

'And what might they be?'

'Confusion and error,' muttered Leeming.

Colbeck smiled. 'We've encountered both since we've been here,' he agreed, 'but I had two different words in mind – coal and silk.'

'Explain,' said Tallis.

'The products define the battle for the chairmanship of the Midland Railway, sir. Mr Quayle made his fortune out of coal while Mr Haygarth lives in luxury on the profits of his silk mills. Coal is hard while silk is soft. In some ways,' argued Colbeck, 'they help to characterise the two men. We never knew Mr Quayle but we met his elder son who's been likened to him in every way.' He turned to Leeming. 'How would you describe Stanley Quayle?'

'Cold and hard.'

'Just like a piece of coal. What about Mr Haygarth?'

'Smooth and snake-like.'

'Just like a bolster of silk.'

'I'm trying hard to follow your reasoning,' complained Tallis.

'It's quite simple, sir,' said Colbeck. 'The one has ousted the other. From what we can gather, Mr Quayle was a natural leader, respected, strong-willed and resilient in the face of the many difficulties that have afflicted this railway company. He's been supplanted by a more subtle, guileful and sinister rival.'

'Are you saying that Mr Haygarth is behind the murder?'

'He's the one who stands to gain most out of it, sir.'

'Then why insist on calling on you to lead the investigation?'

'He wants to gain kudos by appearing to make every effort to solve this crime while confident that a solution is beyond me.'

'I still think that Hockaday had a part in it,' asserted Leeming. 'He's not clever enough to set the whole thing up by himself but he'd be a willing helper if there was money in it. That brings us back to the person best placed to employ the cobbler to do his dirty work for him – Superintendent Wigg.'

'That's a ludicrous suggestion,' said Tallis.

'We've met corrupt policemen before, sir.'

'You hardly need to tell me that, Leeming. I've had to dismiss too many of them. Inspector Alban Kee was an example. I'll have no fraudsters or bribe-takers under my command. Now, I've never met this Superintendent Wigg,' he went on, 'but I find it hard to believe that anyone in his position would condone – let alone, incite – murder. Haygarth stands to gain from the death but Wigg was bound to lose. He'd merely be replacing one person he loathed by another. What's the point of that?'

'The superintendent's brother is a pharmacist, sir,' Leeming reminded him.

'That's an irrelevance.'

'I don't think so.'

'Then you must learn to focus your mind, Sergeant.'

Tallis went on to give a searching analysis of the evidence so far gathered and showed that he'd been listening very carefully. While conceding that Haygarth had to be a major suspect, his instinct was that a much younger man was involved.

'Gerard Burns is the most likely killer,' he concluded.

'I thought that until I met him,' said Colbeck.

'What changed your mind?'

'I tried to look at him from the point of view of his employers, sir. He was well paid and given an important job by Mr Quayle. Burns clearly did it very well. It was only when he strayed away from it that the trouble started.'

'He suffered physical injury on Quayle's orders. An urge for revenge must still burn inside him.'

'It does, Superintendent, and he won't gainsay that. But think of the man who indirectly pays his wages now. Every servant and gardener at Melbourne Hall would have been subjected to rigorous scrutiny before they were taken on. Rare as his visits to Derbyshire are, the prime minister would not want potential killers among his staff. In essence,' said Colbeck, 'Burns is an excellent gardener so committed to his trade that he doesn't have the time or the inclination to avenge an old slight.'

'It was much more than a slight,' said Tallis. 'My money is on him.'

'We know that Burns was in Derby on the night of the murder,' added Leeming. 'Why won't he tell you where he went?'

'Perhaps I should have a word with him.'

'No, no, sir,' said Colbeck, hastily, 'that would be unwise. If Gerard Burns *is* our man – and I'm not convinced of that – we should leave him alone and let him think he's got away with it. If he really is the killer, we'll amass the evidence that will put a noose around his neck. However, I still think him innocent.'

'You prefer to see him in terms of his work,' said Tallis, 'and choose to forget the scandal he caused at the Quayle household. In my opinion, that's a more accurate reflection of his character. He's sly, deceitful and a practised libertine.'

'What he was drawn into was a genuine romance, sir.'

'Burns has no moral compass.'

'Miss Quayle doesn't believe that, sir,' recalled Leeming. 'She loved him for his good qualities. I told you how well she spoke of him.'

'The fellow was bent on deflowering her.'

An awkward pause ensured. When he realised that he was talking about a gardener, Tallis was embarrassed that he'd chosen that particular word. Colbeck and Leeming traded a glance but said nothing, all too conscious that romance had passed the superintendent by. Tallis neither understood nor approved of relations between the two sexes. If the subject came up, therefore, it was better to let him rehearse his prejudices without challenging them.

'Where do we go from here?' he asked.

'There's a rather tempting dessert menu in front of you,' Colbeck pointed out.

'I'm asking whom you will question tomorrow.'

'Well, I'm going to see that pharmacist in Belper,' said Leeming.

'Save yourself the trouble. Colbeck?'

'I plan to visit the Quayle family again, sir.'

'Good,' said Tallis. 'I'll come with you.'

Colbeck sighed. 'Oh, I wouldn't impose on you, sir.'

'Never spurn the assistance of your superior. Besides, a second opinion is always wise.' He stroked his moustache. 'Now pass that dessert menu and I'll see if it contains anything to tempt my palate.'

* * *

Jed Hockaday was a different man in uniform. He looked bigger, broader and more upright. His swagger became more pronounced. Having finished work at his shop, he'd closed it up, eaten a frugal meal then stepped out into the streets of Spondon as a police constable. His footsteps took him in the direction of the railway station. Long before he reached it, he heard the train that he was supposed to meet arriving with its customary pandemonium. The cobbler soon saw a uniformed figure leaving the station amid a knot of other passengers. He waited until Elijah Wigg reached him.

'I expected you on the station platform,' said Wigg.

'I'm sorry, sir. I was late closing up.'

'Punctuality matters. It's a mark of respect.'

'It won't happen again, Superintendent.'

Wigg fell in beside him and they walked back towards the village.

'What do you have to report?'

'They've found nothing.'

'Are they still burrowing away?'

'Yes,' said Hockaday, 'but it won't do them any good.'

'I hope that's the case, Constable.'

'It is, sir. What I don't see with my own eyes, other people tell me about. They've both been here – Inspector Colbeck and the sergeant – but they don't know where to look.'

'That's good to hear.'

'The real nuisance is that reporter from the *Mercury*.'

'Do you mean Conway?'

'That's him,' said Hockaday with a malevolent smile. 'He's too clever for his own good. Ever since it happened, he's been here like a bloodhound in search of a scent. And he's more likely to find one than the detectives.'

'Has Conway been bothering you?'

'Yes, sir – do you know him?'

'I make it my business to know all the staff on the *Mercury*. Most of them are well-intentioned bumblers but Conway sticks out. Young men with ambitions are always dangerous.'

'He and Sergeant Leeming are becoming good friends.'

'I'm not sure I like the sound of that,' said Wigg, caressing both of his side whiskers simultaneously. 'We don't want them to get too close.'

'No,' said the other, 'Conway is enough of a nuisance as it is.'

'I'll see what I can do. Perhaps I'll have a word with the editor and see if he can move Conway away from Spondon.'

'I tried to frighten him off, Superintendent.'

'Did it work?'

'That's the trouble. I'm not sure.'

They were almost late for their train. As the cab was about to set off, Madeleine Colbeck remembered something she'd forgotten and rushed back into the house. During the long minutes her friend was away, Lydia Quayle was fretting, afraid that their train would go without them and that they'd be forced to wait for a later one. As it was, Madeleine came out with a flurry of apologies, clambered into the cab and asked the driver to take them to King's Cross. In spite of heavy traffic, they got there with plenty of time to spare. Since they shared a first-class compartment with other travellers, the two women found it impossible to have a proper conversation. It was only when their companions got off at Bedford that they were able to talk properly.

'You look uneasy,' said Madeleine.

'I'm very nervous,' admitted Lydia.

'That's understandable.'

'I don't know what sort of a reception I'll get.'

'You know that your younger brother will welcome you and your mother is sure to be pleased that you've come home.'

'It's not my home any longer, Madeleine. I'm going there to make a gesture and not to move in again. That's out of the question.' She smiled gratefully. 'I couldn't do this without you. It's so kind of you to come all the way to Nottingham with me. It would have been much easier for you to stay on this train to Derby where you'd have a chance of seeing your husband.'

'I can do that afterwards, Lydia. We'll change at Kettering and catch the train to Nottingham. It's the least I can do.'

Madeleine was not just prompted by sympathy. At their first encounter, Lydia had given her a privileged insight into the Quayle family and, after her visit home, might be able to furnish other details that had a bearing on the investigation. While acting as a friend, therefore, Madeleine had not entirely shed her role as a detective.

'How long will you stay?' she asked.

'They may not wish me to stay.'

'It's your *home*, Lydia. They'll insist on it.'

'Stanley won't, that's certain, and I don't know how Agnes will react.'

'Blood is thicker than water. You'll all be drawn together.'

Lydia was dubious. 'Will we?'

They were passing through open countryside and they took time off to admire the landscape that was speeding past. The rural serenity was a sharp contrast to the tumult of the capital with its urban sprawl and constant smoke. Lydia had grown up in such surroundings but Madeleine could only yearn for them.

'What will you do afterwards?' she asked.

'Well, I hope to see *you* at some stage, Madeleine.'

'I'll be staying at the Royal Hotel – if my husband permits that, of course.'

'He's hardly likely to turn you away,' said Lydia with a laugh. 'Judging by what you've told me about him, I'd say that he'd be thrilled to see you.'

'And your family will be equally thrilled to see *you*.'

Lydia grimaced. 'I've no illusions on that score.'

'You reached out to them – that's the main thing.'

'I could only do that when I knew that my father was dead.'

Madeleine wanted to ask her about her plans for the future but felt that it would be too intrusive. Lydia was in a fragile state. While she was prepared to talk about her family, she'd said almost nothing about the woman with whom she'd been living. Madeleine recalled how Beatrice Myler had done her best to send her and Victor Leeming on their way when they called, and how resentful she'd been when they were invited into the house by Lydia. There must have been tension in the wake of their departure. Madeleine wondered if and how it had been resolved.

It was almost as if Lydia could hear the question that her friend was posing.

'The answer is that I don't know, Madeleine,' she said.

'You don't know what?'

'The situation in London became increasingly difficult. I had to leave.'

'But you haven't left for good, surely?'

'I may have done.'

'I thought you'd be going back eventually to Miss Myler's house.'

'Beatrice may not want me there.'

'Oh, I'm sorry . . .'

'I'm an orphan,' said Lydia. 'I'm travelling between two homes that each may rebuff me in turn. My family may well find that what I did in walking out was unforgivable and Beatrice is entitled to feel the same. I'm just a poor orphan, Madeleine. I don't belong anywhere.'

Robert Colbeck opted for the lesser of two evils. Determined to keep Edward Tallis away from the Quayle family, he agreed that the superintendent could instead confront Gerard Burns. It would keep him out of the way and give him the feeling that he was helping in the investigation. It might also make him less certain that Burns was the killer. Had he accompanied Colbeck, he would have been a real hindrance. Tallis had intervened before and not always with beneficial effect. In the previous year, he'd insisted on being involved in a case of abduction and got in Colbeck's way. On another occasion, he'd thrust himself into a murder investigation in Exeter and been injured in the process. His most troublesome intervention had been in a case involving the death of an old army friend in Yorkshire. Because his emotions had got the better of him, Tallis had been a severe handicap and it was only when he'd been persuaded to return to London that Colbeck and Leeming had been able to solve what turned out to be a complex crime.

Arriving on his own at the Quayle residence, Colbeck was able to have a free hand. For the first time, he met the brothers together. Lucas was pleased to see him but Stanley was more reserved. After an exchange of niceties, Colbeck gave them a brief account of the progress of the investigation.

'When will you make an arrest?' demanded Stanley.

'When we have sufficient evidence, sir,' replied Colbeck.

'You must have *some* idea who the villain is.'

'As the sergeant explained to you, we have more than one suspect.'

'Haygarth is behind it somehow,' decided Lucas.

'It's either him or Burns,' said his brother. 'Have you considered that the two of them may have been acting together, Inspector?'

'We've considered every permutation, sir,' replied Colbeck. 'The one you've suggested is the least likely. The only connection between the two individuals is that Mr Haygarth once tried to coax Mr Burns away from you.'

'They're two of a kind.'

'I fail to see any likeness. They come from the opposing worlds of masters and servants. Mr Haygarth is an entrepreneur with soaring aspirations while the other man has secured what is for him the perfect post.'

'Except that he can't play cricket for this county any more,' said Lucas, sadly.

'He's bound to regret that.'

Stanley was irritated. 'Let's not talk about that despicable man,' he said, peevishly. 'We're well rid of him. I want to know why it is taking you so infernally long to gather evidence.'

'The killer left no discernible trail, sir.'

'Have you come all the way from Derby to tell us that?'

'No,' said Colbeck, 'I came to ask you a favour.'

'If we can be of any assistance,' said Lucas, helpfully, 'we will.'

'That depends what you want,' added Stanley. 'We can't have you poking around here at a time like this. I'm sure you understand that.'

'I do, sir.'

'So what is it that you're after?'

'I need permission to speak to your coachman.' The brothers were baffled. 'I assume that he used to drive your father to and from the station on a regular basis. Who, therefore, is in a better position to tell me about his movements?'

'Cleary can't help you,' said Stanley.

'You never know,' argued Lucas.

'I've spoken to him myself. He has no idea where Father was going on the day of the murder. Talking to him would be pointless.'

'Nevertheless,' said Colbeck, 'I'd value a word with him.'

'I have no objection,' said Lucas. 'Stanley?'

'Is it really necessary?' asked his brother.

'It's what brought me here, sir. You're welcome to be present, of course, and that goes for both of you. Well?' asked Colbeck. 'Do I have your permission?'

Leeming's rooted dislike of train journeys was intensified by the fact that he had to share a compartment with a garrulous farmer whose clothing gave off such powerful agricultural vapours that the sergeant had a fit of coughing. Fortunately, the man gave him no opportunity to speak and that was a blessing because Leeming found his broad Derbyshire dialect almost impenetrable. What he did gather was that the major landowners were the Strutt family, who owned the local cotton mills, and that they'd complained about the projected railway line so strongly that its direction was radically altered. Leeming could see through the window that the construction must have been a highly expensive process because the train passed through a long, deep cutting and passed no less than eleven bridges within a mile. The Strutt family, he suspected, would not have been popular with the North Midland Railway, as it was at the time.

Glad to escape the stench of the soil and the interminable lecture in a foreign language, Leeming made his way towards the centre of Belper. It didn't take him long to find the shop owned by Reuben Wigg. When he stepped into it, he was greeted by a blend of bewitching aromas. Superintendent Wigg and his brother bore little resemblance to each other. While the policeman was hirsute, the pharmacist was singularly lacking in hair. Bald-headed and clean-shaven, Reuben Wigg wore a white coat and an expression of severe disapproval. His brother had patently monopolised all of the arrogance allotted to the family and left a residue of umbrage for the pharmacist.

Before Leeming could speak, a customer came into the shop and was served first. After his departure, the sergeant was able to introduce himself and state his business, only to be interrupted by two more customers. When it happened for a third time, he asked if he could speak to Wigg in private. The pharmacist reluctantly called his assistant into the shop before taking his visitor into a back room with an even more pleasing pungency. Leeming asked the question that had brought him there.

'Have you ever sold poison to your brother?'

'No, I haven't.'

'Is that the truth?'

'I haven't sold anything to Elijah,' said the other, 'for one simple reason. He doesn't think he'd have to pay. Because I'm his brother, he expects to get everything free. You can't run a business like that.'

'How often do you see him?'

'We see precious little of him.'

'I have the feeling that you're rather glad about that.'

'Elijah and I are not the best of friends, Sergeant.'

'Why is that?'

'It's a personal matter.'

'Has he ever asked you for advice about poisons?'

'Why should he? There are pharmacists in Derby.'

'Yes, but you're his brother.'

'Only in name,' said Wigg, sourly. 'In answer to your question, I've never sold Elijah any poison but there have been many times when I've been tempted to administer some to him.' The bell tinkled as someone else came into the shop. 'I'll have to go, Sergeant. My customers rely on me.'

Leeming was deflated. All that he'd gained from his visit was the news that the Wigg brothers were hostile to each other. Trudging back towards the railway station, he hoped that Colbeck and Tallis would have more productive encounters.

John Cleary was cleaning some harnesses when Lucas Quayle arrived with Colbeck in tow. After introducing the two men to each other, Lucas left them alone. Cleary put the harness aside and wiped his hands on a cloth.

'I'm told that you're a good cricketer,' said Colbeck.

Cleary smiled. 'I do my best, sir.'

'You and Gerard Burns were outstanding.'

'Ah, well, we've lost him, I'm afraid.'

'Are you sorry about that?'

'Very sorry.'

'Why is that?'

'Gerard was a friend. There are not too many of those around here.'

'Have you played any cricket matches since he left?'

'Yes, sir – we lost them all.'

Cleary was saddened rather than embittered. Since he excelled at cricket, the game was important to him and he'd enjoyed a run of success in the past. Without Gerard Burns in the side, the team was condemned to a series of losses.

'What I'm trying to find out,' explained Colbeck, 'is where Mr Quayle went on the day of his murder. You drive him to the railway station, I understand.'

'That's true, Inspector, but he never said where he was going that day.'

'Where did he usually go?'

'Oh, he went to his office in Derby, even on Sundays sometimes.'

'Did he catch a particular train?'

'Yes, he kept to a strict timetable,' replied Cleary. 'Mr Quayle always caught the same train in the morning and if he needed me to meet him in the evening he'd tell me what time to be there.'

Colbeck warmed to the man. The coachman answered questions without hesitation and looked him in the eye as he did so. There was no hint of the evasion he'd met elsewhere. Cleary wanted to help.

'What sort of a man was Mr Quayle?'

'I'm not the best person to ask that, sir.'

'Why not? You saw him almost every day.'

'Yes, but all he did was to give me my orders. In all the years I've been here, we never talked properly. Don't misunderstand me,' he went on, 'I had the greatest respect for Mr Quayle. He was a good employer and treated me well but I never really got to know him as a person.' He waved an arm that took in the stable yard. 'This is where I belong, sir.'

'I'm not asking you to tell tales about him, Mr Cleary.'

'There are none to tell.'

'What about his row with Mr Burns? I'd call that a tale worth hearing.'

'All I know is that we lost a good gardener and a decent man. Not that I'm taking sides,' said Cleary, quickly. 'Mr Quayle did what he felt was right. I've no argument with that.' He removed his cap and ran a hand through his hair. 'But I do miss Gerard on the cricket field. I've never seen a bowler like him.'

'Has he ever been back here?'

'No, Inspector.'

'Are you sure?'

'He told me he was going for good.'

'Was that before or after he was beaten up?'

Cleary was surprised. 'You *know* about that?' he asked, replacing his cap.

'I've spoken to him twice.'

'What happened to him was bad. Gerard could hardly walk.'

'Did that make you look at Mr Quayle in a different way?'

'I do what I'm paid to do,' said Cleary, levelly.

Colbeck studied him. He could see why the coachman had befriended the gardener. Apart from cricket, they had much in common. They were younger than most of the servants and had positions that they cherished. In his mind's eye, Colbeck could see them slipping off to a local inn together after the day's work was done.

'Did he ever talk to you about Miss Lydia Quayle?'

Cleary was emphatic. 'No – it was none of my business.'

'Were you shocked when the truth came out?'

'We all were, Inspector.'

'Did it cause a lot of upset here?'

'Yes, it did. But that's all in the past.'

'The murder of Mr Quayle has brought it alive again,' said Colbeck, 'because Mr Burns is bound to be viewed as someone with a strong motive to kill his former employer.' Cleary shook his head violently. 'You disagree?'

'Gerard would never do such a thing, sir.'

'Have you seen him since he moved away from here?'

'Only once – but I don't need to see him. I *know* him. He's not a killer.'

'People can change, Mr Cleary.'

'Our sort stay the same,' said the other, steadfastly.

His identification with the gardener was complete. Cleary and Burns were kindred spirits. The coachman refused to believe that his friend was capable of murder. While he admired the man's loyalty, Colbeck doubted his judgement.

'Did Mr Quayle ever stay away from home?' he asked.

'Yes, sir – he often went to London on business.'

'Where else did he go?'

'I don't know. All I was told was when he was coming back.'

'Let me ask you a final question, Mr Cleary,' he said, 'and I want you to take all the time you need before answering it. On the day of the murder, you took Mr Quayle to the railway station at the usual time. Presumably, he caught the usual train but you are in no position to confirm that. Was there *anything* – anything at all – that was different that day? Did Mr Quayle say or do anything out of the ordinary? Now, please – think carefully.'

The coachman needed only a few seconds to recall something unusual.

'I could be wrong, of course,' he warned.

'What do you remember?'

'Well, Mr Quayle took very little notice of me as a rule. When he got out of the carriage, he just muttered his thanks.'

'Was there something different on the last day you saw him?'

'Yes,' replied Cleary, 'there was. He didn't say a single word to me at the railway station and . . . I had a feeling that he'd been crying.'

CHAPTER EIGHTEEN

As the wheel of the cab hit another deep pothole, Edward Tallis cursed the fact that Melbourne did not have its own railway station. The drive to the village was an ordeal of bumping, jerking, twisting and sudden lurches that threw him against the side of the vehicle. Every possible hazard in the road seemed to have been explored, leaving the passenger with unwelcome bruises. It was almost as if the driver had set out to injure Tallis. When he finally reached the Hall, he paid the man his fare and left a series of stinging complaints in lieu of a tip. Having introduced himself to the housekeeper, he asked to see Burns in his own domain. The gardener was poring over a catalogue when Tallis appeared. He scrambled to his feet.

The housekeeper introduced the visitor then left them alone.

'Can I help you, sir?' asked the gardener.

'I believe that you've met my colleague, Inspector Colbeck.'

'I spoke to him a few hours ago. There's nothing else I wish to add.'

'*My* wishes are paramount here, Burns. I require your attention.'

Burns sighed and put the catalogue aside. He indicated the bench and they both sat down. During his career in the army,

Tallis had dealt with a large number of men and developed a knack of summing up a person's character at a glance. Burns might seem polite and open-faced but the superintendent saw a hint of the unspoken insolence that broke out in the ranks from time to time and on which he'd always stamped firmly. In his opinion, the gardener looked as if he might have a mutinous streak.

'How long have you worked here, Burns?'

'Does it matter?'

'I'll ask the questions.'

'Then talk to the inspector before you ask the same things he did. He'll tell you my history. There's no point in going through it again. I was honest with him about my setbacks. I'm much happier with my lot now.'

'Is your happiness connected with the death of Vivian Quayle?'

Burns was jolted. 'That did give me pleasure,' he said, slowly.

'It must have been a cause for celebration.'

'I'm too busy here to think about such things, sir.'

'The inspector told me about the weedkiller you use.'

'I'm not the only gardener who's experimented with it. I could name two or three. When I worked for Mr Quayle, I used a similar preparation on weeds. Perhaps you should be talking to the head gardener there.'

'There's no need for flippancy.'

'Then I apologise.'

Tallis gazed around. The gardens were spectacular and the man in charge of them was clearly knowledgeable. It seemed unlikely that he'd desert his post to plot the murder of an old enemy. Yet he had a strong motive, access to one of the poisons found in the dead man and was known to have been close to Spondon on the night in question. Added to that was the calculated stubbornness he was now displaying.

'I'm told that you're a fine cricketer,' said Tallis.

'I used to be.'

'Did you never wish to play for the All-England team?'

'Gardening always came first.'

'But you were encouraged to play the game when you were in Mr Quayle's employ. It seems that your bowling was the crucial ingredient of the team's success. You must miss the chance to play to such a high standard.'

'There are compensations, sir.'

'In your position, I'd resent the man that took that chance away from me.'

'I still play cricket now and then,' said Burns, arrogance showing through, 'and Mr Quayle had more cause for resentment than me. Since I left, his team haven't won a single game.'

'How do you know that?'

'Gossip travels.'

'I thought you'd lost all interest in what happens on his estate.'

'I can't help it if I hear rumours, Superintendent.'

Tallis removed his top hat carefully and used a handkerchief to dab at the light perspiration on his brow. His next question came without warning.

'You're hiding something, aren't you?' he challenged.

'No, sir, I'm not.'

'You're hiding the fact that you've kept in touch with your old place of work so that you could be aware of the movements of the man you hated. You've been biding your time, Burns, haven't you?'

'I've not seen Mr Quayle since the day I left.'

'You didn't need to if you had a confederate who still worked there.'

'But I don't.'

'We only have your word for it.'

'I'm telling the truth.'

'It doesn't sound like it to me – or to Inspector Colbeck, for that matter.'

Burns was angry. 'What has he been saying about me?'

'He thought that you couldn't be trusted. I'm inclined to agree. It was his suggestion that you might have someone working on Mr Quayle's estate who reported back to you.'

'I haven't been anywhere near the place,' yelled the other.

'There's no need to shout.'

'I don't like being accused of something I didn't do.'

'Where were you on the day that the murder took place?'

'You know quite well,' said Burns with exasperation. 'I played cricket in Ilkeston then went to Derby in the evening.'

'But you refuse to say what you were doing there.'

'I went to see a friend.'

Eyes glinting, Tallis put his face close to that of the other man. 'Was it a friend or an accomplice?'

The directness of the question made Burns recoil slightly. For the first time, he looked uncomfortable. As Tallis glared at him from close range, the gardener lapsed into a bruised silence.

The visit to the Quayle house had been profitable. Colbeck had learnt far more than he'd managed on the first occasion when he called there. It was the conversation with John Cleary that had been revelatory. He'd made some illuminating comments about his former employer. Colbeck was interested in the news that Quayle often stayed away from home at some unknown location. If the man had been crying on his way to the station on his last day alive, it was highly uncharacteristic. After taking soundings from a number of quarters, Colbeck had built up a picture of a man who savoured power and exercised it mercilessly. It was an image reinforced by the portrait of Vivian Quayle that hung in his house. The man in that, Colbeck recalled, looked as if he'd never shed a tear in his life.

Against the excitement of finding new and important information, Colbeck had to set the discomfort of having Tallis as an unwanted assistant. Apart from the fact that the superintendent would insist on leading the investigation, there was the certainty that he would get under the feet of Colbeck and Leeming. The inspector had devised strategies of dealing with Tallis but the sergeant had not. As long as the older man was there, Leeming would be working with reduced effectiveness, always looking over his shoulder. With the arrival of the superintendent, a complicated case had instantly become even more difficult to solve. If there was some way to dispatch Tallis back to London, it had to be seized.

Colbeck was still enjoying fantasies about how to get rid of him when his cab rolled up outside Nottingham railway station. After paying the driver, he went onto the platform and looked up and down. At the far end, a smartly dressed woman was perched on a bench. She looked so much like Madeleine that he stared at her for a minute before deciding that it couldn't possibly be his wife because he didn't recognise the hat she was wearing. He was about to turn away when she glanced in his direction for the first time.

'Robert!' she exclaimed, jumping to her feet.

Fired by his good fortune, he ran the length of the platform to embrace her.

'What on earth are *you* doing here?' he asked in disbelief.

'I came with Miss Quayle. She's decided to return home.'

Bolstered by Madeleine's presence, Lydia Quayle had felt confident that she would be given a welcome at the house. As soon as her cab turned in through the main gates of the estate, however, that confidence was replaced by apprehension and, in turn, by cold fear. Her break from the family had been so dramatic and final that she couldn't imagine that any member of it would wish to see her, let alone be delighted by her reappearance. Lydia was tempted to abandon the visit altogether and ask the driver to take her back to the station. Somehow she fought off that temptation. Memories flooded back to please and unsettle her simultaneously. She passed a glade where she and Gerard Burns had often met in secret, and there were other places that brought their romance fleetingly alive again. It died instantly as the grotto where she and Burns had been discovered together appeared in her mind's eye. Her memories darkened at once and she shook her head in an effort to get rid of them but they were too vivid to be dislodged. She had returned to an estate that had held joy and terror for her. When the house came into view, her heart sank. It looked so forbidding.

The cab drew up on the gravel in front of the portico and she needed time to compose herself before she stepped uncertainly out of the vehicle. As she stood alone in front of what had once been her whole world, she felt lonely and unwanted. Someone must have seen her through the windows but nobody came out. The door remained closed as if delivering a blunt message. Lydia waited for minutes. She was on the point of leaving when the door suddenly swung open. Her brothers and her sister stepped out together, staring at her as if she was a complete stranger. The sense of rejection was like a physical blow.

In a flash, the mood changed. Her younger brother suddenly ran out to greet her and threw his arms around her.

'Welcome home!' cried Lucas. 'Thank God you've come at last.'

* * *

There was so much news for Colbeck to hear that it wasn't until the train arrived, and she sat opposite him in an empty compartment, that he noticed how pale his wife was.

'Are you unwell?' he asked in concern.

'No, no, I'm just tired after the journey. Trying to keep up Lydia's spirits has put a lot of strain on me. I do hope that the effort was worthwhile.'

'She obviously has great faith in you.'

'I don't think she'd have come back without me.'

'I'm glad that you were able to offer her support, Madeleine. The murder of a father – even if one dislikes him – is bound to have a profound impact. She needs to be with the rest of the family at such a time.'

'Only if they want her there,' she pointed out.

He peered at her. 'You're wearing a new hat.'

'I bought it the day you left. I needed something to cheer me up.'

'It's wonderful to see you again,' he said, beaming.

'I had no idea that you'd be in Nottingham today, Robert.'

'It's a case of happenstance, my love.'

'What stage is the investigation at now?'

'After my visit this morning,' he explained, 'it's moved forward in the right direction. But there's still a long way to go.'

'In your first letter, you mentioned that Mr Haygarth was a possible suspect.'

'He still is, Madeleine.'

'If he's the acting chairman of the Midland Railway, you ought to ask him why Nottingham isn't on the main line. Lydia told me that her father had plans to make it easier to reach by train.'

'Quayle was a man with vision. Haygarth is merely a man with a vision of power and monetary gain. The one loved railways for their own sake and the other loves them for what they can deliver to him.'

'Lydia spoke very harshly of Mr Haygarth – but even more so of her father.' She pursed her lips. 'Oh, I do hope that she's reconciled with her family.'

'What will happen if she isn't?'

'Then she'll try to join me in Derby. Having come this far, I wasn't going to miss the chance of seeing my husband. I know it was presumptuous of me but I hoped I'd stay with you at the Royal Hotel.'

'I can't think of anything nicer, Madeleine.'

She saw his brow corrugate. 'Is there a problem?'

'Yes,' he replied, 'and I've just remembered it. But it's an obstacle we can circumvent. Superintendent Tallis turned up out of the blue. You can imagine how Victor and I feel.'

'Doesn't he trust you to run the investigation?'

'He always thinks he can do our job better than we can. Stay at the hotel with me, by all means,' said Colbeck, 'but be on your guard. With the superintendent on the prowl, you may have to play a game of hide-and-seek.'

Lydia Quayle was so touched by the warm reception she was given that she burst into tears. Her brother Lucas was the most demonstrative of her siblings, putting an arm around her to shepherd her into the house. Agnes rose to a kiss on the cheek and even Stanley, aloof though he was, abandoned his earlier hostility and raised no objection to her return. The domestic servants who glimpsed her were thrilled to see her and rushed off to spread the news of her return. But the major test was the reunion with her mother. Having heard from the others how poorly the old woman was, she went upstairs on her own and tapped on the door of her mother's bedroom. Since there was no response, she let herself in and heard a gentle snore. Not wishing to disturb her mother's sleep, she sat beside the bed and waited, noting the bottles of medicine and boxes of tablets on the bedside table. Her mother was even older and feebler than she remembered.

The others had insisted she went into the room on her own. Though Lydia had been grateful at first, she now wished that they'd been with her so that her mother would awake to see familiar faces instead of one she had learnt to forget. It might have been better if Lydia had been seen as part of the family again instead of as a lone visitor from the past. The longer the wait, the more uncomfortable she became and the greater the urge to tiptoe out of the room to summon help. When she tried to move, however, she seemed to be bolted to the chair. There was no escape.

It was half an hour before Harriet Quayle stirred. She opened watery eyes.

'Is that you, Agnes?' she whispered.

'No, Mother, it's not. It's me – Lydia.'

'Who?'

'It's Lydia, your daughter,' she said, putting her face closer. 'I came back.'

Harriet was confused. 'Am I dreaming?'

'No, it's me and I'm here with you.'

'Agnes usually sits beside the bed.'

'She wanted me to come in here instead,' explained Lydia, softly.

'Oh, I see.'

The old woman drifted off again and Lydia thought that she'd gone to sleep but the eyes opened after a few moments and struggled to focus. It took time and patience. Eventually, Harriet was convinced that her elder daughter had returned to the fold. She began to sob quietly.

'Don't cry, Mother,' said Lydia, leaning forward to kiss her. 'I wanted you to be happy. That's why I came.'

'I *am* happy. I'm very happy.'

'Is there anything I can get you?'

'I have all that I want,' said Harriet. 'I can die in peace now.'

When the cab arrived outside the hotel, Colbeck first slipped inside the building to make sure that the coast was clear. Relieved to see no sign of Tallis, he came out to collect her. Even though Madeleine was his wife, he felt embarrassed having to smuggle her into the building and up to his room. Once they had real privacy at last, they were able to embrace properly.

'What will you tell the management?' she asked.

'I'll say that this room will have double occupancy tonight.'

'Won't they be suspicious?'

'Oh, I think they've learnt to trust me,' he said with a grin. 'I don't anticipate having to dangle your wedding ring in front of them. My only regret is that I can't stay long. I have an appointment.'

'Please don't worry about leaving me, Robert. I feel quite exhausted. To be honest, I'd relish the chance of a nap. I'd much rather you stayed, of course,' she added, 'but I realise that work comes first. Where are you going?'

'I'm about to indulge myself, Madeleine. Why come to a railway town without taking full advantage of the fact?' He reached for his hat. 'I'm going to have a tour of the Derby Works.'

Donald Haygarth went through the agenda for the next board meeting. They were quite happy to work on a Saturday. He and Maurice Cope discussed each item at length before moving on to the next. Anxious to be confirmed as the next chairman of the company, Haygarth wanted to leave nothing to chance. Covertly, the other man had been acting as his campaign manager.

'You'll have more than enough votes,' he assured Haygarth.

'That's largely your doing.'

'Thank you, sir.'

'I always reward good service.' He consulted his watch. 'What time are you seeing the inspector?'

'He should be here at any moment.'

'I can't see the point of traipsing around the works. You'd never get me doing that. The noise is deafening and there's grime everywhere. I'm surprised that a dandy like Colbeck would risk soiling his fine clothes. However,' he continued, 'it's what he asked for and we must be seen to be helpful.'

'It does mean that I'll be there to watch him,' said Cope. There was a tap on the door. 'That will be the inspector now, I daresay.'

In fact, it was a secretary who entered the room to say that Superintendent Tallis was requesting an interview with Haygarth. The acting chairman asked for him to be sent in and was soon shaking hands with his visitor. He introduced Cope, who remained standing when the others sat down.

'We were expecting Inspector Colbeck,' said Haygarth.

'Yes, I know. It's one of the reasons I came. I'm hoping that I might join him in his perambulation around the Works.'

'Do you have any idea *why* he wishes to have a tour of inspection?'

'No,' admitted Tallis, 'but a reason will emerge. The inspector is a man of unorthodox methods. The extraordinary thing is that they almost invariably produce good results.'

'We've seen none so far,' said Haygarth with a meaningful glance at Cope.

'No,' said Cope, taking his cue, 'we'd hoped for more progress by now but both the inspector and Sergeant Leeming have failed to turn up any decisive evidence. The board meeting for the election of the new chairman will be held at the end of next week. For obvious reasons, we'd like the murder to be solved *before* that takes place.'

'I appreciate that,' said Tallis.

He'd already been given a good description of the two men by Colbeck and, looking at them now, he realised how accurate it had been. Haygarth was plainly a man who gloried in power and Cope was his lickspittle lieutenant. Within the Midland Railway, they were a formidable team and it said much for the character of Vivian Quayle that he would have been able to defeat them in the battle for control of the company.

'Have you taken charge of the case, Superintendent?' asked Haygarth.

'No, I'm simply here to monitor it.'

'You've been given the names of possible suspects, I take it.'

'Oh, yes, Mr Haygarth. I spoke to one of them early today.'

'Who might that be?'

'A fellow by the name of Gerard Burns,' said Tallis. 'He's a stubborn individual and is very defensive when the name of Vivian Quayle is mentioned.'

'He has every right to be,' said Cope. 'I'm told he can be prickly.'

'You must have formed your own judgement about that, Mr Cope. I hear that you once approached him to leave Mr Quayle's employment to work for Mr Haygarth instead. Why did the two of you conspire to snare someone else's gardener? For the life of me, I can't see why that would help in the running of this railway.' He shared a bland smile between them. 'Perhaps one of you can enlighten me.'

Victor Leeming alighted from the train in Spondon. After his visit to Belper, he was delighted to be back in the village. It was where the murder victim had been found and where one of the prime suspects lived. On his way to Hockaday's shop, he reflected that his conversation with Reuben Wigg had not been entirely a waste of time. He'd learnt something about the character of the pharmacist's brother, Elijah, which served to keep the superintendent's name on the list of suspects. The latter had a compulsion to achieve a position of power and would even discard a member of his family if he offered no professional advantage. Reuben Wigg had clearly matched his bewhiskered brother in his capacity to bear a grudge. He'd even talked of committing murder, albeit with a macabre jocularity.

The arrival of Edward Tallis had jangled the sergeant. He hated the feeling that he was being spied on by his superior. Tallis had poured scorn on the notion of going to Belper but Leeming felt that it could now be justified. His assessment of Superintendent Wigg had been ratified. The pharmacist's brother would have been far too careful to get blood on his hands. Murder would have been assigned to someone else. Leeming wondered if he was about to meet the man who actually did the deed. Before he did so, he had a more enjoyable encounter. He saw Philip Conway coming around a corner. Each was pleased to see the other.

'It would be easier if you actually *lived* in Spondon,' said Leeming. 'You've been here every day so far.'

'I like the place, Sergeant, and the local people seem to like me.'

'Why do they have to talk in that weird language?'

'Derbyshire folk are proud of their dialects,' said Conway. 'If they came to London, they wouldn't be able to understand a word of Cockney slang.'

'It takes getting used to.'

'As for staying the night here, this may be my last visit to Spondon. The editor says I won't be coming again.'

'But you've turned up vital information.'

'Somebody doesn't want me here and spoke to my editor – Wigg, probably.'

Since it was Conway who'd told him about Wigg's brother, Leeming felt obliged to say that he'd been to Belper and to give a short account of what he learnt there. The reporter was not surprised. Elijah Wigg only cultivated people who could be useful to him, such as the editor of the *Derby Mercury*. A pharmacist brother had no social or political leverage to offer.

'As it happens, he was here last night,' said Conway.

'Superintendent Wigg?'

'Yes, the stationmaster saw him arrive.'

'Well, there's no reason why he shouldn't be,' remarked Leeming. 'He and his men are still supposed to be helping us with our enquiries though they've not given us much assistance so far.'

'They work slowly but surely.'

'I know. It takes them three years to solve a murder.'

'The Stone case is still awaiting a solution.'

'I wonder why,' said Leeming with irony. 'If he came here, Wigg would certainly have been in touch with Hockaday. Indeed, that may have been the main reason for his visit.'

'You could be right, Sergeant – as long as you don't ask me to confirm it by challenging him. I'm keeping out of Hockaday's way.'

'He can't harm you, Mr Conway. He'd lose his position as a constable, for a start. We've had to get rid of a number of our men who are too ready to use their fists to pay off old grudges.'

'Well, he certainly holds a grudge against me.'

'It's because you're a threat. You might find out the truth about him.'

'I'll leave that job to you, Sergeant.'

After exchanging information with him for a few more minutes, Leeming took his leave and made his way to the cobbler's shop. Hockaday was in the process of serving a customer. When the woman departed, he turned an unfriendly stare towards his visitor. The sergeant fired off his first question immediately.

'Where did you go by train yesterday, Mr Hockaday?'

'Why do you want to know?'

'You don't deny it, then?'

'If you've been talking to the stationmaster again, he'll have told you I caught a train. Is that how you spied on me?'

'No, it isn't,' replied Leeming. 'I happened to be sitting in the window of the Malt Shovel when you strode past. You were so eager to get somewhere that I wanted to know where it was. I followed you.'

The cobbler sounded hurt. '*I* never saw you.'

'I thought you were going to Duffield to warn the people whose names you'd given that they might get a visit from us. It looked as if you went to concoct an alibi.'

'I didn't need to,' said the other, incensed.

'I know that now, sir. Mr Verney confirmed your story and he struck me as an honest man. He told me that you did call there on the night of the murder but that it was late and you'd been drinking.'

'I'm entitled to a pint of beer now and then.'

'I agree. Where did you go *before* you visited Mr and Mrs Verney?'

'That's no concern of yours, Sergeant.'

'Was it the same place you went to yesterday when you stayed on the train instead of getting off at Duffield?'

'Why are you paying so much attention to me when there's a killer on the loose?' demanded the cobbler.

'It's because you're concealing things from us, Mr Hockaday. For instance,' said Leeming, 'you didn't tell us that you had family in Duffield. Mr Verney made sure that nobody overheard but he told me that you were his son. Is that true?'

Hockaday's anger changed immediately to alarm. He suddenly looked very vulnerable. Reaching out, he grabbed Leeming by both arms.

'Don't tell anybody that,' he pleaded. 'People here don't need to know it. I beg of you to keep it to yourself, Sergeant.'

Maurice Cope astounded him. Colbeck's assumption was that the man was there to watch them as much as to conduct them around the works. In fact, Cope turned out to be as fascinated by trains as the inspector. His knowledge of the Midland Railway was almost encyclopaedic and he spoke with a muted passion. Most of the technical information was lost on Edward Tallis, who trailed behind the two men with mounting boredom.

'When the Midland Railway was authorised in 1844,' said Cope, 'we inherited an assortment of locomotives from the constituent companies. There were 95 in all, plus 282 carriages, 1256 goods wagons and a number of horseboxes, post office vans and carriage trucks.'

'The Midland Counties had tiny Bury locomotives,' recalled Colbeck, 'but the North Midland had those sturdy, sandwich-framed ones.'

'So did the Birmingham and Derby Junction.'

'Is all this relevant?' wailed Tallis.

But the other two men ignored him. They were inspired by everything they saw, from the turning of the huge wheels on massive lathes to the riveting of the boilers and the ingenuity of the bending tubes. The pounding of the giant steam hammers made Tallis put his hands over his ears but the others took the hullaballoo in their stride. It was in the roundhouse that Colbeck simply stood and stared in awe. It was the largest structure of its kind in the whole country, with a turntable at its centre and a series of parking bays running off it like the spokes of a wheel. There was a fearsome compound of smells and sounds. Cope indicated points of interest and Colbeck evinced an almost childish glee.

'How much longer is this going on?' complained Tallis.

'You may leave if you wish,' said Colbeck.

'I thought we came here to learn something.'

'We've learnt *dozens* of things, Superintendent.'

'All that I've learnt is that it was an act of madness to accompany you. The stink is unbearable and I think my eardrums are perforated. How can anyone work in such appalling conditions?'

'Employees adapt very quickly, sir,' said Cope. 'Apprentices start as young as thirteen years of age. They work an eight-hour day and are controlled by a steam whistle. Only when it rings for the sixth time can they end their shift.'

'It makes our day seem soft by comparison,' said Colbeck.

'Nonsense!' exclaimed Tallis. 'We work longer hours and often have to be on duty all night. Also, I should remind you, we face danger on a daily basis.'

'So do the employees here.'

'It's true,' said Cope, sadly. 'We have far too many accidents. Railway workers need to keep their wits about them. Some men have been incapacitated for life, and I'm ashamed to admit that we've had fatalities.'

'You'll have another if *I* have to stay here any longer,' grumbled Tallis.

'At least stay to see the turntable in action,' urged Colbeck.

'I've seen enough.'

'There's something I've always wanted to do.'

'I think I can guess what it is, Inspector,' said Cope. 'Give me a moment and I'll arrange for your wish to be fulfilled.'

'What's this about a wish?' asked Tallis.

After removing his hat and his coat, Colbeck handed them to him.

'Please look after those for me, Superintendent.'

'Where are you going, man?'

'You'll soon see.'

A locomotive had been driven onto the turntable and stood there throbbing with latent power. Cope was speaking to the fireman who gave an affirmative nod. It was the signal for Colbeck to hurry over to them. After taking instructions, he and the fireman went to one side of the turntable while two other railwaymen went to the other. After rocking the vast wheel to and fro for a little while, they put all their strength into a heave. To the amazement of the watching Tallis, four men were making a locomotive of immense weight turn as if it were made of paper. They pushed on until it had completed a semicircle then locked it into position so that it could drive frontwards out of the shed again. Colbeck was overjoyed to have been part of the operation. Ignoring the fact that the fireman's hand was covered in coal dust, he shook it gratefully.

Tallis was both bewildered and annoyed, mystified by what Colbeck had done and infuriated that he was holding the inspector's hat and coat. There was worse to come. A steam whistle suddenly went off only yards away and Tallis was so startled that he took a few injudicious steps away, only to get his foot jammed under a rail and to fall backwards on the ground. His yell of anguish brought Colbeck running over to him. Picking up his discarded hat and coat, he bent over the superintendent.

'Are you all right, sir?' he enquired.

'No, I'm not,' howled Tallis. 'Thanks to you, I may have broken my ankle. Why did you ever bring me to this hellhole?'

'The visit has paid a handsome dividend, sir.'

'Is that how to describe my injury?'

'Didn't you see what happened?' asked Colbeck with controlled excitement. 'I just discovered how to solve this murder.'

CHAPTER NINETEEN

It was strange. Lydia Quayle had been living in London for a few years yet nobody in her family asked her about the sort of existence she led there. Their minds were instead fixed on the murder inquiry and on the imminent funeral of the victim. Even her mother showed no curiosity in where she'd been and what she'd been doing. The mood in the house was sombre. Faces were drawn and voices low. Lydia found it oppressive. Having left her sister alone for so long with their mother, Agnes began to feel territorial, insisting that it was her place to maintain the bedside vigil and refusing to be supplanted by Lydia. She therefore returned to her accustomed position and left her sister free to reacquaint herself with her brothers. Before she did that, Lydia made her way to her father's study so that she could look at the portrait of the man who'd become such an ogre in her perception. Almost bursting out of the gilt frame, Vivian Quayle seemed horribly lifelike with his abiding sense of achievement and his air of unassailable confidence. Even though she knew that he was dead, Lydia felt a cold hand run down her spine.

She was struck anew by the incongruity of a room with

many bookshelves yet few books. It was so different from the well-kept library that she shared with Beatrice Myler in London. There was no place for paintings or decorative objects there. Every shelf was occupied by a book of some sort and piles of them stood on the table and on the window sill. Beatrice was far too self-effacing even to consider the idea of having her portrait painted. Lydia's father, by contrast, filled the room with his personality.

'What are you doing in here?' asked Lucas.

He'd entered so quietly that she twitched in surprise at the sound of his voice.

'I'm sorry, Lydia. I didn't mean to give you a shock.'

'Being back in this house has given me a series of shocks, Lucas.'

'There haven't been many changes.'

'In my opinion, there have been lots. It may look the same to you but it seems vastly bigger than I remember. That could be because I've been used to a much smaller house, of course. It's gloomier and less welcoming here than in the past. Then there's mother,' she said with a note of self-reproach. 'That's the major change. If I'd know she was so unwell, I'd have come sooner.'

'I did urge you to do that in my letter.'

'I'm ashamed to say that I didn't even read it properly. Father was alive then and . . . well, let's just say that his presence kept me away.'

'We missed you, Lydia.'

'You did – and I'm grateful for that. Stanley would never have bothered to track me down and Agnes is already showing signs of her old envy.'

He took her by the shoulders and placed a gentle kiss on her cheek.

'It's a tonic to see you again.'

'Thank you, Lucas.'

'I wish we could have met in other circumstances.'

'That would have been impossible,' she explained. 'It took a dreadful event like this to bring me back. I'd never have returned to Father's deathbed. I'm here for the family, not for his sake.'

'I understand.'

'I don't think that you do, Lucas.'

'Then *make* me understand.'

'I didn't come to burden you with my troubles. I just want to take my place alongside you all during this time of trial.'

'We're delighted to see you,' he said, releasing her. 'Stanley may appear distant but he's always had difficulty showing his emotions. In her own way, I'm certain, Agnes still loves you enough to want you here. As for Mother . . .'

'What does the doctor say about her?'

'He's not very sanguine.'

'She seems to have shrunk and lost all her spirit.'

Lucas nodded. 'It's only a matter of time.'

In the wake of the visit to the Derby Works, the priority was to get medical attention for Edward Tallis. He was evidently in distress and could not place much weight on one foot. Maurice Cope felt obscurely responsible for the mishap and wanted to make amends. He sent for a doctor to attend the patient then helped Colbeck to support the superintendent as he was taken to an office. Cope withdrew and left them alone. Tallis was in obvious pain but bore it well. His anger was reserved for the blast of the steam whistle that had caused the accident.

'It's my own fault,' he confessed. 'I should never have been misguided enough to go into that mechanical Hades. It was one long, cruel, ear-splitting obstacle course.'

'One has to keep one's eyes peeled,' said Colbeck.

'I only came because it gave me an opportunity to appraise Haygarth and that cringing, over-polite henchman of his. I endorse your opinion of both of them.'

'Let's not worry about that now, sir. Your injury takes precedence.'

'I've had far worse.'

'Indeed, you have, Superintendent. In Exeter, you were stabbed in the arm.'

'Such things happen in the line of duty.'

Though Tallis was trying to brush the incident aside, Colbeck remembered the bravery he'd shown in trying to foil the escape of a prisoner. On that occasion, too, the superintendent had been more concerned with the inconvenience caused by the injury than the associated pain.

'You forget that I was in the army,' said Tallis. 'One is almost bound to suffer injuries in action. Like any trained soldier, I learnt to shrug them off.'

'You're much older now, sir.'

'What's that got to do with it?'

'Nothing,' said Colbeck, seeing his eyes flash. 'Nothing at all.'

Cope popped into the room to see if the patient was comfortable and to issue another string of apologies that the accident had occurred. Since he'd been in charge of showing the two men around, he felt that he was partly to blame. After treating them both to an ingratiating smile, Cope went out again.

'Thank heavens he's gone,' said Tallis. 'I hate sycophancy.'

'I undertake never to lapse into it,' promised Colbeck with a smile.

'Are you being ironic?'

'It's wholly foreign to my nature, sir.'

'Poppycock!'

'We haven't really discussed your visit to Melbourne,' said Colbeck, changing his tack. 'What was your estimate of Gerard Burns?'

'He was shifty and disrespectful. I'm fairly certain he's the killer.'

'Why didn't you place him under arrest?'

'I chose to stand off for a while,' explained Tallis. 'It transpires that the prime minister is arriving to stay at the house in a few days' time, and he is justifiably proud of his gardens. I didn't wish to incur Lord Palmerston's displeasure by putting his head gardener in custody when we don't yet have enough evidence for a jury to convict Burns.'

'I'll keep looking for that evidence, sir.'

'You'll have to, Inspector. I can't dash around the countryside here. I need to be back in London with my foot up.'

'That's the best place for you,' said Colbeck, suffused with a sense of relief.

'You sound as if you're *glad* that I had that accident.'

'Then the pain may have distorted your hearing, Superintendent.'

It was not long before Cope entered with the doctor he'd summoned earlier. Colbeck took the opportunity to slip out and make his way quickly back to the hotel. Arriving in haste, he almost bounded up the stairs. When he let himself into his room, he expected a greeting from Madeleine but he was disappointed. Stretched out on the bed, she was fast asleep.

On his way back to the railway station, Victor Leeming caught sight of the vicar, talking to Superintendent Wigg. He waited until the conversation had finished. When the vicar walked away,

Leeming moved in swiftly to intercept the other man. His attitude to the two superintendents was markedly different. While he tended to cower in front of Tallis, he was prepared to be more outspoken with Elijah Wigg.

'What brings you here?' he asked.

'Someone has to solve this crime, Sergeant, and – for all your credentials – you and the inspector seem wholly unequal to the task.'

'That's because we've had so little help from the local constabulary.'

'We can't help if you don't take us into your confidence.'

'You know every move we've made, Superintendent.'

'Yes,' agreed Wigg, 'but only because I've had reports from my men. Neither you nor Inspector Colbeck have had the courtesy to keep me abreast of every new initiative you've taken.'

'Events sometimes move too fast for us to do that.'

'That's a lame excuse, Sergeant.'

Leeming was irritated. 'When we need you, sir, we'll call on you.'

'And how long will it be before that happens?' asked the other, teasingly. 'My feeling is that time is running out for you. Haygarth's patience will soon be exhausted. He'll see that it was a mistake to bring you from London and he'll hand the case over to someone who knows this county and its people far better than you ever could.'

'You are right about that, Superintendent. There's only so much I *wish* to know about Derbyshire and I've almost reached that point. But if you're in the mood to solve a murder,' said Leeming, daring to provoke him, 'why don't you start with the one that took place in this village three years ago?'

'That case is under review.'

'It's good of you to be so honest about your blunders, sir. If the case remains open, you keep reminding people of your failure. Most constabularies try to bury their mistakes and flaunt their successes. That means they have to be on good terms with the editors of their local newspapers, of course.'

Wigg was roused. 'What are you implying?'

'I merely made an observation, Superintendent.'

'If you bandy words with me, I'll complain to the Inspector.'

'Then I must make a confession,' said Leeming. 'The observation was not mine. I was only quoting what Inspector Colbeck said to me. He thought you were unhealthily close to a certain editor.' He enjoyed Wigg's irate gurgle. 'By the way, did you know that Philip Conway is being moved away from Spondon?'

'The movement of reporters is of no concern to me.'

'It ought to be. Mr Conway has been far more useful to us in this village than any of the six constables who live here. He knows how to dig out the little secrets that people prefer to keep hidden.'

'I don't care two hoots about Conway.'

'Then why did you have him shifted from this village?'

'I did nothing of the kind,' said Wigg, whiskers bristling.

'Someone used his influence with the editor.'

'I resent that charge, Sergeant. I'm on good terms with the *Mercury* because I know the important part that a newspaper can play in the war against crime. The facts that I provide for publication are there to inform and reassure people. Any responsible constabulary would do the same.' He jabbed Leeming in the chest. 'Take back that vile slur you made against me. I did not have Conway moved.'

'Then we must be mistaken,' said Leeming, feeling that he'd prodded the man far enough. 'If I offended you, sir, I apologise.

But we would be grateful to hear *all* the evidence you and your men have so far gathered.'

'What I'm seeking is an *exchange* of evidence.'

'I'll pass on that request to the inspector.'

'Please do so.'

'Oh, and there's something else I must pass on,' added Leeming, getting in a valedictory dig. 'Your brother sends his regards.'

Wigg spluttered. 'Why bring Reuben into this?'

'I called on him in Belper, sir. I thought you should know that.'

Word of Lydia Quayle's return had spread quickly throughout the staff and it had reached the ears of John Cleary. He was puzzled by her reappearance after so long an absence. Since she was now inside the house, he didn't expect to catch sight of her at all. He was therefore astonished when she came in search of him. He was polishing the phaeton at the time and saw her mirrored in the shining side panel. Cleary spun round to face her.

'Good afternoon, Cleary.'

'Oh, good afternoon, Miss Quayle – I heard that you were back.'

'How long I'll be staying, I don't really know.'

'While you're here,' he said, 'you're very welcome.'

It was a sincere comment. Cleary had always liked her because she'd treated him well during her time on the estate. Lydia found him pleasant, willing and very efficient. He was also quietly unobtrusive. Some of the servants were always courting attention in the hope of gaining favour but the coachman simply did as he was told. Cleary had a gift for fading into the background.

'I'm rather surprised to see you out here,' he said, tentatively.

'Why?'

'After all this time away, I'd have thought you had a lot to say to the rest of your family. They must have been wondering where you've been.'

'They're preoccupied with other things at the moment.'

'Of course – I'm very sorry about what happened to your father.' When she made no reply, he pressed on. 'We all respected Mr Quayle. We can't imagine that anyone would want to harm him in any way. Do the police have any idea who committed the murder?'

'I believe that they have suspects in mind.'

'That's good.'

'Inspector Colbeck has an excellent reputation.'

'Yes, I met the inspector. I was impressed by him.'

Cleary was still trying to work out why she'd come to the stables in the first place. She seemed so uncomfortable and hesitant. For her part, Lydia was battling with demons from the past and trying to summon up her courage. During her time in London, she'd made a conscious attempt to put Gerard Burns out of her mind but he'd seeped back in the moment she'd seen their old haunts. Lydia did her best to sound casual but the question was nevertheless blurted out.

'Do you ever see anything of Mr Burns?'

'No, I don't,' he replied.

'You were such good friends at one time.'

'We lost touch.'

'I remember watching the two of you play cricket,' she said. 'You and Mr Burns were the best players in the team.'

'Your brother was a fine cricketer as well, Miss Quayle.'

'Lucas was never as good as either of you.'

'Oh, you can't compare me with Gerard. He was very special. I'd hate to have faced him when he was bowling.'

'Have you . . . had any word of him?'

'I can only tell you the tittle-tattle,' he said, apologetically, 'and there's no knowing how reliable that is.'

'I'd like to hear it nevertheless.'

'Well, the rumour is that Gerard has a position as head gardener at Melbourne Hall. When he left here, he managed to better himself.'

'Good gracious!' said Lydia with genuine pleasure. 'That *is* a feather in his cap. It's a just reward for all that studying he did about horticulture. Well, well,' she went on, trying to absorb the news, 'that's very gratifying. We all know who lives at Melbourne Hall. Gerard . . . Mr Burns, that is, must be so proud to serve the prime minister. His life has changed so much since he was here.'

'There's another rumour I heard about him,' he said.

'What was that, Cleary?'

'He got married.'

'Oh.' In a flash, all the joy had left her. 'Oh, I see.'

'Someone told me that Gerard was going to be a father.'

She mustered a brave smile. 'How nice for him!' she said.

But there was no conviction in her voice. Lydia felt suddenly hollow and bereft. After thanking him for the information, she walked back towards the house. Cleary was unable to see the anguish in her face.

When he got back to the hotel, Victor Leeming expected to deliver a report of his visit to Spondon and to receive congratulations on what he'd found out. Instead, he was confronted with the news that he had to take the superintendent back to London. After examining the injury, the doctor had told Tallis that he'd been fortunate. Though it was swollen and badly sprained, the ankle was not broken. Rest was prescribed. The superintendent decided to leave immediately and to press Leeming into service.

The sergeant was hopeful. 'Does that mean I can spend the night in London?'

'I'm afraid not,' said Colbeck. 'I need you here, so you must catch a train back to Derby at once. We've lots to discuss and you'll have a chance to meet Madeleine.'

'I didn't know that your wife was here, sir.'

'I'm keeping her hidden in my room until the superintendent has gone.'

'I wish that I had Estelle hidden away in *my* room,' said Leeming, longingly. 'I might even start to enjoy Derby then.'

'I'm sorry that it can't be arranged. Estelle is not directly involved in the investigation, you see, whereas my wife is. Miss Quayle prevailed upon Madeleine to go to Nottingham with her because she needed a friend for company. I met Madeleine at the railway station there and brought her back here.'

'If he knew about it, Superintendent Tallis would be outraged.'

'That's why I'm so glad that we're getting rid of him. That accident he had was a godsend and so was the visit to the Works. Watching that turntable in action opened up a whole new line of inquiry.'

'Did it, sir?'

'We've been approaching this case from the wrong angle, Victor. I only realised that when I saw a locomotive being spun around so that I could view it from the other end, so to speak. That's what we must do with this case.'

'I don't understand.'

'All will be explained when you return,' said Colbeck. 'I daren't even mention my theory to the superintendent. After what happened to him in there, he won't listen to a single syllable about the Works. The place is anathema to him.'

They were standing in the foyer of the hotel. A porter had brought down the luggage from Tallis's room and stood ready to load it into the waiting cab. When the door of the manager's office opened, Tallis hobbled out with the aid of a borrowed walking stick.

'Ah, there you are, Leeming,' he said. 'Come and help me, man.'

The sergeant went across to him and let Tallis lean on him.

'I'm sorry to hear about your ankle, sir,' he said. 'Does it hurt?'

'It hurts like blazes!'

'You'll be much better off in London.'

'Pain takes no account of geography. It will hurt just as much there as here.'

'We hope you have a swift recovery,' said Colbeck, nodding to the porter to take out the luggage. 'We'll miss the benefit of your guidance here.'

Tallis was curt. 'Don't lie any more than you have to, Colbeck.'

'I hope that you have *some* pleasant memories of Derby, sir.'

'The only thing that will give me pleasure – and soothe my ankle at the same time – is the news that you have finally solved this crime.'

'That news will not be long in reaching you,' said Leeming.

'I'll hold you to that. Leeming?'

'Yes, sir?' said the sergeant.

'Get me out of this accursed place.'

'Lean on me, sir.'

'Slow down, you imbecile!' said Tallis as Leeming moved off. 'Every step is a separate agony. Let me set the pace.'

Colbeck watched them move gingerly towards the door. He was sorry to lose Leeming for several hours but consoled by the fact that the superintendent was going as well. Freedom of action had been restored. It was a vital factor because Colbeck could do what he wanted now. He escorted the two men out to the cab and helped to ease Tallis into it. Leeming was palpably unhappy about having to spend so much time in the company of the irascible superintendent but someone had to shoulder the burden. Inevitably, it fell on the sergeant. When the cab rolled away, Colbeck gave it a farewell wave then hurried back into the hotel and raced up the staircase.

In trying to pass on information to the acting chairman, Maurice Cope only succeeded in annoying him. Donald Haygarth flapped a hand in the air.

'You don't need to take me stage by stage through the Works,' he protested.

'But that's what the inspector wanted to do, sir.'

'Colbeck *likes* trains. I only like them when they take me on a journey.'

'Superintendent Tallis is of the same opinion,' said Cope. 'He did nothing but grumble and his accident will not endear him to locomotives. He's gone back to London with the sergeant.'

'Are you sure of that?'

'I'm absolutely certain.'

They were standing outside the headquarters of the Midland Railway. Wanting to know the bare facts of what had happened during the tour of the Works, Haygarth was irked when Cope brought in so much technical detail about the production process. He had sent him there to watch the two detectives and not to enjoy what he saw around him. They were about to part when Superintendent Wigg hailed them. Trotting up to them, he reined in his mount.

'I didn't know you were a horseman, sir,' said Cope.

'It's the best way to travel sometimes,' argued Wigg. 'Trains run to timetables so there's always waiting involved. A horse is there when and where you want him.'

'You've no need to tell that to Cope,' said Haygarth. 'He rides everywhere.'

'Yes, I've seen him on horseback.'

'Do you have anything new to tell us, Superintendent?'

'I will simply observe that your much-vaunted detectives have been as much use as a silk kettle. You have three of them on the case now and they're still no nearer solving it.'

'We have to correct you,' said Haygarth.

'Yes,' added Cope, receiving a signal from the acting chairman, 'the three detectives have now been reduced to one. Inspector Colbeck is the only survivor.'

He described how the accident had occurred when Tallis was startled by the steam whistle. Wigg couldn't believe what they had done.

'What could they possibly learn there?'

'It teaches you everything you need to know about the way that locomotives and rolling stock are made.'

'That has no relevance at all to the murder inquiry.'

'Inspector Colbeck believed that it did. Mr Quayle loved to go on a tour of inspection at the Works. The inspector was keen to follow in his footsteps.'

'It's a pity he doesn't clear off back to London with his colleagues.'

'What have *you* learnt, Superintendent?' asked Haygarth. 'We know that you have a high opinion of yourself as a policeman.'

'Confidence is an essential part of leadership.'

'And what have your men discovered under your leadership?'

'The noose is slowly tightening around the killer's neck.'

'You don't even know who he is yet.'

'Yes, I do,' said Wigg, looking down at them. 'The murder was the result of a conspiracy. Someone was hired to do the deed because of his past association with Quayle. In my opinion, that "someone" is Gerard Burns. The people who suborned him are more difficult to unmask,' he said, looking shrewdly at each of them in turn. 'But I'll soon have enough evidence to do so.'

'Inspector Colbeck has been to Melbourne Hall twice,' said Cope, 'and the superintendent has also paid a visit to Burns.'

'Then why is he not in custody?'

'You'll have to ask them, sir.'

'And before you criticise Inspector Colbeck again,' said Haygarth, 'you might like to know that he provided us with a detail that passed by you and your men. In view of what you say about Burns, it might be significant.'

Wigg was piqued. 'What detail is this?'

'Miss Lydia Quayle has returned home.' He was rewarded by a look of surprise on the other's face. 'Events in Nottingham are important. You should have had the Quayle residence under surveillance.'

'I don't have the resources for that, Mr Haygarth.'

'You have large numbers of men at your beck and call. Inspector Colbeck is acting entirely by himself at the moment yet he is gathering more telling evidence than you. That's why I sent for him,' said Haygarth, complacently. 'When I wanted the best available man for this assignment, your name did not even cross my mind.'

Wigg was furious. Tugging on the reins, he turned his horse in a semicircle then dug his heels in to send it cantering away. Haygarth grinned.

'That should be enough to keep him away for a while.'

* * *

Alone in their room, Colbeck was able to luxuriate in the company of his wife and to hear a fuller report of what she'd been doing in his absence. He could understand why Lydia Quayle had turned to her for help.

'You obviously impressed her, Madeleine.'

'My charm didn't work on her friend, Miss Myler.'

'Yes, Victor told me how unwelcoming she was.'

'She was guarding Lydia like a mother hen.'

'Then she wouldn't have been in favour of her returning to Nottingham.'

'No,' said Madeleine, 'I fancy that she'd have opposed the decision. Lydia has said very little about Miss Myler to me but there's clearly been an upset between them. I'll probably get the blame for that.'

'Murder always causes upsets. It alters sensitive balances.'

Madeleine explained how nervous Lydia had been and how uncertain she was about spending the night at the house. In the event of her leaving Nottingham, she planned to come to the Royal Hotel to meet up with her new friend again. Colbeck was pleased at the prospect.

'It would be good to meet her,' he said. 'She can tell me things about the family that neither of her brothers have deigned to do so.'

'What sort of things?'

'I want to hear more about her father.'

'She despises him.'

'I know that, Madeleine, but you've been telling me what an intelligent woman she is. I like intelligent women,' he said, caressing her hair. 'That's why I married one. Like you, Miss Quayle will have keen intuition. She'll have picked up signals that went unnoticed by her brothers.'

'Something's happened, hasn't it?' she said, taking his hand between hers. 'I can sense your excitement.'

'That's because I'm with you,' he said.

'It's something to do with the visit to the Works, isn't it?'

'Yes, Madeleine.'

'It's the accident,' she decided. 'You're overjoyed to get rid of Superintendent Tallis, aren't you?'

'Not at all – I'm heartbroken.'

'I know you better than that, Robert.'

He laughed. 'Then it would be folly to try to deceive you,' he said. 'Though I'm sorry that the superintendent was injured, I regard the accident as providential. With his departure, a great cloud has lifted. But the real bonus of the visit was the chance I had to operate the turntable. It was a revelation.'

'Father always says that you should have worked on the railways. That's your real passion in life, isn't it?'

'No, Madeleine – it will always be secondary to you.'

'Thank you for the compliment – now tell me about the turntable.'

'It taught me how little effort is required to move an immense weight and it changed the direction of our investigation dramatically. We've been looking so intently at the murder victim that we completely ignored someone else.'

'And who is that?'

'Let's go back to the start,' he advised. 'What do you remember?'

'The body of Mr Quayle was found in an open grave in a village churchyard. Nobody could understand how it got there because he has no connection whatsoever with the place.'

'That's what we were told.'

'It's what Lydia confirmed. She couldn't remember her father

301

ever mentioning Spondon, let alone going there. His social life revolved around Nottingham.'

'She was wrong, Madeleine. We all were.'

'You've *found* a connection?'

'Not exactly,' he admitted, 'but I know it's there. The choice of that churchyard was not a coincidence. It was a deliberate statement by the killer. Mr Quayle was put in a grave reserved for a Mrs Cicely Peet. *She* is the person on whom we should be concentrating.'

'Then you must believe there's a link between her and Lydia's father.'

'Heaven knows what it is, Madeleine, but it's there somewhere.'

'What makes you think that?'

'It's something that Cleary said to me. He's the coachman at the Quayle residence. On his last day alive, Mr Quayle was driven to Nottingham station by Cleary. As they parted, the coachman noticed that his employer had been crying.'

'That sounds very unlikely. Lydia told me how stoic and hard-hearted her father had always been. He never showed any real tenderness to her and to her sister.'

'That doesn't mean he was incapable of it.'

'No,' she conceded, 'that's true.'

'Can you see the way that my train of thought is heading?'

'Yes, Robert, I believe so. Until now, you were baffled by the fact that Mr Quayle had somehow ended up in that village. You now think that he had a good reason to be there.'

'I'd go further than that, Madeleine. My guess is that he wasn't killed elsewhere and taken to Spondon so that the body could be disposed of there.'

'How do you explain his presence in the village, then?'

'He went there deliberately because he was drawn to do so.'

'Was he set on in Spondon?'

'It's beginning to look that way.'

'So who was the killer, Robert?'

He leant forward to kiss her gently on the lips.

'That's the one thing the turntable was unable to tell me.'

CHAPTER TWENTY

As soon as she'd entered the house, Lydia Quayle had felt its
suffocating effect. Any pleasant memories it might have held
had been smothered beneath a pillow of pain and recrimination.
Though he was no longer there, the place was still dominated
by her father. She could hear his voice ringing in her ears. The
reconciliation with her mother had brought Lydia a satisfaction
fringed with despair at the old woman's poor state of health.
Except for Lucas, her relations with her siblings were uneasy. Agnes
came close to resenting her return and Stanley had signalled his
profound disapproval of what he saw as her air of independence.
There was another blow to absorb. Vague hopes of hearing that
Gerard Burns had been pining for her had been shattered by what
the coachman had told her. The gardener was married and forever
beyond her reach. Lydia was therefore in a house stalked by the
ghost of her father and surrounded by an estate redolent of happier
times with the man she'd loved and lost.

'I'm sorry,' she announced, 'but I can't spend the night here.'

'But your old room has been prepared,' said Agnes, crossly.
'When you turned up unannounced, I gave order for it.'

'You must stay, Lydia,' said Lucas.

'Yes,' added Stanley, peremptorily. 'The funeral is the day after tomorrow. We need you on the premises.'

'I'll be here for the funeral,' promised Lydia, 'but I won't spend a night under this roof.'

'Don't be ridiculous – you *must*.'

'No, Stanley. I will not.'

Lydia's robust response led to an uncomfortable silence. The four of them were seated in the drawing room. Stanley had been reminding them about the arrangements for the funeral and assuming that Lydia would fall into line with the rest of them. Her minor act of rebellion angered him.

'All that we're asking is that you behave in a civilised manner.'

'That's what I've been trying to do,' she said.

'Life in London has obviously coarsened your manners.'

'That's unfair,' insisted Lucas. 'Lydia didn't deserve such a comment.'

'I agree with it,' said Agnes.

'Then you should have more sense.'

'There's no point in Lydia's coming back unless she becomes one of the family again and she can't do that if she refuses to spend a night here.'

'I'll come back tomorrow,' said Lydia.

'What use is that?'

'You should be here, mourning with us,' said Stanley.

'All that we're doing at the moment is arguing,' said Lucas. 'Lydia has her reasons for not wishing to remain here tonight and we should respect them.'

'Thank you, Lucas,' said Lydia.

'Your return has made a world of difference to Mother.'

'I haven't noticed it,' said Agnes, waspishly. 'If anything,

Mother is even worse since Lydia came back. I've had to give her some of her tablets.'

'Well, I think that Lydia rallied her.'

'That's what you want to think, Lucas, because you were the one who got in touch with her again. Stanley and I would never have done such a thing.'

'It's true,' confirmed Stanley.

'Thank you for the warmth of your welcome,' said Lydia with light sarcasm.

'You see what I mean about her coarseness?'

'Oh, don't be so pompous, Stanley. You're too young for pomposity.'

'I disagree,' said Lucas with a grin. 'He's been pompous since the age of five.'

'And you've been frivolous since the day you were born,' his brother retaliated with a sneer. He turned to Lydia. 'Where will you stay?'

She did not wish to admit that she was going to the Royal Hotel in Derby to see her friend, Madeleine Colbeck, because they would wonder what the inspector's wife was doing there and how she'd befriended their sister. That might cause problems for Colbeck and his wife, so Lydia feigned uncertainty.

'I'll find somewhere,' she said.

'You could always go to Aunt Dorothea,' Stanley pointed out.

'I could but I certainly won't.'

'Why do you say that?'

'It's because it would defeat the object of my leaving here. Aunt Dorothea is family. She lives less than five miles away. I'd still be trapped overnight in a part of the county with unfortunate associations for me,' said Lydia. 'I'd rather get well away from here.'

'We should accept that,' suggested Lucas.

'I don't accept it,' said Stanley. 'It smacks of desertion.'

'Lydia always had to be different to the rest of us,' said Agnes. 'Let her go.'

'I'd prefer her to stay.'

'You've no call to stop me from leaving,' said Lydia, looking from one to the other. 'I've already sent word to the coachman to harness the phaeton. Cleary will take me to the railway station and I'll make my decision there.'

During his many appearances in court, Victor Leeming had watched the reaction of criminals as they were sentenced. Some were impassive and others attempted boldness but the majority were plainly terrified. When he was told to accompany Tallis back to London, he'd belonged to the third category, responding to his dire sentence with a quivering fear. The superintendent was in a vengeful mood. Suffering pain and deprived of the pleasure of leading a murder investigation, he'd be a scary companion on the train journey. Leeming prayed that they'd occupy a compartment with other passengers so that Tallis's fire would be banked down somewhat. In fact, the superintendent chose an empty compartment in which he could, if he so wished, rant and rave at will.

Yet the anticipated tirade never came. Tallis was calm and reasonable.

'I have this feeling about Burns,' he said.

'Do you, sir?'

'It's a feeling I've had before when I've been questioning a suspect. All of a sudden, I *know* that he or she has committed the crime. That's what happened at Melbourne Hall. A sense of certainty welled up inside me.'

'What should we do about him?'

'Gather more evidence then perform the arrest.'

Tallis was no longer troubled so much by his injury. At Leeming's suggestion, he was reclining lengthways on the seat so that his feet were off the floor. While the pain was dulled, his mind was stimulated.

'Who did he see on the night of the murder?' he asked.

'He wouldn't tell the inspector that.'

'He refused to give me a name as well and I can guess why. He didn't wish to disclose the identity of his accomplice.'

'Would it have needed two of them?' said Leeming. 'Burns is powerful enough on his own, surely.'

'He's hiding someone, Sergeant. I want to know who he is.'

'How do you know it's a man?'

'It would hardly be a woman, would it?'

'If he wanted someone to assist in a murder, he'd probably choose a man. But perhaps he went to Derby that night for a different reason altogether. Suppose that he paid a visit to a woman?'

'Adultery!' exclaimed Tallis, making it sound a crime more heinous than any in the statute book. 'No, I got no sense of that. He's concealing an accessory.'

'You could be mistaken, sir.'

'The feeling I get rarely lets me down.'

Leeming was less dogmatic. He'd had a similar conviction about suspects on many occasions and it had often been misplaced. As a result, he'd learnt to be more cautious before he actually arrested anyone.

'I had that same feeling until today, Superintendent,' he said. 'I was almost ready to let Mr Hockaday feel my handcuffs click into place.'

'Is he that cobbler?'

'Yes, sir.'

'What held you back?'

Leeming told him about the visit to Duffield and the discovery of the father.

'Why didn't he give you that information at the start?'

'It's because he has *another* father,' explained Leeming. 'Seth Verney, a farm labourer, is his real father but the son was born out of wedlock. He was brought up by a Mr and Mrs Hockaday who live twenty miles beyond Duffield. That's where he went first on the night of the murder and on the day that I followed him. When he realised that I'd spoken to Mr Verney, he begged me not to reveal his true parentage because it would destroy his reputation in the village.'

'Did you believe him?'

'I did, sir. For once, he was being honest with me.'

'Why did he keep in touch with the father who abandoned him?'

'That was a surprise to me,' said Leeming. 'Most sons would feel betrayed but Hockaday took the trouble to find out who his real parents were. The mother was a kitchen maid who died in childbirth but the father, Mr Verney, was still alive. When he discovered that his real father had fallen on hard times, Hockaday used to give small amounts of money to him and his wife.'

'What did the wife think about that?'

'Mrs Verney was told that he was her husband's nephew. She didn't know that her husband had a child before he married. That was the reason Mr Verney made sure he was not overheard when he confided to me that he was Hockaday's father.'

'Lust is a fearful thing,' said Tallis. 'You see the deception it causes?'

'I was the person deceived, Superintendent. I had a feeling that

Hockaday was the killer and I was hopelessly wrong about him. You might be wrong about Burns.'

'That's impossible.'

'You've made errors of judgement before.'

'If you're referring to the fact that I promoted you to the rank of sergeant,' warned Tallis, 'you may be right. I thought you would be reliable and respectful.'

'I strive to be both, sir.'

'Then let's have no more questioning of my judgement.'

'No,' said Leeming. 'Thanks to you, the killer has finally been named.'

'Remind the inspector of that when you return to Derby.'

'Is there no chance that I could go home to see my wife first?'

'What!' roared Tallis.

Leeming went into retreat. 'Forget that I said that, sir.'

'You're a detective, not a doting husband. Domestic concerns must be put aside when you're on duty. It's a strict edict of mine, Leeming, as you well know. There is no place whatsoever for a wife in a murder investigation.'

After listening to his copious notes, Madeleine Colbeck felt that she was well versed in the intricacies of the case. Her husband had collected a mass of material during his time in the town and she was grateful to be there when an important new development had taken place. Colbeck was embarrassed that he knew so little about the family of Cicely Peet. He promised to repair his ignorance quickly. Meanwhile, he'd been liberated from any fear of bumping into Tallis at the hotel so he felt able to take his wife downstairs on his arm. They arrived in the foyer at the same time as Lydia Quayle and the two women embraced affectionately. Standing back, Madeleine introduced her husband.

'I'm delighted to make your acquaintance, Miss Quayle,' said Colbeck.

'And I'm delighted to meet you, Inspector,' she replied. 'Madeleine has given me the most flattering biography of you.'

'Pay no attention to her.'

'Every word was true,' said Madeleine.

'Let Miss Quayle be the judge of that,' said Colbeck, indicating the lounge. 'Shall we go somewhere more comfortable?'

When they were seated together in a corner of the room, they ordered drinks from the waiter. Colbeck was able to appraise the newcomer properly and had the same reaction as his wife and Victor Leeming. Lydia was a striking young woman. Her self-possession reminded him of Madeleine when they first met and it was not the only resemblance. When he asked why she'd chosen to stay at the hotel instead of at her home, Lydia was not afraid to tell him the truth. The drinks soon arrived and they engaged in casual conversation for a while. Colbeck then ventured on to a more serious subject.

'Miss Quayle,' he began, 'I'm fully aware of the reservations you have about your father but I'd like, if I may, to ask some questions about him.'

'You may ask whatever you wish, Inspector,' she said, tensing slightly. 'I want the killer caught.'

'We all want that,' said Madeleine.

'Have you ever heard of a Mrs Cicely Peet?' asked Colbeck.

Lydia shook her head. 'No, I haven't. Who is she?'

'She was the lady buried in the churchyard where your father's body was found. Inconveniently, he was occupying the grave dug for her.'

'How eerie!' she exclaimed. 'Mrs Peet was not mentioned in the newspaper reports I saw. What do you know about her?'

'I was hoping that *you* could tell *me*.'

'I'm sorry. I can't help you.'

'What about the husband, Roderick Peet?'

'That name is new to me as well, I'm afraid.'

'Mr Peet is a well-respected member of the local gentry. You can imagine how he felt when he learnt that his wife's grave contained the body of a murder victim. He insisted that another one should be dug for her.'

'I don't blame him,' said Madeleine.

'Neither do I,' added Lydia. 'Where is all this leading, Inspector?'

'That's what I'm trying to establish,' he said. 'It's my belief that the choice of Spondon was not accidental. Your father had some as yet unknown link with the village or with the Peet family. It may be, for instance, that Roderick Peet was a former business associate of his.'

'You'd have to ask my brothers about that, Inspector. I know nothing about my father's business affairs beyond the fact that they consumed every minute of his time. Our mother once told me she felt more like his widow than his wife.'

'Unfortunately, that's the role now assigned to her.'

'I did get to meet some of Father's business associates,' said Lydia, searching her memory, 'but I can't recall a Mr Peet. It's a name I'd remember. Father liked to use my sister and myself at social gatherings. We had to be nice to certain people.'

'That must have been a trial,' said Madeleine.

'It was – we both hated it.'

'Did your father ever talk about Spondon to you?'

'No, he never did.'

'So what was he doing there that night?'

'More to the point,' said Colbeck, 'who was with him?'

'I have no idea,' said Lydia.

'What sort of man was he?'

'I've already told you how badly he treated me.'

'But until that point, you and he must have got on reasonably well. If he was away a lot, the two of you would have met infrequently.' Lydia nodded. 'Yet he was always there for the cricket matches, I suppose.'

'Father would never miss those.'

'He loved the game, I'm told.'

'No, Inspector,' she corrected, 'it went deeper than that. He loved to use the game as a way of showing off and humbling his rivals. And as long as he had the head gardener and the coachman in the team, he could rely on winning, especially as my brother, Lucas, was a talented cricketer as well.'

'Cricket and railways – it's an odd combination.'

'Cricket was only seasonal and very few games were played. Railways, by contrast, absorbed him every day of the year. There's a portrait of him in his study. That tells you a lot about my father.'

'I saw it on my first visit,' said Colbeck. 'I'm only sorry that Madeleine didn't paint the locomotive in the background. It would have been more realistic.'

'Don't exaggerate, Robert,' said his wife, modestly.

'Mr Quayle hired a portrait artist and the result must have been satisfactory or he wouldn't have hung it on the wall. But the artist lacked your draughtsmanship.'

'I'd like to see more of your paintings,' said Lydia. '*Puffing Billy* was wonderful. How many other locomotives have you painted?'

'Oh, they're not the sort of thing that would interest you.'

'Why do you say that?'

'Your taste is very different,' said Madeleine. 'When I came to your house with Sergeant Leeming, I noticed that the house had a few paintings on the walls. Every one of them was a pretty landscape.'

'They were not my choice.'

Beatrice Myler popped up in her mind again and caused a jolt. Wherever there was a wall without space for a bookshelf, Beatrice had hung a picture. Lydia had had no part in its choice. She was reminded once more of the fact that she'd left no real imprint on the house. It belonged to her friend and mirrored her taste in every way. A feeling of sadness washed over her. Beatrice had gone and she had definitely lost Gerard Burns to another woman. Her future lay elsewhere. Lydia might be forced to move through a series of hotels again. Conscious that the others were waiting for her to speak, she apologised.

'If you saw my father's study,' she said, 'you'd have noticed his collection of fine porcelain.'

'At first,' recalled Colbeck, 'I thought it might belong to your mother.'

'She has no interest in it at all.'

'How long has your father been a collector?'

'Many years,' said Lydia. 'After making his fortune out of coal, he developed a fondness for something that was less filthy and more delicate. He spent a great deal of money on that collection.'

'Where did he find the items?'

'He went to auctions in London. If you'd met him,' said Lydia with bitterness, 'you'd have found my father essentially a man's man. The last thing you'd expect is that he was a regular visitor to Christie's to buy teacups and saucers.'

The temptation was there but Leeming managed to resist it. After escorting Tallis to the apartments where he lived, the sergeant made sure that he was comfortable then he left. His wife and children were only fifteen minutes away by cab and he was desperate to see them again. What held him back from going home was the certainty that he'd spend much longer there than he intended and would be late setting off. Colbeck had been specific. Armed with his copy of *Bradshaw*, he'd told Leeming which return train to catch. If he arrived hours later, the sergeant would be in trouble. Besides, he told himself, the investigation took precedence. The sooner the case was solved, the sooner he could enjoy the fruits of family life. Leeming therefore turned his footsteps towards the railway station.

'I'm glad to see you, Inspector,' said Elijah Wigg. 'I have a complaint to make.'

'What is it?'

'Your sergeant insulted me.'

'I find that hard to believe.'

'He accused me of having a reporter moved from Spondon because he was collecting more evidence than the constables there.'

'Why *did* you have him moved?' asked Colbeck, mischievously.

'I didn't – that's the point. It was the editor's decision.'

'I'll explain that to Sergeant Leeming when he returns from London.'

'What's he doing there?'

'He's probably in flight from your wrath, Superintendent.'

Colbeck had walked to the police station in Derby in search of information but he first had to provide some. When he described Tallis's accident, he drew a grim smile from Wigg and the observation that a visit to the Works had no bearing on the investigation and was therefore a needless diversion.

'On the contrary,' said Colbeck, 'it's shown the whole case in a new light. That's why I'm here, Superintendent. What do you know of the Peet family?'

Wigg was incredulous. 'You're not going to arrest one of *them*, are you?'

'Tell me about Roderick Peet.'

'He's wealthy and well connected. He owns one of the finest houses in Spondon, another in Devon and a third in France. As someone who can only afford to buy one house, I should be envious of Mr Peet but I'm not and I'm sure that nobody else is either.'

'Why is that?'

'He's a man of such decency and uprightness that you can't begrudge him anything. Roderick Peet has given thousands of pounds to charity. He's been particularly generous to the village itself.'

'What about Mrs Peet?'

'Some people say that it was she who encouraged him to open his wallet so wide. Cicely Peet is his second wife, by the way. His first died after a bad fall from her horse during the Boxing Day hunt. The second Mrs Peet was much younger than him,' said Wigg, 'and she got very involved in local activities. Since she had money of her own, she led the way in charitable donations.'

'Were they happily married?'

'They were devoted, Inspector.'

'Did you meet them as a couple?'

'I did so many times,' said Wigg. 'Roderick and Cicely Peet were kind enough to make a substantial donation to the Police Benevolent Fund.'

Colbeck smiled. 'They obviously recognise a good cause.'

'As to their private life, I can't speak with any authority. I was never invited to their home. I know someone who was, however. If you want to learn more about the Peets, you might speak to him.'

'Whom do you mean, Superintendent?'

Wigg scowled. 'Donald Haygarth.'

* * *

317

Haygarth slapped the desk so hard with the flat of his hand that the inkwell jumped an inch into the air and sheets of paper were sent flying. Too frightened to say anything, Maurice Cope sought to win favour by retrieving the papers that had floated to the floor. Haygarth was hoarse with fury.

'Who's behind this, Cope?'

'I can't be certain.'

'You're *paid* to be certain.'

'It's one of three people.'

'Earlier today, you were assuring me that I'd be elected as the new chairman without opposition. Now you tell me that there's to be a contest, after all.'

'I'm as disappointed as you, Mr Haygarth.'

'I want names.'

'They're not easy to find,' admitted Cope. 'People say one thing and do another. When I canvassed opinion, the majority of board members were firmly behind you. There was no whisper of a challenger.'

'You failed me, Cope.'

'All is not yet lost, sir.'

'I should have been warned that they're plotting against me.'

'I was quite unaware of any plot. In any case,' said Cope, 'I don't think that it will command enough votes against you. I still think you're home and dry.'

'That's not enough,' snarled Haygarth. 'I want to be elected unanimously.'

The late appearance of a rival for the post of chairman had mystified Cope and fuelled Haygarth's rage. Both men had assumed that the latter's election was a foregone conclusion. His supporters had all been impressed by the prompt way he'd stepped in when Vivian Quayle had been murdered and the speed with which he made executive decisions. Those same attributes were not viewed by everyone as assets. Behind the scenes, evidently, some people had changed their minds because they resented the way that Haygarth had appointed himself to the position of control without any prior discussion with board members.

'Why are we losing support?' he asked, rancorously.

'I wish I knew, sir.'

'You must have heard *something*.'

'There have been whispers,' said Cope. 'Where they've come from, I don't know, but they've damaged you.'

'What sort of whispers are you talking about?'

'Not everyone accepts that it was a coincidence, sir. They argue that you were poised to take advantage of Mr Quayle's death. Indeed, you were so prepared to react to his murder that you must have been party to it.'

'That's slanderous!'

'I'm only reporting what I've heard, Mr Haygarth.'

'Then you must go back to the whisperers and warn them. I'll not be tainted by the murder of Vivian Quayle. He was never my friend but I had respect for him. Everyone knows that. Who has been circulating this foul calumny?'

'It has to be Superintendent Wigg, sir.'

'I'll get even with that meddling fool, if it's the last thing I do.'

Hitting his stride, Haygarth unleashed a torrent of vituperation against Wigg. It soon descended into a string of expletives. The intemperate language was still echoing around the room when the door opened and a secretary showed in Robert Colbeck. His arrival silenced Haygarth at once and made Cope freeze on the spot.

'Have I come at an awkward time?' asked Colbeck.

As the train drew up alongside the platform, Victor Leeming sighed with relief. The return journey to Derby seemed to him to be even longer and more tedious than the one he'd earlier made to London. The saving grace was that he didn't have Tallis as a companion this time. Alighting from the train, he took a cab to the hotel and was astonished to see Madeleine sitting in the lounge with Lydia Quayle. He'd known that Madeleine was in the hotel but had not expected to see the other woman again. When he joined them, he exchanged greetings and slumped wearily into a chair.

'You look exhausted, Sergeant,' noted Lydia.

'I've been to London and back.'

'That means you've travelled hundreds of miles.'

'It felt like a thousand. But what are *you* doing here, Miss Quayle?'

Lydia explained why she couldn't stay at the family home and how she would be returning there the following day. Meanwhile, she claimed, she was able to hear the latest news about the murder inquiry.

'Then I wish you'd pass it on to me,' said Leeming. 'The truth is that I don't know what's going on. Inspector Colbeck said something about a turntable.'

'I can tell you about that,' volunteered Madeleine.

'Please do, Mrs Colbeck. I'm very confused.'

When she told him about her husband's theory, he was only mildly interested at first but that interest became more intense as Madeleine presented Colbeck's argument to him. By the time she'd finished, he was completely won over.

'That would explain so much,' he said.

'It's only a supposition,' said Lydia.

'Robert's suppositions are usually reliable,' said Madeleine.

'Yet he hasn't made much progress so far.'

'That's because we've had so much contradictory evidence,' said Leeming. 'If you start from the wrong place, as we did, you end up at the wrong destination. I think that the inspector has got us on the right track at last. All we have to do is to find the link between Mr Quayle and the Peet family.'

Lydia was sceptical. 'I'm not sure that there is one.'

'You said yourself how little you knew of your father's business affairs,' Madeleine reminded her.

'Yes, I own that I did.'

'The link may have nothing to do with business,' ventured Leeming. 'It may be of a more personal nature.'

A waiter arrived and the sergeant took the opportunity to order a glass of whisky. He needed something to revive him and he always enjoyed buying something at the expense of the Midland Railway. Leeming was able to relax properly for the first time in hours. The only danger, he feared, was that he might fall asleep out of fatigue.

Entering the hotel, Colbeck made straight for the lounge. He was pleased to see the sergeant ensconced with the two ladies.

'Ah, you're back, Victor,' he said. 'How was the superintendent?'

'I can't say that I enjoyed his company, sir.'

'You'd obviously prefer to travel to London alone.'

'It would be much more restful.'

'I'm glad that you think that,' said Colbeck, 'because I'm sending you back there immediately. Something has come up and it needs verification.'

'I can't leave now,' protested Leeming. 'I've just ordered a whisky.'

'It won't be wasted. I'll drink it in your stead.'

'That does seem unfair on the sergeant,' said Lydia.

'Necessity is often unjust. In this case,' Colbeck went on, 'the loss of the whisky is offset by the pleasure of spending a night with his family.' Leeming brightened at once. 'You won't be able to make enquiries until tomorrow.'

'Do I have to go this minute, Inspector?'

'There's a train in twenty minutes. That will give you time to collect your bag and take your orders from me.'

'But I've already made an arrangement, sir.'

'It's just been cancelled.'

'I feel bad about letting him down,' said Leeming. 'It's Mr Conway's last day in Spondon. He's making the most of it by staying well into the evening. I promised to meet him here to see if he has anything new to tell us.'

'I can listen to Mr Conway as well as you, Victor.' Colbeck turned to Madeleine. 'He's a reporter from the *Derby Mercury*. We'd better not be seen together. If he discovered that my wife is here, it might just creep into his newspaper and that would cause ructions.' His head swung back to Leeming. 'Fetch your valise then take the next cab on the rank.'

'Will you give my apology to him?'

'Have no fear, Victor. I'll take care of Mr Conway for you.'

It was dark when Philip Conway came out of the Union Inn. The stiff breeze was like a slap on the face that reminded him just how much he'd drunk in the course of the evening. His legs were rubbery and he took a moment to steady himself. Since he would be working on another story the next day, he'd done his utmost to gather a few last clues relating to the murder. Though he went to three public houses in a row, he heard nothing of consequence from any of the patrons there. Everyone was glad to see him and to offer their versions of what must have happened on the night in question but no hard facts emerged. The large reward had failed to produce the significant evidence needed.

Before leaving the town, Conway decided to take a last look at the churchyard where the body of the murder victim had been found. Letting himself in through the gate, he walked across to the plot where Cicely Peet should have been buried. When he'd passed it earlier, the grave was still yawning wide. During his time in the village, it had somehow been filled in. Conway bent down and took up a handful of earth before letting it fall through his fingers. He didn't hear the footsteps behind him. When the blow struck him on the head, he pitched forward on the ground and lapsed immediately into unconsciousness.

CHAPTER TWENTY-ONE

Gerard Burns was deeply troubled. He'd now had to endure visits from a Scotland Yard detective, each one more searching than its predecessor. The next time he had to be questioned, he was warned, it might well be in a police station and he would be under arrest. The threat made him pause for thought. After being dismissed from one post in the most brutal manner, he had done his best to start afresh in the neighbouring county and had impressed everyone with his industry and horticultural expertise. There had been years of continuous repair. He'd repaired his confidence, repaired his career and repaired his heartbreak by finding someone else to love. At a time when his life was better than it had ever been before, the hated name of Vivian Quayle had risen up in front of him like a spectre.

The situation had to be resolved. It would involve the breaking of a solemn promise to a friend but Burns had to put himself first. His whole career might be in jeopardy. If he was dismissed from Melbourne Hall, he would never find a position remotely as prestigious and remunerative. Lord Palmerston and his wife would be returning soon and they would expect to be shown the improvements in the garden. If Burns was not there to act as their guide, it would be frowned upon. If they learnt that he was being held in custody, and was being interrogated about a murder, they'd have second thoughts about the wisdom of employing him. With a wife to support, and with a child on the way, Burns had to secure his future. Someone might suffer as a result but it could not be helped.

The first thing he did that morning was to saddle his horse. Instead of riding to work at the Hall, however, he cantered off in the opposite direction.

Lydia Quayle had also opted for an early start. Spurning Madeleine's offer to go with her to Nottingham, she'd had breakfast alone and taken a cab to the station. On the fretful journey back home, she determined that she would make more effort to conform to the family's expectations. On the eve of her father's funeral, she didn't wish to introduce discordant elements. On the previous day, she'd been the only one who was not dressed appropriately in black. Lydia made more effort this time. The first thing she did when she eventually got there was to go up to her room and take mourning wear out of her wardrobe. Though she still had misgivings, she changed into the dress.

Lydia joined her brothers in the drawing room. Lucas was glancing at the morning newspaper while Stanley was marching up and down with his hands behind his back. Both of them took notice when she entered the room. Even her elder brother had a kind word.

'Thank you for coming back,' he said. 'We appreciate that, Lydia.' He ran his eye up and down her. 'I'm glad to see that you've started to take this event with the requisite seriousness.'

'It's lovely to see you again,' said Lucas, putting his newspaper aside and getting up to kiss her on the cheek. 'I knew that you wouldn't let us down.'

'I always keep a promise,' she said. 'The only exception to that rule is the promise I made to myself never to enter this house again.'

'Where did you spend the night?'

'It doesn't matter, Lucas.'

'Was it in a hotel?'

'I'm here again, aren't I? Be satisfied with that.' She glanced upwards. 'How is Mother?'

'She's not at all well,' said Stanley. 'The doctor has promised to call later this morning. We're hoping that he can give her something to help her through the welter of emotions she's bound to feel tomorrow.'

'Agnes is sitting with her at the moment,' said Lucas.

'I'll go up in due course.'

'Mother will be pleased to see you.'

She looked around the room before taking a seat on the sofa with a rustle of black silk. Her brothers also lowered themselves into chairs. Lucas was smiling and Stanley dispensed with the accusatory stare he'd used the previous day.

'When is the inquest?' she asked.

'The date has not yet been set,' replied Lucas. 'Let's get the funeral out of the way before we worry about any inquest. Tomorrow will be the real ordeal.'

'Will you be sleeping elsewhere tonight?' asked Stanley.

'I don't know.'

'I take that as a hopeful sign.'

'I want to sit with Mother and Agnes when you all go off to church.'

'That's as it should be, Lydia.'

There was a tap on the door then the butler entered with a silver salver.

'Oh, I quite forgot,' said Lucas. 'There's a letter for you.'

Lydia was surprised. 'Really? From whom, I wonder?'

'Why not read it and find out?'

She took the letter from the salver and thanked the butler with a smile. He glided out of the room. Lydia recognised the handwriting at once. It had been sent by Beatrice Myler and her immediate thought was that it contained a demand for her to remove all her things from the house. She felt a sharp pang of regret.

'Well,' said Stanley, 'aren't you going to open it?'

'I'll do that later on,' she decided. 'It's nothing important.'

Colbeck was shocked when he saw the bandaging around Philip Conway's head. When the reporter had failed to turn up the previous evening, Colbeck had assumed that he'd simply forgotten the arrangement he'd made with Leeming. Clearly, he'd been prevented from getting there.

'What happened, Mr Conway?'

'I don't rightly know. I was attacked from behind last night. All I can remember is that I felt this fearsome blow to my head.'

'Where were you at the time?'

'I was in the churchyard in Spondon.'

'That's getting to be a very hazardous place.'

When they adjourned to the lounge, Conway described how he'd been interested to see that the earlier grave had now been filled in. His curiosity had been his downfall. He was knocked out cold and, when he finally recovered consciousness, he'd crawled to the vicarage and asked for help.

'The vicar sent for Dr Hadlow and he dressed the wound.'

'How do you feel now?'

'I've still got this pounding headache, Inspector.'

'Have you any idea who might have assaulted you?'

'Yes,' said Conway, teeth clenched. 'I have a very good idea.'

'What's his name?'

'Jed Hockaday.'

'Why are you so sure about it?'

'We've had verbal tussles with each other almost every time I've been to Spondon. On the last occasion, I thought he was going to strike me.'

'Did you provoke him in any way?'

'I annoyed him once too much, Inspector.'

'So what are you going to do?'

'I'm going straight back to the village so that I can confront him. My editor has shown compassion for once. He wants to know who the culprit is. He's not having his reporters set upon at will.'

'Yet it was only one blow, by the sound of it.'

'One was more than enough, I can tell you.'

'Then it was delivered by a strong man who knew how to wield whatever it was that hit you.'

'I think it was a truncheon,' said Conway. 'Dr Hadlow picked a few splinters of wood out of the wound. Like other constables, Hockaday carries a truncheon.'

'Don't be misled by that,' warned Colbeck. 'I carried a truncheon when I was in uniform. They were always made of male bamboo or lancewood. In both cases, it's a hard, shiny wood that doesn't splinter easily. Mine never did and I had some use out of it. The standard length in the Metropolitan Police is seventeen inches. I should imagine that they have something of similar length here.'

'It was Hockaday,' asserted the reporter. 'I'm certain of it.'

'Then you must take care what you say to him or he may turn

violent. If he really was your attacker, I'll make sure that charges are brought against him.'

'Thank you, Inspector.' Conway rose to his feet. 'Will you give my apologies to Sergeant Leeming, please? I was supposed to meet him here last night but I was far too groggy.'

'As it happens, you couldn't have met him here.'

'Oh – why was that?'

'The sergeant was sent back to London,' said Colbeck. 'I wanted him to wake up there in his own bed so that he'd be refreshed and ready to carry out some important research.'

Victor Leeming had only ever been to an auction once. When he and his wife bought their little house, it needed furniture so they went to a saleroom that specialised in cheap, second-hand items. He'd proved an impulsive bidder and ended up paying far more for a rickety table and four chairs than he need have done. Leeming remembered the smell of damp and the careless way that the sticks of furniture had been piled up on each other. Christie's auction house presented a stunning contrast. Located in King Street, it was surrounded by impressive buildings and exclusive dwellings in the wealthy district of St James's. One look at the premises was enough to give Leeming a spasm of social inferiority. He envied Colbeck's ability to feel at ease in any company, however exalted it might be.

Geoffrey Sheldon blocked his way as soon as the sergeant entered.

'There's no auction today, sir,' he said.

'I know that.'

'But I can show you a catalogue of the next auction, if you wish.'

'No, thank you. I'm only interested in events held here in the past.'

When Leeming gave his name and explained the reason for his visit, Sheldon was both shocked and intrigued. He'd never been involved in a murder investigation before. It excited him.

'Mr Quayle was one of our best customers,' he said. 'I was horrified when I read of his death in the newspaper. He was an expert on fine china and we were privileged to add to his collection.'

Sheldon introduced himself. He was the auctioneer, a tall, slim, elegant man in his forties with a flowing mane of curly brown hair and a voice like dripping honey. He took the opportunity to give his visitor a history lesson.

'Christie's is celebrating its centenary this year,' he said, waving a hand in the direction of the opulent saleroom. 'It's just been renamed Christie, Manson and Woods, actually, but to serious collectors, it will always be known as Christie's. In the last forty or fifty years, this city has become a centre of the international art trade and we have been its leading auction house. Sotheby's cannot compete with us.'

After letting him praise the company for a few minutes, Leeming asked for a favour. It was refused point-blank at first but, when the possibility of a search warrant was raised, Sheldon slowly changed his mind. Reluctantly, he conducted his visitor into his plush office. Pictures of various kinds adorned every wall. One gilt-framed painting was of a picnic beside a river and Leeming was startled by the fact that the three women reclining on the grass were completely naked. His cheeks burnt with embarrassment. He couldn't understand how Sheldon could work in a room that had such a worrying distraction in it.

'You must understand that this is very irregular, Sergeant,' said the auctioneer. 'We pride ourselves on offering a confidential service. What is recorded in our ledger is sacrosanct. No unauthorised eyes are permitted to view it.'

'But you've just authorised my eyes, sir.'

'That was under compulsion.'

'You may be helping to solve a murder case, Mr Sheldon.'

'The only thing I feel is that I'm betraying our clients.' He opened the thick ledger on his desk. 'Art is our primary concern, of course. China only appears in our catalogue every six weeks or so.'

'That should make my job a little easier,' said Leeming.

'How far back do you wish to go?'

'Two years should be enough for me to confirm our suspicions.'

'You're not suspicious about the activities of Christie's, I hope.'

'No, sir – all I'm looking for is a chain of coincidences.'

At Sheldon's invitation, he sat behind the desk and began to work his way through the list of auctions that Vivian Quayle might have attended. He spotted the man's name at once. It was not long before he found the other name he was hoping to find. Leeming looked up. 'What are these initials after some of the purchases?'

'They're code for the addresses to which certain items are to be sent. When a client buys a large painting or a collection of oriental porcelain, he or she can't just tuck it under the arm and walk out. Every item has to be carefully packed. It can either be picked up from here later or we deliver to the address we've been given.'

'What does this stand for?' asked Leeming, pointing to some initials.

Sheldon looked over his shoulder. 'That would be Brown's Hotel.'

'Thank you very much, sir.'

'It's in Albemarle Street.'

Leeming closed the ledger and got up. 'I know where it is, sir.'

'Did you find what you were after, Sergeant?'

'No, Mr Sheldon,' said the other, grinning, 'I found a lot more.'

Jed Hockaday had just finished putting new soles on a pair of boots and applying cobbler's wax around their edges. He stood the boots side by side on the counter to admire his handiwork. The customer would be pleased. A sizeable tip could be expected. If he served their needs, people usually paid more than he asked. They also passed on any gossip they'd picked up and he seized on any small detail. Being a constable meant that he had to know the minutiae of village life. He'd learnt the names of every inhabitant and he, in turn, was known to them. He was Mr Hockaday, the cobbler, a man who'd served his apprenticeship in Spondon after attending school there. Everyone knew the biography he'd carefully crafted for himself. If they discovered that he was, in fact, the bastard son of a Duffield labourer, they'd regard him as a fraud and a liar. His trade would suffer badly as a result.

He had to rely on the discretion of a Scotland Yard detective and that unnerved him slightly. His worst fear was that his personal history would be exposed and that there'd be adverse publicity in the newspaper. When he saw Philip Conway come into the shop, therefore, he went numb. Conway was a friend of Sergeant Leeming. The cobbler was worried that he'd been betrayed by the detective. Then he noticed the bandaging under his visitor's hat.

'What happened to your head?'

'You, of all people, should know that,' said Conway, angrily.

'Why?'

'You knocked me out with your truncheon.'

'No, I didn't.'

'First of all, you threatened me, then – when I took no notice – you waited for your moment and attacked me in the churchyard.'

'Who told you that?'

'Don't lie, Hockaday. You know what you did. Dr Hadlow found some splinters from your truncheon in the wound. How do you explain that?'

'I don't *need* to explain it,' said the other, trenchantly. 'Wait here a moment.'

Hockaday went into the back room and could be heard rummaging around. When he returned, he was carrying a bunch of keys and a truncheon. He handed the latter to Conway.

'Show me where the splinters could have come off,' he challenged.

The reporter inspected the truncheon. It was exactly as Colbeck had described, hard, shiny and of the stipulated length. The wood had not splintered anywhere. It was certainly not the blunt object that had smashed into Conway's skull. Doubts began to ripple in his mind. His assumption had been too hasty. With a murmured apology, he handed the truncheon back. Hockaday bent down behind the counter to retrieve something. When he stood up again, he was holding a stout length of timber with a jagged end.

'This is what might have hit you, Mr Conway.'

'Where did you get that?'

'I took it off a man I arrested last night. He was rolling drunk and waving this around in the air.' He put the weapon down. 'Come with me.'

He took the reporter out of the shop and along the road to the local lock-up. Finding the right key, he inserted it in the lock then opened the heavy metal door. Half-asleep and smelling of beer, Bert Knowles peered at them through one eye.

'This place stinks,' he complained.

'You brought the stink with you, Bert. Why did you hit Mr Conway?'

'Who?'

'He was attacked in the churchyard last night.'

'Yes,' said Knowles, grappling with a vague memory. 'I filled in thar grave yest'day and I finds some bugger playin' with the earth. Nobody was goin' to ruin another grave o' mine so I bashed 'im good and proper.'

'This is the gentleman you bashed,' said Hockaday, indicating Conway. 'You'll be had up for assault, Bert.'

'T'were only a tap.'

'Oh, no it wasn't,' said Conway, removing his hat to reveal the bandaging. 'You cracked my head open, Mr Knowles.'

'Serves yer right for messin' wi' my grave.'

Knowles broke wind with thunderous effect and burst out laughing. Closing the door, Hockaday locked it and turned to his companion.

'I told you so, Mr Conway. It wasn't me.'

He offered his hand. The two men would never like each other but that was not the point at issue. Conway had made an unfounded allegation. The extended palm was a sign that Hockaday was ready to forget the whole thing. Conway reached out and they exchanged a handshake. Inside the lock-up, Knowles began to kick the door mutinously and demand to be let out. The two men walked away.

In the privacy of their room, Colbeck studied the notes he'd made throughout the day spent in Derbyshire. Madeleine looked on fondly as he went over and over the evidence he and Leeming had gathered. In the end, he sat back in his chair and ran a hand through his hair. She crossed over to him.

'It's not often that you're baffled, Robert.'

'We've taken too many wrong turnings.'

'You always say that's unavoidable.'

'It is, Madeleine. Detection is a case of trial and error. So far, I have to admit, there's been rather too much error.'

'You should have visited Derby Works earlier,' she suggested, 'then you'd have seen that roundabout. Better still, you should have remembered my painting of the Roundhouse in Camden. That might have alerted you.'

'It might indeed. But I'm not despondent,' he said, getting up. 'In fact, I feel remarkably optimistic this morning. We're almost within touching distance of solving this murder.'

'Does that mean an arrest is in the offing?'

'Who knows? There may be more than one.'

'You think it was the work of accomplices?'

'Anything is possible, Madeleine,' he explained. 'I've just been going through the things that bother me about this case.'

'What are they?'

'Well, that top hat keeps worrying me. Why would anyone wish to steal an unusually tall top hat?' He gave a short laugh. 'Was the thief a very short man who wishes to appear of more normal height?'

'It may not have been stolen. It could just have been thrown away.'

'Then someone would have found it.'

'Not if it was deliberately hidden.'

'Thieves don't discard or conceal assets. That hat was expensive. The least he would have done was to get good money from a pawnbroker. No,' he decided, 'the man still has it, either as a souvenir or for some other reason.'

'What else bothers you, Robert?'

He smiled sadly. 'It's the fact that I'm embroiled in a murder case when I'd rather be showing my dear wife the delights of Derbyshire. You'd love Melbourne Hall, and the countryside around it is breathtaking.'

'All you have to is to arrange for the prime minister to invite us there.'

'Oh, I don't think that's a possibility,' he said with a laugh. 'If I arrest his head gardener, Lord Palmerston is going to be exceedingly annoyed with me.'

'*Are* you going to arrest him?'

'I think that I probably shall. Gerard Burns was in the vicinity of Spondon on the night when the murder took place. He's admitted that he visited a friend but refuses to divulge a name. His alibi is therefore unreliable.'

'He does sound like the culprit, Robert.'

'Superintendent Tallis met him and felt convinced he was our prime suspect. Mr Quayle, you must remember, was killed by a corrosive poison that contained elements from a weedkiller favoured by Burns.'

'It was ministered by injection, wasn't it?'

'Yes,' he said, 'but the victim had been given a sedative beforehand. Where could Burns have got the sedative and how could he get hold of a syringe? They're not the kinds of things you'd find in a garden shed, are they?'

'So where *could* they be found?'

Grouped around the bed, they were in a solemn mood. It was very close to the end. Harriet Quayle was fading away before their eyes. On the eve of her husband's funeral, she was about to join him. Stanley's face was a mask of grief, Agnes's eyes were moist and Lucas, wrestling with his own emotions, put an arm around his younger sister to steady her. Lydia stood apart from them, sad, lonely, out of place, yet glad that she was there at the moment of death.

The doctor opened the bedside drawer and took out a small black case, lifting the lid to reveal a syringe.

'Nature is providing its own sedative now,' he said, softly. 'I could inject her again if you wish, but – quite frankly – it would be too late. I'm afraid that we must all prepare ourselves for the inevitable.'

* * *

He answered the summons at once. When Colbeck was told that someone had come to the hotel in search of him, he thanked the messenger then descended the stairs to the foyer. Waiting beside the reception desk, to his amazement, was Gerard Burns.

'What are you doing here?' he asked.

'I thought I'd save you the trouble of coming to Melbourne again.'

'That's very considerate of you, Mr Burns. Are you also going to save me the trouble of proving your guilt by making a confession?'

'It is a confession of sorts, Inspector.'

'Let me hear it in private, then.'

The lounge was fairly empty and they sat in armchairs that were well away from the few other occupants. Burns needed time to gather his thoughts. Colbeck could see that his visitor had ridden to Derby. He wore riding boots and had the dishevelled look of someone who'd been in the saddle on a windy day for a length of time. Tucked into the side of one boot was a riding crop.

Colbeck spread his arms. 'What have you come to tell me?'

'I was less than honest with you, I'm afraid.'

'We all know that, especially Superintendent Tallis. You were lucky that he didn't haul you off to the police station. He's convinced that you're our man.'

'Then he's wrong, sir. I'm not.'

'I thought you came to confess.'

'The confession is not about me, Inspector,' said Burns, uneasily. 'It's about someone else.'

'Is it the person you spent time with on the night of the murder?'

'Yes, it is.'

'Why didn't you tell me this before?'

'He's a good friend, sir, and I didn't want to let him down.

338

When we met here in Derby that night, he made me swear that I'd never tell a soul about it. To be honest, I couldn't see why but I gave him my word nevertheless. And I've kept it.'

'Why have you changed your mind?'

'You and the superintendent have been breathing down my neck.'

'Oh, so it's a case of survival, is it?' said Colbeck. 'In order to save your own skin, you're ready to incriminate a friend.'

'No,' replied Burns with passion, 'that's not why I'm here. He has nothing to do with the murder. The reason he didn't want me to breathe a word of our meeting is that he was frightened it might cost him his job.'

'Why should it do that?'

'If it got back to his employer, my friend could have been dismissed.'

'Why should the employer want to dismiss him?'

'It's because of *me*, sir. He didn't know that we'd stayed in touch but we did. As it was, of course, my friend was in the clear but we didn't know that at the time.'

'I'm not sure that I follow you, Mr Burns.'

'He worked for Mr Quayle. A dead man can't give you the sack.'

Colbeck's mind was racing. He thought about two young men who excelled at cricket and had been drawn together. He remembered thinking how the pair of them would bond easily and spend free time together whenever they could.

'You're talking about the coachman, aren't you?'

'That's right, sir – John Cleary.'

Harriet Quayle's death was slow, gentle and uneventful. She just passed away before their eyes. They had been ready for it for so long that there was no outpouring of grief. Each of them contained his or her own sorrow and watched as the doctor examined their mother. He confirmed her death with a faint nod. Lydia shed the first tears. Unable to mourn a murdered father, she was moved by the loss of her mother.

Within minutes, the news reached the servants below stairs and they expressed themselves with less restraint. A beloved mistress had been taken from them. Their weeping and moaning soon bordered on hysteria. John Cleary stayed long enough to comfort some of the women. When the wailing eventually gave way to maudlin reminiscences, he took his leave and went off to his room above the stables. The coachman had his own reasons for mourning the loss of a woman he liked and respected. Kneeling beside a wooden chest, he took out a key and used it to open the chest. Cleary then reached in and took out a tall, cylindrical hat. He then placed it gently on his head as if crowning himself.

It was rare that Victor Leeming was able to gather such comprehensive evidence in so short a period. When he caught the train, he was still congratulating himself on his success. The sense of triumph lasted all the way to Derby and made the journey seem ridiculously short. Alighting from his compartment, he expected to take a cab to the hotel so that he could pass on the fruits of his research. But he got no further than a dozen yards along the platform before Colbeck stepped out to greet him.

'Welcome back, Victor!'

'Thank you, sir.'

'Was your visit a profitable one?'

'Oh, yes,' said Leeming. 'I've so much to tell you, sir.'

'Get back onto the train and I'll be happy to listen to it.'

Leeming was taken aback. 'Where are we going?'

'We're off to Nottingham to make an arrest.'

They found an empty compartment and jumped into it. Saving his own news, Colbeck asked for details of the evidence that Leeming had managed to gather.

'It was as you suspected, sir,' explained the sergeant. 'I found a number of occasions when Mr Quayle and Mrs Peet visited Christie's together. Each of them not only bought items at the same auctions, they had them delivered to the same hotel.'

'Which one?'

'It was Brown's Hotel in Albemarle Street. The manager wouldn't let me see the booking register at first but he changed his mind when I told him that we'd discuss the matter at Scotland Yard.'

'What did you discover?'

'The two names cropped up time and again, sir. Mr Quayle and Mrs Peet stayed there – in separate rooms – when no auctions were being held at Christie's. It was obviously their meeting place.'

'You've done very well, Victor.'

'It was your idea to look more closely at Mrs Peet.'

'But it was Mr Haygarth who supplied the information about her obsession with oriental porcelain. He'd seen her collection at the house and had heard her praise the auction house which she patronised. Haygarth also told me what a handsome woman she'd been.'

'She was a handsome woman with a much older husband.'

'Significantly, Mr Peet had no interest at all in her collection. He once told Haygarth that china was something that ought to be used and not put on display in glass-fronted cabinets. But he loved his wife,' Colbeck went on, 'so he indulged her. At some point, Mrs Peet met a man with the same love of porcelain as herself. That friendship developed to the point where they had clandestine trysts.'

'Now we *know* what he was doing in Spondon that night.'

'He wanted to see the plot where her body was to be laid. If he'd turned up at the funeral, his presence would have been noted. The visit had to be surreptitious.'

'How did he actually get to the village, sir?'

'Thanks to Gerard Burns, I finally worked that out.'

'Has he given himself away?'

'No, Victor – without realising it, he's just handed his friend a death sentence.'

Leeming was bemused. 'So who are we going to arrest?'

'It's Mr Quayle's coachman – John Cleary.'

Everything he needed was stuffed into the saddlebags. After several happy years there, Cleary was about to leave. As long as Harriet Quayle had been alive, he felt that he had to stay. She was the lonely, ailing, neglected wife of a wealthy man. The one pleasure in her life was to be taken on extended drives in the country. Over the years, she and Cleary had become more than mistress and servant. He offered a sympathy that she didn't get from anyone in the family. Long before the detectives had found a link between Vivian Quayle and Cicely Peet, the coachman knew that his master was betraying his wife. When he returned from visits to London, Quayle was always in a mood of uncharacteristic bonhomie. Harriet, too, was keenly aware of it.

Reaching into the wooden chest, Cleary took out the last object in there. It was the appointments diary he'd stolen from Quayle on the night of the murder. A casual glance would suggest that it was merely a list of endless meetings about the Midland Railway. To the coachman's eye, it was also a record of adultery. The dates of auctions at Christie's had a tick beside them as did other occasions when Quayle had stayed at Brown's Hotel. Each rendezvous with Mrs Peet was there.

Cleary had not needed to search through the ledger at the auction house or inspect the booking register. Harriet Quayle had insisted on ocular proof. She trusted her coachman enough to engage his services, sending him off to follow her husband to London. Cleary soon got conclusive proof for her. He saw the couple entering Christie's together and he watched them getting out of the same cab at the hotel. While Harriet was in no position to fight back at her husband, the coachman was. All that Cleary had to do was to choose his moment to strike.

In a fit of anger, he tore the diary to shreds and tossed it away. Then he stood the top hat in the middle of the room and stamped on it several times until it was virtually flat. It was his final act of rebellion against a master he'd come to hate.

'Why didn't Burns tell you all this before?' asked Leeming.

'He'd given his word to his friend.'

'He's not the sort of friend that *I'd* want, sir.'

'You've never played cricket,' said Colbeck. 'I have. It's a game that breeds camaraderie. Burns and Cleary were the solid foundation of the team. It must have irked them to see Stanley Quayle receiving the plaudits as captain when the players who actually won games were them, the gardener and the coachman – with some help from Lucas Quayle, I fancy.'

'Cricket's not for people like me,' Leeming said. 'It's too difficult. I could never hold a bat properly because I'm all fingers and thumbs. The only sport I ever liked was the tug of war. This case has been a bit like that,' he added, reflectively. 'First of all we were tugged in one direction and now we're pulling in the opposite one.'

'That's a good metaphor, Victor.'

'I loved the feeling of the rope in my hands.'

'Cleary is going to feel it around his neck fairly soon,' said Colbeck, wryly.

They were in a cab that had just passed between the main gates of the Quayle estate. Overawed as a rule when he visited mansions, Leeming felt no queasiness now. They were on their way to arrest a killer and that concentrated the mind. When the house rose up before them, he ignored it altogether. Like Colbeck, he turned his attention to the stables. As their cab got closer, they saw a lone horseman emerge and kick his mount into a canter. Colbeck recognised him at once. It was John Cleary.

'Follow him!' he barked.

The cabman obeyed the command, cracking his whip and making his horse jerk forward with sudden speed. The cab rocked and rattled. The chase was on.

The house was in turmoil over the death of Harriet Quayle. Nobody was taking the slightest interest in the stables. Cleary had therefore expected to steal quietly away and that his departure wouldn't be noticed for several hours. Yet a cab was now in pursuit of him. Who the passengers were, he didn't know and he wasn't prepared to wait in order to find out. The horse felt his heels again and was soon galloping hell for leather along the track.

Inside the cab, meanwhile, Colbeck and Leeming were urging the drive to go faster but they knew it was an impossible task. A horse with one rider was always going to outpace a cab with three people aboard. The detectives were in luck. What the chase had done was to instil panic in the coachman. Fearful that he might be caught, he rode off the main track towards a stand of trees, hoping to dash through spaces that were far too narrow for the cab. It was a sensible course of action and it would have ensured his escape if it had not been for the badger's sett in amongst the trees. Galloping wildly, the horse caught a foot in the cavity and lost its balance, tumbling forward and rolling over. Cleary was thrown free and he hit soft ground before somersaulting a few times. Dazed but unhurt, he got to his feet, grabbed the saddlebags from the stricken animal and began to run as fast as he could.

Unable to go into the trees, the cab was pulled to a halt. Colbeck and Leeming jumped out of the cab at once and ran towards the sound of the frantic neighing. When they saw Cleary lumbering off with the heavy saddlebags, they knew that they'd catch him easily. Colbeck gave the sergeant the honour of making the arrest. He let him surge ahead and dive onto the coachman's back, knocking him to the ground. Leeming got up, dragged Cleary to his feet then stumbled backwards as a hefty punch caught him on the chin. Snatching up the saddlebags, the coachman used them as a weapon, swinging them hard to keep the detectives at bay. Colbeck was outraged when, as he tried to duck beneath the flailing saddlebags, his top hat was knocked off. He stepped back several yards then ran forwards and flung himself at Cleary's legs, grasping him round the ankles and pulling his feet from under him.

The ensuing struggle was fierce. It took the two of them to overpower and handcuff the coachman. Colbeck retrieved his top hat and brushed off the dirt.

'This is one hat you're *not* going to have, Mr Cleary.'

Edward Tallis was not going to let a sore ankle keep him away from work. He sat behind his desk with one shoeless foot resting on a velvet footstool. Seen from the front, he looked to be in rude health. In addition, he was in unusually good spirits. A murder had been solved and a full report lay in front of him. Local and national newspapers had congratulated two of his detectives and he'd received further praise from the commissioner. After being ridiculed in the pages of *Punch*, Sir Richard Mayne had been delighted by the ringing endorsement of his leadership that came after the events in Derbyshire had finally been resolved.

It was the day after the arrest of John Cleary. Now in custody, he'd taken full responsibility for the murder so that the victim's wife was not in any way implicated. Colbeck knew that there was something missing from the prisoner's sworn statement. When he and Leeming called on the superintendent that morning, it was the first thing that the inspector raised.

'He had an accomplice.'

'It must have been that friend of his,' said Tallis. 'Gerard Burns.'

'No, sir. He's completely innocent.'

'Then why was he so evasive when I questioned him?'

'He wanted to protect his friend.'

'Aiding and abetting a killer is an indictable offence.'

'That's not what he did, sir,' said Colbeck. 'When he was asked to say nothing of that meeting with Cleary, he thought he was simply saving the man's job. He had no inkling of the coachman's real motives.'

'So who was his real accomplice?'

'We can never prove this, of course, because the person is dead and Cleary is determined to take the secret to the grave. The real killer was not a loyal coachman. In my opinion it was a vengeful wife.'

Tallis's mouth was agape. 'Mrs Quayle?'

'It surprised me, too, sir,' said Leeming.

'But the woman was extremely poorly.'

'Much of her illness,' argued Colbeck, 'was caused by the immense stress she was under from being overlooked by her husband in favour of a younger and healthier woman. The irony is that it was Mrs Peet who died first. I believe that Harriet Quayle instructed her coachman to exact revenge on her behalf. She lived in a huge house filled with people but the one who got closest to her was John Cleary. Look at the way the victim died. Poison is often thought of as a woman's weapon.'

'How did Cleary get hold of the poison?'

'His explanation was that he used a weedkiller that Burns bought when he was a gardener there. It was mixed with other toxic elements. Where he got them from, and how he got hold of a syringe, he refused to say. But if Mrs Quayle had been unwell for so long, it's likely that she'd have been given a variety of drugs, some of which would be administered by a syringe. On the night of the murder,' said Colbeck, 'Cleary had been told to pick up his master from Derby station and drive him to Spondon. Before that, of course, he spent the evening with Burns. According to the coachman, Quayle was so drunk when he arrived that he had to be helped off the train. Cleary had brought a brandy flask, spiked with a strong sedative. Thinking it would steady his nerves, Quayle took several swigs from the flask. The sedative made him defenceless. By the time they reached Spondon, he was fast asleep.'

'So the coachman was able to inject the poison,' said Leeming.

'Yes, Sergeant, he confessed it. He hid the carriage near the church then waited until Quayle was dead. When he felt it was safe to do so, Cleary borrowed a wheelbarrow from a nearby garden and used it to push his master up the hill and into the grave dug for Mrs Peet. Though he denies it, I'm certain that he was obeying instructions from Mrs Quayle and I'm equally certain that she supplied the sedative.'

'Have you confided this theory to anyone else?'

'No,' said Colbeck. 'The sergeant knows but nobody else will.'

'I think Mrs Quayle's memory should be unsullied, sir,' asserted Leeming. 'There's no need to reopen the case because nothing can be gained by doing so.'

'What the world will see – and that includes her children – is a sick and lonely old woman collapsing under the weight of her bereavement. I think that's all they should be allowed to see, Superintendent.'

Tallis was worried. 'I don't like the thought that she got away with it.'

'You can't prosecute a corpse, sir.'

'It means that this case has loose ends hanging from it.'

'You have your victim and his killer is in custody,' said Leeming, bluntly. 'What more do you need, Superintendent?'

'I'm troubled. Colbeck's theory is oddly convincing.'

'But it is only a theory,' said Colbeck. 'My view is that it can never be substantiated with proof and is best left unexplored. Everyone is happy at the outcome of the case. The family is relieved, you are feted in the press and there is a glowing testimonial of the sergeant's tenacity in the *Derby Mercury*.'

Leeming grinned. 'Mr Conway was kind enough to show me a copy before it was printed in today's edition.'

'The praise was well deserved.'

'Both of you are worthy of a commendation,' said Tallis. 'I will be pointing that out to the commissioner at our meeting later today.'

'Thank you, Superintendent.'

'Whoever first gave you the name of Burns set you off on a false trail.'

'That had to be Maurice Cope,' guessed Colbeck. 'He actually had the reward posters printed and sent me one before the others had even been put up.'

'I didn't take to the fellow,' said Tallis. 'He looked too sly and devious. I'm grateful that we'll have no more dealings with him.' His smile was almost paternal. 'Mr Haygarth must be overjoyed with what my detectives have done. In solving the murder, the pair of you removed an ugly stain from the Midland Railway.'

'Some people think that Mr Haygarth *is* the ugly stain,' observed Leeming.

'What makes you say that?'

'We heard rumours in Derby, sir.'

'They're more than rumours,' said Colbeck. 'According to Superintendent Wigg, there's been something of a revolt. Mr Haygarth thought that his election simply needed to be confirmed but he now faces a challenger and many board members are turning to the new man. To quote an old adage,' he went on, 'there's many a slip between cup and lip. I fancy that Donald Haygarth has contrived to drop the chalice altogether.'

As he was driven towards the church, Haygarth was still seething. The latest information from Maurice Cope was that some of those who'd agreed to support the acting chairman were now wavering. It was now likely that victory could be snatched away from him. Every board member would be attending the funeral of Vivian Quayle. Though he would not be wanted by the dead man's family, Haygarth had decided to go in order to defy them and to be seen by the colleagues who'd anoint him as the successor. Dozens of vehicles were converging on the church. The local aristocracy and gentry were coming to pay their respects to a man who'd built a towering reputation in the county. Representatives from each of his coal mines had been given the day off to be there, miners whose whole lives depended on the Quayle family. A veritable multitude was coming to honour Haygarth's hated rival.

When the carriage got within fifty yards, he lost his nerve completely.

'Turn around,' he shouted. 'I'm not going to the funeral, after all.'

It was mid-evening before Colbeck finally got back home. Madeleine was waiting for him in the drawing room. After a welcoming kiss, she sat beside him on the sofa.

'What did the superintendent say about your report?' she asked.

'He was very impressed.'

'It's just as well he doesn't know the full story.'

'Your role had perforce to be suppressed, my love,' he said. 'Superintendent Tallis is in enough pain with his ankle. If I told him that you'd helped to further the investigation by befriending Miss Quayle, he'd be in complete agony.'

'I'm glad that you mentioned Lydia. I had a letter from her today.'

'Really? What did it say?'

'Well, it was written in the wake of her mother's death,' said Madeleine, 'so it's very emotional. I was touched that she chose to turn to me. Recent events have made her think twice about what she's going to do. She's staying in Nottingham until the funerals of both her parents are over then she's coming back here. I thought that she and Miss Myler had parted company for ever,' she explained, 'but it appears that she's been invited back by her friend. How long she'll stay there is debatable. I fancy that Lydia will strike out on her own one day. The death of her parents has made a difference to her. It's given her total independence. For the time being,' she went on, 'she'll be living in London again.'

'Until her father's murder, she was perfectly contented here.'

'She was such a pleasant woman. I'd like to see her again.'

'Then you must invite her here at some point, Madeleine.'

'I will,' she replied. 'I'm going to need female company if I'm to spend more time alone here. I can talk to Lydia. We got on so well together.'

Colbeck was startled by what he suspected might be a wonderful revelation. He remembered the fatigue she'd shown in Derby and how pale she'd seemed. He smiled tentatively and looked at her with nervous hope. When Madeleine nodded, he laughed with joy and grabbed her hands.

'When is the . . . ?'

'Early in the New Year,' she told him.

'How long have you . . . ?'

'Does it matter, Robert? It's certain now. Are you happy?'

'I'm delirious,' he said, taking her gently in his arms. 'I feel as if that turntable is on the move again. There'll be three of us from now on. We'll have to look at life from a wholly different angle.'